BEACH HOUSE RULES

A NOVEL

Kristy Woodson Harvey

G

GALLERY BOOKS

New York   Amsterdam/Antwerp   London
Toronto   Sydney/Melbourne   New Delhi

G

Gallery Books
An Imprint of Simon & Schuster, LLC
1230 Avenue of the Americas
New York, NY 10020

First Gallery Books hardcover edition May 2025

GALLERY BOOKS and colophon are registered trademarks of Simon & Schuster, LLC

Manufactured in the United States of America

10 9 8 7 6 5 4 3 2 1

Library of Congress Cataloging-in-Publication Data is available upon request.

ISBN 978-1-6680-7480-0
ISBN 978-1-6680-7482-4 (ebook)

To my summer "mommune":
Jessica Wilder, Dorothy Coleman, Caroline Mooring,
Heather Wiggins, and Megan Fader.
Raising our kids together has been the greatest joy.

Charlotte

The May Flower Moon

It was the cicadas that sold me. That, or maybe the May Flower Moon. *The May Flower Moon.* Has there ever been a more beautiful term? Even now, I can close my eyes and picture the otherworldly orangeness of it, the way it glistened on the surface of the ocean. I remember leaning my head on my husband Bill's shoulder, watching our daughter, Iris, walk down the beach a few yards away with a neighbor girl.

Thinking of our friends back in New York City—the place I thought I would call mine forever—unable to leave their apartments, I felt guilty. I envisioned them finding scraps of joy by performing nightly singing and cheering rituals for the healthcare workers leaving the hospital, world-weary in their hazmat suits. It was a small dose of reality, of remembrance that what they were living was terrifying, that what we were facing, even down here, was unprecedented.

What had given us the foresight to escape to Bill's stepmother's house in Juniper Shores, North Carolina, while we still could, I wasn't sure. All I knew was that that apocalyptic scene felt a world away right now as the spring warmth wrapped around us, the cicadas singing their song in a way that, if you listened closely, felt in time with the ebb and flow of the tide, in rhythm with the croaking of the bullfrogs, in step with the sweet sound of crickets.

Iris hadn't wanted to leave the city, of course. But even she—at the sometimes surly but often very sweet age of eleven—had managed to make new friends in this socially distanced world we had been dropped into. Everything was outdoors here anyway. Covid numbers were low. I knew how intensely lucky we were.

Lulled into contentment by the feel of Bill's arms around me, the sand beneath my bare feet, that mesmerizing flower moon, I didn't hesitate when Bill broke the silence. "Maybe I'm crazy, but, well, what would you think about building a house here, in Juniper Shores? With everything virtual, my work is online. I could fly back to the city some, maybe keep a smaller place there?"

He said it quickly, the way he did when he was nervous, a fact I knew about him so very well after thirteen years together. I marveled at that, at how one person could come to know another person so intimately that their quirks and tiny traits simply *were*. They required no thought at all.

"Yes," I said. *Yes.* As easy a yes as when he asked me to share his banana split the night we met. As easy a yes as when he asked me to marry him. As easy a yes as when the doctor asked if I was ready to bring Iris home from the hospital. Above me a million stars shone, showing off for the flower moon, as if declaring that they still belonged amid its fierce beauty.

Bill pulled away from me and looked down at my face. "Yes? Just like that?"

"Just like that," I said. "Sure, in some ways it feels like we've plunged into an alternate universe, but it's a universe where, against all odds, I want to stay."

If you had asked me, even during the chaos of the beginning of the

Covid-19 pandemic, if I would move to a sleepy beach town in North Carolina, my home state, I would have said no way. Not a chance. But here, now, I felt like I had found where I was meant to be.

We were a family here. We were happy here. We were part of a small town that, somehow, seemed like it could protect us.

That's the thing about protection, though. It's fleeting. Because the people who know best how to protect you also know the very thing that will rip your heart out.

At that moment, though, I only knew the happiness of the sand beneath my feet, the water lapping my ankles, that mesmerizing flower moon. And the cicadas singing me into complacence, chanting a lullaby that I would hear forever, even in my dreams.

Sharing bad behavior and delicious drama in North Carolina's most exclusive coastal zip code. DM with tips, pics, and juicy deets.

AUGUST 24, 11:08 A.M.
1 Post
4 Followers
0 Following

You didn't hear it from me, but . . .

PIC 1: Which hunky investment guru's multimillion-dollar waterfront gem is covered in caution tape? If you guessed Bill Sitterly's, you guessed right. Juniper Shores' beloved Member Guest Golf Champion is socializing at a brand-new club: Club Fed. Can't pay the Amex Centurion bill? No biggie. Just swipe from your clients' retirement funds! But the big question remains: With Bill, um, otherwise occupied and their house a crime scene, where are Charlotte and Iris Sitterly?

PIC 2: High school heartthrob Merit McDonald is looking as draft-pick-worthy as ever at preseason football practice. Is this the season our beloved Marlins win State? More important, is it true that this junior star has snagged the hottest senior girl in school? Stay tuned for Friday Night Lights—and quite likely some fireworks.

PIC 3: Sources say that Alice Bailey has been spending an *awful* lot of time at St. Mary's Episcopal Church. Could our own widower Father Matthew be the Black Widow's fourth . . . victim? Hold on to your vestments, Father Matthew. It could be a bumpy ride!

PIC 4: The RoséStream in Juniper Shores Village's Airstream Park is closed for renovations. To all the soccer moms who can't get through the afternoon without a rosé slush: thoughts and prayers.

Stay tuned for news about which Juniper Shores golden boy has returned to our sun-drenched slice of heaven.

TNT ('Til Next Tide . . . and maybe a little dynamite!)
JUNIPER SHORES SOCIALITE

The Low Point

This was my low point. Even I knew that. Standing in the lobby of Suncoast Bank, saying, in a louder-than-appropriate voice, "But why should I be punished for what Bill did? It wasn't like *I* had anything to do with it!" was pretty much the closest to a total meltdown I had come. Three days ago, I'd arrived home from dropping my daughter at tennis lessons to find police cars and FBI swarming the five-bedroom, four-and-a-half-bath cedar-shake beach house that we had just spent two years building. Two years of paint samples and fabric choices with one of the country's finest designers, flown in from Palm Beach, to give my family our dream home.

And in an instant, it had become a nightmare.

The fact that I was in a bank lobby nearly yelling this at Enid Plyler, who was in her late sixties with short gray hair and had, it seemed, been born behind the loan officer desk at Suncoast Bank, made it even worse.

I loved Enid, stopped by her office to chat each week when I came in to make deposits and get cash. We were a bit of a study in contrasts. Enid was short and wore an ill-fitting lady's suit, paired with tan orthotic shoes that I would need too if I were pacing back and forth on this beautiful but very hard white marble floor every day. I am nearly five ten, so I was towering over her in my three-inch wedges paired with one of my old dresses I had found stashed at my parents', a little rose-pink number with a deep V-neck that I knew complemented my summer tan. I should not have been taking my panic out on her. Fortunately, while I was losing it, Enid remained very calm. "Charlotte, I hear you, sweetheart. And I want to help you. I do. But I think you understand that convincing the board of directors at a financial institution to hire a woman who is married to a man awaiting trial for stealing massive sums of money from his clients might be a hard sell."

Ten points for frankness. "So, what am I supposed to do, Enid?" I asked in a frantic, high-pitched voice that made Paul Lucas and Gabe Montoya, who were both waiting in the teller line, turn and take notice. Well, that was just great. Of all the women who had been unfriendly and unwelcoming to me when we moved here from New York three years ago, their wives might have had spot number one and number two on the list. I was sure they would just *love* this. "I've called *everyone*," I said, suddenly feeling light-headed, the room starting to go soft and blurry around the edges. "All those big New York firms who promised they would have a job for Charlotte Nicholson who stepped away from finance too soon? No one will touch me now." Enid grimaced, and I shuddered at the thought that I might be back to my maiden name. Would I be a Nicholson again? But, no, Iris was a Sitterly. I would remain one too. I continued, realizing that I was sounding more like a lunatic by the second: "My degree is in finance. My master's is in finance. My job history is in finance. I realize an investment firm might not be jumping to have me, but I assumed my local bank might throw me a bone. All my assets are frozen." My voice going an octave higher, I added, "I have a *child* to raise, Enid."

Enid took my elbow and said, "Why don't we step into my office?"

It was a kind gesture. I wasn't being exactly polite, after all. I took a deep breath, tried to calm myself, realizing that all the tellers, several with cash in their hands, were staring at me. The lobby had gone silent.

"Actually," an even voice from behind me said, "Charlotte, why don't you come with me?"

I turned to see a woman I was sure I knew, but couldn't quite place. She was petite and thin, a little older than I was, and had this sort of ethereal glow about her. She had on no makeup, her hair was long and looked as if it had perfectly, naturally fallen into waves, and she was wearing a loose, flowing dress that screamed *I live at the beach*. She had a preternaturally calm presence that I obviously needed right now. The room was starting to come back into focus, and the full weight of my humiliation was sinking in. What was I *doing*? "I'm sorry, Enid," I whispered. "This isn't about you."

Enid smiled encouragingly. "I know, sweetheart. I will see what I can do to help you," she promised. "It's going to be okay. This town loves you."

I turned back to the woman behind me, realizing that what Enid said wasn't really true. I wasn't from here, wasn't "local," and, while everyone knew who I was—well, everyone knew everyone, to be fair—I wasn't exactly *beloved*.

"From church," the woman behind me said. "You know me from church."

A little laugh-sound escaped from my nostrils. "I know," I said, as if it had been obvious to me from the beginning. "You're in the choir." I snapped my fingers, actually recognizing her. "Your solos always make me cry!"

That was true. She had the most angelic voice. I smiled at her and ran my fingers through my hair, trying to seem relaxed and nonchalant to mitigate some of the damage I had done with my outburst. Just what I needed: everyone in town would be talking about *this* now. Well, that was great. Maybe that would be more interesting than Bill's arrest, the tidbit that, much to my chagrin, they were still discussing three days later. Not that that was a long time, of course. In fact, it was probably just enough time for the news to have reached fever pitch. In a larger place, full of scandal, people moved on to the next thing. Here, there was no next thing to move on *to*. Well, no, maybe that's not true. The usual appetizers of small-town bad behavior—who left his wife for the babysitter, who got *way* too drunk at Coterie Club and skinny-dipped in the pool, whose facelift was entirely too drastic— were always available to gobble up. But Bill's arrest was an entrée that everyone was eating in teeny, tiny bites.

"My name is Alice Bailey."

"I'm Charlotte Sitterly," I replied. Under my breath, I added, "But I think everyone in the country—or at least the state—knows that."

"Things are never as bad as they seem," she said. Then she scrunched her nose. "I don't know why I said that. Sometimes things are even worse than they seem."

That made me laugh—and remember. There was something shadowy about this Alice person. I tried to ignore rumors because this town had so many of them, but she definitely had a story. And I got the feeling that Alice knew all about things being worse than they seemed. But I didn't have time to sit around and share sob stories. I had to figure out my next move.

"Okay, well . . . I think I'll call the Shores Shuttle and head back to the hotel now. Maybe yell at an unsuspecting waiter." I was try- ing to lighten the mood. I knew I was lucky that the town offered a public transportation system that I could call for pickup, but I was dreading waiting in the parking lot for it to come. I was dreading going back to the modest hotel that I could afford for two more weeks. Then what?

Just a few weeks ago, I had been ignorant about the lack of affordable housing here. I had also taken the basic, simple amazingness of car ownership completely for granted.

"I'll drive you," Alice said.

I gestured toward the teller. "Don't you have banking to do?"

Alice shrugged. "It's okay. I can come back later."

I was about to protest, but then I thought better of it. I was used to having enough money and agency that I didn't need anyone else. I was going to have to depend on other people if I was going to make it through. So I said, "I would appreciate that so much, Alice. That's very kind of you."

We walked outside, Alice hit the unlock button on her key fob, and I got into the passenger side while she slid into the driver's seat. She pushed the start button. "Charlotte," she said. She looked at me, and I found myself locked in her cool, appraising gray stare. I saw something there. It wasn't pity, wasn't sadness. It was something more like determination. "I can help you."

I had always been leery of people who wanted to help other people. I knew that said something unflattering about me. Yet now I was surprised to find that those words out of Alice's mouth made every tense and tightened muscle in my body and jaw relax just a squidge. "Why would you do that?" I asked.

"Let me rephrase that," Alice said. "Charlotte, I think maybe we can help each other."

Now, that was more like it. Pity was hard; transactional relationships I could manage. "I like the sound of that, Alice," I said, feeling a smile grow across my face. "What did you have in mind?"

The Mommune

It was a basic life rule: never get into a car with a stranger. But Alice wasn't a stranger really, was she? I mean, it was true that I had seen her sing in the choir at church. Of course, church affiliation, as every good Southerner knew, didn't equal a lack of bad behavior. But there was something so warm in Alice's face, something so soothing. She had this dewy, glowing skin and long dark hair with a strip of gray that framed her face and made her look terribly elegant. I guessed she was maybe seven or eight years older than I am, forty-five to my thirty-eight? I wondered if the gray was natural or if she dyed it that way. It made her seem enigmatic. Bewitching, even. Oh! That was one of the rumors I had heard about her: she was a witch. But what did that even mean? I hoped she could cast a spell to take me back to a few days ago, when life was perfect.

"Charlotte, do you have anywhere to be?" Alice asked in her warm, syrupy voice. Just the sound of it soothed me. I wanted her to keep talking. I closed my eyes, leaning my head against the passenger seat.

"Court," I said.

She laughed. "Okay. Well, besides that."

I opened my eyes and looked out over the water beyond the

road, remembering that we lived in one of the most beautiful places on earth. Usually that calmed me. Now, nothing could dislodge the boulder that was sitting on my chest. What in the world was I going to do?

"I have to pick Iris up at two thirty," I said.

"I can take you." There was a question in Alice's voice.

"What?" I asked.

"I hope this doesn't hurt your feelings . . ."

I laughed. "Alice, if anyone is going to hurt my feelings, it certainly isn't going to be you."

"Well, it's just . . . how do you not have any friends to loan you a car, take you to run errands, set up a job interview?"

"Well, Alice, I have been asking myself that same very pertinent question."

"I know you haven't been here long, but I would think you'd make friends quickly."

That second part was untrue, though I wasn't quite sure why. Juniper Shores seemed like an idyllic place to live. It was obvious that this was a beautiful Southern coastal town with a charming beachfront village and white sandy beaches, great restaurants, historic churches, and stunning houses. But what I hadn't quite understood was that Juniper Shores was a town caught in the in-between, old versus new, the families whose cottages had dotted the oceanfront for a hundred years who wanted nothing to change and the people like Bill and me, the newcomers, who wanted to build their dream home and stay forever. Development was everywhere you looked; that wasn't *our* fault. But some of the women who felt like natural friends for me saw us as part of the problem.

I didn't let it bother me that much, though. Overall, people were friendly. We were regulars most places. Everyone knew our names. I got all the cozy small-town feels I was looking for. I just hadn't quite found my best friends yet.

Bill was my only true confidant, the only person I trusted. And now I had to face the fact that maybe even he had betrayed me. *Maybe.* I felt the tug around my heart that I felt every few minutes lately. I closed my eyes and pretended, as was my habit now, that he was wrapping his arms around me. Could the man who'd always made me feel so safe really have done this?

I opened my eyes and looked out the window, at the charming Juniper Shores Village, the downtown area, which was filled with work-and-live spaces with shops on the bottom and condos on the top, the old-timey light-blue lifeguard station, the beach volleyball court, and the Airstream Park that held food trucks and pop-up shops and won this town more awards than I could count.

I didn't know quite how to explain my complicated feelings about my place here to Alice. So I said, "We've been here three years, but two of those were in the midst of Covid. We moved to Bill's stepmom's house as a respite from our New York apartment once everything went virtual. It was supposed to be temporary, but we fell in love with it."

"Who wouldn't?" Alice asked.

I smiled. "Iris wasn't in school here, so I wasn't meeting school moms at first. I quit my job when Iris was born, so I don't have a job to help me meet people—or, as I'm now seeing, to get me out of scrapes. I certainly have acquaintances. I'm in a book club, a mah-jongg group. But I don't have anyone I can call to say, 'Help! Can I come live with you?'" I paused. "But does anyone have a friend that good?"

Alice smiled in a way that made me know that, yes, people had friends that good. *She* had friends that good. My friend situation hadn't bothered me all that much until right this minute.

I'd never really seen grown-up friendships modeled, but I longed for them all the same. My parents had fellow professors they socialized with at university cocktail parties. But their friends were their books, their papers, each other. Bill had been my friend. Then I said what was perhaps truest: "You know, Alice, I think I was making headway, but let's be honest: People want to distance themselves from you in situations like this, like you have a contagious illness. I don't one hundred percent blame them."

"You're preaching to the choir."

Alice and I pulled up in a driveway behind a beautiful two-story home, raised up a floor with a garage underneath. It was only a block or so from my house, the house that, because of my current situation, I couldn't so much as enter the door of. I had driven by this beachfront beauty many times. The front doors were perfectly symmetrical, and the sides were arranged in what could only be described as wings. The house was massive, and, when I opened the car door, the salt air and rhythmic shush of the waves enveloped me. I had missed this sound for the past few days. I followed Alice wordlessly up the steps, unsure where we were or why. Again, basic not-getting-murdered rules would dictate not going inside. I could hear Oprah urging, from the TV when I was a child, *Never let them take you to the second location!*

Well, I was a goner because here I was. Second location. Alice opened the back door—no key. I wasn't surprised. She seemed like a no-key kind of gal. We stepped inside the most beautiful hallway, and I turned to face an open-plan dining room on the right and an elegant chef's kitchen to the left. Beyond that, the living room stretched the entire width of the house and was really more like two sitting areas, furnished in unstuffy French Provincial style with bleached-wood furniture, oversized cushions, and throws, with a built-in bar on the far-left wall and a shell-covered fireplace to the far right. It looked comfortable. It looked like the kind of place where a woman could curl up with a book and a glass of wine. *Wine.* Oh, how I missed wine. I certainly wasn't wasting any of the precious money I had left on wine when I had a daughter to feed and only two weeks of lodging money left. My heart fluttered nervously. *I'll be okay,* I thought. Even if I had to get a job I was way overqualified for, I would find something.

Mentally, I kicked myself for ever quitting my job. I had only myself to blame for this situation. Then again, I wouldn't trade one single second of being home with Iris. And also, what about love? What about trusting a man who swore he only wanted to take care of you? Shouldn't a woman be able to put her faith in that?

I followed Alice through the house and onto the front porch, where oversized rockers swayed in the wind. As we sat, looking out over a clear blue pool and onto the ocean, I was green with envy. Not over the house, per se, although it was very beautiful, but that Alice had a home of her own. When would that happen for Iris and me again? The things that, only a few days ago, I had taken for granted were astonishing.

"This house looks like you," I said. "Earthy and elegant, simple and refined."

She smiled. "This used to be a bed-and-breakfast. I ran it with my husband. Until he died."

Having lived here only three years, I had missed out on so many people's life details, like this.

"I'm so sorry, Alice. What happened?"

I had never even known Alice's name until today, much less felt the pain she must feel, and here she was driving me around. I suddenly felt guilty. Maybe this was why I hadn't found my "people" yet. I should be a better friend. A better church participant. A better school volunteer. Although, when would I volunteer now? I'd be working nonstop to try to put a roof over our heads. And who was going to drive Iris to tennis lessons? *Oh my gosh.* Who was going to *pay* for tennis lessons? And lawyer's bills? I was getting ahead of myself. One thing at a time. Job. Money. House. Then we'd worry about tennis lessons. Bill always paid our club dues for the year up front, but I was fairly certain that once you stole money from other members you were kicked out. The board members were probably adding a bylaw right this minute, scratching their heads and saying, *Who would have imagined we'd have to create a provision for* this?

Alice shook her head and waved me away in a gesture that indicated the death was too painful to even speak about.

"About the time he passed away, my niece Julie's husband left her with three kids under five and a mortgage she couldn't pay. So, I asked her to move in here with me."

I was suddenly jealous of this Julie character. Imagine having a generous aunt to move in with. I had spent the first few nights since I fled Juniper Shores at my childhood home with my parents. But they were not generous. At least, not in spirit. I had reached the point yesterday that figuring out what to do next on my own had seemed more palatable than one more moment in Chapel Hill. Plus, Iris started school today. I wanted to maintain as much normalcy for her as possible, so I would just figure this out. Surely the feds wouldn't keep us out of our house more than a week or so. Two weeks, tops.

"And then her best friend, Grace, split with her husband when he decided to take a job in Tokyo. It was amicable, but she was left with two kids, and she felt, um . . ." Alice paused. "Overwhelmed by the idea of doing it all alone."

There was definitely more to that story . . . "It's nice to have community," I agreed.

"So she moved in here too."

My eyes widened. "Are you kidding me? You just took these women in? With all their kids?"

She laughed. "I never had children, and I'd always wanted to experience a slice of motherhood." She shrugged. "Plus, it was a bed-and-breakfast, so we were already set up for communal living."

"Wow," I said, incredulous. Who *was* this woman? She was either a saint or a lunatic. Did I want to find out which?

"Then Joy, the mom of a student I taught at the elementary school, lost her job and had to sell her house and needed a place to stay while she got back on her feet. So she moved in here too with her two teenagers."

"So, you're running, like, a lost ladies' hostel?"

She laughed. "Sort of. We call ourselves the mommune."

I laughed too. "The mommune. That's really cute."

"Everyone has responsibilities around the house based on what they do best. I do a lot of the driving because Julie and Joy have traditional jobs. But Grace works from home, so she does most of the cooking and shopping—she's a fabulous cook. We split up chores and bills, and it just generally makes life a lot easier."

I couldn't tell if this was the weirdest thing I'd ever heard or the most sensible. "Like a sorority house for grown-ups?" I asked.

"Does it sound crazy? I've lost perspective."

"No, not crazy," I decided suddenly. "Kind of brilliant, actually. When you can't be around, there's another mom there to do your mom things."

"I'm glad to hear you say that," Alice said. "Because I was thinking maybe you could be one of those moms."

I was at once totally sure of what she was saying and not sure at all. "What?"

Alice got up and walked inside, and I knew I was supposed to follow her, so I did. She walked up the cream-carpeted stairs, and I couldn't help but wonder whose job it was to keep those clean while I looked at the eclectic art lining the stairwell. She took a right at the upper landing into a bedroom with a charming pair of twin beds and a dresser made entirely of light-colored shells. The walls were covered in a pale-blue bamboo wallpaper. Then she led me through a bathroom with double sinks—the countertops had bits of oystershell embedded—and marble mosaic tile floors, a huge soaking tub, and a separate glass shower, into another bedroom with a king bed. I couldn't even take in how lovely it was because, right in front of me, outside the wall of windows with one door in the center that led to a porch, was an expansive view of the ocean, which was very calm today, retreating and then returning to the sand. Shorebirds flitted to the water's edge and, as the waves came in, pranced toward the beach again, which was full of umbrellas and intact families eating sandwiches and building sandcastles.

A sob I didn't even realize was building burst out of me. The last few days hadn't even felt real, and my sole focus had been trying to get in touch with my lawyer, trying to keep a roof over my daughter's head, trying to figure out what to do until—God willing—some court somewhere had mercy on me and released our money. Our clothes. Our house. *Something.* I hadn't even had a moment to realize that the family Bill and I had created was gone. That the man who swept me off my feet, and spent sixteen years doting on me, had lied to me the entire time. Hadn't he? Alice pulled me to her as I cried. "Things are very bad right now, and that's okay," she said. "It's okay to let them be bad."

She stroked my hair, and it occurred to me that, of all the women in the world, she should have been a mother. She was so soothing. Her house was a magical oasis of beauty, and her light shone over all of it. I finally composed myself enough to pull away from her. I wiped my eyes. "I'm so sorry," I said.

"You aren't the one who should be sorry."

"Wow. Tantrum in the bank, sobbing in a stranger's house. Is this what a complete nervous breakdown feels like?"

"You haven't shaved your head yet, so I think you're still on the right side of the line."

I couldn't help but smile. "I suspect my marriage is over," I said. "My family is over."

"You don't know that," Alice said. "Have you even talked to Bill? Maybe it's all a misunderstanding."

I considered that briefly. And that's how I knew that I was a little to blame here too. Because my husband, the man I had pledged my life to for better or worse, had been sitting in jail for three days, and I hadn't been able to make myself go over there to see him. At thirty-eight, a woman has a certain level of knowledge about herself, and I knew I was bad in a crisis. Bill was great in a crisis. I felt frozen. Deep down, I knew I hadn't gone because I didn't believe he was a criminal. But the minute I looked at him, the minute I saw his face, I would know for sure. And if he was guilty, I wasn't sure how I could survive it.

When I closed my eyes at night, while I was trying to sleep, I would think of that face, of the first moment I ever saw Bill. I had just graduated from college, just moved to New York. But I wasn't exactly living out my *Sex and the City* dreams. I had interned for Bank of America the summers after my sophomore and junior years of college and was incredibly lucky to have been offered a job—albeit an entry-level one—right after graduation. I didn't want to admit it, but I was scared. I was scared of leaving the safety of the small-town existence that I'd had in Chapel Hill and going out on my own. I was scared, that is, until my great-aunt asked me if I wanted to come live with her, save on rent. She lived way up Fifth Avenue, in a dated apartment in a beautiful prewar building that overlooked Central Park and the reservoir. The kitchen appliances were old (but who cooked anyway?), all my cool friends were living in Tribeca, and, well, my roommate was a seventy-eight-year-old woman. But I had my own bedroom and bathroom, and, what's more,

I had what I needed to make that leap: a sense of security. I was leaving the nest without leaving the nest.

I told people that my parents had insisted I live with Aunt Mary, which was completely untrue. She gave me a gift that year. Not only did I save a ton of money, but I also found the courage to take the next step, to find a career I loved, a man I loved, and friends who helped me grow up.

That first, sweltering summer, I felt like I was the only person in Manhattan. I was working nonstop and had neither the money nor the cachet for a summer place in the Hamptons or any other chic city-adjacent locale. By the time I left work around eight each night, I was exhausted and hot and the last thing I felt like doing was eating. Every now and then, I would walk the dozen or so blocks from the Bank of America Tower to Serendipity 3, decompressing from my day, to get my favorite banana split. Maybe it was childish, but, well, I was twenty-one: part of me *was* still a child.

That particular night, I was dreaming of that perfect dish with the delectable ice cream and light, fluffy whipped cream, but when I took my seat in the colorful restaurant right beside a flying unicorn and tried to order, the server said, "I'm so sorry. We're out of bananas. We just served our last banana split." As luck or fate would have it, he pointed to the person at the table beside me, a man in his midtwenties, with blond hair swept casually over his forehead, his blue eyes sparkling. My heart skipped a beat when he smiled at me. "I'll share," he said, gesturing to the seat across from him.

The good Southern girl in me should have protested, but even I—young and inexperienced in the ways of the world—knew when a man was flirting with me. I took the seat and his extra spoon and Bill said, "You can't call ice cream dinner if it doesn't have produce."

"That's what I always say!" I smiled and whispered, "But the frozen hot chocolate is really my favorite."

"Then we should get that for dessert," he said.

I had fallen in love with that sweet, charming man on the spot—or, well, maybe while we were sipping one frozen hot chocolate out of two straws. I had found him to be kind but passionate, thoughtful yet driven. Sure, he had made some mistakes. But hadn't we all?

And now people were saying my husband had defrauded dozens of people out of millions of dollars. Why wouldn't he have come to me if he was in trouble? After days of first-class, hard-core avoidance, I felt desperate to know the answer. I was swamped with guilt over not attending his arraignment. But now I was ready. I would march myself, like many, many scorned women before me, down to the county jail where my husband was being held without bond because he was a "flight risk." And, well, he might have had a teeny, tiny, nothing, stupid prior conviction for check fraud. (The mistake . . .) It was only a state misdemeanor, and it was years ago. But it was enough to justify holding him without bond, enough to make me doubt him. . . . And I wasn't the only one.

I had spent three days with my parents' *I told you so*s. Three days of humiliation that my life had fallen apart. Three days of, quite honestly, missing the man I thought I knew. I needed to see Bill; I needed to know the truth, good or bad.

But I didn't mention any of that to Alice. To her, I just said, "Maybe so."

Alice opened the glass door, and I stepped out onto the porch, taking a deep breath. "These would be your rooms," she said. "Joy's children have graduated and she has left us, so we have the space."

I studied her, my heart quickening. "Seriously?"

"If you and Iris choose to join us here at the mommune, we'd be happy to have you. There are responsibilities, but I think you'd find that, overall, being in a friendly, loving environment in the company of other women and children is quite satisfying. I feel that it would be a good fit for you. A step in your healing journey."

I wanted to fall into her comforting, motherly arms again. I wanted to sink into the king bed and take a nap. Instead, I said, "Alice, I'm so flattered, but there's no way I could afford the rent."

"Get on your feet and then we'll worry about rent."

My breath caught in my throat. Bill was the only non-relative who had ever been this nice to me. I was suspicious of that at first. I wondered how it could be real. Maybe it hadn't been, in the end. And so this, too, seemed too good to be true. "But why?" I whispered.

Alice took both of my hands in hers, and I found myself, not for the first time today, unable to look away from her. "Charlotte," she said with so much emotion, "I know how it feels to have nowhere to turn. And when I saw you in the bank this morning, I knew that's how you felt."

I bit my lip to keep from crying *again.* But I nodded because she was right. That was exactly how I felt. Trying to lighten the intensity of the moment, I said, "Wait. In the car, you said we'd be helping each other."

She nodded. "Oh yes. Well, we have homework time at night and each of us helps the kids with a subject. Julie is language arts, Grace is history, and I am somehow stuck with science and math. I am terrible at math. So you can take math."

I burst out laughing. I was overwhelmed by so many emotions I wasn't sure which one was at the forefront. But then I recognized it. Relief. Because my daughter wouldn't be on the street.

"It's perfect here," I whispered, getting choked up again.

Alice squeezed my shoulders. "Charlotte, darling, welcome to the mommune."

Two Things

Starting school three days after your dad was plastered all over the news as Juniper Shores' most wanted was, um, not the greatest. It was like all the girls' moms had specifically told them not to mention it, so they walked around like, "Oh, hey, Iris," in these really squeaky, high-pitched voices and then ran off to their corners to be awkward. I mean, whatever. I can handle it. My only real friend in first-period Honors English was Ben, anyway. I loved my girls, but they were in English 1. Plus, if I had to choose one friend for right now, it would be Ben.

"Hey, girl," he said in a faux high-pitched voice, sauntering over to me in his Peter Millar khakis and matching collared shirt, our school uniform, the uniform that I was wearing for the fourth year, which seemed hard to believe. Ben was cute. Like, really cute. He was taller than most of the boys in our class and had soft brown hair that got blondish and surfer-like in the summer. He had to cut it during the year because boys' hair can't touch their collars here at this prison they call school that basically serves to completely subvert our individuality. *Subvert* was one of our summer vocab words, and I was super into it.

Anyway, Ben was cool. And I know how that sounds, but I didn't like him. Not like that. Or maybe sometimes I thought I did? But I'd seen enough movies to know that making out with your best friend meant he wasn't your best friend anymore. I mean, sure, on TV it's because he was destined to be your great love who had been there all along and you lived happily ever after. But we were in ninth grade, so happily ever after seemed unlikely.

"Hey," I said to Ben, dropping my shiny, happy, everything-is-great-even-though-we-lost-all-our-money-and-my-dad's-in-prison act. He hugged me. He smelled like the ocean and the woods and something a little spicy. If I thought about it, he was obviously wearing cologne. But I liked it better when that was just the smell of Ben.

"I'll pay for your cookie in the lunchroom from now on," he said, grinning at me. "Because I know that was your primary concern."

We both laughed. I was surprised I could think something was funny, but I really did. I think because I knew Ben loved me no matter what.

"For real. You okay?"

I shrugged. "I have no idea." I looked around. Everyone was sneaking glances at us but pretending to be super caught up in their own conversations. I was the giraffe at the zoo today. It was kind of like my first day after we moved here from New York. I reminded myself how quickly that had passed, how quickly I had made best friends and felt like this had been home all along. "I mean, this is bad. And it's my dad, you know? I love him. And he's such a good dad. And, Ben, I *know* he didn't do this."

Ben nodded at me in a sympathetic, *oh you poor thing, you think he's innocent* way that irritated me. I crossed my arms.

"Okay," he said, putting his hands up. "He didn't do it."

Then I let my scariest thought sink in. "What if he did do it?" I whispered. "I mean, I guess that changes things."

"Two things can be true at once," Ben said importantly.

This was why I loved him. He was so *wise*.

"Yes. Right. So, worst case, he can be a good dad and a criminal." That made me feel better. Maybe my life wasn't a lie after all. "But to be clear. He didn't do it."

"Noted," Ben said. I thought about my mom. Poor Mom. She obviously had quit her job and her whole life to stay home with me, which had to suck. I mean, can you imagine if Taylor Swift had to cancel the Eras Tour because she was home with a preschooler? Shiver. And the reality was that, while I was sad and confused and kind of scared, I really wasn't all that scared because my mom would take care of me. Full stop.

Her first attempt at that, our three days with my grandparents in Chapel Hill, had been *interesting*. My grandparents were very cool for a day at holidays, but more than that was a lot. Plus, I missed my friends, and I hadn't really believed that Mom would pull off getting us back here before school started, so that kind of compounded things. But she had.

"Ladies and gentlemen," Mr. Friedman's voice boomed. "Let's take our seats please."

Ben winked at me and, for just a second, I forgot that my entire life was up in flames; I forgot that everything was falling apart. My friend Chloe texted me and our other best friend, Dabney. *Have you seen Juniper Shores Socialite today?*

We were allowed to have our phones at school; we just weren't allowed to text in class, a rule I was 100 percent breaking right now. I rolled my eyes because that lady hadn't been particularly kind to my family. Although, to be fair, she was great at spreading all the gossip, so the conversation definitely wasn't *only* on my dad anymore.

Yessssssss! Dabney texted back. *Principal Windsor and Callie's mom?? Wasn't she, like, a for real model?*

I winced and tried to think: If Principal Windsor wasn't my principal was he any kind of hot, even in an old-man way? Nope. Nope. Couldn't see it. *Ewwww,* I texted back. *What is she thinking?*

I didn't follow Juniper Shores Socialite quite as closely as Dabney and Chloe because I was always a little afraid of seeing more bad stuff about my dad. But what I couldn't figure out was how she knew all the high school drama *and* all the adult drama. And what was really crazy was that adults were, like, scandalous. I just figured that you got married and had kids and that was that. Nope. Not the case, apparently. I found adults infinitely more interesting now.

Sleepover at my house this weekend? Chloe texted.

I felt like my heart had just grown three sizes. I texted back *Yesssss!!!*

They weren't ostracizing me, like I had feared so deep down that I hadn't admitted it to myself yet. Everything was going to be okay.

At least, that's what I thought—until the end of the day. Mom had prepared me that she wouldn't be picking me up since, well, she didn't have a car. What a shitshow. So I was looking around the carpool line when I saw her hang her head out of this newish-looking small Lexus SUV. For just a second, I had the best thought: this was all some misunderstanding and Dad had bought Mom a new car today and was out of jail. They had proven that he was innocent!

But as I walked over, I realized some other lady was driving. "Hi, honey," Mom said in her mom-tone, with the mom-eyes that meant, *You behave yourself, young lady, or there will be hell to pay.*

I reminded myself that whatever was going on here, no matter how bad it was, I could always try to get a scholarship to boarding school next semester.

I opened the back door and tried to gently launch my overstuffed backpack into the seat. Juniper Shores Prep was all about the homework. Which was okay because I always had straight As, and I was fast at homework, hence my confidence I could get the scholarship to boarding school if I wanted to go off. "Um, hi," I said. For just a second, I wondered if this was some long-lost family member of Mom's. It certainly wasn't Grammy, with whom, seriously four hours into our stay, I had been so annoyed that I suggested to Mom that perhaps camping under the overpass wouldn't be *that* bad.

"Iris, this is Alice," Mom said. "She owns a beautiful bed-and-breakfast on the beach, and she's going to let us stay there for a while until we get this mess cleared up."

I could tell by the way Mom glanced at Alice that she was lying. Or, at least, doing that mom-lie thing that isn't a full-on lie, but also isn't totally true. Butterflies flipped around my stomach. Was this place gross? Dirty? In a bad neighborhood? But wait. Juniper Shores didn't have bad neighborhoods, right?

We were taking the beach road—our road—so, I mean, come on. How bad could it be?

But when we pulled up in front of the massive beach house, my heart stopped. My blood turned to ice water. "Here it is," Alice said in this calm tone that I suddenly found creepy instead of soothing.

"Great," I said, trying to keep the panic out of my voice. As we all got out of the car, Mom smiling like we had won the lottery, I grabbed her elbow, the way she used to do to me when I was little and in trouble. "Mom, can I speak with you a moment?"

Alice smiled that angelic smile at me again and pointed. "I'll just go ahead up and let you two have a second."

As soon as she was out of earshot, I whisper-hissed: "Are you *insane*? You moved us into the *mommune*?"

Mom laughed. "Wait. You've heard of the mommune?"

"Does this seem like I'm making a cute joke, Mom? We cannot live here. These people are creepy."

"Alice is the nicest person I've ever met. She is offering us a place to live for free while I get us back on our feet. It's beautiful, sweetheart. You'll see."

I looked around, then whispered, "Alice murdered *three* of her husbands, Mom. Not one, not two, *three*."

Mom put her hands on her hips. "That woman did not murder her husbands."

Okay. So maybe it did seem like kind of a stretch that the chic goddess up there in the house was a cold-blooded killer. But everyone at school said that. Everyone. I felt my eyes widen, trying to make my point. "How do you think she got this big house on the ocean?" I asked. "Life insurance, that's how."

"This is just like when you and Kelsey were seven and got the idea that the lady we used to see in the elevator from the floor above us was a witch because she had that long black index fingernail."

Kelsey was my best friend in New York. "Well, that made sense, Mom. Admit it."

She laughed. "When really she had dropped a pan on her finger, and it grew out just fine."

I wanted to argue, but maybe it *was* a little like that. I couldn't imagine the rumors flying around about my family right now. Well, I could imagine some, thanks to Juniper Shores Socialite. But I would hate it if people believed something false was true. Although the truth seemed pretty bad. . . .

Mom sighed, and I realized how tired she looked. "Honey, I always want to protect you—"

"By moving me in with a murderer and a bunch of creepy ladies who will make me call them 'Mom'? Yeah. I feel really safe."

She cut her eyes at me, and I knew I was taking it too far.

"As I was saying, I always want to protect you, but you need to know that things are precarious right now. I don't know how long our accounts are going to be frozen, and I'm not the number one draft pick in the finance world."

I could feel anger rising in me. "Well, that's not fair. You didn't have anything to do with Dad's stuff!"

I knew Mom would never steal from someone. We'd sleep on the sidewalk first.

"I know, honey, but you and I both know that's how the world works."

"Well, that's just sucky. I am so tired of living in a world where a woman is judged by a man's actions. A man that she has no real control over, by the way. It's not fair. Eff the patriarchy."

I had to say *eff* because the last time I said the real sentence, Mom had grounded me for a week, specifically from all my music accounts until I could be mature enough to learn which Taylor lyrics I was allowed to quote.

Mom sighed. "Honey, please?"

I crossed my arms. "Fine."

"Fine, you'll stay here?"

"Do I have a choice?"

"Sweetheart, look, I'm sure we'll be back in our house soon. But for now, we don't have a lot of great choices."

That was a harsh, scary reality, and I decided right then and there that I would shut my mouth and go with the flow. Things were hard enough for my mom. I didn't need to make them worse.

"I'll do it on one condition," I said.

She raised her mom-eyebrow.

"You let me go see Dad."

She sighed and nodded.

I smiled. Gosh, I missed him so much. "When?"

"I'll go see him tomorrow and put in your paperwork. You can go as soon as it gets approved."

I nodded, realizing how absurd this was, how much my life had changed.

"So can we go up?" she asked.

Mom put her arm around me. I leaned my head on her shoulder and turned my head up to kiss her cheek. "Fine. This will be a really great chapter of my memoir one day."

She laughed. And as we paused just a moment to stare at the ocean, I felt fortified by its presence. By her presence. "We're Lorelai and Rory Gilmore now," I said.

"The Sitterly Girls," Mom solidified.

"Mom, we don't have to, like, wear long skirts and keep our hair in buns now, do we?"

"Well, you pretty much always wear your hair in a bun anyway, so I don't know that much will change for you."

"Mom!"

"It's just a place to stay, Iris. We'll be out of here in no time."

As I stepped over the threshold and into the open-floor-plan kitchen, dining room, and living room that looked over the pool and then to the ocean, I had to admit I was kind of impressed.

"Wow. It's so pretty," I said.

"Oh, honey," said Alice, who I hadn't even noticed coming down the steps, "that's so nice."

I studied her. *Three dead husbands,* I remembered. She seemed nice enough. But I reminded myself not to get too close. If my dad debacle—and Juniper Shores Socialite—had taught me anything, it was that adults had secret lives.

For now, I would play a part. I would help my mom. But let's get one thing straight: I'd be sleeping with one eye open.

JUNIPER SHORES SOCIALITE

@junipershoressocialite

Sharing bad behavior and delicious drama in North Carolina's most exclusive coastal zip code. DM with tips, pics, and juicy deets.

AUGUST 27, 9:16 A.M.
4 Posts
893 Followers
7 Following

You didn't hear it from me, but . . .

PIC 1: We've heard that Charlotte Sitterly put the "char" in charges this week when she failed to appear at her husband's arraignment. Innocence 101? Have your grieving wife appear distraught and very, very virtuous at your first court appearance. We hate to say it but . . . her lack of court appearance didn't exactly do Bill any favors!

PIC 2: Juniper Shores Prep's favorite tennis coach seems to have slinked off into the night, leaving no trace and no word—not even for us! Could the rumors about his alleged affair with a now-graduated senior star who's making the pro-am tournament rounds be true? Either way, he didn't even say goodbye. Come on, Coach: We know love means "nothing" in tennis, but does it mean nothing in real life either?

PIC 3: It seems that perhaps our darling Growing with Grace's divorce rumors might be true. Troy doesn't seem to be coming home anytime soon, and the most telltale sign of all . . . Grace was spotted on the beach sans whopping diamond—with the damning un-tan white line of a recently removed ring to prove it. We'll keep our eyes peeled. In the meantime, let the rumors about who will be next to snag everyone's favorite domestic goddess commence!

TNT ('Til Next Tan Line!)
JUNIPER SHORES SOCIALITE

Charlotte

~~~~~~~~~~~~~

Cool Instagram Mom

The thing about my daughter was that, while so much of what she said was overdramatic, even when I pretended to brush her off, what she said stuck. Did Alice really have three dead husbands? Was that how she had gotten this house? And, even if that was true, could she actually have killed them? The minute Iris said that it all came flooding back to me. *That* was what I had heard about Alice. That was what Juniper Shores Socialite had meant by "the Black Widow's fourth victim." She meant it literally. I couldn't shake my very, very unsettled feeling.

But for the moment, we were here. Worst-case scenario, we could pack our bags tomorrow. Since we had next to no stuff, it wouldn't take long. Or maybe we could at least wait until I found a job?

I had sent out a dozen or so résumés to investment firms in New York and North Carolina while I was in Chapel Hill, and, as I expected, crickets. No one was really thrilled about hiring a woman whose husband was in jail for suspected wire fraud, one who, sure, had been a rising star at one point, but who hadn't worked in fourteen years. Tomorrow I would start making phone calls. It was harder to turn someone down voice to voice when you were old friends.

Alice was looking out the window, onto the pool deck. Three little girls were splashing around with an older one watching them.

I turned back toward the kitchen. A woman who looked vaguely familiar walked down the steps barefoot, in a pair of fitted pants that just skimmed her ankles and a sleeveless gauze top half-tucked in the way chic Instagrammers did but I could never quite—"Oh my gosh!" I said, recognizing her. "You're Growing with Grace! That's why you can do the cool Instagram Mom half-tuck!"

I put my hand to my mouth, immediately embarrassed. Iris was glaring at me, as well she should. That was not my finest moment. But Grace just laughed. "I think you'll find I'm decidedly less cool than I appear on Instagram."

I scrunched my nose. "But certainly cooler than I am. Forgive me. I lived in New York for years and never once accosted a celebrity."

"Grace," Alice said, saving me from myself, "this is Charlotte Sitterly and her daughter, Iris. They are going to be staying with us for a while."

Grace shook our hands. "I can't wait to get to know you both."

She walked over to the kitchen island and pulled a pan out of the drawer.

Trying to add some levity to the situation, I said, "And I will pretend that I don't already know everything about you."

She laughed. "Oh, you'll have plenty to learn. I've mastered the art of showing people what they want online while very skillfully avoiding anything real."

Grace opened the fridge and started removing ingredients, and I wondered if I was like that in my regular life, if maybe we were all a little like that.

"Grace is the most incredible vegan chef, and she has taken it upon herself to become our mommune cook," Alice said.

"So that part is real!" I said almost gleefully. I couldn't figure out why I was so excited. Wasn't I cooler than this? But I loved *Growing with Grace*. I watched her content every single night. Had I ever tried one of her recipes? No. But she seemed to have everything so together in a way I never would. Maybe she didn't have it as together as I thought, though. She was living at the mommune, after all. "Well, of course it's real," I amended. "I bought your book."

Grace turned back to the stovetop, which was in the island and made it easy for her to interact with everyone in the house coming and going as she cooked. "The cooking part is as real as the butternut squash risotto with leeks and spinach I'm about to make," she said.

"That's just too good to be true!" I was loving this situation more by the moment. I absolutely despised cooking.

Grace nodded. "Sure, but you repay me in football pickup or something."

"I wasn't vegan before Grace," Alice said. "But I feel so fantastic, I doubt I'll ever go back to bacon."

I laughed, but I had to wonder again what Grace was doing here. I didn't know her situation with her ex, but I was 100 percent sure that she was popular enough that she could support her family on her career alone. "That's great," I said, already (unlike Alice) missing bacon and being 99 percent sure I was still going to eat cheeseburgers outside the house. Iris was glaring at me again. That girl loved a chicken nugget. I gave her a *you're fine* look.

"You'll love it here," Grace said, pouring olive oil out of a chic bottle with a silver spout with the same flourish I had seen her use about a million times on *Growing with Grace*. "I didn't want to raise my children alone, and Alice and Julie have been such a godsend."

Grace and Alice shared a look I couldn't quite decipher.

"I can't wait for you to meet my kids. Emma is twelve and Merit is sixteen."

Iris stopped, the smile frozen on her face. "Like, Merit McDonald?"

"The very one," Grace said, winking at me.

"Oh, wow," she said.

"Well, I can't wait to meet Julie," I said.

"Oh, I'm sure you have," Grace said. "At least at school."

At that moment, three soaking-wet girls, and the older one, who I now assumed was Emma, came tearing through the house. "Mommy's home! We heard the garage door!"

I heard footsteps up the stairs from the garage and mudroom, and a woman in a dark suit didn't flinch as those drenched children practically attacked her on the landing right below the kitchen.

I was smiling at how sweet the whole scene was, missing for a moment the exuberance of Iris's youth. I loved Iris's current stage, but sometimes I missed having a little one who ran to me with relief and excitement.

Julie looked up and caught my eye, and I froze. The Julie in question was none other than Julie Dartmouth, the Julie who had seemed to absolutely revel in writing about Bill's arrest, our fall from grace, everything salacious she could get her hands on. I refused to talk to her for her articles for the *Juniper Shores Sun*, obviously, and I soothed myself with the notion that it was a paper in a town of ten thousand people. How much damage could it do? But still. That woman was not who I wanted to live with.

Julie walked up the few stairs into the kitchen. "Charlotte Sitterly?" she asked, confused. She pointed toward what I assumed was a private room and said, "If you want to talk, we can—"

"Julie!" Alice interrupted her. "Charlotte and her daughter, Iris, are going to be staying with us for a while."

Julie's face lit up, and I started to feel sick. "That is amazing news! Welcome to the mommune!"

I didn't know what to say. I couldn't stay here with *her*. After all the things she had written about Bill, about my family, after how relentlessly she'd badgered me to talk to her for her articles . . .

"Hi, Iris," Julie said.

"Hi, Mrs. Dartmouth," Iris said back. Julie knew my daughter?

I wasn't sure I could stay here, that I could put myself and my daughter in the situation of living with the local reporter who seemed hell-bent on making our lives harder. I needed some quiet; I needed to think.

"All right, girls," Alice said. "Let's go get your things put away and get some laundry started. I'm sure you have plenty."

"Great," I said. My usually quick mind felt stuck, unmoving. It was unsettling.

For the second time today, I followed Alice. I had plenty of reasons not to trust her. But for tonight, my daughter and I had a place to stay. And for that small mercy I couldn't help but feel grateful.

Iris

~~~~~~~~~~

Killing Me

I didn't know what Mom was getting so freaked out about. Sure, yes, Mrs. Dartmouth was annoying. She was always trying to stir something up in town to write about. But she was nice and cute and basically harmless if you asked me. Exactly zero people took her seriously. Plus, I mean, if we were trying to get Dad out of jail, wouldn't it be nice to have a newspaper reporter on our side?

When we walked into my new room, I was so excited that I couldn't even care about Mrs. Dartmouth. It wasn't as nice as my room at home, obviously, but it was really pretty and so cozy and had twin beds so I could have a friend spend the night—if any of my friends' moms would let them spend the night at the mommune, that is. Which I kind of doubted. I was only a kid, and even I had heard that Julie and Grace were Alice's murder accomplices, that they'd plotted to kill her husband so they could all live at the big beach house together.

"Darling," Alice said, "your mom and I grabbed your things from the hotel before we picked you up. Let's get your clothes in the washing machine—including that uniform you have on. You can borrow something of mine."

Three days ago, I wouldn't have had a choice. But, as annoying as staying with my grandparents was, they did get us stocked up on clothes. Well, in a minimal way, at least. I thought of my closet down the street overflowing with beautiful dresses and cute shoes and my favorite jeans, and let out a little sigh. I missed them. But Mom kept reassuring me that we would get them back soon.

I didn't answer, which Alice must have taken as a yes because she said, "Let's go to my room and get you two something to put on. I'm about to throw a load in right now."

"Oh," Mom stuttered, "no, don't worry. You don't have to do our laundry. We can do it."

Alice patted her hand. "It's not your week to do laundry."

A question formed on Mom's face.

"We'll get you all up to speed over the next few days."

There was a tap at the door, and Julie, now in sweats instead of that pool-water-drenched suit, leaned against the doorway. "I just wanted to clear the air," she said.

"Iris, let's go get that dress," Alice said.

Julie shook her head. "No, Iris needs to hear this too."

Mom crossed her arms.

Julie pointed vaguely toward the front of the house. "Out there, I'm a reporter. In here, we're friends, co-moms, a weird little family. Anything you say in here about Bill or your life or anything is forgotten."

Mom looked skeptical.

"I promise you, Charlotte," Julie said. "You too, Iris. I have a very firm separation between my work and my life."

Mom looked at Alice, who nodded encouragingly.

Mom bit her lip then said, "Okay. Well, I appreciate your saying that. Because this obviously wouldn't work if someone writing about my life was living it alongside me."

Julie nodded. "Obviously not."

"You can trust her," Alice said.

"I would like to discuss a few things with you," Mom said to Julie.

Alice nodded at me, and I grabbed an armful of laundry and took my cue to leave. I could have made some excuse to stay, but really, I wasn't that interested in whatever old-lady drama was boiling between them.

I followed Alice into her room. "Wow," I said. It was right on the ocean and bathed in soft blues, pinks, and yellows.

"The palette highlights the water, the sunrise, or the sunset, depending on what time of day it is," Alice said, opening her drawers. "I love sitting on my little balcony early in the morning, writing in my journal, sipping tea."

"That does sound nice," I said. "I mean, I get up at the last possible second in the morning, but theoretically." I paused, realizing something. "I've really missed falling asleep to the sound of the ocean." Just thinking of that made me so incredibly homesick. "Do you think I'll ever get to go home?" I sighed.

"I do think so, sweetheart. I really do." Alice opened her drawer and pulled out a bikini. "Do you need bathing suits?"

"Well, I have one," I said as she handed it to me.

"You can have this," she said.

"Seriously? This is so cute. Don't you want me to borrow, like, an old, dusty one?"

"No," she said, laughing. "You can keep that. Alas, my bikini days have passed."

I followed Alice into her closet. "Alice! Your clothes!"

"My clothes will be a little big, but you can borrow anything you'd like until we get you squared away with enough."

"Why would you do this?" I asked. "Seriously. Why would you just take in total strangers and their random kids?"

She shrugged. "Because it's the scariest thing in the world to feel like you've lost control over your own life. When I saw your mom this morning, I could see that feeling in her face. And I could make it better for her. So I did."

"Okay, sure. But there have to be, like, a million people who have the same situation as you, and they aren't letting random kids borrow their dresses."

"Well, there are also people giving up their cushy lives to volunteer in refugee camps, so I wouldn't say I'm a candidate for sainthood."

I smiled. "So are you going to tell me more about your stuff?"

"My stuff, as in my emotional baggage?" she asked, looking amused. I nodded.

"Maybe one day. But right now, I want to get *this* stuff in the washing machine."

"I'll help," I said. "I like to do laundry. I like how it makes everything smell fresh and clean. It's like starting over again."

"We use natural, fragrance-free detergent, so no smell," Alice said.

I shook my head. "You're killing me, Alice. Killing me."

But as I followed her downstairs to the laundry room, I knew Alice wasn't killing me—even if she had killed her husbands. Not at all. In fact, I got the feeling that, in more ways than I would ever truly understand, Alice had saved me.

Charlotte

Beach House Rules

A change in scenery has always been able to help me change my mind. If Bill and I were having a fight or I wasn't feeling my best, a book club meeting could make me forget all about it. Likewise, when I was climbing the ranks of the financial world, no matter what was going on, when Friday at 5 p.m. hit, I felt lighter somehow. Even if I was working through the weekend, nothing felt as serious or as stressful.

So maybe it shouldn't have shocked me as much as it did that, while sitting on a bistro stool at the counter, sipping Sancerre and watching Grace—whom I had watched cook dinner on Instagram countless times—cook dinner in real life, as Alice helped Iris with her school clothes and I snacked on grapes, I felt slightly less panicked than had been my status quo the past few days. What everyone was saying about my family, how Bill was faring in prison, why our freaking lawyer had failed to return *seven* of my calls . . . well, those were problems for someone else to deal with, another Charlotte on another day.

Or maybe it was just that this felt like the Twilight Zone, like my late-night Instagram friend had stepped through the screen and come to life. And now I was getting to know the real Grace.

She was detailing her split with her husband, how he got offered an amazing job in Tokyo and she wasn't willing to relocate. She added a splash of wine to the risotto pan, making it hiss, and said, "I think if he had stayed here, we would have stayed together. But the fact that he was dead set on moving and I was dead set on staying just revealed a deeper crack between us, this fissure that neither of us wanted to acknowledge. We didn't hate each other; we just didn't care."

That's when I had to realize that I wasn't a different Charlotte. I was the same Charlotte. Tears sprang to my eyes. "But, see, that's the thing," I said, my voice cracking embarrassingly. "I love Bill so much. And I just don't think he could possibly do something like this."

Grace smiled supportively. "So what does Bill say?"

I bit my lip, my face growing warm. "I don't know because I haven't gone to see him." I was bathing in shame. My eyes filled again, and I looked down into my glass so she wouldn't see.

"Hey," she said, "this is tough. There's no handbook. You're doing your best."

"Right. I'm doing my best." I shook my head, realizing that this half glass of wine might have gone to my head already. Was I seriously sitting here pouring my heart out to a stranger? After days with no one to really talk to about this, I think it just felt good to have someone listen. So I leaned into it. "I think I'm scared that, if he did do this, I'm going to have to look at my part. Like, was he stealing that money because he thought I needed more?" I had relished our big life, sure. I loved our beautiful house and our fancy decorator and how I could offhandedly say things like, "Wouldn't it be fun to have a restored Defender Ninety?" and one would magically appear a few days later. I loved planning our dream vacations and working them around Iris's school schedule and my perfect wardrobe. But all those things sort of evolved as we did.

I sighed.

"Either way, this isn't your fault," Grace said.

I took a deep breath. *It isn't my fault.* That was a relief, actually. "I went to great lengths to let him know that I loved him for him." My eyes filled. "And I did. I *do.* I love him so much. I miss him more than I can even say, and it's only been a few days."

I trailed off, and Grace leaned over the island toward me. "What is your favorite memory of Bill?"

I was surprised by the question. But I smiled at what instantly popped into my mind. "Bill is, like, a man, you know? He's serious and a little stoic and other people find him very intimidating. I knew he'd be a good father in all the ways that checked the boxes. He'd provide, he'd show up, he'd love our child." I had to take a deep breath to keep the wave of feelings from swamping me. "But I had no idea how great he would be with Iris. I remember when we brought her home from the hospital and it was the first time she had really cried and cried, and I was at my wits' end. And he put on beach music and danced with her all over the house. She loved it." I paused, the tears swelling in my throat. "And that kind of became their thing."

Grace reached out and squeezed my hands. "That's what you're going to think of," she said. "In those moments you don't think you're going to survive, that you aren't sure you can trust the man you loved, that's what you're going to remember." She smiled at me. "You're going to get through it. I promise you."

She locked eyes with me, and I knew she understood what I was going through.

"You certainly are," Alice said behind me, alerting me that she was back, meaning Iris wasn't far behind.

I raised my glass to Grace. "Thank you for the therapy."

I got up and walked around to her side of the island. "May I use these plates to set the table?" I grabbed a stack of plates from a glass-front cabinet.

"Sure," Alice said. "I'll help."

"Why don't you relax and let me take care of this?"

Grace held a spoon out for me. "This is the real therapy."

My mouth watered before I even tasted the risotto. It was complex and at once salty and sweet. It was so decadent I felt lost in it for a full five seconds.

"This is the best thing I've ever tasted," I said, swallowing reluctantly.

"And it's all very healthy for you," she said.

"It's official. I've arrived in the Garden of Eden. This completes the picture."

Julie walked into the kitchen too, hair wet from either the pool or the ocean or the shower. "Hello, beautiful ladies." She kissed Alice on the cheek, then turned to smile at me. "Charlotte, I am just so glad you're here. Glad we could chat through everything."

I was glad too. On both counts. I knew it was going to take some time to truly be certain I could trust Julie, but I was sure enough for now.

Alice smiled in agreement. She was placing a rattan placemat at each seat—which I took as a sign that she didn't want to relax—and I put a white plate that seemed to have little fish fins and a tail at each spot. "These are the cutest things I've ever seen!" I said.

"Alice's ex-boyfriend got them for us," Julie said in a tone that indicated, *He's her ex because she's crazy!*

I hadn't imagined Alice with a boyfriend. I was pretty set on her widow persona, which was ridiculous. Of course a woman could have a second act. I thought about what Iris had said earlier. A fourth act? Surely she was exaggerating. There was no way this gorgeous forty-five-year-old had lost three husbands in her young life so far. And if she had . . . well, that was just terribly sad. A little ripple of *something* did pass over me. Was that suspicion? I chastised myself. I was basically in the same position right now. Everyone and their brother was out in the world saying that I knew, I must have known, that I was in on Bill's scheme. And I decidedly was *not*—if there even was a scheme in the first place. So I was the last person in the world who should be judging anyone.

"Tell us about this boyfriend!" I said, wiggling my eyebrows, trying to seem like we were teenagers gossiping, not that I was wondering about Alice's secret past and if said boyfriend was actually Father Matthew at church, as Juniper Shores Socialite had predicted. But I didn't want them to know how closely I followed her page.

Alice smiled at me, but I could see the sadness behind her eyes. "There might have been something once, but he's gone. Moved away."

"Because someone broke his heart," Grace said matter-of-factly.

I wondered about the hole Alice had dug herself into. She was responsible for all of these people's fates. How could she even be free to date? What if she decided to remarry? I planned on this being a very temporary situation for us, so I wasn't worried for myself. I just couldn't imagine what pressure she must feel and how her own life must be tarnished in the pursuit of taking care of everyone else.

Iris bounded down the stairs in a flowing spaghetti-strap maxi dress that was a little too big. But she wore it well. She wore everything well, that awkward stage of two years ago fully behind her. Her hair was in a messy ponytail, and in the light streaming through the windows, she was both her future and her past. A little girl collecting seashells on the beach and a grown woman about to be out on her own. I didn't want this hardship for her. I wanted her to stay as young and carefree as possible for as long as possible. And I knew that this situation would steal some of that from her. I put the last plate down, walked to the foot of the stairs, and wrapped her in a hug, kissing her cheek. She smelled like a mixture of the sunscreen she wore every day and some sort of earthy-yet-expensive lotion that I was certain came out of our new shared bathroom. It smelled like Alice, like this house, like peace.

"You okay?" I asked.

Before she could answer, a teenage boy who I assumed must be Merit trotted down the stairs behind us, rushing by and grabbing a grape out of the bowl on the counter. He popped it in his mouth, turned, and smiled a smile that I knew had left a trail of longing girls in its wake. "Hey," he said, obviously to my daughter, not even noticing me.

Oh, crap, I thought. I had unwittingly put my daughter under the same roof as the high school heartthrob. I knew all about Merit from *Juniper Shores Socialite*, damn her. She talked about my husband and my family, but even still, the gossip she spewed was too delicious to look away. I wondered who she was.

"Hey," Iris said back. Merit walked over to the table and took a seat. Iris wriggled out of my embrace and whispered, "I think I'm going to like it here," as she walked to take the seat beside him.

As we all made our way to the table, Alice introduced me to Julie's three precious girls, Brenna, Jamie, and Audrey, and Grace introduced me to Merit's sister, Emma. She was in seventh grade, just two years younger than Iris, and I hoped they would get along well. Again, I was planning for this to be a very, very impermanent situation.

As everyone sat down, Alice said, "I thought this might be the right time for us to go over the beach house rules." I sat up a little straighter at that. *The beach house rules?* Well, okay. I guessed it made sense for a house to have rules. If I was going to be living here, I should know how things worked.

"Since you call your mom 'Mom,' Iris, you can call me 'Mama Grace,' and Julie prefers 'Mommy,'" Grace said.

My stomach lurched. Iris's face, now locked on mine, was white. But before I could get myself too worked up, Merit burst out laughing, and Alice, Grace, and Julie followed suit.

"I'm sorry! I'm sorry!" he said. "I couldn't keep it in any longer." He pointed at Iris. "Your face!"

My heart was returning to a normal beat.

"She's just teasing you," Alice confirmed. "Don't worry. There's nothing weird!"

"There's one that's a little weird," Julie said under her breath, as she helped herself to a large portion of risotto and scooped smaller portions onto her daughters' plates. *Those babies are going to eat risotto?* I thought. But there was no whining, no fussing, no complaining. Wow. Maybe these house rules worked.

"A little weird?" Iris asked.

"It's not weird, and it's really not hard at all once you get used to it," Alice said, which was when the hair on the back of my neck stood up. "But at dinnertime we all put our cell phones over on the front hall table at the charging station."

"That's great," I said, feeling relieved. "Then dinnertime is sacred, and no one is tempted to look at his or her phone."

"She isn't finished," Merit said.

"We don't retrieve our phones until the next morning," Alice added.

"What?" Iris practically spat. "But that's when everything happens! My Snap is fire at night. That's, like, half my social life. I can't just ignore it."

She was flushed, and I could tell she was panicking. I was sort of panicking too. How would it even be possible to not have our phones at night? I thought, idiotically, *How will I keep up with* Growing with Grace*'s reels?* But, well, now that I was sitting across the table from her, I guessed that was kind of a moot point. "Sweetheart," I said soothingly, "let's just hear Alice out."

"Well, that's really it," Alice said. "The average American child won't have the attention span to read a book by the time he or she is thirty-five. I won't contribute to that."

That really was horrifying. And I had read all those studies about social media contributing to unhappiness and depression in girls. Maybe I just hadn't been brave enough to take Iris's phone; I guess I'd reasoned that, if she didn't have a phone, she couldn't communicate and how would she have any friends? And wouldn't having no friends contribute to unhappiness and depression too?

"Okay," I said. "But, just playing devil's advocate, since I'm looking for a job, I might need to return emails or take phone calls in the evenings."

"There is a phone in every room," Alice said. "It used to be a B&B, after all. You just click on a new line if you want to talk. And computers are allowed. Just not the scrolling time-suck of cell phones."

I was telling myself that I was a grown woman and Alice wasn't my mother. She couldn't *make me* give up my phone. Then again, was it normal or healthy for me to feel this panicked by the idea of not being attached to a device for a few hours a night?

"We go out on the beach at night!" Brenna said with such seven-year-old enthusiasm that I thought I might cry.

"Yeah!" Jamie chimed in. "So we can see the moon and the stars."

"It really isn't bad once you get used to it," Julie said.

"You feel sort of . . . free," Grace added.

Free. When was the last time I'd felt free? And, come on, Grace had almost a million followers. If she could separate from her phone, surely I could too.

I pinned on a semifake smile and shot my daughter a look across the table as I said, "Well, then, we will adjust."

"It seriously only takes like a week to get used to it," Merit said. He grinned at Iris.

She grinned back. "Well, if you can do it, I can do it."

Grace caught my eye and shook her head. I knew what she was thinking: we might be in dangerous territory.

"Okay," Alice said. "Well, now that that's over, everything else is pretty simple. There's a board in the laundry room that details all the jobs for the week and whose responsibility they are. We chip in for a housekeeper once a week, so the major cleaning gets done. With so many of us, they are all very small time commitments, with the exception of Grace's."

Alice grinned at Grace, and I suddenly, irrationally, was jealous of her. Alice was like a flickering candle, and I was a moth. I felt drawn to her, like I wanted to be best, her favorite, her person. But that was ridiculous. I was in my late thirties. I didn't need to spend my time worrying about whether Alice liked me best.

Iris was shooting daggers at me with her eyes. I raised my one mom-eyebrow at her. I knew she didn't care about the chores; it was the phone. I would never hear the end of it.

"I already mentioned the vegan thing," Grace said.

I wondered if being vegan was unhealthy. Didn't children need a lot of protein? But then I looked at six-foot-tall, sixteen-year-old Merit with his shiny hair and perfect skin and ultra-white teeth, and I decided that he was getting everything he needed. And nothing that he didn't, which was probably more important.

"If every meal tastes like this," I said, "I think we're on board with anything."

"And we have homework time immediately after dinner," Alice said. "And all the adults are around to help with their assigned subject if any of the kids need help."

Iris didn't balk at that one.

"And then it's family beach time!" Brenna exclaimed.

She really was so cute. They all were.

"Forced family fun!" Merit said, matching her enthusiasm.

Alice held up her fingers. "The others are easy: everyone inside the beach house is treated like family."

Brenna piped up: "What happens in the beach house stays in the beach house!"

We all laughed at that. But it did make me wonder: Were there secrets to be kept here?

"Wet hair and sandy feet are highly encouraged," Julie said, smiling.

"And when you make a snack, make extra," Grace added. "Coffee too."

These were sweet rules. Warm and fuzzy rules that lulled me into contentment, that reminded me of childhood summers. Even so, my mind began to wander to Bill, to wonder how he was holding up. I decided that I would definitely go see him tomorrow. I had to. I needed answers. For a brief moment, I let myself sink down into my delusion: maybe he wasn't guilty after all.

~~~~~~~~

Big Brother

I was liking this *Alice* less and less by the minute. Until now, she had seemed like that cool aunt you went to when your mom was being a total drag. But no phones after dinner? This woman couldn't be serious.

"I mean, how am I supposed to keep my Streaks alive?" I moaned to Merit as we sat side by side at the top of the porch steps after our assigned homework time. He was wearing blue Patagonia baggies with a white Juniper Shores Surf Shop T-shirt that might as well have been a tux for how irresistible he was in them. He had legendary hair. It was shaggy, sun-streaked blond, and kind of flipped up around his face. He was perfect. And I was with him. So, that part of the mommune wasn't all bad.

I was half whining to Merit, half aware that every cell in my body felt more alive from the mere fact that it was this close to Merit's body. Was it even possible for a human to be as hot as he was? I'd seen him plenty, sure. But not this close up. He was flawless. I mean, what sixteen-year-old guy didn't have even a hint of acne?

He did this little snort thing out of his nose. "Oh, Iris, Iris, Iris, thank goodness I am here. I have so very much to teach you."

The way he said it made my breath catch. I hoped he didn't notice. Maybe I shouldn't have been complaining. When you thought about it, I had won the lottery. I was getting to live with the hottest guy in the junior class, which gave me ample opportunity to get in his good graces. If he couldn't so much as text another girl after dinner, it definitely gave me an advantage. I mean, I guessed he could call someone on that landline in his room. But who would even talk on the phone? The idea was totally ridiculous. I could think of many, many things I wanted Merit to teach me. I was, like, practically the only girl in the ninth grade who hadn't been kissed. Well, maybe not the *only* one. But the only one of my friends. It was definitely a goal for the year. And now it suddenly made sense. Why have a boring, run-of-the-mill kiss with some rando freshman when your first kiss could be the hottest junior in school? I felt like, for the first time since my life fell apart, God was smiling on me.

"Iris, you just have to get a burner phone."

Um, phone customs of teenage delinquents weren't high on the list of things I wanted to learn from Merit. But okay. Whatever. "I'm sorry. What? A burner phone? Like a drug dealer?"

I'd basically only seen burner phones on twisty dramas about criminals on the run. *Oh my gosh. Did my dad have a burner phone?* I was sort of in denial about my dad being, you know, in jail. It just didn't seem like it could be real. But he was innocent until proven guilty. Why didn't the rest of the world see that?

"Exactly like that," Merit said. "You just keep the burner in your backpack, and when dinnertime comes, you put your phone in the bag on the hall table like a good girl and you do your cursory family time on the beach. And then, when it's just you in your room, you get your burner and continue your Streaks to your heart's content."

I was so relieved. "I have spent so much time cultivating my

Snapchat life," I said, realizing how incredibly dorky I sounded. But Merit laughed. Good. He thought I was joking. I totally was not, but I would take it.

"So . . . how does one get a burner phone?"

He turned his head toward me and gave me this kind of half-smile that made sweat break out behind my earlobes.

"Leave it to me," he said.

Then something hit me. "Um. I can't exactly pay for said burner phone right now. I don't know if you've heard, but my financial situation has shifted."

I was trying to make light of things.

"Don't worry about it. I've got you. We in the mommune have to stick together."

I was dying to text my friend Chloe to tell her *I was living with Merit McDonald*. But, of course, I couldn't text her because I didn't have my phone.

"You can't do that," I protested.

He shrugged. "My dad throws plenty of pity allowance my way. I might as well share the wealth." He gave me a once-over, and for just a second I thought maybe he was checking me out. But then he said, "If your dad ever gets out of jail, you'll totally be owed pity allowance. It doesn't fix anything, but it's not the worst perk. Two Christmases aren't that bad either, once you get used to them."

I shook my head vigorously. "No, no. My dad might be in jail, but my parents aren't getting divorced."

That half-smile again, except this time it was sad. "Ah. Okay."

"You don't believe me!" I said, elbowing him flirtatiously at a time that wasn't really appropriate for flirting.

"I don't know your life," he said. "Maybe your mom is different. Maybe she can hang in there through all this."

A horrifying realization washed over me. It wasn't just that my dad was in jail; it wasn't just that we had lost our house and all our stuff and all our money—things that I had spent the past three days panicking about and somewhat coming to terms with. My parents were going to get divorced. Of course they were. How hadn't I seen it before? I was an idiot. I felt that burn in the back of my throat that meant I was going to cry. And then, horrifyingly, I did. I was sitting on the raw wood steps down to the beach crying in front of the hottest junior at Juniper Shores Prep. This was the most embarrassing moment of my life.

Well, it was . . . until he put his arm around me. "I want to tell you that I'm wrong, but I'm not going to lie to you, kid: I don't see how they get through this one."

Kid. That couldn't be good. But I was so close to him, and he smelled so great, like salt air and pine trees and something just a little spicy like cinnamon. Maybe calling me *kid* wasn't a setback.

I pulled away and wiped my eyes, and he put his thumb in the cleft of my chin and his fingers underneath it, turning my face toward his. He was going to kiss me. Oh my gosh, Merit, god of juniors, was going to kiss me. And while I acknowledged that it was probably a pity kiss, I would take it. I would take it all day long.

"I'll teach you how to surf."

"What?"

"I'll teach you how to surf," he said. "I swear, the waves healed me when I was dealing with my parents' split."

Surf. Uh-huh. Because that's what Merit could do to take my mind off of things. Boys were so dumb. But it was a nice offer. And I *did* want to learn how to surf. I wanted to be one of those cool girls with the saltwater dried in her hair making effortless beach waves. Although I kind of figured those girls never gave much thought to their hair. Well, whatever. It was more time with Merit. I'd worm my way in there somehow.

"A burner phone *and* a surf teacher all in one?" I asked demurely.

He nodded. "Just consider me the big brother you never had."

Big brother. That was going to be hard to come back from. But I could do it. The waves and Alice's new bikini would be all it took to get Merit thinking about me like I wasn't just a little sister. I mean, I thought. What did I know? I'd never even been kissed.

Merit stood up to go inside. "Burner phone time," he whispered. I smiled and gave him a thumbs-up.

As he turned to leave, I internally groaned. Could I possibly have done anything lamer? I mean, really? A thumbs-up.

But as I watched him walk away, I felt myself sigh without even meaning to. So, no, I wasn't 100 percent sold on the idea of living at the mommune. It was, admittedly, pretty weird. But if it meant spending more time with Merit, I thought it was a life I could get used to.

@junipershoressocialite

Sharing bad behavior and delicious drama in North Carolina's most exclusive coastal zip code. DM with tips, pics, and juicy deets.

AUGUST 29, 7:47 A.M.

9 Posts

2,173 Followers

11 Following

You didn't hear it from me, but . . .

PIC 1: A brand-new pair has moved into Juniper Shores' most-gossiped-about house: the mommune, a.k.a. Alice Bailey's beachfront compound, the creepy and surely haunted site of the death of one of the Black Widow's three deceased husbands. The disgraced Charlotte and Iris Sitterly have taken refuge from their troubles alongside its glittering ocean views. But one source questions: Will someone under that roof be the Black Widow's next prey? And another asks: Is the mommune a cult, and are Charlotte and Iris its newest members? Stay tuned. . . .

PIC 2: In your daily dose of high school drama, freshman Chloe Montoya has indeed snagged the reigning heir to the Juniper Shores automotive throne from a certain junior co-cheer captain. Chloe, we hope your new man gets you a fast getaway car. . . . Said junior girl also holds the Juniper Shores sprint record.

PIC 3: Boozy moms, rejoice! The RoséStream has reopened—just in time for the Juniper Shores Country Club Bar to undergo a full renovation. Do people around here not know that alcohol sales are the majority of our GTP (Gross Town Product)? Again, thoughts and prayers.

TNT ('Til Next Tequila!)

JUNIPER SHORES SOCIALITE

Charlotte

Before

"Miss," the Uber driver said gently, "are you, um, going to get out?"

Miss.

I couldn't remember the last time someone had called me *miss*. I didn't hate it. But then a cold chill washed over me. Was he calling me *miss* because he intuited that I was going to be unmarried in short order? I looked down at the sparkling carats on my left hand and my breath caught in my throat. This was one of the only things I had left. Was someone going to come take it from me? Should I try to sell it before they did? Would that be a crime?

And why isn't my freaking lawyer calling me back?! Three days ago, Oliver had left me a message letting me know the date and time of the arraignment and urging me to be there. Then he had left a message telling me that Bill was being detained because he was a flight risk since he had the means to flee and plenty of ties to offshore companies . . . and because of that stupid, nothing prior conviction for check fraud that I kept trying to ignore in case it made me think that Bill could have done this.

And, no, I had not called Oliver back then. So maybe he was

giving me a taste of my own medicine. But the idea that he had abandoned Bill too panicked me. Was it because we couldn't pay him with our assets frozen? But Oliver had been with us for almost three years. Not a lifetime, but long enough for us to deserve some loyalty. Surely he wouldn't desert us now. Part of me thought about calling someone else. But who? It wasn't like lawyers were filed under "wire fraud" in the Yellow Pages. Plus, I couldn't pay one anyway. I felt sick.

"I have another ride, but if you need me to drop you somewhere else . . ." the driver interrupted my thoughts again.

"No, I'm sorry," I said, collecting my purse and my phone and sliding out of the hot black leather seat. "Thanks so much. I'll be sure to give you five stars." And a good tip that I could ill afford for a half-hour ride I didn't want to take. I knew I was going to have to figure out a bus route or something if I came here often.

"I get it," he said. "No one's really dying to walk into jail."

I grabbed the bag I had brought and inhaled as I stepped out, somewhat relieved not to be bathing in the scent of pine air freshener anymore even if I was walking toward a fate that felt out of a fairy tale, one of the dark Grimms ones where people died and children were eaten by witches. But we never think about the bad parts of the fairy tale, do we? We remember Cinderella's glass slipper, not the evil stepsisters trying to keep her from the ball—or, in the original, cutting off their toes to fit the shoe. This was toe-cutting level.

I looked up at the building, which, to my immense relief, wasn't surrounded by a fence or barbed wire. It was long, white, and boring. It looked like a suburban high school. I was in a fog as I pushed a call button on the door and heard the buzz that meant I could open it. I walked into what looked more like a bank lobby than a prison. A woman in uniform with short, curly red hair sitting behind the desk said, "ID, please." I tried to smile at her as I handed her my license, but I couldn't quite do it.

"What's that?" she asked, taking my bag as I walked through a metal detector.

My new housemates had been so kind as to put together some treats for Bill. "Oh, just clean sheets, body wash, some snacks, things like that. Do you want to go through it?"

Her smile conveyed that I was the dumbest person she had ever met. "Ma'am, you can't bring that in here."

Now I was confused. "Why?"

"This isn't *Legally Blonde*. This is *prison*. You can leave that on the counter and get it when you leave."

I was embarrassed, mostly because she had read me so clearly: we had based this whole thing on the scene in *Legally Blonde* when Elle Woods visits her exercise instructor in prison. So, yeah. The woman rifled through my bag and handed me the two paperback books I had packed for Bill. One was *Killers of the Flower Moon*, a tale of the grizzly Osage murders. But I knew he would get the subtext of the flower moon, remember our perfect night on the beach, hopefully be transported there. "Here," she said. "You can take these."

I changed the subject. "Um, what do I need to do if I want my daughter to be able to come visit my husband?" Nausea roiled in my stomach. *Stop it,* I scolded myself. This was the reality. I had to handle it. Plus, this would be over so soon. I hoped.

She handed me a stack of papers. "Fill these out."

"Thank you," I said, quietly, my throat feeling dry. As I wrote, I said, "I mean, I'm sure we don't even need these. There's no way they can just keep holding him here. He didn't even do anything wrong in the first place. So my daughter will just see him at home and . . ." I realized I was rambling, and the look she was giving me was so *oh you poor thing, you think he's innocent* that I wanted to smack her.

A man, also in a uniform, smiled jovially at me. "You ready, Mrs. Sitterly?" he asked.

I wanted to say no. I wanted to run away. I wanted to see Bill, but I didn't want to see him.

I had no idea what to expect. I'd never been to jail, after all. I'd only seen it on TV, watched prisoners and their visitors talk on black phone receivers through panes of plexiglass.

"I guess so?" I asked.

"He's going to be mighty glad to see you." He was awfully *cheery*.

I was surprised to be taken to an open room with floor-to-ceiling windows, quilts hanging on the walls, five or six sets of tables and chairs. It smelled of a familiar cleaning solution. Windex, maybe, or 409? It wasn't an offensive smell, and it thrilled me that the entire place felt so bright and tidy. A family was clustered in the right-hand corner, and it broke my heart to see a toddler on what I presumed was her father's lap. In the middle were two men huddled together talking. And in the left-hand corner, in an orange jumpsuit he looked quite sickly in, was Bill. Huh. It was shocking to see how tiny a six-foot-two man could look.

Bill's once-blond hair had darkened to light brown and, now, begun to tinge with gray around the temples. He was a stickler for an every-three-week haircut, which he was definitely at the tail end of now. Bill had a commanding presence, broad shoulders, a strong jaw. He was the kind of man who looked like he would always protect me. What about now? He gasped when he saw me. He jumped out of his chair and practically leapt toward me, wrapping me in his arms and kissing me passionately. I let him. He smelled like metal and industrial soap, not the Byredo Black Saffron body wash he favored. And he was so *thin*. How was he ever going to survive in here?

It felt like a stranger kissing me, but I still found myself melting into him. I missed him; I missed him *so* much. As I pulled away and hugged him tightly, I felt myself exhale a breath that I didn't know I had been holding for the past four days. And out with the breath came an absolute reservoir of tears. I looked into the face of my husband, the man I loved. "I'm so sorry," I said. A physical pain gripped my insides. Through my tears, I touched his face and said, "You needed me, and I just left you here."

He pulled me to him again. "Hey," he said quietly, in that same kind voice he always used to comfort me. "It's okay. I know this has been hard for you too." He stroked my hair. "I knew you had to go home to your parents. You didn't have anywhere else to go."

"Home is where you are," I choked.

He kissed my tearstained cheeks. "I know."

And I knew he did. I knew that Bill knew—was the only one who knew—that he was my rock, my safe place, my port in the storm. Without him, I was totally adrift. Trying to hold it together had nearly killed me. I knew then that not coming here had been a protective move in more ways than one. If I saw him, I would default to letting him fix things. That wasn't an option. I needed to be strong for Iris; I had to be the one with the plan. He held my face in his hands and said, "Look at me."

I nodded, and I did, suddenly not caring what he had done, or how bad it was. I just had to get him out of here.

"I did not do this," he said firmly.

I nodded because I knew he was telling the truth; I'd known it the moment I saw him sitting so small in the corner. I believed him with all my heart, and then I felt even worse because I'd been mad at him when I should have been helping him.

"I know," I whispered. I bit my lip. "I'm so sorry I wasn't there for the arraignment." I had let myself off the hook, told myself that not standing beside my husband as he faced the federal magistrate was because I was getting Iris and me set up for our next move. But the reality was that I just couldn't face it.

Over Bill's shoulder I finally noticed the man I had once believed held the key to solving all our problems: Oliver Engle, the refined, fortysomething British attorney Bill had hired as his head counsel at Sitterly Capital three years ago. He always wore horn-rimmed glasses and wool sports coats that made him seem as if he'd just come from a hunt. And he smelled faintly of pipe tobacco, though I'd never seen him smoke. Something about his mere presence soothed me.

Upon spotting him, I remembered it wasn't just Bill and me here. I took a deep breath, wiped my face, and walked to him. "Well, well, well . . . you aren't dead in a gutter or on vacation on a deserted island."

He looked sheepish. "Apologies, Charlotte. I've been working nonstop to get Bill out of here until his trial—at least get him on house arrest."

"House arrest," I repeated. "You mean, like, at the house I'm not allowed to go into?"

Bill slumped back down in the chair. "I'm so sorry, sweetheart. I'm so sorry. As soon as we figure out how to get me out of here, Oliver and I will put all our effort into getting your and Iris's lives back to normal—or as normal as possible."

I loved Bill, and I missed him, and I wanted him out of here, but I have to say, that irked me. Was he not worried about us at all? I had gone to stay with my *parents.* That's how bad things were. I mean, I'm exaggerating, obviously. Kind of. My parents were great people. They volunteered for causes that mattered, protested when there was a wrong to right, spent their lives in the pursuit of making the world a better, more equal place for all who lived in it. They were both professors; to my friends, my parents were brilliant paragons of knowledge and truth. And I never gave them a reason to doubt that. But the problem had always been that they were more concerned with the pursuit of knowledge than anything else. Including their daughter.

I read once that there comes a point in childhood development when daughters begin to cling more to their mothers, while sons begin to separate and break away. I might have been an exception to the rule because I broke away from both my parents. When I was more interested in playing outside than spending hours with my nose in a book. When numbers came to me easily and quickly, but I was never that interested in history or politics. And, most glaringly, when, instead of signing up with a nonprofit, I took a job at Bank of America. And then married Bill, who also worked in finance.

My actions were stabs at everything my parents—who thought that capitalism was the devil and the downfall of society—believed in. They told me not to get mixed up in that world. They told me not to marry Bill. And so, when I showed up at my childhood house in Chapel Hill and my mother said, "Well, Charlotte, what can I tell you? When you deal with the devil, you get burned," I almost left. But I had frozen assets, no home, no clothes, fourteen hundred dollars in cash that, thank goodness, was in my wallet, on my person, when our house was raided, and a daughter to think about. So I swallowed my pride, shook my head, and spent three days holding my breath and shrugging off their holier-than-thou attitudes.

They loved us, of course. They helped us enormously, finding us clothes, feeding us, lending me money until, God and Oliver willing, we could get back in our house. But I needed love and sympathy, nurturing and chicken soup. That, however, was too much to ask for.

Now I had to face the fact that my husband was still locked up, that my life was still a disaster, and that I finally felt ready to look for answers. Now that I knew Bill was innocent, if I could help prove it, my parents wouldn't be able to give me those *I told you so* looks anymore.

"I love you, Char, and I'm going to fix this. But please don't be mad at me. I'm telling you, I have been framed. Everything's going to be back to normal soon. You'll see."

I looked around the room, realizing that we certainly weren't alone, and that even if we had been, there were cameras everywhere. I wanted to yell up at them, *Do you hear him? He didn't do this!* But I guessed guilty people lied all the time.

I studied Bill again in that orange outfit and was swamped with horror. I squatted down in front of him, my hands on his knees, the fabric rough and thick and industrial. "I will get you out of here," I said.

He nodded. He kissed my hand. "I never had any doubt." He paused. "What are people saying?"

I didn't know as much about what people were saying because of Alice. The time away from my phone last night had proven to be blissful, restorative. Sitting on the beach, sipping wine with the other moms, had given me a gift I wasn't expecting. Alice had told me that if I didn't read what people were saying, then it didn't apply to me. That wasn't exactly accurate, but it had done wonders to keep my sanity intact.

I shrugged. "Time heals all wounds," I said. "You know how it is. People move on."

"Hey," Oliver said, "I hate to interrupt, but we've got some work to do. Charlotte, can I walk you out?" He looked at Bill. "I'll be right back."

Bill squeezed my hands and kissed me again. I savored that kiss, breathed it in. I knew it would be a while until I had another. "I love you," he said. "Don't forget it."

I was in that fog again, my eyes full of tears, as Oliver led me out to the parking lot, stopping to retrieve my bag on the way. My heart was pounding in my chest. How do I fix this for Bill? How do I get our life back? I noticed Oliver looking around.

"Tell me you aren't looking for my car," I said.

He touched his palm to his forehead. "I'm sorry, Charlotte. I'm exhausted. I'm not thinking straight." He walked over to his car, and I followed. "Let me take you home."

"Since I can ill afford another Uber fare and the extra twenty-five percent I feel inclined to tip since they are dropping me at, you know, *jail*, I would appreciate a lift more than I can say."

As we pulled out of the parking lot, I gave Oliver the address, then asked, "So, how much trouble is he in?"

Oliver pursed his lips. "Char, I'm not going to sugarcoat it: I don't know yet what the feds have on him. They conduct these investigations in secret, and I don't have any of their evidence yet." He paused. "But at the indictment, Bill was charged with wire fraud and wire fraud conspiracies with companies known and unknown to the grand jury."

I looked at him blankly.

"Meaning other people were likely involved, and they know it. They just haven't made arrests yet."

I nodded. "But how can they just keep him there?"

"Look, I'll level with you. Sometimes people are free on bond who probably shouldn't be, and sometimes they keep people who it seems kind of ridiculous to keep." He sighed. "But the prosecutor had concrete reasons to keep him."

That fired me up. "Well, what about . . ." I searched my brain and pulled out the only legal term I could think of. ". . . habeas corpus!"

"The prosecutor is arguing that he can be detained until trial because letting him out would give him the opportunity to cover his tracks, get his story straight with his staff, flee to another country. . . . And, Char, I hate to remind you, but he has a previous charge."

"Wait. *Habeas corpus* was the right term?"

Oliver laughed a little out of his nose. "Look, Charlotte, between us, I'm worried about how high-profile this has gotten."

I flicked Oliver on the shoulder, and he looked surprised. "Oliver, you are the fixer. When things are bad, you make them better. I need that right now! Come on!"

He smiled half-heartedly. "Charlotte, my dear, it is all going to be right as rain! I will wipe this away like it never happened."

I nodded. "That's more like it."

We both tried to laugh, but it didn't quite take. Nothing was funny. I wanted Bill. He was the one who took care of me. I wasn't sure I could face all of this without him. My head began to pound.

Oliver pulled up to the beach house and turned to look at me seriously. "Charlotte, the indictment was very clear, so I waived Bill's preliminary hearing." He put his fingers to his nose, backing up, since I obviously looked confused. "It will take two or three weeks for the discovery—basically the evidence against Bill—to come in. And then we will exercise our right to a speedy trial."

Trial. My stomach rolled, and I felt like I might be sick.

"And if we go to trial . . ."

Oliver didn't have to finish the sentence. I knew what he meant. Without concrete proof Bill wasn't involved, if we got to a court date, the outcome was anyone's guess. Even if Bill was innocent, could we prove it?

Oliver said, "Look, Charlotte, Bill isn't one hundred percent sure how he feels about this, but I have to tell you . . ."

My stomach turned.

"You can technically go back to your house. The investigation there is finished."

I felt a little light inside of me, but, as soon as it flickered, the look on Oliver's face dimmed it. And then I remembered: all those people had all those hands in all my things. My *underwear* drawer would have been searched. Things had been seized from our house. I felt so violated, and, as much as I missed home, I knew I would feel that violation ten-fold if I were back there.

Most of all, Bill wasn't there. How could it feel like home without Bill?

"And why doesn't Bill want me to know?" I asked.

Oliver sighed. "He's worried about your safety and Iris's safety. He's afraid that, with all these people out there believing he's guilty, someone could come after you and Iris."

The mere idea of someone coming after my child made a cold chill run down my spine. I was surprised that I felt relieved Bill didn't want us to go home. For now, at Alice's, I felt safe. I wanted to keep it that way.

I nodded. "Yeah. Okay. We'll stay put for now. We're fine where we are." I paused, thinking about my daughter. I didn't want to lie to her, but sometimes protecting your children meant glossing over the truth. "Maybe don't mention this to Iris? If she knows, it will just be this whole thing."

"Mum's the word," Oliver said.

I smiled because the phrase was so cute in his British accent.

"For now, we just concentrate on getting Bill out of there and getting you all back home, together, lickety split," Oliver said.

I was suddenly filled with purpose, like hot concrete was growing inside of me and then solidifying, making me strong. Bill would save me if I were in a situation like this. I was going to save him right back.

A Beautiful System

I stole money from the offering plate once. I was eight years old. I had been chosen for a high honor that day: post-church lemonade server. My prize? Leaving church straight from communion—before the post-communion prayer, before the final hymn—to get ready. Knowing I was walking down the aisle to break out early, escape the confinement between my two brothers in the hard wooden pew, and burst out of the huge double doors into the vast, enveloping light and warmth of the spring day, was a heady type of freedom that made me feel powerful and reckless. So maybe that's what made me so bold.

Two gleaming brass offering plates sat on the long table behind the last, empty pew, overflowing with checks, envelopes, and cash, barely contained, like the stream of water from the fountain at school. With no premeditation whatsoever, I reached my hand over and grabbed a crisp, new five-dollar bill from the top.

That's when my trouble began.

I knew that somewhere, way deep down, that was why I found myself now, at barely 6 a.m., in the back room of the wooden A-frame church on the water that had felt like home to me for decades. Behind the holy, public spaces, in the private, workhorse one,

I polished, ironically, the same offering plate I had stolen that five dollars from. Then I moved my silver cloth onto the chalice that the congregation drank wine out of every Sunday morning, admiring the way it gleamed in the fluorescent light of the sterile altar guild room, which was lined with old, utilitarian wood cabinets with cheap white plastic knobs. It seemed incongruous that the interiors of such simple cabinets were crammed full of priceless, antique silver. The story goes that, when this church was founded in the late 1700s, the women got together and donated their jewelry. It was melted down to form pieces like this engraved silver chalice, which was lined with gleaming gold.

I never could be sure how I felt about all these shiny things in relationship to the God I felt I knew, the one who was kind and loving and forgiving—even toward someone like me. I didn't think that God cared all that much about the ostentatious urns we filled with opulent displays of roses and lilies each week. Even still, I loved them. I loved getting to be the one here with them, maintaining them, caring for the vessels that would hold Christ's body and blood.

This simple space with its perfectly ordered cabinets—organized by me—soothed me. It was where I felt closest to God. I didn't pray to him anymore, not in any sort of personal way outside of the prayers I recited in church. After I'd begged him to rescue Jeremy from that avalanche and Glen from that car accident, after I'd pleaded with him through tears in the back of the ambulance with Walter, whose head and face were swollen to proportions that didn't even look human, I stopped. I still believed in God. I just no longer believed that he cared what I wanted.

Maybe church was now just another ritual that helped me get through the days. But I'd always been a church person. It was the first place I felt real comfort and joy as a child, as a little angel in the

Christmas program, singing a solo of "Silent Night." I couldn't understand why people were crying, but I felt in my heart it was a good thing. After that, I was hooked. These days I loved to be alone in my austere church by the sea early in the morning. I often woke around four thirty or five, and I needed something to occupy my thoughts, to distract me from the sadness and loss that were bound to creep in during those early, silent moments. I could walk in the dark down the beach and use the key I had been entrusted with after many years of service, to spend time in the holy silence of my most grounding place.

If they knew about the five dollars from the offering plate, would they have given me a key? If they knew that I was so shameless that I used the money to buy the Hello Kitty erasers I'd had my eye on, would they let me back here?

The door to the altar-guild room flew open, startling me out of my thoughts, and I couldn't tell if my heart was racing because of the noise or because of the man walking through the doorway. Elliott Palmer. *My* Elliott. Only, he hadn't been mine for almost a year for reasons that, as he stood in his jeans, cowboy boots, and slightly rumpled collared shirt, holding the silver ladle that was used for baptisms, I couldn't quite remember for a moment.

I wasn't sure if he was still angry at me for the way I ended things; he hadn't reached out since he moved away, a few hours inland, to take over the antiques business his great-grandfather started generations before. But he grinned when he saw me like no time had passed, like nothing had changed, like I had never broken his heart.

After Walter died, I had sworn off men. Three dead husbands in the span of twelve years was three too many. I knew people said I'd killed them. And if it weren't so ridiculous, it would have crushed me. So, not only could I not live through that sort of loss again, but I also had to imagine that men wouldn't be lining up to lend me their arms. Plus, I was beginning to wonder if I was cursed.

Too stunned to delve into anything real with Elliott, too rattled to formulate something sensible, I said, "You shaved." Oh, how I wished he hadn't. Because his bare face was even more handsome. And I was kicking myself because *that* was all I could find to say to him, to this man I had cried into my pillow over for months.

"I had forgotten how beautiful you are," he said.

I realized that maybe Elliott wasn't winning any *bright things to say to your ex* competitions either. But I felt a blush coloring my cheeks all the same. Elliott could do that to me, make me feel girlish. I fell in love with him too quickly; I wanted a future with him right away. And that was why I had to let him go. Because maybe what everyone said was true: I had killed three men I loved. I couldn't kill a fourth.

After the first two deaths, I had joined a support group for mourners. By the time I lost Walter, I felt like I had memorized the program. I was embarrassed to go back there *again*. I wondered if this was what it felt like when alcoholics fell off the wagon, got back on, and had to start AA from scratch. It wasn't their fault; they were fighting a lifelong battle with a hideous illness. But in both situations, going back again and again presented some sort of element of failure. I had once again failed to keep a husband alive.

If I had gone back to that widows' support group I felt like I was flunking, I never would have met Elliott. Unable to haul myself into the converted gas station that held the group every Monday, Wednesday, and Friday, I had instead taken my lonely heart to the brewery across the street for a beer. I had sat, feeling numb, wondering how a woman could even begin to make a start after so many losses.

Elliott had walked in that cold, dreary Wednesday night in February, when the island's population was at its lowest, with a full beard and a flannel shirt tucked into his jeans. I didn't consider him all that much. I wasn't in a place to. But we were the only people in the bar, and, once he got his beer, he sat right beside me.

"Is this seat taken?" he asked.

"Only by all my ghosts," I said in the most macabre voice I could muster. I didn't necessarily want him to leave, but I wanted to be clear that I wasn't in a Susie Sorority mood. I wasn't going to give him some friendly, chatty banter and leave him with a smile—or end up in his bedroom.

As he settled onto the stool, he said, "There's room for them and for me."

He was trying to make me laugh; he succeeded. But his words turned out to be prophetic too. Because, much to my shock, there was room for Elliott and my three dead husbands. And my niece. And her three children. And the various and sundry other families who had been a part of ours. The man was not only a saint, he was also fun. He was light and free in a way I envied. He didn't worry all the time, didn't sweat the small stuff. He was five years my junior and mid-divorce from his high school sweetheart. He, like me, had no biological children. His wife, however, had gotten pregnant. With a baby that wasn't his. He had his ghosts, I had mine.

Why did I throw that away? I asked myself now. I remembered something about protecting him, about saving him from me, but none of that seemed important as I felt my pulse speed up at his mere presence.

"Elliott," I said, his name tasting like honey in my mouth. I was going for a scolding tone, but it didn't quite take.

He stepped closer to me, and I felt a familiar thrumming in my chest that only Elliott could produce. "No. I hadn't forgotten how beautiful you are. I just thought that I must be remembering you with rose-colored glasses. Because no one could be as beautiful in real life as I remembered you."

I shook my head, reminding myself. I hadn't seen him a week ago. It had been almost a year. "What are you doing here?" I asked. I knew what I wanted him to say. But how could he when I had discarded him?

He gave me his amused look, my favorite one. "Well, see, I came back here for you."

Yes. That was what I wanted him to say. But why? Hadn't I felt almost relieved when he left?

"But Juniper Shores Socialite said you had something going on with Father Matthew, and considering that you're here before sunrise, I have to wonder if she might be right."

I rolled my eyes. "Yes. I'm so glad you put serious stock in an anonymous Instagram account."

He nodded. "It's the only place I get my news. All facts. All the time."

I laughed.

"So, Father Matthew?"

I put my hand to my heart. "As you can see, Father Matthew, the grumpiest, quietest man alive, and I are in the middle of a torrid affair."

He laughed. "So that's a no, then?"

I gave him a *please* look. My heart was racing out of my chest, and I just needed a second to compose myself. Because, sure, I had pushed him away. But in my heart of hearts, hadn't I hoped and prayed that he would come back to me? Hadn't I spent more nights than I could count missing that laugh of his, that smile, the way he always had an arm around me, a hand in mine, as if he could protect me from the world? I knew I had. I wanted to close my eyes and lean into this and rewind like no time had passed. But I was a woman with too many scars. "Are you serious, Elliott?"

"Have I ever, ever lied to you?"

I took a step closer to him, the only thing between us the ladle.

"Nothing's changed," I whispered. I thought back to that night on the beach, crying into the sleeves of my sweater. "You don't understand," I had sobbed to him. "I'm cursed. Every man who loves me dies. I love you too much to hurt you."

He had held me to him. "Al, that's ridiculous. You aren't cursed. Unlucky, maybe, but not cursed."

He couldn't convince me. And as much as it had broken me to watch him walk away, I felt like I had saved him.

Now he said, "You're right. Nothing has changed." He put his hand to my cheek. "This thing between us is still very, very real."

"But . . ." My heart was thudding too loudly in my ears to finish, my pulse pounding in a rhythm that wanted only Elliott. "Is this ladle for me?" I asked, trying one last time to deny the connection I felt with him.

He nodded. "I fixed it. That's what I do, Al. I fix things."

Elliott's family owned a huge antiques importer just a few hours away where people came from all over the country to shop for authentic pieces they couldn't find anywhere else, from true one-of-a-kind heirlooms—chairs sat in by Louis XIV or campaign chests that once resided in George Washington's battle tent—all the way down to inexpensive trinkets you might find at a flea market. When we dated, he was always bringing me some token of his affection, and it was always perfect. A four-leaf clover preserved in glass, a vintage locket that happened to bear his initials (that was underneath my dress right now, still close to my heart), a set of incredible china that he insisted I use every day, an antique sewing basket that perfectly held my magazines. In his professional role, he had learned to fix and repair any number of priceless old objects, to save them from destruction.

I took the ladle in my hands, setting it delicately on the counter on a piece of felt, admiring its soft curves and delicate etching. Elliott, from behind me, took my hand in his. "It was beginning to split right here," he said, his rough, callused finger over mine. He ran my finger over an area of the silver. "So I soldered some sterling silver into the space and made it as good as new."

His breath, which smelled of coffee and peppermint, was so warm in my ear.

He turned me around toward him, my back on the counter, my legs touching his. He put his hands on the space where my neck met my shoulders, and I remembered how, when we were together, he always had his hand there. "Just because something is broken, Alice, that doesn't mean you throw it away. It means that, if you love it enough, if you care for it exactly right, you can make it whole again."

Looking up into his blue eyes, I felt like I was melting into a puddle, like all the mushy parts inside of me were going into all the mushy parts inside of him. I knew then that I couldn't be away from him, that all the nights I'd lain awake missing him with a deep pain inside my bones hadn't been wrong. I didn't want to need him; I didn't want to love him. Because I didn't want to hurt him. Well, no, I didn't want to *kill* him.

His hands ran down my bare arms, resting on my hips. "Elliott," I said quietly. "They died. All three of them."

He nodded. "I wasn't worried about that a year ago. I'm not worried about it now."

My eyes filled with tears. Here was someone who knew the truth and loved me anyway, someone I had pushed away who came back here for me. Yet I didn't know if I was brave enough to start over again. I didn't know if I could let him love me.

He leaned his forehead on mine and whispered, "How about we

finish here, go get some coffee, and talk about how I'm too big and strong to die, even at the hands of the Black Widow."

I couldn't help but laugh. I knew people called me that. And if I hadn't before, that damn Juniper Shores Socialite had certainly spread the word. I didn't even blame people, but it was still hurtful. In other people's voices—not in Elliott's. Because he loved me, and I knew it as well as the lines of his abdomen that I put my hands on now. My heart was racing. This heat between us was what had been impossible to resist.

I tilted my head up to his, remembering that I'd broken up with him because I wanted to protect him, reminding myself that nothing had changed. Just as I was about to move my mouth the last inch toward his, that heavy old door with the ancient, creaky springs began to open. Elliott literally jumped away from me, and not a moment too soon.

"Father Matthew!" I said. "I'm just here doing altar guild," at the same time Elliott was saying, "I fixed your ladle!"

He looked from me to Elliott and back to me, an expression on his face like he knew he should probably care about what was happening here, but he decidedly did not. Father Matthew was a man in his late sixties with gray hair and a world-weary expression. But he came alive behind the pulpit. It was an interesting thing to watch, a moment that felt like callings were real.

"All right, then," Father Matthew said. "Have my vestments been altered for morning prayer?"

Right. Morning prayer. Which was now, or, well, almost now.

"We're here! We're here!" Leslie called as she bustled in with a basket that smelled like it contained some sort of baked good, Bonnie on her heels. My altar-guild partners in crime were both wearing slim black pants with different-colored ballet flats and printed blouses, as though they were in middle school and had coordinated their outfits but didn't want to match exactly. Bonnie's shoulder-length hair was held back by a thin tortoiseshell headband. Everything about her style screamed *efficient!* She made fun of Leslie incessantly for growing her hair out long again and coloring it back to the red of her youth. I thought it was cute.

"Thank goodness for you, Alice," Bonnie said. "Seven just gets earlier and earlier, doesn't it?"

Leslie handed Father Matthew the basket. "I was late because I was making these muffins for you," she said sweetly.

"Suck-up," Bonnie said quietly, only to me.

Elliott laughed. "I should be going," he said as I pulled the plain silver handle of the small closet that held Father Matthew's vestments. It stuck a little, the paint catching in the humidity.

I looked over Father Matthew's head. Elliott winked and mouthed *Call me.* Bonnie's eyes went wide. "It's true! He's back!" she whispered. "Are you two an item again?"

Great. That news would be all over town by afternoon. No one had bigger mouths than Bonnie and Leslie. Were *they* Juniper Shores Socialite? Nah. I doubted they would venture into the world of Instagram. Why would they when plain old word of mouth had served them so well?

Leslie slipped the vestment on Father Matthew, and he wordlessly left the small room, seeming relieved to get away from all these women, as usual.

"Leslie, you are shameless," I said, remembering that this was the other reason I loved this church, this altar guild. In my heart of hearts, I often felt so numb. By comparison, they were so animated that some days I felt like they rubbed off on me.

She smiled demurely at me. "Why, Alice, I have no idea what you mean."

Bonnie rolled her eyes. "Father Matthew is great behind the pulpit. There's no denying that. But I just can't see him being a very exciting husband."

Leslie put her hands on her hips. "Bonnie, I am seventy-seven years old. I don't need exciting. I don't need dramatic. I have you for that."

I laughed, and Leslie looked back at me. "What about you, Alice?" she said. "Are things exciting and dramatic with our beautiful antiques man?"

Bonnie literally clutched her pearls. "Oh, how I hope so! Please let me live vicariously through you!"

"Bonnie!" I scolded. "What would Dean say?"

She scoffed. "Oh, call me when you've been married fifty-four years." Then she bit her lip as if realizing that might be the wrong thing to say to a woman who'd never managed to be married more than seven.

"So, are you going to call him?" Leslie asked. "Because if he had mouthed that to me, I can tell you I wouldn't be in this room right now."

I laughed again. "Leslie! What would Father Matthew say?" These women.

Would I call him? Maybe he was right: he was man enough to overcome any curse from any woman. Even the Black Widow.

"Just don't wait too long, darling," Bonnie advised.

Leslie nodded. "A man like that has *choices*."

I gasped.

Bonnie shook her head. "We aren't saying he's interested in his choices."

"We're just saying that the town is aflutter with the news of his arrival and a lot of women would like to be in your position, with Elliott pining for them," Leslie added.

I studied them as they flittered about and twittered on about Elliott and me. I wondered if, inside, they were as light and uncomplicated as they seemed. And, maybe even more, I wondered if they could see past my perfectly cultivated exterior, all the way to the darkness inside of me. And, more important: Could Elliott?

@junipershoressocialite

Sharing bad behavior and delicious drama in North Carolina's most exclusive coastal zip code. DM with tips, pics, and juicy deets.

AUGUST 29, 4:42 P.M.
12 Posts
3,214 Followers
13 Following

You didn't hear it from me, but . . .

PIC 1: Yes, as predicted, the golden boy—well, man . . . he is forty, after all, but it doesn't have quite the same ring—has indeed returned! Elliott Palmer, once the pride of the Juniper Shores Marlins, fled (for his life?) after a reportedly traumatic breakup with Alice Bailey—who seemed to have landed the whale—nearly a year ago. Speaking of rings . . . is he back for the Black Widow? Or back to his playboy ways?

PIC 2: From headline sponsor to MIA . . . Everyone's favorite Mommy Blogger was notably absent from her chairwoman position at this year's Save the Turtles Tea. Did she have a fall from, well, Grace? Or are outside activities not allowed at the mommune? GWG, DM us for deprogramming!

PIC 3: Spotted! The oh so glamorous and almost too beautiful Charlotte Sitterly, leaving the county jail in an ultra-chic sheath and oversized sunglasses that practically scream *Stand by your man!* After being noticeably absent at his arraignment, it would now appear that Charlotte is officially Team Bill. So, what does that mean about his guilt . . . or innocence? And when does this poor woman get her house back? Did she know about the crime? Was she in on it? So much to uncover. One of our sources says that Charlotte Sitterly was actually the mastermind, and Bill took the fall for his wife. (We get it, Bill; she's a fox.) But all we can say is: innocent until proven guilty.

PIC 4: Plus, we have a bigger question: Who was the hunky Brit driving Mrs. Sitterly home? If he's your new paramour, we say, more power to you. If not, be a doll, Char: Send hunky Brit our number!

TNT ('Til Next Transmutation, i.e., converting joint property into sole property for our beautiful Charlotte, we hope, God willing . . .)
JUNIPER SHORES SOCIALITE

Most Powerful
Woman in the Room

I was already beginning to love the flurry of the mornings at the mommune. All the kids together, Alice being the one to nag them about plans and whether they had everything they needed. Julie had told me that the key to life here was to pretend that you were at summer camp. Grace, Julie, and I were the counselors-in-training, Alice was head counselor, and the kids were campers. Because if you thought about it too much, Juniper Shores Socialite—who had, for better or worse, become the running inner dialogue of the people—was right: living at the mommune was weird. A bunch of grown women raising their kids in the same house? Unconventional. But if you thought of it like summer camp, then it wasn't weird. For a brief period of time, we were under one roof, eating together, laughing together, making new friends that I hoped we'd have forever. It was great. If I could set aside the deep, painful longing for the man I loved, that is.

I walked down the stairs, feeling determined to make the best of every situation today. I wondered, briefly, if Iris and I should go back home.

But then Audrey flew from around the corner from the first-floor bunk room. "I want to go on the beach!" she shrieked to me.

And I remembered how much being here felt safe and comforting. I decided I would be honest with Alice that we could go home. But I distinctly hoped she'd let us stay anyway.

"Me too! Me too!" Jamie chimed in, racing down the hall, already in her kindergarten jumper, Julie on her heels.

"Hi!" she said to me breathlessly but sunnily. "Audrey! There you are. We have to get you ready!"

I shook my head. "I'll get her ready. You get to work. There's nothing worse than being rushed."

"I'll take them to school!" Alice said, standing up from the living room couch. I hadn't even seen her.

"I made lemon muffins!" Grace called from upstairs. She appeared on the landing, still in her flannel pajamas, toothbrush in hand. "Grab one on your way out. They are divine, if I do say so myself."

Julie kissed my cheek and then Grace's. "The two of you are angels from heaven. I swear that you are. I can't live without you, and I love you so." She rushed out.

"I need milk," Audrey said, studying my face. "So I can grow big and strong." She flexed her muscles.

Organic milk and butter from a local farm were the only non-vegan items Grace allowed in her kitchen. She believed the fat was good for little brains and the probiotics were good for all our bellies. After growing up in the fat-free era, I still found it surprising that all that whole-fat milk was now considered good for us. But things were always changing. I was Exhibit A.

Speaking of change, Iris was helping Brenna butter her muffin and Jamie up on a stool. She peeled a banana for Jamie and handed it to her. She had slid right into this crazy world.

I kissed Iris, who was all ready for school in her plaid skirt and white blouse, picking blueberries out of the communal bowl of fruit salad.

I smelled Merit before I saw him. Teenage boys and their cologne . . . Emma was hot on his heels. I could tell she was smitten with Iris, already worshipping the ground she walked on. Merit pulled Iris's ponytail playfully, and the two older girls rolled their eyes at each other. But Iris blushed.

"Do you have your lunch?" I asked.

"Yes, ma'am," Iris said. She brightened. "Look at what Grace made me!" She opened a bento box with what appeared to be pinwheel veggie and hummus wraps, fruit skewers, potato wedges, and cookies that were, no doubt, homemade. That irked me, but I didn't have time to feel irritated right now.

"Homework?"

Iris nodded, her mouth full of muffin.

"Charlotte, I can take Iris to school," Merit said. "Emma and I have to go anyway."

I tried to ignore how Iris's face lit up.

Under ordinary circumstances, I wouldn't have let Iris ride around with a sixteen-year-old boy. But these weren't normal circumstances.

"Well, that would be amazing, Merit. Because I, for one, have a full day of . . ." I paused dramatically. "Job interviews!"

"Yay, Mom!" Iris said.

"Go, Charlotte," Merit said.

Brenna and Jamie broke out in applause right as Grace reappeared in the kitchen, dressed, toothbrush nowhere to be seen. "I have tons of errands to run today. Why don't I drive you to your interviews?"

"Oh, I couldn't ask you to do that. . . ."

"I insist," Grace said.

"We're here to help!" Alice sang.

Did this really work? It seemed like it. Crazy. But I guessed under this roof, you knew when someone did something for you, it was coming back your way.

I smiled. "Okay. Well, if you're sure, I'll take you up on it."

"Good luck, Mom!" Iris said.

"Okay, okay!" Alice said. "Morning mommune meeting time!"

The kids rolled their eyes, but they all congregated.

"Middle school and high school drop-off?" she asked.

"Me!" Merit said.

"Elementary school drop-off, me," Alice said. Then she asked, "Pickup?"

"Charlotte and I have elementary school pickup at two forty and Emma at three, and Merit has post-sports," Grace said.

Merit nodded in agreement.

"Lunches?" Alice asked.

Six lunch boxes went up in the air.

"Computers?"

Five hands went to computers in their backpacks, and Emma said, "Oh, shoot!" and dashed upstairs.

"Water bottles?"

Brenna grimaced and ran around to grab hers from beside the sink, but the others gave Alice a thumbs-up.

"Yay!" Grace said. "Love you all! Have a fabulous day and learn a lot!" She kissed Emma's cheek as she flew back up the stairs.

"Let's go, middle and high school crew," Merit finished.

"I love you, little girl!" I said to Iris, kissing her on the cheek.

"Mo-om," she said, pulling away from me.

I'd take that as she loved me too.

"Charlotte, let's get our stuff and I'll meet you down here in five for interview domination!" Grace said.

In a flurry of backpacks and car keys, they were all gone.

I ran upstairs to freshen my makeup even though I'd done it twenty minutes ago, as if that would be the thing to secure me a job. As I swiped my left eye with mascara, I heard a light tap on the door and turned to see Julie. True to her promise, she hadn't said one word about Bill or his scandal since I arrived. She was a funny little bird. She had told me straight out that she believed she was doing our town an incredible service by providing local news stories in an in-depth way that they would never get from a bigger publication, that they would never see on national news. She had a master's degree. She'd won a daytime Emmy for her on-air reporting back in Charlotte, for crying out loud. She was very proud of herself, and why shouldn't she be? I admired her confidence. I would need to borrow it to help Bill. But first, I needed a plan.

Julie's face, pretty and symmetrical, was covered with way too much makeup, her blond hair sprayed into place so that even the beach wind couldn't muss it, a holdover from her days as a TV journalist, I imagined. Without all that makeup, when her hair was free and flowing and beachy, she was downright beautiful. I wondered when she would get her second act. She certainly had her hands full with her girls, but wasn't motherhood the art of juggling?

"Hi," I said, smiling. "I thought you left."

She smiled back. "I did, but I forgot . . ." She held up her phone. "The negative to storing them at dinner is you sometimes forget them in the morning!"

I nodded.

"Before I left, I just wanted to wish you luck. Remember, you are the most powerful woman in any room you walk into." She paused. "That I'm not in, of course."

We both laughed. "Thank you," I said. "To be honest with you, Julie, I needed that. This has really shaken my confidence."

"What do you mean?"

I sighed and perched on the edge of the bed. "I always had this idea that companies would be clamoring to hire me. And now no one will even return my calls."

"It will get better, Charlotte. I promise you, it will. Either way, you'll land on your feet." She paused. "And if you don't, you can just stay here with us."

We both laughed again.

"For real," she said. "I just wanted to say that Gabe Montoya will love you, but he's kind of old school. He's of that 'little woman' ilk, which is annoying, but he's a good guy. He just doesn't quite get it. Don't be thrown by it."

That was very helpful. I was interviewing with Gabe today.

"Paul Lucas is kind of an ass, but once he knows you're smarter than he is, he'll calm down. Weirdly, he likes to be in charge, but he loves an employee who knows more than he does." She paused. "Which you do."

I smiled. "Thank you, Julie. Seriously."

"They'd be idiots not to realize that your misfortune is their best day ever." She squeezed my shoulder. "Okay. I'm off to the mean streets of Juniper Shores to correct injustices and spread the good word."

I laughed, remembering that, in Julie's capable hands, one lunch lady's cold turned into "Possible Covid-19 Tsunami Sweeps Juniper Shores Prep." That a councilwoman sleeping with her male assistant bloomed into "Sex Ring Overtakes Small Town."

Then I had a thought. I gasped. "It's you!"

"What's me?"

"You're Juniper Shores Socialite!"

She laughed and shook her head. "Please. Charlotte, I'm kind of offended. I'm a serious journalist."

Sort of, I thought.

"Would you tell me if you were?" I asked, raising my eyebrows.

"Definitely not," she said. "But I wouldn't write about my own aunt—or you. Because I promised."

That did make sense. Just then my phone rang, and I jumped up to grab it off the dresser, seeing a 917 number—a New York City area code—that I thought I knew. "Ah!" I squealed. "This is about a job!"

Julie nodded and waved as she stepped out of the room.

"Hello," I said breezily.

"Well, well, well, if it isn't Charlotte Nicholson," the voice on the other end of the line said.

Yup. Bradley (not Brad!!) Mellon. I wanted to correct him, to say it was Sitterly, a fact I was feeling more confident about now that I was 99 percent sure my husband hadn't stolen millions of dollars from his clients. But, well, I needed Bradley's help, and I didn't exactly want to remind him either that I was married or that I was associated with Bill in any way.

"Hi, Bradley! Long time no talk."

"Uh-huh. I'm hoping you're calling because you've come to your senses after sixteen years and want a second chance at love with Bradley. But I presume you want something else."

I laughed. I had to take a deep breath, to pretend that I was still that same nerves-of-steel Charlotte he had once known. Well, once been almost-engaged-to, to be exact. I had told him I wasn't ready to get married, and then had met Bill and gotten engaged five months later, which hadn't gone over that well. *Bill* . . . I had been up half the night, my mind racing with how to get him home, with how much I needed a job, with how Iris was faring in these new circumstances. Usually when I was worried in the night, Bill would roll over and pull me to him, wrapping me in his arms, his breath soothing and rhythmic in my ear. Remembering only made it harder to fall asleep, but I'd eventually drifted off. I had to put that aside and be as cheery yet tough as possible. I needed to sound employable.

"Well, Bradley, I'm finally ready to come back to work, and I'm calling you first."

Bradley had done very well and had his own midsize investment firm that got great returns. He was a smart cookie and very well-connected. He just wasn't the love of my life. And, no, under normal circumstances, I wouldn't even consider working for an ex, but, under these circumstances, I had a daughter to support—and if New York and Bradley were the way to do it, then sign me up.

"Uh-huh." He was a little breathless, and I could tell his feet were pounding the treadmill. "Char, look, I have a soft spot for you. You're smart as a whip and a real ballbuster. But you've got to give me some time here. I can't hire you until your name is good and cleared."

I felt deflated—but wasn't it Bradley who had taught me that you had to overcome three objections before you'd get someone to say yes? "Bradley, I get that. I do. But the thing is, not only am I innocent, so is Bill. We have everything we need to get his name cleared. We're just dotting some i's and crossing some t's."

So, yeah. No way around it. That was a big, fat lie.

"Oh, Char. Do you believe that?"

Okay. Now he was pissing me off. "Bradley, it doesn't matter. This isn't about Bill. It's about me."

"Call me in four months," he said, getting more out of breath. I heard the motor on the treadmill stop. "Hey, Char. Are you serious? You think he's innocent?"

"I mean it, Bradley." Not Brad! Never Brad! "He's innocent. Some-one set him up."

"Well, Oliver Engle is the best. He'll figure it out. In the meantime, I promise I'll help you any way I can."

My eyes puddled at the kindness. "By giving me a job!" I said, with faux brightness.

"Four months!" he said.

"Two!" I countered.

He sighed. "Call me in three." The treadmill started up again. "Hey, in the meantime, do you need money? I heard all your assets were frozen."

I wasn't expecting that, but Bradley was a very frank person, so maybe I should have. "What I need from you is to figure out how millions of dollars that Bill rightfully invested just disappeared." I obviously did need money, and Bradley had so much of it that he wouldn't even sneeze. But I would *never*.

Bradley made a dubious sound. "Sounds innocent to me."

"Bradley!" I scolded.

"I hate Bill Sitterly, but I've always liked you. I'll think about it, and I'll help you if I can. But, for now, you're killing my mile time."

I smiled. Some things never changed. He'd been working on that mile time the whole time I'd known him.

"Okay. Hope you beat your record. Thank you!"

He hung up. And I couldn't help but smile at myself in the mirror. So, no, nothing was fixed. I hadn't gotten a job. But someone—anyone—had called me back. Someone would give me a job, even if it was in four months—no, three. It wasn't perfect, but it was a start.

I made my way down the stairs and took a deep breath, trying to calm my nerves. I closed my eyes, thinking that, if Bill were here, he would tell me I was smart and confident and beautiful, and he would *defy* anyone to tell Charlotte Sitterly no! I smiled just thinking of it. It helped a little.

I was just turning toward the side door when someone knocked on it. When I opened it, the FedEx driver's scanner made a little beeping noise, and he handed me a package. "Here you go, ma'am."

"Thank you!" I said as he jogged down the steps.

To my surprise, the package was addressed to me. I knew I needed to leave for my interviews, but I couldn't resist grabbing the scissors from the kitchen drawer and tearing into the box. As I unwrapped the packaging, I laughed: Serendipity Frrrozen Hot Chocolate Mix. I didn't need to read the card to know it was from Bill. Or, well, Oliver, since Bill had no money and no internet ordering access. But still. What an amazingly thoughtful gesture. The card inside read: *I love you more than iced hot chocolate—and you're going to knock 'em dead today. Thanks for believing in me.* It was a somewhat awkwardly phrased one-hundred-twenty-characters-or-less typed enclosure card. But it was from Bill. And I couldn't have loved it more.

I was holding the card to my chest as if it could hug me back when Grace walked in. She smiled. "Oh, hot chocolate!"

"Definitely not vegan," I said.

She linked her arm in mine. "That's okay. It seems like, whatever it is, it was just what you needed today."

I nodded, slipping the card in my pocket. It was like having Bill right there with me. And a reminder that today I was going to knock 'em dead.

Iris

The Full Moon

I am in Merit McDonald's car, I wanted to text *everyone.* But the hope that people would actually see me get out of his car in the parking lot was even cooler. That would say more than any text ever could and would deliver the kind of wow factor that would leave people talking about my potential maybe "thing" with Merit instead of my imprisoned father. So, that would be a nice change of pace.

Wordlessly, Merit handed me a phone. Then he handed Emma twenty bucks. "Is this it?" I gasped.

"Must be," Emma said. "Because Merit only gives me twenty bucks when he wants me to keep quiet."

"What about beach house rules?" I said, trying to swallow my nerves. "Wouldn't this fall under *what happens in the beach house stays in the beach house?*"

"Nope. Because what happens in the school parking lot, I'm going to tell Mom."

I couldn't help but laugh.

Merit said, "Your bright, shiny new burner phone."

Guilt pulsed through me. I didn't want to lie to my mom. Plus, I thought of myself as a good person. But I wasn't really lying to my mom. No. I was lying to Alice. And, while I liked Alice, I didn't really owe her anything. Right? Although, I mean, yeah, she was currently keeping us from being homeless. No way around it: I sucked.

"Wow," I said, trying to seem thrilled and grateful. Merit didn't have to know how nerdy my thoughts were. "I don't know what to say. But I need to pay you back for this."

"Nah," he said. "It's not fancy. But it can handle your apps. Basic texting. Obviously, you'll have to give your friends your number. But if I were you, I'd be careful who you give it to. You don't want to give it to someone who's just going to get mad at you and tell their mom or something."

"Did you ever think that maybe it's kind of sad that you guys can't be without your phones for, like, two hours?" Emma interjected.

"Maybe if you had a social life, you'd understand," Merit shot back.

Kind of mean. I glanced over my shoulder at Emma, who rolled her eyes. "Yes, Merit. You are God. How could your subjects exist on a planet where they didn't have access to you for a few hours after football? The world would surely end."

Merit gave me a look that said, *This baby doesn't understand.* My heart raced. Merit McDonald was giving me secret looks. Could he possibly like me? Did you get burner phones for girls you didn't like?

"Anyway," he said, "just make sure you keep it in your backpack when you aren't using it."

I nodded seriously.

"Because if you get caught, that implicates me too. If anyone gets suspicious about you, they'll get suspicious about all of us."

"And then Merit can't text his *girlfriend*," Emma said in a singsong voice.

My heart sank.

"I don't have a girlfriend, Emma," Merit said as he pulled into a parking spot.

"Yeah, okay. Tell that to Sophie Parker," Emma said.

Not only was Sophie Parker the prettiest girl in school, she was a senior. Merit was cool, but he was only a junior. Sure, he was a cute, smart football star, but could he get Sophie Parker? I wasn't sure. As if clearing up the situation, she walked up to the car only seconds after we pulled in. Merit rolled the window down and gave Sophie a smile that I had never seen Merit give anyone. That wasn't a good sign.

I mean, if I was really honest with myself, I had to admit that any flirtation Merit was sending my way was probably in my head. I was a freshman. He could get a senior girl. But next year I'd be a sophomore, higher up the food chain. That would help, right? I just had to bide my time until then, keep him from falling in love with Sophie, and, most of all, keep him from demoting me to the role of "sister."

As Sophie kissed Merit on the cheek, I realized I was staring. Emma sighed. "Come on, Iris. We have to get to *school*."

I shot her a look. "Bye, Merit," I said.

He threw me a wave but never took his eyes off Sophie. Sophie was amazing. She had big boobs and a tiny waist and wore fake eyelashes and hair extensions and had these perfectly pink glossy lips. In comparison to her, my tinted ChapStick and the tiny bit of mascara my mom let me wear seemed babyish and ridiculous.

I got out of the car and fell in beside Emma, putting on my backpack. I glanced once over my shoulder, to see that Sophie had her arms crossed on Merit's windowsill and her chin resting on her hands. She was inches from his face. I hated her with every fiber of my being.

Emma and I walked up the steps and along the sidewalk that led from the high school building to the middle school building. The high school was unadorned brick, while the middle school doorways were flanked by huge wooden cutouts of flowers that said, *Juniper Shores Middle Picks YOU.*

"Iris, you're going to get in trouble for that phone," Emma said. "It's totally not worth it. Merit just has one to seem cool, and he's really just a huge nerd who can play football. He's probably using his phone to play Wordle or something. He's the last person you need to act cool for."

That surge of guilt pulsed through me again. I was not only lying to my mom, but I was also being a bad example for Emma. This multi-family household stuff was tricky. I'd never had anyone younger looking up to me. "Emma, you'll get it when you're older," I said. "It's a dumb rule."

Before she could respond, my best friend, Chloe Montoya, ran up to me, squealing. "Oh my gosh! Is it true? Were you in Merit Mc-Donald's car?"

"Chloe, I think you know Merit's sister, Emma?" I said, smiling at her while simultaneously throwing darts at her out of my eyes.

"Oh, sure," Chloe said. "You're in sixth grade, right?"

"Seventh. And I'm going there now." Emma rolled her eyes like we were too much and headed off toward her classroom. Maybe she did have it more together than the rest of us.

Chloe and I turned and started walking toward the high school building. "How do you already know about me being in Merit's car?"

"Um, you've been scooped!"

"What? Whoa. That JSS works fast."

"Are you guys, like, a thing?" Chloe asked right as Jessica Frazier ran up too. "Oh my gosh! Oh my gosh! Does his car smell as good as he does?"

Apparently good news traveled fast, and, as I had hoped, no one was even thinking about my dad anymore.

I wanted to be cooler than this, but I wasn't. So I squealed right along with them and said, "It does! It totally does!"

"What is he like?" Jessica asked. "Wait, does he like you?"

Dabney Collins, my other best friend besides Chloe, ran up. "Who? Does who like Iris?"

"Merit McDonald!" Jessica and Chloe squealed simultaneously.

Dabney put her hand over her heart. "You have won freshman year. I bow down to you."

I shook my head, but I couldn't wipe the grin off my face. "It isn't really like that," I said. But I kept my tone and body language noncommittal in a way that meant, *He totally likes me; I'm just not telling you.*

"You have to tell us *everything* . . ." Dabney paused. "You know, later." She couldn't say *at the sleepover* in front of Jessica because we hadn't invited her.

Chloe's sleepovers were the best because her mom had the best snacks. Double Stuf Oreos, Cheetos, Hershey's Kisses, our favorite Cheerwine soft drink . . . anything amazing you could think of was in their pantry. And she always made us chocolate chip pancakes for breakfast. I mean, I liked my friends too, obviously, but when given a choice of sleepover houses, Chloe's would always win.

"Yes! Oh my gosh! Tell us *everything*," Ben said in a high-pitched voice, mocking us, coming over to see what was going on.

I punched him in the arm.

"Iris rode to school with *Merit McDonald* this morning," Jessica said, eyes wide. "Can you even?"

"I can't even," Ben said, again mockingly.

The first bell rang, warning us that it was time to get to class. "See you at lunch!" I called to my friends. Ben and I walked inside together, to Honors English. We were reading *Little Women*, and it might have been the best book I had ever read in my entire life.

"So what's that about?" Ben asked.

"Well . . ." I started. "It's kind of a long story, but my mom and I are living at this awesome beach house—just temporarily, of course—with Merit's family and this other family."

He stopped and put his arm out. "Wait. You're living at the mom-mune?"

I laughed. "Ben, come on. Yes, okay. We're living at the mommune."

"Blink twice if you're in danger."

I slapped him lightly on the arm. "It wasn't like we had a lot of choices. We literally can't get to any of our money or our house or anything. Alice is really nice."

"Is it true that you have to do a share-your-feelings ritual at dinner? And yoga with the sunrise?"

Honestly, neither of those things sounded that bad to me. And at the couple of dinners I had been to there so far, all we did was talk about the best part of our day, something we were grateful for, and something we wanted the group's advice on. Sure, it was a little weird. But it was also kind of great, you know? Like this big family I would never have gotten otherwise.

"And sacrifice virgins on the full moon?"

I laughed at that one. "Ben, it's totally fine. Although the meals are vegan."

Ben made a gagging sound.

"No, you won't believe how good a cook Merit's mom is," I said. "She's, like, next-level. You have to come over sometime to have her cooking."

He smiled at me. "You name the time. I'll be there." Then he held up *Little Women.* "So, do you like this?"

"I think it is magic. The sisters. The family. The love and the bond between them."

"I have sisters, and it's basically a lot of screaming and clothes stealing."

I laughed, but it occurred to me that maybe that's what I liked about the mommune. At home, it was just Mom, Dad, and me. And for a minute, it seemed like it was just going to be Mom and me. And now I had this whole big family to hang out with and laugh with. And even when the little kids kind of got on my nerves it was fun to be a part of it.

"Your sisters are great," I said.

"Uh-huh. Right. Try having them nag you all day every day and then see if you can still say that."

We walked into the classroom and took our seats beside each other.

"All right, class," Mr. Friedman said, turning on the smart board. "Let's talk about last night's reading."

My hand shot up. I was eager to discuss all the ways that Jo was so forward-thinking and ahead of her time. In fact, it was the very thing I had talked about with the group at dinner last night, and the other moms—and Merit, surprisingly—had had some cool insights to share.

Before Mr. Friedman could call on me, Ben leaned over: "Don't forget about dinner."

"I won't. I promise."

Mr. Friedman pointed to me, and as I started to talk, I couldn't help but notice that Ben never took his eyes off me.

Charlotte

~~~~~~~~~

Joint Property

"Wow," I said as I buckled myself into Grace's Mercedes. "This is something I never thought I'd be doing."

"Getting a job?" Grace asked.

"Well, not exactly. I could always imagine myself going back to work. But I imagined if I did it would be all about companies wining and dining me, not me begging some small-town office to let me be its secretary." I winced and looked over at her. "That makes me sound really awful, doesn't it?"

Grace laughed. "Are you kidding me? Women never fight enough for what we deserve. We roll over and roll over until we lose our minds, at which point we get labeled crazy bitches." She looked over at me. "So, no. It doesn't make you sound awful. It makes you sound like a woman who knows she's been shafted."

I thought back to fourteen years ago, when Iris had just been born, when my six weeks of maternity leave—which, let's face it, had been peppered with calls and questions from work—was coming to an end. I was crying over having to leave her, over the nanny being the one she would call "Mommy," over how I could work sixty hours a week when I had a baby who needed me.

"So quit," Bill had said.

I'd laughed, assumed he was kidding. Quit? I couldn't quit. That was ridiculous.

"I mean it," he said. "Quit your job, stay home for a little while. It's not like everyone won't be begging you to come back when you're ready."

It was such a kind gesture. My quitting my job would be harder on Bill. There was no doubt about that. But he was only worried about Iris and me.

"But I've worked so hard," I said then. Even as I said it, I knew that, if he was serious, I wasn't going back to that job. I loved it. I ate it, breathed it, slept it. I dreamed about clients and money and deals. But now I had Iris. And everything seemed different.

"I don't know," I said to Grace now. "I mean, I *was* upset about going back to work. Maybe I did the right thing."

"Every woman in the world is upset about going back to work. But then they go. And they get used to it in, like, two weeks and sometimes it's hard as hell, but they make it work."

"Is that how it was for you?"

Grace laughed. "Oh, God no. I quit working the absolute day Troy and I got married. I hated working. It was the thing I did because I had to. But that doesn't mean I'm not a little jealous of people like you who have a real passion for it."

"But then you started *Growing with Grace*?" I asked. I was a bit of a latecomer to the heavily trafficked site. I'd probably only followed Grace for a year or two, which was so dumb because Iris was mostly grown. But there was something about her Instagram page that was so soothing and lovely that I liked to watch it just for the pleasure of it.

"Yes," she said. "When Merit was two." She shook her head. "Wow, fourteen years ago. That's hard to believe."

I looked over at her contoured cheek and her shiny ponytail. She really was the image she was selling. Well . . . mostly. "Can I ask you something?"

She glanced at me. "You can ask anything you'd like. I probably won't tell you the truth, but I'll definitely answer." She grinned.

"Why not let your readers in on your real life? They love you. They would be Team Grace and support you all the way through your divorce and everything. You don't have to be so perfect all the time."

Grace laughed as she turned at the stoplight. "Oh, Charlotte. That is so sweet and so naïve."

"Which part?"

"My darling, Grace from *Growing with Grace* isn't a person. She is a product. A bright, shiny silver Bergdorf box with a signature purple bow. That Grace is a rerun of *Gilmore Girls*. She makes you feel good about your life. She makes you feel calm, like maybe you can pull the disaster that is your family together. Maybe it's an illusion, but it's an illusion that keeps you going. Do you know what I mean?"

I stared at her as she pulled up in front of Montoya & Sons Insurance. "That is awful," I said.

"It's not *awful*," she said. "It's just the way of the world. Look, it's fine. I give people an image that makes them want to buy cast-iron skillets and creaseless ponytail holders from companies that pay me to sell them. Everyone wins."

I gasped. "I love those ponytail holders!"

She put her hand to her own ponytail. "See? I know. If I'm crying in my pjs about my husband leaving me, you're not buying life-changing ponytail holders. We all lose."

I put my hand on hers. "Well, you can be real with this follower."

She nodded. "You can be real with me too, you know."

I bit my lip. "Well, if that's the case . . ."

She raised her eyebrows.

"Look, I know this seems silly, but I'm reading this book about raising an adult, and I've really been trying to let Iris fix her own lunch to teach her responsibility and . . ." Grace was looking at me with such an amused expression that I paused.

"So, you don't want me making your child's lunch?"

Something about the way she said it was so disarming that I found myself stuttering. "Well . . . I mean . . . I just . . ."

"So, your daughter who makes straight As and plays three sports and is a member of six clubs and doesn't get in trouble. She needs to make her own lunch to prove she is a productive citizen?" She paused. "I'm not baiting you. I'm just wondering."

Well, when she put it that way, it did seem sort of stupid. Iris had a lot on her plate for a fourteen-year-old. All our high-achieving kids did. I looked out the window and then back at Grace. "It's just that the book said—"

"I wrote a book too, Charlotte," she interrupted. "And, trust me, I don't know what the hell I'm talking about."

That made me laugh.

"Look," she said, "there are four grown women under this roof. We are going to have major differences of opinion about how we parent our children, and I'm never going to tell you what to do with Iris because I get that we won't always agree. But, for heaven's sake, let the child sleep ten extra minutes in the morning. Let me make her lunch." She smiled. "When you make a snack for yourself, you make one for someone else. It's beach house rules."

I couldn't help but laugh—and realize that she was right. "Fine, Grace. Thank you. That's a very nice offer." Between games and homework and extracurriculars, Iris never got enough sleep. Every little bit helped.

Grace cocked her head and exhaled. "So, with that behind us, anything else you need to get off your chest before you go nail that interview?"

I sighed heavily and nodded. "Do you want to know the worst part?"

"Always."

Grace put the car in park and turned to face me.

"A nice chunk of that 'frozen' money is mine, some I saved from working and then a nest egg my great-aunt left me when she died. I thought I was protected if the worst happened."

Grace patted the dash of the Mercedes. "Nope. Joint property, baby."

We both laughed, but I was worried I had offended her. "You birthed his children and raised them. You deserve the joint property. My money is just sitting there for a crime my husband didn't even commit."

"He's innocent?" Grace asked, shock written all over her face.

"Don't look so surprised! Yes. He was definitely framed. Now we just have to figure out how to get the prosecution to see that."

"Whoa." Grace put her hand up. "This is serious. We're going to need to unify the mommune on this one."

I laughed, because what were we going to do?

I pulled out my phone and texted Oliver, *Any updates?* Three dots appeared, and then, so quickly that I knew he must be voice-texting:

I'm doing everything I can, Char.

Everything he could was definitely not enough. I was down to four hundred dollars. Two weeks ago, I would have dropped that at Whole Foods without a second thought.

"Okay," Grace said. "Deep breath."

We both inhaled, and she locked her eyes on mine. "You are going to nail this interview. You are going to be the best . . ." She trailed off. "What are you interviewing for?"

I sat up straighter, cleared my throat, and said authoritatively, "Customer care associate."

"Uh-huh. So you deal with pissed-off customers?"

"I would say so. Yes."

"Okay. Well, today you are going to be the best pissed-off customer handler they have ever seen there. You are going to wow them with your grace and poise, and you are going to come out of here gainfully employed."

I nodded. "And if I don't, we have three other interviews to drive around to today."

"Right," Grace said. "But we aren't going to need them because you, Charlotte, were born to work at Montoya and Sons Insurance."

We both burst out laughing. I was grateful for the opportunity, sure. But my, how the mighty had fallen.

The inside of Montoya & Sons was exactly how one would picture a small-town insurance agency. It had bad fluorescent lighting between water-stained ceiling tiles and green carpet squares that it seemed they had forgotten you could replace. The walls were a neutral tan that needed to be painted and the halls were lined with insurance company posters that had to have been decades old. Jake from State Farm wasn't in a single one. No LiMu Emu. And where the heck was Flo? I snickered to myself.

A lady wearing a name tag that read AGNES with a perm and a jaw that could chew gum like I'd never seen was very inconvenienced to be walking me down the hall. Well, yes, I could see that things at the front desk of the empty office were *very* taxing. She led me to a closed door. "Any tips?" I whispered.

She rolled her eyes and walked away. Cool. All for one and one for all at this office. Woman power. Agnes might not have said it, but I was sure that was how she felt. I couldn't help but smile. I cracked myself up today.

I tapped on the door.

"Come in!"

"Hi, Mr. Montoya," I said. He stood up, wearing a rumpled gray suit with a green patterned tie that felt like it went with this office somehow. He reached out to shake my hand, the fluorescent light shining on his cue-ball bald head. He was probably in his late fifties—a solid fifteen years older than his wife, Chloe's mom—and had a nice smile.

"Just call me Gabe, sweetheart. Please, sit down."

I should have told him not to call me *sweetheart*, but I remembered what Julie had said—he was old school. And, if I was really honest, his kind demeanor soothed me. I didn't want to admit it to Grace, but I was very nervous. I had no idea how long my money would be on lockdown. I absolutely had to have a job.

As I settled into a chair, he picked up a piece of paper—my résumé, I realized—and looked at it, then back up at me. "Charlotte, you can't sit here and answer phones."

My heart fell to the floor, and I stumbled. "Oh, no, Mr. Montoya, I am great with customer service. Just ask my daughter. I'm basically her personal rep."

He laughed. "I sure do like that daughter of yours. She and my Chloe are as thick as thieves."

I smiled and nodded. I'd been planning to remind him of our daughters' connection to help me, but it seemed I didn't have to.

"No, I just mean a brilliant gal like you can't sit at a desk in this rattrap all day."

I put my hands on the desk and leaned forward. "Mr. Montoya." I paused. "Gabe, I'm going to level with you. My husband is in jail—wrongly, I might add, but there all the same—my accounts are frozen, and I have a daughter to raise. So I'm not really in a position to be picky. I need a paycheck. I'm super smart, and I'm the hardest worker you've ever met."

He was studying me but didn't say anything, and my nerves almost got the better of me, but then I thought of Bill. He needed me to do this. He needed me to be strong for our family. If he were beside me, he would say, "Char, you're brilliant and resilient and you can do anything." And so I would.

I read Gabe for a moment, and then, remembering Julie's advice and deciding he would think it was funny, added, "If I told you how much cocaine those finance bros were doing to keep up with clean and sober me, you wouldn't even believe it."

He burst out laughing. The gamble had paid off. "Charlotte, honey, I'm not trying to make you beg here. I'm just thinking." He chewed the end of his pen and said, "As soon as we heard about your situation, the Mrs. and I wanted to help you and Iris."

I had to control my eye roll. "The Mrs." a.k.a. Ruth Montoya a.k.a. the ringleader of the snotty moms who seemed bound and determined to keep me on the fringes of their little clique. But that was fine with me. As long as Iris was happy, I was happy. And, as standoffish as Ruth and the other moms had been to me, the girls had been equally as accepting of and loving to my daughter. And that was everything. I nearly choked on my "That's very nice of you, Gabe. Of both of you."

"I'm just saying that you need to be out in the field; you need to be with people. How about I make you a sales rep?"

I would be amazing at that. Overcoming objections was my jam. I wanted to ask him if this was a pity hire. But I couldn't. Because, even if it was, I needed it. I had literally no pride left. "Here's the problem: no one trusts me right now. How am I going to sell insurance to people who think I'm a thief? Or thief-adjacent, anyway." I wanted to tell him that his lovely wife was keen on spreading that not-so-nice rumor. But obviously, Gabe didn't believe I was involved. So that was something.

He leaned over the desk. "I bet you'll figure it out." He paused. "And, look, your base as a salesperson is the same as the salary for the customer service rep, so it's really a no-lose for you."

I put my hand to my heart. I thought I might cry, I was so overwhelmed by his generosity. But I knew from experience that a woman crying in the workplace got her branded a certain type of way. And it wasn't great.

"You'll get your base pay for a couple weeks while we're getting your licensing requirements done."

I nodded. "I've kept up with my securities licenses and my certified financial planner, so I should just need insurance licenses."

"Amazing. You can shadow me out in the field for a while. I have enough clients coming in that I could really use some help, so you should have a steady stream of sales right off the bat. I'm sure it's not what you're used to, but it's decent money. It'll get you back on your feet."

He stood up to shake my hand again. I wanted to hug him, but even in a small town I felt like that might be frowned upon.

He walked me to the front desk. "Agnes," he said, "Charlotte's going to be our new saleswoman."

"Great," she said with as much disinterest as possible.

"She's excited on the inside," I whispered as he walked me to the sidewalk.

He laughed. "Agnes is a pill, but she shows up, which is more than I can say for most people. Although sometimes I wonder if it would be better if the phone didn't get answered at all."

I smiled at him, feeling overwhelmed with gratitude. "Thanks for taking this chance on me, Gabe. I know you're doing it for Iris, but I really can't tell you how much it means to me. I'm so grateful, and I'll never forget it."

"It's not a chance, sweetheart. You're a sure thing."

There were a lot of things wrong with that sentence, but I was so happy I didn't care. And I knew that Bill was going to be so proud of me.

I gave Grace a thumbs-up and she was clapping before I even got back to the car.

"You are looking at Montoya and Sons' newest insurance saleswoman!" I said.

"What? You got a promotion already?"

I just grinned.

"Then I'll be your first client."

"Aw, Grace. You're the best." It struck me how, just a few days ago, I didn't know this woman. And now she felt like my best friend. But, again, the summer camp effect.

"Let's go get lattes to celebrate. On me."

"Obviously," I said. "It's not like I've gotten a paycheck." I paused. "But once I do, the first bottle of Sancerre is on me."

"Hooray!" she said as she pulled out of the parking lot. "Charlotte's got her groove back."

Charlotte had her groove back, indeed.

@junipershoressocialite

Sharing bad behavior and delicious drama in North Carolina's most exclusive coastal zip code. DM with tips, pics, and juicy deets.

AUGUST 30, 5:45 P.M.
18 Posts
7,776 Followers
16 Following

You didn't hear it from me, but . . .

PIC 1: Juniper Shores Prep's hottest new couple is none other than Merit McDonald and Sophie Parker. Head cheerleader + star quarterback = a match made in yearbook superlative heaven.

PIC 2: What infamous newspaper reporter's ex was spotted canoodling with his twenty-two-year-old assistant at the Tavern near 2 a.m.? Oh, Houston, never change.

PIC 3: Charlotte Sitterly might be down, but she's also *in*. In demand, that is. Montoya & Sons' latest sales rep is open for business and ready to help you with all your insurance and investing needs. Word to the wise: make your checks out to Gabe. . . . We're kidding. We're kidding. (Well, kidding-ish.)

TNT ('Til Next Tip—from you! And make it juicy!)
JUNIPER SHORES SOCIALITE

Alice

The Rhythm

Dinner was my favorite time of day at the mommune. The electric buzz of everyone around the table together, passing dishes, laughing and chatting. Every night, every time, it was a reminder of how it used to be in my family, while my parents were still here, before my siblings and I drifted apart. And tonight, it was a good distraction from the text messages that Elliott had been sending me all day—and my thoughts about whether I was going to text him back.

Merit whispered something in Brenna's ear, and she laughed so hard I thought she was going to fall off her chair. Iris scooped cabbage stir-fry on top of the buckwheat noodles on Audrey's plate. She scrunched her nose but then brightened as Iris said, "No, it's so good! I promise you!"

"And it will make us grow big and strong too," Jamie said. "Right, Grace?" she asked, looking up at the woman who had prepared all this goodness for us.

Multiple times a day, in moments just like this, my heart felt like it stretched to accommodate how much I loved these children. But I had always loved children, and not just the ones under my roof. For years I had been a first-grade assistant in our local elementary school.

Being in a school environment comforted me, maybe because, even when my life was falling apart as a kid, school was consistent.

I relished that job, and the brightness and innocence of the children I taught, for almost twenty years. But after Walter died, I found that I wasn't able to do it well anymore. I was having so much trouble sleeping that I would arrive tired and cranky, and the challenges that used to inspire me panicked me. Something simple—a child skinning a knee on the playground, a sick teacher needing me to take over the lessons for the day—would throw me into a spiral. I needed consistency; I needed rituals and routines. And, well, what people around town said about me was true: with three dead husbands, I could support myself.

It wasn't until Julie and Grace moved in that I realized that a family provided me with the stability I so desperately needed. I loved getting the little girls dressed and ready for the day, knowing that, while Julie was at work, I would manage their schedules, that we would all sit around the table for dinner together. I went to bed very early each night because I had realized that around 10:30 p.m., my anxiety began to get the best of me. In the beginning, I felt guilty about not helping Julie with middle-of-the-night feedings, but I couldn't handle the stressors and demands of the day without a good night's sleep.

Of course, with that many kids in the house, things went wrong all the time. But in the context of "family," they were things I could handle. Or maybe I was simply coming back to myself and was able to deal with small inconveniences better. It was a heartening thought. But did it mean I was ready for another relationship? I wasn't sure.

"Right," Grace said enthusiastically, responding to Brenna, then looked over at Merit and jumped up to fill his water glass.

"Mom," Emma said, "can you get me some red pepper flakes?"

"Of course, honey," Grace said.

Charlotte locked eyes with me and nearly imperceptibly shook her head. She'd asked me earlier why Grace acted like her children's personal assistant.

"Grace," I said, knowing I should stay out of it, "why don't you let one of us help you. You've worked all day on this, and your food is getting cold."

Grace bustled back to the table, hands full, and passed things out. She smiled tersely at me. "I'm just taking care of my children."

I knew that smile. I knew I had crossed a line. So I looked at my plate and said, "You have outdone yourself. This looks divine."

I said a blessing. Then Grace tapped her glass and said, "Everyone, I believe we need to let Charlotte begin our nighttime proceedings."

Charlotte beamed from the head of the table. "Ladies and gentle-man," she started. Poor Merit. The only gentleman. He was either going to turn out to be the kindest, most empathetic man or a hen-pecked disaster. It was a grand social experiment. "You are looking at Montoya and Sons' newest sales associate!"

"Mom!" Iris shrieked. The little girls loved her shrieking so much that they joined in.

Julie clapped and Emma whistled, and Grace said, "We're having homemade ice cream for dessert to celebrate!"

When everyone quieted down, I asked, "So, what exactly does this new job entail?"

Charlotte paused for a moment, then laughed, saying, "Alice, I really don't have any idea."

We all laughed.

"A job is a job," Merit said. "Congratulations, Charlotte."

He really was mature and sweet. So far, things pointed toward very good man.

"So, what can we help you with, Charlotte?" Emma asked, as was our tradition.

"Well, Emma, I was thinking you looked like you needed an insurance policy."

She giggled.

"Seriously," Julie said. "We're here for anything you need."

Inside, I smirked. I took Julie's kids to school and picked them up and watched them all afternoon. How was she going to help Charlotte with whatever she needed? Not that I minded. I looked over at Brenna, Jamie, and Audrey. They were the joy of my life. They were, if I was really being honest, a huge contributing factor to why I hadn't moved forward with Elliott when we broke up a year ago. I couldn't, wouldn't leave them. And, beyond that, life at the mommune worked. I was good at it. I had failed miserably at marriage. But the thought of Elliott's beautiful, work-worn fingers on my neck . . .

"Well," Charlotte said tentatively, breaking me out of my thoughts, "I hate to ask. But, depending on what my new schedule is like, I might not be able to pick Iris up from school or practices."

"We've got that covered," I said. My afternoons were spent driving around to ballet, tennis, swimming, and gymnastics anyway.

"I can help too," Merit said. "Iris's tennis practice and my football practice are usually at the same time."

"Well, we will take it day by day and work out something that makes sense for everyone." I raised my wineglass. "For now, cheers to Charlotte!"

"Cheers to Charlotte!" everyone chimed in, the little girls raising their milk glasses, the teens and tweens raising their wineglasses of sparkling water.

The glasses clinked—and just like that, I was thrust back thirty-five years, to my ten-year-old self. I could see her, that little girl, in sepia tones, feel the way the house shook, how the shards of glass hit my skin, smell the gasoline, the fire, hear the shrieks of my brothers and sisters. But most of all, it was the shatter of glass that got me. The clatter, the clang. Maybe it was because it was the last thing I could remember that it always launched me back into that moment. The last thing before I woke up in a sterile hospital room all alone. I had been in the hospital once before when my eardrum burst, and my mom had never left my side. What she did with my four brothers and sisters I'll never know. I'd never thought about it; I hadn't had to. She kept us safe. Until she couldn't keep us safe anymore.

"Alice, you go next!" Jamie shrieked.

I pinned on my most serene face. Jamie. My love. She, Brenna, and Audrey were the reason I could hear shrieks again without having to hide away; they were the reason that I could experience real laughter. *You aren't alone,* I reminded myself. *They're all here. They aren't going anywhere.*

"The best part of my day today," I said, "was coming home and seeing all of these kids running around together on the beach."

I caught the smile that Emma and Iris shared, and it made my heart jump. Kids had such an easy connection, made such fast friendships. It was part of what made the mommune work.

"I am grateful," I said, "for the sunsets and how much I love sharing them with all of you. And I need help with . . ." I paused and put my finger to my chin as if I was thinking really hard. ". . . deciding which toppings I'm going to put on my ice cream tonight!"

"Oh! Oh! Sprinkles!" Jamie said.

"Chocolate chips!" Audrey added.

"And chocolate syrup too!" Brenna added in a very mature voice. I had noticed that she had these moments now where she was trying to seem more grown-up than her sisters, I think to distinguish herself as more like Emma and Iris and less like Jamie and Audrey. It broke my heart a little, but it was also the most natural thing in the world.

I took a bite of my noodles and cabbage, savoring the salty, tangy goodness of the flavors combining in my mouth.

Grace started to get up, her plate already clean. "Oh, I'll help you," I said.

"No!" she said, a little snappily. "I would like to get my children's dessert, please," she added in a tone far colder than I was expecting. But I should be used to this by now, Grace's obsession with feeding her children, with feeding us all. It was how she showed her love, and I understood that. But I hated how clearly we all watched her pay her penance.

But we all had our penance to pay. Grace paid hers in homemade ice cream. I paid mine in taking in those who needed me, in trying to save those I could to make up for not being able to save the ones I should have. It might not have been an even trade. But what was even anyway? What was fair? The thought began to overwhelm me, so I looked out the window, focused my eyes on the waves rolling to the shore, then retreating.

Find the rhythm, Alice, my mother used to say to me when I was scared, when I couldn't sleep. *Focus on the patterns.*

The waves, my heartbeat, my breath in and out. There was a rhythm, a pattern, a reason. And I knew that, if I just kept looking for it, if I kept seeking it out, I could make it through another day.

Grace put a bowl down in front of me, a beautiful creamy white with diced peaches inside. I smiled up at her. She smiled down at me. I put my hand on her wrist for the briefest moment, to remind her that she was okay too. I felt it, her pulse, her beating heart. The rhythm helped. It always did. The ice cream didn't hurt either.

Charlotte

Amicable, Chic Separation

"Are you sure this is okay, Julie?" Grace asked as the three of us sat, side by side, on the last inch of dry sand before the tide line. Merit, Iris, and Emma each had a boogie board that Brenna, Jamie, or Audrey was stretched out on. They were running through the shallow surf, pulling the little girls as they shouted with glee.

"They are having the time of their lives!" she said. "What could not be okay?"

I smiled at her. Iris and I were settling into life here. I had even gotten so used to giving up my phone these past few days that today, on a Sunday night a solid hour before dinner, I had left it at the house. I had argued that I needed to prep for work, but Brenna had reminded me that beach time every day was one of our beach house rules. So I had relented.

And Brenna was right. I felt so much lighter as I watched my daughter as she gathered steam and then ran through the waves, laughing, her hair damp from swimming and the spray. I would never have asked for any of this, obviously. And missing Bill was a beating pulse that ran through my every thought, my every breath. But, with the help of these women, I had pulled myself up by my bootstraps. We were getting through.

"So, how're you doing, Charlotte?" Julie asked.

I scrunched my nose and looked out at a line of birds gliding through the sky. "Maybe you could be more specific?"

She laughed. "Well, how is your life? And how are you settling into the mommune?"

"My life is a swirling pile of garbage. But the mommune is perfect," I said.

"And Bill?" Grace asked.

My stomach turned. "He is being incredibly stoic, but this is so hard. I mean, the man who has been perfectly paleo for five years is living on white carbs from the cafeteria because he's saving the generous forty cents an hour he makes mopping so he can have internet time instead of spending it on the vaguely healthy tuna packets from the commissary." I shook my head. "He didn't even *do* anything and he's allotted three hundred minutes a month to talk to his family. This is just so unfair and I—" I realized their wide-eyed attention was set on me. "I'm sorry. I'm ranting."

Grace put her hand on my shoulder solidly, to calm me, to hold me in my place. It helped. "Don't be sorry," she said. "This is unimaginable."

"Right?" I said. "It's unimaginable! In true Bill fashion, he has himself on this strict reading and workout schedule to keep from going insane, but, y'all, this is bad, and what if they can't prove that he's innocent?" I took a deep breath.

"What day is his hearing again?"

"Discovery should arrive to Oliver in a couple of weeks, and we'll know after that. But soon." I paused. "You guys, what if he has to serve a sentence for a crime he didn't commit?"

Julie shook her head. "We won't let that happen."

I rolled my eyes and immediately felt guilty. "I'm sorry. That wasn't about you. I'm just scared. People are unjustly incarcerated all the time."

"Not Bill," Julie said firmly. Something in her eyes made me know that she was plotting for me. And, well, if nothing else, the woman was a Grade A plotter.

Grace bit her lip just the tiniest bit. It was so small, almost nothing. Even so, it sent a chill down my spine.

"What?" I asked.

"Me?" she asked. "Nothing."

"Come on, Grace," Julie said. "That lip bite of yours is never nothing."

Grace shot Julie a look. "Fine. It's just . . . well . . . Charlotte, what if he isn't innocent? I mean, what if he's just putting on a good front?"

And just like that, the kumbaya, sisters-forever mirror shattered. I picked up a shell and drew little lines in the sand with it distractedly. These virtual strangers had already stood by as I unpacked so very much of my baggage. I believed Bill. I truly did. But only a total moron would be so convinced of his innocence that she hadn't even considered the alternative. After all, he had crossed the line before. But I *needed* Bill to be innocent. I needed Iris to have the stable, safe life that I had always dreamed of.

"He's innocent, Grace. He can't lie to me. He's never been able to. And he certainly couldn't convincingly lie about something this big."

Grace nodded like she understood. I couldn't open that *what if* can of worms. So I deflected. "I feel like you've heard nothing but my sob story lately," I said. "What about you two? How are you doing?"

Julie smiled and Grace sighed. "I'm really great," Julie said. "I'm starting to feel a little guilty, like maybe I've imposed on Alice too long. But we're all so happy here that I can't bear the thought of leaving."

We all laughed as Brenna rolled off her boogie board and Merit scooped her up. Yet my heart palpitated nervously. If Julie left, that meant we all left, didn't it? I felt so safe here, so protected. I didn't want to leave.

"Noooo!" Grace said, echoing my thoughts. "If you leave, we have to leave!"

"Yeah," I said. "At least you're actually her family."

"No, I know. And I know she loves us fiercely. But we are a full-time job. You guys are basically bed-and-breakfast tenants, but even easier because you cook and clean up after yourselves! I rely on her so much." She paused. "Maybe too much?"

"Do you know what I think?" I asked. "I think that we, as women, are terrible at accepting help, even from the people who love us. I think that you and your girls bring an equal amount of joy to Alice as she brings help to you."

Julie rested her head on my shoulder. "That is beautiful. Thank you."

Audrey ran up. "Mama! I have to tinkle! Now!"

"Can't you just go in the ocean?" I asked.

She shook her head. "Nooo!" she wailed. "The sharks will get me."

"Sweetheart," Julie said, "the sharks aren't going to get you if you tinkle in the ocean."

"Yes, they will," she said, her little teeth chattering.

Julie smiled and stood up. "Okay, I think it might be time to get you in the bath." She wrapped Audrey in a towel and shouted, "Girlies, it is officially bath time!"

"I don't want to take a bath!" Jamie whined. But Brenna, looking up at Iris and Emma, kept her cool.

Julie raised her eyebrows at Grace and me. "She is so into looking like a big girl in front of your big girls. Thank you for that."

Grace nodded seriously. "It will backfire one day soon, but for now, you're welcome."

Julie trudged up to the house carrying Audrey, her two little duck-lings following her.

"I miss that stage sometimes," Grace said.

I nodded my agreement. Merit and Iris had ditched the boogie boards and grabbed two surfboards, a soft-sided small pink one for her and a green longboard for him. They were paddling out side by side. I bet my daughter thought she had won the high school lottery. "I miss it in some ways," I said. "But I think I'm a better mom at this stage, when she's more independent."

"The worries are so much bigger now, though," Grace said.

I nodded. "I am constantly worried about her safety. Will she get in a car wreck with a friend? Drink at a sleepover? Get kidnapped by a random stranger or raped by someone she trusts . . ." I trailed off and looked at Grace. "Sorry. That got dark."

She shook her head. "It's just reality. Merit on that football field might be the death of me."

I squeezed her forearm. "At least he's the quarterback with all those big linemen to protect him."

What I was really thinking was that Jason Street in *Friday Night Lights* was the quarterback and that didn't help. But that was a TV show. "We can't worry about every little thing," I said. "Bottom line, we have to teach them everything we can, hope they make good choices, and pray that God will figure out the rest."

Grace nodded. "This is when I need Troy, you know?"

I squeezed her arm again. "I can only imagine." I knew that having a son with no father around was complicated. Iris was my person; I was hers. But Merit had so many interests that I knew were probably from his dad, questions that Grace couldn't answer; male influence was desperately lacking from the mommune.

"I keep thinking that if I'm the perfect wife, the perfect mother, the perfect cook, Troy will somehow intuit that all the way from Tokyo and come to his senses, come back to me."

It felt like a gut punch, the way her pain was just so raw and on display. "Oh, gosh, Grace. I'm so sorry. I thought you wanted the separation."

Even through her sadness, she yelled encouragement as my girl managed to stand all the way up on her board for a full two seconds before she plunged into the water. We both jumped to our feet and cheered. But that was motherhood, right? Compartmentalizing your own pain to accommodate your children's joy. "That's a good boy you've got right there," I said. "Teaching Iris to surf like this? What a great distraction."

She smiled. "Merit has this relationship with the water that I'm envious of. The ocean scares me, whereas he is just so at peace with it. He understands it in a way that is lost on me."

I nodded, looking over at her. "Yeah. I get that. You can tell the local kids from the vacationers right away. That saltwater runs through their veins."

"Troy was one of those locals, and he certainly had no trouble leaving."

"Grace, I imagined this amicable, chic separation for you. But I think that's because I'm still reconciling the Instagram Growing with Grace with the real Grace."

"I know I made it seem that way when we met." She sighed. "But the truth is that I would have done anything for him, gone anywhere for him, managed any distance for him," she said with a cool ferocity that caused the hair on the back of my neck to stand up. "After he left, after we cried and promised this would be short-term or the kids and I would move, he told me he wanted a divorce. Over the phone."

I shook my head. "That's awful."

She nodded. "I don't know if that was his plan the whole time or he met someone else or what. But suffice it to say, I am devastated."

Merit and Iris were paddling out again. "I am so sorry." I gave her a small sideways hug as best I could and almost jumped as Julie reappeared between us—with a bottle of wine and three plastic cups.

"It's like you read our minds!" I said.

She smiled. "What did I miss?" she asked as she poured.

"Not much. Just my sad story for the hundredth time," Grace said. "Nothing like a hugely heavy mental breakdown to kill a Sunday vibe!" She laughed.

"Thank you for sharing with me," I said. "I mean it. I want to know you more. You too, Julie. And Alice."

"I'm a pretty open book," Julie said. "Girls. Nosy, pushy reporter. Mommune."

"But you'll never know Alice," Grace said.

"You don't feel like you know her?"

Grace shook her head. "Oh, Charlotte," she said flippantly, "no one really knows Alice."

"Not even you?" I asked Julie. "You're family."

Julie shook her head. "I love Alice. She's an amazing woman. But I've never gotten that deep with her." She shrugged sadly. "I'm not really sure even Alice knows Alice."

The hairs on the back of my neck stood up again as I wondered who I had moved my child in with. *But this is temporary,* I reminded myself. I could go home any time.

Iris, board in tow, paddled through the water, then stood and slogged the rest of the way toward us. "I am exhausted!" she said, flopping down beside me on the sand. I scooted close to her and put my arm around her wet shoulders, planting a kiss on her temple. "You were great out there!"

She looked at me skeptically. "Mom. I was fair at *best.*"

I laughed. "No, I mean it. You were great. I am so proud of you for trying something new." I paused. "No, I'm proud of you for diving into this new life. I'm proud of you for not even complaining about not having your cell phone!"

She laughed and rested her head on my shoulder. "It's not so bad."

I took a deep breath, wrapping my arms around her, smelling the saltwater on her skin, savoring this moment of my girl being just a girl, softening around the edges. It was bliss.

One of the best things about living on this beach was the way the sunset was just a little different every single day. Tonight, the sky was the palest pink, a soft baby blanket dotted with fluffy clouds. It was a lullaby sky that could soothe me into believing that everything was going to be okay.

As Merit popped up on his board and rode a wave all the way to shore, I thought about Bill, about what an athlete he was, how important his physical shape was to him, how disciplined he was in what he loved. Grace's earlier question seeped into the corners of my mind. But no. Bill was strict and sure, and his moral compass was strongly intact now. As Iris cheered for Merit, I thought about bringing her here, about the situation I had put her in. And that unsettled feeling returned with the echo of Julie's words: *I'm not really sure even Alice knows Alice.* But my teeny, tiny doubt about Bill made me wonder: How well did we ever really know anyone?

Alice

Eligible Bachelor

I met my second husband, Glen, in the ordinary way: at the eligible bachelor auction to support Juniper Shores Elementary. Okay, so maybe that wasn't *ordinary*. I didn't even want to go to the auction, but it had been nearly two years since Jeremy's death and, while I wouldn't say my friends were still rallying around me in quite the same way, they were still conscious of making sure I got out and about. "Come on!" my friend Kate begged. "It will be fun. You don't have to bid on anyone."

I hadn't planned to. All the bachelors were dancing onto the stage when it was their turn, gregarious and extroverted. And then there was Glen. Shy and quiet, cheeks flaming, he took his hands out of his pockets long enough to wave tentatively to the audience. He was tall and broad-shouldered—a former Juniper Shores Prep basketball benchwarmer turned math teacher—ten years my elder.

Our paths had never crossed. But when I saw him up there, so uncomfortable, and realized that he wasn't getting as many bids as the other men, I couldn't let him flounder. So I raised my paddle and my voice. The previous bid had been twenty-five dollars—and it had taken three bids to get there—so I said, "Two hundred seventy-five dollars!" That was twenty dollars more than our super-hot UPS driver, who was clearly the most eligible of the eligible bachelors.

I'd been careful not to spend my inheritance from Jeremy, saving every penny for a rainy day. I lived meagerly and quietly on my very small teaching assistant salary. But this was an emergency. All I could think about was what I would do if I were standing up there, mortified and alone. And so, I bid.

The auctioneer, a.k.a. the principal, said, "Going once, going twice, sold to Alice Bailey for two hundred seventy-five dollars."

Glen practically melted off the stage and over to me. "Thank you," he whispered.

I hadn't planned on actually *going* on the date. But then Glen said, "I promise I make a beach picnic so good it will be worth your investment."

He had dimples when he smiled and so much hope in his voice I couldn't possibly say no. I didn't plan to fall in love with him; I didn't plan to marry him. But, well, Glen was quiet and soft-spoken. He held me like I was a porcelain doll. We sort of quietly coexisted, spending evenings in, cooking and watching movies. We pooled our salaries to rent a small town house two blocks from the ocean. We never could have afforded it, but Glen had tutored the owner's child to a B+ in AP Calculus, and he had rented it to us for a steal. I look back on those years as tinged with a sort of solemn happiness, like the golden glow of early-morning light on the water before the showiness of sunrise.

We met when I was twenty-nine, married when I was thirty-one. A few months later, over a messy cake that Glen had made for me himself, he said as I blew out the candles, "Is one of your birthday wishes this year for a baby?"

My stomach gripped when he asked. It seems insane now that we hadn't talked about children before we married. It's hard to explain our relationship. It was like I fell into this comfortable moment that made me feel like I was breathing again, and Glen was afraid to push too hard for fear that I would figure out what I had done and run away. Was this mad, passionate, great love? No. But it was safe. We were happy. Or as happy as I could imagine being while still mired in the grief that I was dead set on never letting go.

I had given thought to children, of course. I'd always wanted to feel that type of true, unconditional love. I spent a moment feeling terribly guilty that I could even imagine having children—my dream with Jeremy—with anyone else.

But Jeremy was gone, a fact that washed over me with fresh horror every single day. It certainly wasn't fair to deny this truly decent man the joy of children because of the past I could never change. And so I smiled. "I think a baby would be perfect."

I'll never forget the way Glen beamed. "I think it's time then," he said.

Glen had an old knee injury that gave him the tiniest limp. He knew he needed a knee replacement, but he'd been putting it off as long as possible so that with luck he would only have to do it once. He was forty-two now, which was maybe not quite old enough, but he said, "I want to be able to run around with my children. I want to coach their teams and be the dad playing with them in the yard."

His eyes filled with tears. Mine did too. Glen would be a wonderful father. Patient. Kind. Loving. Any healing I had done had come from his ability to meet me where I was. He would ask about Jeremy, listen when I needed him most. He never seemed threatened or upset with me for holding on to this part of my past. He never minded holding me, stroking my hair, when I woke up screaming from a nightmare about Jeremy. And, in that way, I was able to move forward.

I remember sitting in his lap, putting my arms around him. He kissed me softly. "I'll schedule the surgery," he said.

I was teaching when he went to his pre-op appointment. I went to the grocery store after school, anxiously awaiting his call. The police knocked on my front door right as I was walking in the back. When I saw them, I knew. I don't know how, but I knew. I dropped the bag of groceries, the eggs breaking and seeping through the cardboard into the carpet. I've blocked out the rest.

I blamed myself for years. I should have taken off from school that day. I should have driven him. No matter how many times the priest or friends assured me there was nothing I could have done, I blamed myself.

I left that townhome, used Glen's shockingly generous life insurance and savings to purchase a tiny cottage in downtown Juniper Shores, and saved the rest. I felt so guilty.

I had learned over the years, when I let my mind wander to that horrible night, to "choose a happier thought." It was hard, but sometimes it worked.

Yes, the past was a dark, scary place that I had to save myself from. But every now and then, I couldn't help myself: I looked in the rearview mirror. Tonight was one of those times. Elliott's many, many texts had asked if we could get together, just to talk. As much as I wanted to feel firm in our decision to break up, I decidedly did not. Not when I saw him again. Not before that. And I had to admit that I was more than a little interested in what he wanted to say. I was equally interested in whether being open to this conversation was a step in the right direction for me, if it signaled growth.

So now Elliott had his arm slung over my shoulders as if it had been there every day for the past 341 days since I had seen him. Since I'd told him—in the midst of the terror that I would lose him—that we couldn't be together. Since he had left town.

We were walking slowly through the crowds at Juniper Shores Village. It is one of the most appealing parts of this area, the thing most written up in travel magazines and lifestyle columns, the place that inspires tourists to start saving so they can retire here one day.

Three open-air restaurants grace the oceanfront: a burger place popular with the late-night crowd that has the most eclectic bar scene on the beach, a Mexican cantina where one can eat tacos and drink Modelos from the comfort of a hammock or play cornhole, and the Fish Camp, which makes the best fried seafood on the East Coast. Bar none.

Behind those mainstays is the Airstream Park, a cluster of seven Airstreams: two women's clothing outposts, a rosé slushie truck, a coffee truck, a pizza truck, a fresh juice and smoothie truck, and a vegan health food truck. There's also a long pier with an arcade at the end and a huge NO FISHING sign that is roundly ignored. It's fun and so clean it resists being seedy.

But tonight, even if it *was* seedy, I wouldn't have cared because I was slightly tipsy from a rosé slushie with the man I had missed even more than I'd realized. Elliott was guiding me, and I knew where we were going before he even said it. "In the interest of making you feel loving and nostalgic toward me, I thought it was important to relive our first real date," he said, smiling at me. He was so tan that the creases around his eyes and mouth were a shade slightly lighter than his skin, and his blue eyes sparkled. He had that distinctive look of a man who was made to live beside the ocean, who worked hard but loved every single minute of his life. He looked like a man who had never lost one night's sleep trying to prove himself to anyone else. And he was causing me to take a hard look at the life I had led, at why I was so darn interested in proving myself. Proving myself to whom? *I* knew I hadn't killed my husbands. *They* knew it. Elliott knew it. Why did I care what all those strangers thought anyway?

We walked up to the reception stand at the Fish Camp. "Hi, Elliott," said the hostess, who was wearing frayed jean shorts and a tank top, and couldn't possibly be a day over twenty-three. She wrapped her hair, which was long and wavy and white-white blond, around her finger.

"Hi, Kylie." He smiled. "I have a reservation for two."

She looked from Elliott to me and back to Elliott, making a face like I was the day-old fish they threw out. "That's for you?" She looked at me again. "And you?"

The Fish Camp didn't take reservations. It wasn't a table-for-two kind of restaurant. It was the type of place where they lined raw wood tables with newspaper and dumped oysters or shrimp or clams. You ate wherever there was a seat with whoever else happened to be sitting there. In fact, I thought, panic suddenly rushing through me, that would be great. I knew Elliott was trying to create this perfect night for me. And it had been working. Until this moment when I remembered that so much was at stake here.

"We'll just sit at the community table" burst out of me. Big, scary conversations about why we broke up and whether we could move forward couldn't happen at the community table. I could put off whatever Elliott had in mind, stay in the purgatory of nondecision that, sure, was hard, but was easier than the hell of another clean break.

Elliott put his arm around me and squeezed, calming me, settling me. Could he read my mind? "No," Elliott said. "I called ahead."

"Fine." Kylie took two laminated menus and meandered to our table, smacking her gum, like this was all so boring she could die.

"Tell Roger thanks," Elliott said, pulling out a chair for me as best he could on the sand.

Elliott sat and grabbed my hand hungrily across the table. Elliott always had this almost palpable need to touch me. And it was one of the things that had made him so irresistible to me. I was trying to ignore it, but I had to admit that I felt the same. But I was also afraid of what loving him this much could cost me, could cost *him*.

"Sorry," he said. "I just have to make sure this is real and you're here and this is happening."

I took a deep breath, pulling my hand away. I wanted to sink into how good it felt to be with him, to ignore that every man I had given my life to was gone. But that wasn't reality. For almost a year together, I had ignored that. And then the truth had sunk in. I was in love with Elliott; he was in love with me. And after a year, a couple in their late thirties (him) and midforties (me) had to move forward. I would have to make hard decisions about what came next. We couldn't just sail along with Elliott at his house and me at the mommune. And all the old fear that I'd spent so much time and energy chasing away had crept in. What if I did change my life? What if I let myself really be with Elliott, full-force, all-in? And what if he died? I couldn't let that happen. And so, I had let him go.

"Elliott . . ." I started. I didn't know what came next. This was impossible. I wanted this. I wanted *him*. But I had no idea how to move forward.

Elliott shook his head. "Can I say something before you do?"

He had saved me. Because what was I going to say anyway?

"Al, you broke my heart."

I bit my lip. I knew it, but I hated to hear him say it.

"I have spent three hundred forty-one days blaming you for my pure misery."

My heart fluttered nervously. Had I read this all wrong? Was I here so he could tell me off?

Elliott leaned toward me. "And three days ago, I woke up, and I had an epiphany: I'm just as much to blame here as you are. Because I never should have walked away from you."

I thought back to that night on the beach, me sobbing, telling Elliott it was over. That I was cursed, that I couldn't lose another man I loved. "Elliott, I was pretty firm in that decision," I said. Broken and battered, but resolute.

He shook his head and looked me straight in the eye. "Alice, you love me."

I wondered for a moment if he was trying to hypnotize me, his eyes were locked on mine so intensely. But he didn't have to convince me. I knew I loved him. I loved him so much that I wanted to save him. From me.

"I know you love me because I lived that year with you. I have never, ever felt about anyone the way I do about you." He sighed. "Look, what I'm trying to say is that you insisted on this breakup because you were afraid I was going to leave you. And then I did. I left. And that was the wrong thing to do. I never should have walked away from you. And, if you'll let me love you, if you'll let me be with you, I'll never walk away from you again."

Tears stood in his eyes, and he was so sincere, so beautiful, that I just wanted to sink into him, let him love me, throw caution to the wind. But what I said was, "No, Elliott. I wasn't afraid you'd leave me. I was afraid I'd *kill* you."

At the exact wrong time, a skinny, pale server approached with a bottle of champagne, looking nervous. I couldn't blame him. I'd basically just confessed to premeditated murder. Context is really key in these situations.

"Sir, the 2018—"

"I've got it," Elliott said, motioning for the bottle. The server handed it to him and scurried away.

Setting the bottle down, Elliott stood and took my hand. He pulled me up, away from the restaurant, out into the night on the beach where a humid breeze was blowing softly. He turned toward me, and I wrapped my arms around myself, even though it wasn't cold.

"Al, you're not going to kill me," he said, rubbing my shoulders. "Do you hear yourself? Do you hear how ridiculous that sounds when I say it back to you?"

"It should be ridiculous," I said, my throat thick with tears and fear. "But, with all due respect, Elliott, you have no idea what I've been through. I'm trying to protect you."

Elliott pulled me into him, and I let him. He rested his cheek on top of my head. "I love you, Alice, and I'm not leaving you again. I don't care what you say."

My shoulders relaxed, maybe from his words, maybe from his arms, maybe from the scent of Old Spice body wash and something a little like Old English furniture polish that always clung to him. Because that was what I was afraid of, really, wasn't it? At my core? Being alone? And a knowing coursed through me. He was right. If he had fought me that night on the beach, if he had refused to walk away, we would still be together. I loved him so fiercely that I wasn't only protecting him. I was protecting myself from losing another man I loved.

He pulled away from me. "I'm strong, Al," he said. "You can depend on me. I love you and I want you, but the last three hundred forty-one days have taught me something: I don't *need* you."

I wondered what those words would have sounded like to any other woman. Grace would have been offended, I was certain. But the most delicious feeling washed over me. Julie needed me. Brenna and Jamie and Audrey needed me. To a lesser extent, Grace and Charlotte needed me. I had enough of being needed. I wanted to be *wanted*. I loved my day-to-day existence, taking care of the people in my home. But it was a different kind of love, one that came with stress and structure. What Elliott was offering me was something entirely different.

And I understood then that, as much as I loved him, I had always underestimated him.

I realized, looking into his eyes as the waves crashed on the shore, that he saw me in a way that I hadn't fully recognized. That simple sentence had changed everything.

Elliott took my hands in his. "I'm patient, Alice," he said. "I know you have a lot of scars, and that's okay. I can wait until you're ready. But I'm here. I'm not going anywhere. I'm not going to leave you again."

I never asked for what I wanted anymore, but, for the first time in a long time, I found myself pleading with God that Elliott would finally be the one who got to stay.

Iris

~~~~~~~

Shameless

Chloe leaned over her desk and said, "Psst." I turned and realized that she was leaning over partly so I'd hear her, and partly because it gave her amazing cleavage in her white uniform blouse that she had unbuttoned one button below uniform policy and Greg Saunders—who she had a massive crush on—sat on the other side of me. I glanced at him quickly. Yup. He was looking. "You are shameless," I whispered, leaning closer to her.

She smiled. "I know. Are you nervous about this afternoon?"

"Nah," I said. "Going to see my dad in jail is no big deal. Ordinary, really."

She laughed. "Okay. Well, good. As long as you aren't nervous . . ." She rolled her eyes.

Ben walked over and squatted between us. He looked up at Chloe. "I know Greg is right there, but if you could maybe get those out of my face for a minute."

She rolled her eyes again. "They were here first. Maybe you should get a better handle on where you put your face."

I shook my head.

"My house Friday," Chloe said.

I nodded, and was surprised to find that knowing I would miss Brenna's soccer game made me a little sad. I'd never had a big family, and I was stunned at how fun it was. I'd thought I would miss being alone—at least sometimes—but I didn't at all. Maybe it was because it kept me from being alone with my thoughts about how my life was up in flames. So maybe that wasn't exactly healthy. But, whatever.

"Want me to come with you this afternoon?" Ben asked. Gosh, he was such a good friend. I mean, who else remembered that this was my first time seeing my dad in prison? Chloe had probably already forgotten, and we'd talked about it two minutes ago. But, in fairness, Greg, with his wavy dark hair and killer accent, was talking to her now, so it wasn't really her fault that everything else had probably flown out of her head.

"Don't you have Key Club after school?" Ben was president of Key Club, a volunteer society that, let's face it, we were all in because it looked good on our college applications. I was also in it to be a good friend to Ben, even though I wasn't great at attending the meetings. But I did do the volunteer projects, which I kinda felt was the hard part. Sure, I partly did it because we had to have a hundred service hours a year. But I mostly did it because there was no one I'd rather be around than Ben.

"Yeah, but I can just message the GroupMe. We can do it tomorrow."

"You would do that for me?"

He touched my forearm. "I would do anything for you, Ris."

That made me feel sort of warm and tingly all over. He was such a sweet guy. I was surprised he didn't have a girlfriend. But that was probably good because I would be super jealous that his attention was on her, not me. So I wouldn't be, like, setting him up with anyone. "I don't know if they'll let you in. I had to do a bunch of paperwork and stuff."

He shook his head. "But I can ride over there with you. Be your moral support since you haven't seen him in there yet."

The feeling of dread I had been waiting for all morning finally washed over me. Until now, I had been able to pretend that Dad was on a business trip. I mean, I wasn't literally pretending that. I obviously knew he was in jail. I had talked to him. But I hadn't had to *see* him; Mom was hoping I never had to. But the more days that ticked by, the clearer it became that if I wanted to see him, I was going to have to go.

"I don't want to," I whispered. "It's so bad, Ben. Like, so, so bad."

"But you're okay," he said, putting his hand on my arm comfortingly.

I nodded, biting my lip to keep tears from coming to my eyes. "But I miss him, you know?"

"Of course you do."

"I want things to be back to normal, back to our family together again." As much as I liked the mommune, I didn't like it as much as having my dad home and my mom home with me all the time. I added, "I think Merit is going to drive me over there and drop me off because my mom is going first."

I didn't miss his eye roll. "Why is your mom going first?"

Come to think of it, I didn't really know. It did seem sort of odd that she wouldn't come pick me up. She still didn't have a car, which was more inconvenient than I could possibly have imagined.

"Maybe she's riding with Oliver or something." Oliver had been Dad's attorney for, like, a long time. It made me feel better to know that he was working on all of this because Oliver had always been sort of like our fairy godfather. He was the fixer. He made problems disappear. Although it was notable that my dad was still sitting in jail. So, there was that. How good of a lawyer could he really be anyway? I'd just watched the Bernie Madoff Netflix special. His charges were way worse than my dad's and they put him on house arrest while he was awaiting trial. They let him live in his own plush New York apartment, while my dad was rotting in jail. What kind of sense did that make? *Get it together, Oliver.*

"If Merit's taking you, then I'll just keep the Key Club meeting when it is. It seems like you have all the moral support you need."

The way he turned so quickly sort of surprised me. Was he *mad*?

I didn't have time to wonder because Principal Windsor caught my eye through the door and motioned to me. That was weird. My heart raced, but I knew I couldn't be in trouble. Could I? When I stepped out into the hall, he handed me a little cardboard box that had already been opened. I looked at him questioningly. "It's a gift," he said, then walked away.

I set the box down on the floor, crouching over it. Removing the paper, I found a chocolate tackle box from Dylan's Candy Bar. My favorite. I knew right away who it was from, and my eyes teared up remembering that Dad wouldn't be here to fight over the Peanut Butter Pretzel Poppers with me. The card said: *Break a leg on your geometry test today! All dads love their daughters. I'm a dad. Therefore, I love YOU. (A little deductive reasoning in case you forget!)*

I held the card up to my chest. He was cooped up in jail and had remembered my test—and that I was struggling with deductive reasoning. It made me even more excited to see him this afternoon.

Three hours later, Merit pulled up in front of a long white building that, I'll be honest, didn't really *look* like a jail. There wasn't a huge barbed-wire fence around it like in the movies. And I could see a basketball court and some picnic tables, so maybe Dad was at least getting some fresh air. Vitamin D was very important. "Maybe I'll stay for a pickup game," Merit joked, looking over at a group of men who were playing.

"I'll walk you in," Merit said, obviously sensing my nerves.

But then my mom jogged out the front door, and I said, "Don't worry about it," trying to seem cooler than I felt. "Hey, thanks for driving me."

"Anytime." He smiled at me, and, while I had believed his hotness was affecting me slightly less, butterflies fluttered in my stomach. Don't get me wrong, I knew I had a huge crush on him. But I was getting to know him well enough that I thought I was acting sort of normal. I didn't say one stupid thing during my whole surf lesson Sunday. Although it was kind of hard to talk while waves were smashing me in the face. Maybe that was better.

Mom opened the car door. "Thanks, Merit," she said. Then, looking at me with her *we got this* face, "You ready?"

"Sure," I said with much more confidence than I felt. I got out of the car and slammed the door. Suddenly the thought of walking into that building made me feel sick.

Mom must have sensed my hesitation. "It's not that bad," she said. She paused and put her arm around me. "Well, no. It's bad. But he's in a room with couches and chairs. You don't have to talk to him on a phone through glass."

"Really?" I brightened. "How did you know that's what I was picturing?"

She smiled at me. "Because it's what I was picturing the first time." She whispered, "And the lady behind the counter made fun of me and said everything I knew about jail I'd learned on *Legally Blonde*. And she's totally right."

"Me too!" I said. Old movies were the best.

We walked through the door, and I had to stop at a desk that looked like the concierge at a not-so-nice hotel. Although I guess they didn't have a concierge at bad hotels. Well, whatever. I had to fill out some form verifying that I was me since I'm not old enough for a driver's license yet. Okay, so this was feeling more like jail by the minute. A lady with red hair behind the desk smiled at me and said, "Your daddy is going to be so happy to see you." I knew she was trying to be nice, but it weirded me out.

The whole time I was both terrified to see my dad and so excited to see my dad. It was actually amazing how much a person could feel two opposing things at the exact same time.

Mom looped her arm through mine. A guard smiled at me and walked us to a room that looked pretty much like Mom had described, but with these quilts hanging on the wall that depressed me. I knew without really knowing that prisoners had made them, that some of America's brightest minds had made bad decisions and instead of changing the world were learning basting stitches and French knots.

"Iris!" Dad said, jumping off the couch and practically flying toward me. He hugged me so tight it nearly took my breath away.

"I'm so glad to see you," he was saying over and over. Was he *crying*? I hated it when he cried. I felt sorry for him, but also it made me really uncomfortable.

"I'm so glad to see you too," I said. He smelled kind of like Clorox or something. Not bad, but not like Dad. He smelled liked a stranger.

When Dad pulled away, I noticed he kind of looked like one too. He seemed pale and thin. These dark circles he'd never had before were under his eyes. He hadn't even been here that long.

Oliver got up from where he was sitting in a chair across from a couch. "I'm going to give you three a moment." He moved away.

We sat down, Dad in the seat where Oliver had been, Mom and me on the couch.

"Are you okay, Dad?"

"I'm fine. How are you?"

He didn't *look* fine. He looked pale in this sickly orange outfit, sitting in a room, that, admittedly, had decent natural light but smelled like that cheap floor cleaner they used at school. I just nodded. How was I? I felt kind of okay, but I thought it might hurt his feelings to say so. It wasn't that I didn't miss him. I did. It's just that everything was always so busy around the mommune that sometimes I didn't have much time to even think about how much my life had changed. When I'd told Alice that last night, she'd assured me my dad wouldn't want me to be sad. I guessed that was true, but I still felt kind of guilty.

"Sweetie, we have some news," Mom said.

I could tell from her face that it wasn't *great* news. But, like, the worst had kind of happened. We were talking in a *jail*. So my expectations were low.

Oh my gosh. Merit is right. They had brought me here to tell me they were getting divorced.

"Okay," I said, stalling. "Are we never getting the house back?"

Dad gave Mom a look I didn't understand.

"Honey," Dad said. "I wanted to be the one to tell you, face-to-face, that I did not do this."

I exhaled a breath that I didn't even know I was holding. "What?" Oh my gosh! They weren't getting a divorce! Or if they were, they weren't telling me. Although, if he was innocent, I couldn't really see Mom divorcing him. "You didn't?"

He shook his head. "I did not."

"I knew you were innocent!" I said, rushing over to throw my arms around his neck.

"You did?" he said. His eyes filled with tears again.

"Of course, Dad. What are you even talking about?"

He nodded. "I'm so relieved. I know it's confusing when everyone is telling you something and you don't know what to believe."

I settled back into my seat. "Okay—but, Dad, if you're innocent, why are you here?"

"Well, you know how sometimes we initiate client statements ourselves and sometimes they come directly from the funds our clients are invested in?"

I nodded. I knew very well because I had worked at my dad's office on and off since I was, like, eight years old. In actuality, I worked for him to put in enough face time to justify the Roth IRA he funded for me each year, but he had also taught me plenty of bits and pieces along the way. "Yes. Sure."

I had seen Dad's support staff work on those statements hundreds of times.

"Well, to keep it simple, let's just say that some of those statements or maybe the trades themselves or *something* were falsified and—" He rubbed his temples, and I was flooded with sympathy for him.

"It's okay, Dad," I said. "I get it." And I did. Sort of. But what kind of asshole would do that? And how couldn't someone figure out who it was by now? "Do you think it was someone in your office?" I asked. I had never trusted that Melissa. Of course, I'd always thought she was after my dad and his money. I didn't think she was, like, a full-on criminal.

"If it was, they were convincing liars."

"But that isn't for you to worry about, sweetie!" Mom said brightly, giving Dad side-eye. "Dad, Oliver, and I are going to get this all taken care of."

Dad nodded. "Yup. We'll be back to normal in no time flat."

"Like, *normal* normal?" I asked.

Dad looked confused. "Well, yeah. I'd say so."

I'd always thought Mom and Dad were this perfect, happy couple. Or, well, it was maybe more accurate to say that I hadn't ever given much thought to their marriage at all. They just *were*. The idea of them being apart was unthinkable.

"So, like, the three of us together as a family, under one roof, one Christmas, etcetera."

Mom's face flooded with recognition. "Oh, honey. Dad and I aren't getting divorced."

"Well, that's a relief."

"I'm so sorry about all of this, Iris," Dad said. "I only want your life to be stable and happy and comfortable. I promise you that we will get to the bottom of this."

I just nodded because I didn't know what to say. But I felt like we were going to make it.

"Tell me about school," Dad said. "Tell me something normal."

I looked around, finally noticing that there were, like, ten other people in this sad little living room. This was not normal. But I knew this was harder for Dad than it was for me. I couldn't imagine being locked up in here. Especially being *innocent* and locked up in here.

"Well, I'm going to a sleepover at Chloe's on Friday, so that should be fun. And Belle Epoque on the Beach is Saturday, and Key Club is volunteering, so that will be great."

He nodded. "Hey, Char, we were the head sponsor for that event. I think we got eight tickets. You should go and take your friends."

Mom laughed. "Please, Bill. The last thing I want to do is dress up in some ornate costume and prance around town for everyone to talk about us. No thank you."

Dad put his hands up like he was surrendering, something he did often when it came to Mom.

I laughed, and then filled Dad in on how my geometry test went, thanked him for the chocolates he sent, and got him generally up to speed on my friends and all the Juniper Shores Prep gossip. I purposely left out mentioning Juniper Shores Socialite because I didn't want him to be tempted to look and read anything negative about himself. Our time went by way too fast, especially since I didn't know when Mom would bring me to see him again. Life without transportation was hard. At least I had Merit.

I hugged Dad goodbye so hard and kissed his cheek. "We'll get you out of here soon, Dad, I promise," I said, even though I was fourteen years old, and the world mostly happened *to* me at this point. But if I could help, if I could figure out a way, I would.

Mom put her arm around me, and she turned her head as we walked. I knew she didn't want me to know she was crying, so I pretended I didn't notice, and I made myself not cry so it wouldn't be harder on her. It was life-affirming to know that I could prioritize her.

On the sidewalk, I spotted Oliver.

"Y'all ready?" Oliver asked, looking at Mom.

Mom nodded and sneakily wiped her eyes.

In the car, I pressed my forehead against the cool window, where it left a mark when I pulled away. Oliver and Mom were quiet. I was trying to process what had just happened. Yes, it was a relief to see my dad. But nothing had changed.

Oliver broke the silence, saying, "Well, I know this might not be good enough news to help too much, but I was able to get your car back. We can go pick it up tomorrow."

"That is awesome!" Mom said. "Isn't that awesome, Iris?"

"It's everything I've ever wanted," I said quietly.

What was I supposed to say? All I wanted was to go home. To my real home. Where my mom and dad were together. And my shoes lived. And I didn't have to be a kid with a dad in jail. How had every-thing gone wrong so quickly? And what could I do to make it right?

What can I do to make it right? I knew enough about Dad's busi-ness and his software that maybe if I could get in there and dig around a little, I could figure out where that money had gone. Mom wouldn't want me meddling, of course. So I'd have to get Dad alone. He wouldn't approve of me getting involved, but I could ask him, like, a jillion ques-tions before he'd get suspicious. But it couldn't be with Mom because if I asked even one question, she'd know exactly what I was up to. Mom powers were real. They were to be feared.

"Mom, can I go see Dad whenever I want now that I'm approved?"

She turned to look at Oliver.

"Well, yeah, technically," he said.

"But you can't go without me," Mom said.

But that's the thing about being a teenager. Sometimes you have to tell your parents what they want to hear. Even if you don't mean it one little bit.

@junipershoressocialite

Sharing bad behavior and delicious drama in North Carolina's most exclusive coastal zip code. DM with tips, pics, and juicy deets.

SEPTEMBER 4, 6:49 A.M.
22 Posts
9,247 Followers
19 Following

You didn't hear it from me, but . . .

PIC 1: We have confirmation that the rumors about Greg Saunders and Chloe Montoya are true. They are, in fact, an item. But we can neither confirm nor deny that she gave him a *very* special birthday gift in the Fosters' pool. Just in case, Fosters, we'd give it a good chlorine shock.

PIC 2: Well . . . it's official: the Black Widow is back in action—or so we hear. Alice Bailey has been spotted with Juniper Shores' one and only Elliott Palmer every single day this week. Cue sound effect of a million hearts breaking. (Here's hoping Elliott's isn't about to stop!)

PIC 3: No one loves a good scandal more than everyone's favorite newspaper reporter Julie Dartmouth. But is it possible that she is the subject of one? Julie was spotted with none other than her cheating, lying (innocent until proven guilty, and he has been proven guilty more than once) ex, Houston, practically snuggling at the SmoothieStream. Could more than one of the mommune's illustrious inhabitants be reconnecting with an ex? And, if so, is the cult in jeopardy?

PIC 4: The Juniper Shores Arts Council is hosting its most exclusive event of the year Saturday: Belle Epoque on the Beach. Stay tuned for who made the cut, who wore it best, and, if we're guessing, plenty of seaside scandal. We'll be honest: we'll be there for the gowns, the jewels, and the too-good-to-be-true headwear.

TNT ('Til Next Tiara)

JUNIPER SHORES SOCIALITE

Charlotte

~~~~~~

In the Moment

My stomach was in knots, but I was trying not to let Iris know. Seeing Bill still stuck in jail, realizing that I was totally powerless to change it, had undone me. My mind was reeling, my heart pounding, my brain in a vise grip. I closed my eyes and did what Grace had suggested: I thought of Bill, with Iris, dancing in the kitchen. I couldn't help but smile. It didn't fix things, but I thought my heart might have slowed a little. Progress.

We pulled into Alice's driveway and Iris slammed the car door as she got out, stunning me out of my thoughts. Oliver adjusted himself in the seat next to me. "She'll be okay," he said. "I can imagine that seeing your dad in there would take a toll."

"I'll say. Maybe I did the wrong thing. Maybe I shouldn't have taken her." I looked at Oliver. "Was I prioritizing Bill's needs over Iris's?" It hit me then how deeply involved in our lives Oliver had become. He was a friend. And he knew the little unit of the three of us better than almost anyone. As I studied his face, I had a terrifying thought: *Maybe Oliver was the one who set Bill up.*

"Iris needed to see her father's face and hear his voice when he said he was innocent. That was important. You did the right thing."

Maybe it was that smooth British accent that did it for me, but suddenly I felt guilty for having even considered Oliver. He was on our team. He always had been.

"What do I do, Oliver? How can I help?"

"Look, Charlotte, the reality is that there's not much you can do. The other reality is that the SEC starts these investigations ages before we even know about them, so I don't have any idea what they have. Once the prosecution provides me with their discovery, I'll be able to put the missing pieces together, solve this. I know I will."

I sighed. I certainly hoped he was right. "I want to play *offense*, Oliver."

He nodded. "Me too. But, unfortunately, that's not the game we're in right now."

I let that sink in. He was right, of course. I felt like I was playing defense in every single area of my life. "Let me know if you think of *anything*," I said.

"Will do." He paused. "I'll grab you tomorrow to get your car."

Small mercies.

Grace, Alice, and Julie were waiting for me when I walked in the back door. Silently, Grace grabbed a bottle of wine and four glasses, and we all followed her out the door, down the steps, and onto the beach.

A gentle breeze was blowing, and something about the way the birds were chirping back and forth made me feel like they understood what was going on in my life. But if they didn't, the three women around me certainly did. I had, suddenly and fiercely, lost my footing in the world, just like they had.

"Well, welcome to the lost ladies club," Julie said, putting her arm around me as we walked out to the shoreline.

I couldn't help but laugh. "And what a prestigious club it is."

"Waiting list a mile long," Grace said in a wistful tone totally opposite from what it should have been.

I nodded as Grace handed us each a glass and Julie poured.

We sat down on the sand, which was cool and a little damp. It was soothing to feel a part of this beach.

"So, how did it go?" Grace asked.

I shook my head. "I just feel so powerless. And now I'm questioning whether I should have taken Iris to see him."

"Of course you should have," Julie said. "He's her father. She needs to see him." She put her arm around me. She was so sweet in her private life, which was such a contrast from her work persona that sometimes I had to remember she was the same person. "I know this is hard, but we're here to help you." I sighed, knowing now was the right moment.

"I know that, and you've all been so great. But I have to be honest about something."

All eyes were on me.

"Iris and I can technically go back to our house." I grimaced. "But Bill is worried about our safety. He doesn't really want us to be alone there. But it's also not fair for us to stay here when we don't really need to be here."

Alice laughed. "Charlotte, sweetheart. The mommune isn't about what we *need*. We could all move on. We're strong, capable women. But being together makes us stronger. We want you and Iris to stay here as long as you want."

I put my hand to my heart. "You are amazing. You all are. Thank you so much." I paused. "And, um, I haven't exactly broken the news to Iris that we *could* go home. I would never ask you to lie for me, but if you could perhaps not mention it."

"Of course we won't!" Grace agreed. "We don't want y'all to go anywhere. It's so much more fun when we're all here together, not on our own."

"And we have Alice to take care of us!" Julie said.

Alice smiled, and I raised my glass. "To Alice!" I said.

"Hear! Hear!" Grace said.

"I don't know where Iris and I would be if it weren't for you."

"If it weren't for *you*," Alice said. "Thank goodness you had that total breakdown in the bank. Otherwise, we wouldn't all be here together now."

We all laughed.

Alice reached over me and took Julie's hand. "You saved me." She looked at Grace and me too. "All of you. You have given me purpose. You have given me a family when I thought even the fantasy of that was over for me."

My stomach hurt just thinking about what she had been through. "What happened?" I asked. As soon as I said it out loud, I realized I hadn't meant to. I'd only wanted to think it.

Alice shook her head. "Jeremy died in an avalanche while we were on a ski trip, Glen had a car accident, Walter fell off a ladder while cleaning the gutters."

I shuddered, thinking of the gutters on this house, three stories tall including the garage underneath, and the concrete below. How did Alice stay here?

I looped my arm through hers and sipped my wine. Alice was a chatty, vivacious woman when she chose to be. Her brief answers with no embellishment were all I needed to understand that she wasn't interested in discussing this further. And that was okay. I understood why she wouldn't want to dwell on the past.

Grace cleared her throat and raised her glass. "To second chances," she said.

"Or fourth, as it were," Alice said, laughing lightly.

"To never giving up," I said. That included all of us, didn't it?

"Yes," Julie said. "That. To never giving up." We all clinked glasses. Julie cleared her throat and called, "You can come down now!"

I looked up and could make out two figures on the steps. Merit and Iris.

"Drink up," she said to me. Then to them as they approached, "Kids, sit down. We're having a family meeting."

"Uh-oh," Grace said. "I don't like the sound of this."

"Um, why aren't the other kids at the family meeting?" Merit asked.

"Yeah," Iris said. "Forced family fun usually pertains to them too."

"Not this time," Alice said.

"Oh, um," Merit stuttered. "Well, if I could just explain—"

Julie cut him off, and Grace and I shared a look. She'd just broken Mom Rule Number One: never silence a kid who is about to confess to a crime.

"I want to talk to all of you about Bill and, in a larger sense, our reputation as a house."

My face felt hot. "Julie! You can't just—"

She put her hand up. "No, Charlotte. You and Iris are two of us now, and it is our responsibility to take care of each other. We might not be able to change what happens in court, but we can shape what happens in the court of public opinion, and I think we all know that, in a town this small, it's usually the same thing."

"That's the truest thing I've ever heard," Alice said. She looked at me pointedly. "She's right, Charlotte. They'll get jurors who aren't close to the case and all that, but, come on. Is that true? How do we know that some of those jurors aren't lying? Aren't planted? We have to change people's minds about Bill."

"Well, great," I said sarcastically. "Fan-freaking-tastic. Let me just hop right out and do that."

Grace said, "Julie, apologies, but what does this have to do with the kids?"

"If all of you would let me finish, I would tell you."

Alice made a motion like she was zipping her lips.

"First, I need to write an article in the paper about Bill's innocence. I want to interview him—and, Charlotte, I know I promised, but I hope you too—and his lawyer and his staff and everyone who can sing from the rafters that he is good and honest and has been framed."

"I don't know, Julie . . ." I said.

She charged ahead: "Then, Alice, we'll need you to write an anonymous letter to the editor about some tip or lead or something that hopefully will be real, but even if it isn't, it will get published because it will sell papers, and it's a letter to the editor so it's opinion."

"Sure," Alice said. "Whatever you need."

"Grace, I know this isn't really your speed, but we've got to come up with some way to work Bill's innocence into your massive online following. Maybe you do a special segment with Charlotte and Iris, and it somehow comes up or something."

Grace nodded. "Anything to help."

"I still don't see how this affects us," Merit said.

Julie smiled. "Ah, well, that's where you're wrong, because I've dissected Juniper Shores Socialite's content thus far, and the six of us around this circle are her prime fodder. So at first, I thought maybe we should conduct an investigation, find out who she is—"

"Ohhhh!" Iris said. "We should do that!"

"Too slow," Julie said. "Instead, we're going to make sure that everything we do, everywhere we go, we are preaching the gospel of an innocent Bill. She's everywhere we are, watching our every move. That can't help but make it onto her page."

Honestly, I was impressed. So, no, this wasn't going to get Bill out of jail or prove his innocence, but it was *something*. Julie was right that the court of public opinion could affect Bill's future enormously.

I nodded and said, "Kids, you just live your lives and—"

"Kids," Julie interrupted, "you are fourteen and sixteen, and thus old enough to help. If Charlotte is too proud to accept that, fine. But I'm here to tell you that this is important, and your voices matter."

With that, Julie stood up. "I'm off to start my article. Charlotte, I promised you I wouldn't make you talk. And I won't. But you have the chance to help right this very personal wrong. If I were you, I wouldn't squander that opportunity."

Julie was already marching up the beach. The General had issued the battle plan. "Wow. She is *good*," I said. Finally, someone who would help me play some offense.

"Too bad Julie isn't our attorney," Iris said. "Dad would at least be on house arrest."

"Do you think she's feeling so feisty and sure of herself because she's back with her ex?" Merit asked casually.

"Houston?!" Grace and Alice yelped at the same time.

"She is *not* back with him," Alice said.

"That's not what Juniper Shores Socialite says," Iris chimed in. "And I'm sorry, but facts are facts . . ."

We all laughed, but Julie and Iris had both touched on something here. Whether it was true or not, one anonymous Instagram account was shaping the reality of our entire town. We could use it for good, or we could use it for evil. Julie's plan was the perfect kind: a little bit of both.

Frozen in Time

People say you regret the things you didn't do, not the things you did. Those people don't understand real, true regret. Because those things you never did? You can't know the outcome. Didn't go to Hollywood? Well, maybe you would have made it. But you probably would have come home with credit card debt and the bitterness of broken dreams.

But see, those people who say I'm a murderer . . . well, they aren't entirely wrong. I was the one who wanted to go on that ski trip, to learn a sport that had seemed so foreign and exotic to me. But Jeremy was the one who, in his years of experience, took the gondola to the top of the mountain. Jeremy was the one who got caught in that avalanche. Three years of marriage. Three tiny, precious, precarious years when we were twenty-four to twenty-seven where things were perfect. Three perfect years when it didn't matter that his parents didn't want him with someone like me, someone lost and abandoned and orphaned. Someone who never had the opportunity to go to college, much less graduate. When it didn't matter that I didn't come from money like he did, didn't have a family name like he did.

Jeremy became frozen in time for me, in the honeymoon stage, when it was the two of us against the world. The two of us and a love so big that it would make your heart burst.

I think a part of me realizes that my memories of him aren't totally real, that the time we had together seems so perfect because our love was so young, so untainted. But also because *I* was so young. The Alice I was when I was with Jeremy was so much less afraid of the world. But, whatever the reason, he is still who I see when I close my eyes, whose breath I feel when I'm in that moment right before sleep when the world goes hazy but not all the way dark.

His parents tried to ruin that image for me. As we sat around a shining wooden conference table in their lawyer's office, his mother pointed at me and said, "She killed him. This is her fault!"

She couldn't have known how that propelled me back into my worst memory, how, instead of that lawyer's office, I was suddenly back in my childhood home, sitting on the carpet, buttoning the dress of my favorite baby doll when the plate glass window shattered, when my older brother dragged me across the carpet, leaving rug burns on my thighs and glass embedded in my skin, to pull me away from the 1985 Porsche 944 that I had never been inside of, that my father polished and shined and waxed to perfection weekly. It took me years to understand how that Porsche had come through the window, to grasp that my father had been so drunk—a habit that I didn't know then wasn't an anomaly—that he had driven my mother through the house, into the room where we were all sitting.

It wasn't until that day, sitting in the lawyer's office, that it occurred to me that maybe none of it was an accident. Maybe my father meant to kill my mother; maybe he meant to kill all of us. I only saw him a few times after that, when my mother's sister Mina, who I lived with, could gather the strength to take me, to face him. I was never brave enough to ask. I didn't want to know the truth.

And as that naïve twenty-seven-year-old, I didn't understand the ramifications of what Jeremy's mother was saying, of how grateful I should have been to his father for calming her down. I didn't even know how insurance money worked. All I knew was that, around that table, in the midst of all that pain, they offered me his million-dollar insurance policy if I'd walk away from the rest of his estate, including the house we shared. I remember thinking, *They didn't love him like I did.* No one who loved him like I did could sit across a table from me and negotiate like that eleven days after he died, nine days after we placed an empty urn in the local church's columbarium because his body was never found, buried under feet of snow and ice and fallen rock.

It was the loss that changed me. That steeled me. That nearly killed me. That shut me off for two more years until Glen with his soft-spoken love for me made me feel like I could breathe again. But it wasn't the same. Not that I didn't love Glen. I did. But once you lose your great love, all the others are tainted. You can't help but be closed off from the world when you've lived through the worst that can happen to you.

And that was why, now, at midnight, I was awake, staring at the ceiling, wondering if I could really push past my fear to love Elliott the way that he deserved.

What scared me wasn't just the idea of losing him; it was how very much I loved him. For the first time since Jeremy died, I felt like my heart was fully open, like something in the center of me was blooming and wide.

I heard noise out on the landing. Someone else was awake. Thank goodness. I hated the feeling of being alone in the dark. That's when it was the hardest not to have someone to roll over and touch, someone whose arms could wrap around me and make me safe. I ached at the thought of how easy it could all be, if I were with Elliott right now, letting him hold me, synchronizing my breath with his. The rhythm.

Jamie had been having trouble sleeping lately and would sneak from the bunk room into mine, so I figured it was her creeping up the stairs that I'd heard. But when I tiptoed out of my room, I realized that Iris's door was cracked, and I could hear Merit's voice.

I wasn't trying to listen in on their private conversation, but their voices wafted into the hall as I made my way toward Iris's room. "You should have seen my dad," she said. "He looked so small, so pale. It was just awful."

"I get it," he said. "I know what it's like to lose the person that you thought could always protect you—or at least, the person you knew would always try."

My heart broke for Merit. He'd had to be strong. I tried to be there for him, for Emma too. I tried to be the one to protect them. But I wasn't, would never be, their parent. I couldn't be that person for them.

As I reached out my hand, Merit said, "Julie wasn't wrong about us helping with your dad—"

I opened the door slowly, pushing it with one finger.

"It's really late, kiddos," I interrupted.

Iris was sitting with her back against her headboard, her knees pulled to her chest, on the left twin bed. I knew that pose. I'd spent some time in that pose. Merit was perched at the end of her right twin bed. Still, I couldn't imagine that Charlotte or Grace would be thrilled about them being alone in each other's rooms at midnight.

"We can't sleep," Merit said.

It was so endearing the way he said it. *We.*

"And why is that?" I asked, sitting down on the other end of the second bed, beside Merit and across from Iris.

Iris shrugged. "We're just bonding over being fatherless and alone in the world."

"You will never be alone in the world as long as you have me," I said. I turned to Merit. "But you need to get some rest so that you can be the star player we all love to watch on the field tomorrow."

"It's so much pressure being a star," he said with faux exasperation. He rose, then leaned down to kiss my cheek before leaving the room.

I raised my eyebrows at Iris, who was grinning from ear to ear.

"What?" she asked as Merit disappeared.

"You are not allowed to have a crush on your mommune brother," I whispered.

She scrunched her nose. "Do not ever, ever call him that again, please."

"Fine," I said. "But you understand what I'm saying." I pointed at her bed and said, "And you two in each other's rooms needs to end."

"I wish Merit wanted to be in my room like that," Iris said. "But I'm sorry, have you seen his girlfriend?"

I tried not to make a face. I had. With all her extensions and fake eyelashes and push-up bras. Shouldn't one be a little older before she was laced with so much self-loathing that she had to totally change her appearance? But I was old, so what did I know?

"She is *perfect*," Iris sighed, flopping herself back on the pillow.

What I loved, in this moment, was the resilience of teenagers. She had gone to visit her father in jail and had probably had one of the most traumatic days of her young life, but could still be most upset about her crush's beautiful girlfriend.

"You, my darling, are perfect. And comparison is the thief of joy. Don't get caught in that trap." I paused, then whispered, "And stay away from Merit! You are playing with fire."

She wriggled her eyebrows at me, and I tossed a pillow at her. "Fine,

fine," she said, rolling her eyes. "I'll try to keep him from throwing himself at me. He's so gross."

We both laughed. "You okay? Seriously?"

She nodded. "Just tired."

"I'm here," I said. "One a.m., four in the afternoon. If you need a listening ear or a piece of advice—or someone to talk some sense into you about older boys," I teased—"I'm always here."

She smiled and leaned back on her pillow. "I know."

"Good."

I got up from the bed and turned out the light.

"Sweet dreams," I whispered.

"Sweet dreams."

But I knew I wouldn't sleep. Instead, I walked outside, onto the beach, and watched the moon, the way it shone silvery and almost eerily beautiful on the water. I thought about Elliott. About our walk on the beach this week. About the coffee we'd sipped together. About how he wordlessly slipped into the pew beside me at morning prayer. No expectations.

I looked up at the stars and, as I usually did, thought about Jeremy, wondered if he was out there somewhere, if he could see me, hear me, feel me. And, maybe most of all, I wondered if, wherever he was, he could ever forgive me for moving on.

Screw, Murder, Marry

"If Twizzlers are wrong, I don't want to be right," I said, wrapping one around my wrist. I was lounging in a plush pink beanbag chair in Chloe's very posh and teenager-y playroom. I wondered if her mom had googled "teenage girl playroom" or if she had just added most of the Pottery Barn Teen catalog to her cart. The rug, in shades of pink, green, blue, and yellow that were fun and vibrant, was soft enough to sit on, and white slipcovered couches flanked an armoire holding a TV. The walls were lined with huge vintage photographs of Juniper Shores: the lifeguard station, the food trucks, the ocean at sunset. I didn't know much of anything about decorating, but I got the feeling it was all expensive. Which I guess was to be expected, considering we were sitting in a brand-new house on the ocean in one of the priciest zip codes on the East Coast.

"I'm really Team Oreo," Chloe said, crunching, crumbs dispersing onto the white slipcover. She had told me the housekeepers changed the slipcovers every week like sheets. That's how they always looked so clean despite the havoc we wreaked on them. I probably wouldn't want a bunch of kids eating outside of my kitchen, but Chloe's mom and dad were downstairs with a bunch of other couples having a wine tasting and nibbling on charcuterie, so they probably just wanted the little girls out of the way at all costs.

"Ugh, I'm not team anything," Dabney whined. "How do you eat like that and still stay so thin?"

"Dabney, you are practically a toothpick," I said. She was. She was easily a double zero, with white-blond hair she wore in this impossibly long ponytail down her back. Her legs were ninety miles long, and it was no coincidence that she was the best high jumper at school. "In fact, I think you would be even more beautiful with some Oreo weight on you."

She smirked at me. "I could never."

Chloe and I shrugged at each other like *more for me.*

"Dabney, I can't with this tonight. We love you, you're gorgeous. Just stop it." Chloe was always getting on Dabney. Privately, she believed that Dabney said these things so we would tell her how gorgeous and perfect she was, and she was tired of it.

"Does everyone have their costumes ready for tomorrow night?" I asked. Belle Epoque on the Beach was so fun, and everyone dressed up as if he or she was living in the late 1800s in France.

"Speaking of that," Chloe said, "I think it's time we start discussing our group costume for Halloween."

I felt warm and tingly all over just knowing that I was a part of the group costume. I took a moment to feel badly for everyone who wasn't a part of a group costume.

"I'm so glad you brought this up," Dabney said. "Because I have the best idea."

I smiled. "All ears."

"I think we should be the Spice Girls!" she said excitedly. "I'll be Baby Spice, obviously."

Chloe scrunched her nose. "So, you want to go, like, vintage?"

She nodded. I didn't hate the idea.

"Jessica and Alexis would be our other two?" Chloe asked.

Dabney nodded, and I could tell that Chloe's questioning had taken some of the wind out of her sails. It made me want to defend her, even though I wasn't 100 percent on board with the Spice Girls situation.

"Do you think people will get who we are?" Chloe sounded doubtful.

"When the five of us are all together, for sure," I said. "I mean, everyone's seen the David Beckham docuseries now."

"Oh, that's true," Chloe said. "I didn't think of that. Okay. I'm in!"

"Yay!" Dabney said. Then she paused. "Um, Ris, we can put your outfit together for you."

I shook my head. "You guys already had to do my Belle Epoque costume. I bet Alice can pull something together for me. She has a huge closet full of cool stuff, and she's very generous with it."

"Speaking of, how's life at the mommune?" Chloe asked.

"I think it's good. I mean, kind of weird sometimes when I really think about it, but also awesome to be with all these cool people." I paused. "You haven't lived until you've eaten Merit's mom's cooking. I'm serious."

"What about Alice?" Dabney asked. "What's she like?"

I knew why she was asking. "She's like this really calm, centered goddess. I can't explain it. I didn't know what an 'aura' was until I met her."

"It's probably the Lexapro," Chloe said seriously. Then we all burst out laughing.

"Why do you ask?"

"Oh, you know," Dabney said. "There are just so many rumors about her and all those dead husbands."

I winced. "You don't honestly believe Alice killed her husbands?" Of course, I had believed it mere days ago. Did I still? It was hazier now.

She shrugged. "I don't not believe it." She paused. "Just be careful. That's all I'm saying."

Had Alice ever done anything that seemed strange to me? Well, maybe taking our phones. A cold chill ran up my spine, but I scolded myself. That was for our mental health and development, not so she could murder us all and we wouldn't be able to call for help.

"Is it true that everyone breastfeeds each other's children?" Dabney asked.

I almost spit out my Twizzler. "Ew! Dabs! There aren't even any babies in the house."

This questioning was ruining the night's vibe. I needed to course-correct.

"Okay," I said, sitting up straighter. "How about a game of truth or dare?"

"Yes!" they said simultaneously.

"Me first! Me first!" Chloe said.

She would obviously be first. She was the born leader of the group, and, well, it was her house.

"Iris!" she said enthusiastically, pointing at me. "Truth or dare."

I knew she was just dying to ask me about Merit, so I grinned at her devilishly. "Dare!"

She sighed. "You are the worst."

"I know."

She paused for a minute. "Okay. I dare you to go downstairs and sneak a bottle of wine from my parents' party."

My eyes widened. "Chloe, I can't do that. My mom would kill me if I got in trouble."

"So don't get caught," she said nonchalantly.

I glanced over at Dabney, who shrugged. "Can I be her wing-woman?"

Chloe thought for a minute. "I'll allow it!" she said.

Dabney and I scrambled up, giggling.

"Okay," she said, "I'll create a diversion for the parents."

I nodded. "I think my best bet is grabbing a bottle out of one of the cases behind the bar," I whispered as we walked down the back steps, which were covered in a cool antelope pattern.

"Can you just make sure it's a rosé or champagne or something?" Dabney asked. "I hate red wine."

"Sure, Dab. Any vintage requests while I'm *stealing alcohol*?"

She smiled as she walked into the kitchen, where eight adults were mingling as a bartender stood behind the bar flanked by various bottles.

"Mrs. Montoya," Dabney said loudly, "I wanted to see if I could practice my solo in the school play for all of you." She smiled so sweetly.

I couldn't help but laugh as Mrs. Montoya sputtered, "Oh, um, sure. Why, of course, Dabney."

I mean, what was she going to say, really? I looked at the bartender and shook my head. "You might want to go refill them if she's going to sing," I whispered. He gave me a knowing look and picked up a bottle of red and a bottle of white, stepping from behind the bar.

All eyes were on Dabney as she belted out, "Moonlight, all alone on the pavement!"

I grabbed a bottle of champagne quick as a wink and was on the back staircase before anyone even glanced my way. I was stifling my laughter—because in what world was Dabney in a production of *Cats*? She did have a gorgeous voice, though. Her mom made her sing in the church choir, and she hated it, but she was good.

A few minutes later, she appeared in the playroom, and Chloe and I clapped.

"Thank you, thank you," she said.

We looked at the bottle of champagne. We'd all had a few sips of alcohol here and there, but that was the extent of it. "So, are we opening it?" I asked, suddenly filled with anticipation.

"Do you know how?" Dabney asked.

I shook my head.

"I know!" Chloe said. She whipped out her phone and opened YouTube. I followed the instructions, and after a few attempts, the top shot off, narrowly missing Dabney. We all screamed.

In most houses, we would have shushed each other. But we knew from experience that Mr. and Mrs. Montoya were only coming up here should the house catch on fire. Maybe.

I handed the bottle to Chloe, and she took a sip. She passed it to Dabney, who then passed it to me. It was kind of lukewarm, but pretty tasty.

"Okay," I said. "My turn." I looked from Dabney to Chloe, Chloe to Dabney.

"Chlo, truth or dare."

She laughed.

"Truth! I'm too stressed from the last dare!"

That was just what I was hoping for. "Is it true that you lost your virginity to Greg in the Fosters' pool?"

We had all heard the rumor even before Juniper Shores Socialite decided to out our friend, but Dabney and I hadn't been brave enough to ask her. We assumed Chloe would have told us, but you never knew. She took another sip of champagne and started laughing. "Oh my God, no! Don't y'all know me at all? I only let him touch my boobs because it's what he wanted for his birthday. I'm going to make that boy suffer for as long as possible. Please."

She passed the champagne to Dabney. "Okay, Dabs, truth or dare."

"Truth," she said.

"Fantastic." Chloe looked at me, and then at Dabney again. "Screw, murder, marry. Merit, Ben, Greg."

I shook my head. "You are the worst, Chloe."

"Kill Greg," Dabney said. "Because if I screw or marry him, you'll kill me. Screw Merit, marry Ben. Easy."

They both looked at me. "What? It's not my question."

But I will say my heart rate rose when Dabney said she wanted to marry Ben. I couldn't imagine him being, like, off the table. "But Ben still gets to be my best friend, even when you're married."

"Um, no way," Dabney said.

"Why not?"

Chloe scoffed at me. "Because he loves you, duh."

"He does not. We're just friends."

"Right," Dabney said. "We need to have some conversations about the basics of male/female relationships, but we'll save that for another day. For right now . . . truth or dare!"

I was going to say *truth*. I'd had enough daring for one night. But . . . well . . . I didn't want any questions about Merit or Ben. So, tentatively, I said, "Dare."

Dabney nodded. "All right. I have one." She looked at Chloe, her green eyes flashing. "But it's a triple dare. It's a dare that will take all three of us to carry out."

My stomach started to fill with butterflies. "I don't know, Dab," I said.

"Not up to you!" Dabney said. "Only Chloe can turn down the triple dare at this point."

Chloe grinned. "Oh, I'm in. I'm in all day long."

"That's what I was hoping," Dabney said.

She got off the couch and sat cross-legged in front of me, taking my hands. "Iris. I dare you and me and Chloe to break into your house."

I was confused. "What? Why?"

"Because they have all your stuff, and we're getting it back."

My heart fluttered at the idea. "I don't know," I said. "It's, like, a crime scene."

"It's *your* stuff," Chloe said. "You didn't do anything wrong."

She made good points. My dad hadn't done anything, and even if he had, it wasn't *my* fault. And, come on, were they going to, like, sell my Lululemon on Poshmark and pay back his alleged victims? I sort of doubted that.

"Guys, my mom would seriously kill me."

Chloe handed me the champagne bottle. "Your mom isn't here."

I took a swig, feeling bolder.

"It's three houses down," Dabney said. "How freaking hard could it be?"

I took another swig, the warmth of the champagne rushing through me, giving me the most bubbly, delicious feeling.

Chloe got up and went to her closet, tossing a duffel bag to each of us.

"You in?" Dabney asked.

I took one more swig. It was the fortification I needed. "I'm in," I whispered.

Maybe it was the champagne talking. Maybe it was how pissed off I was to be punished for something that was in no way my fault. But I wanted vengeance. And my Golden Gooses. Tonight, with the help of my friends, I might just get both.

Charlotte

We Ride at Dusk

One of the things that made my boss so successful in this small town was that, even though he had made millions of dollars, Gabe Montoya had that *I'm one of the people, I'm just like you* quality about him.

Earlier this morning he had sat in my office, chewing the Bic pen cap that seemed to be perpetually in his mouth, and said, "I remember what it was like when I wasn't the boss. It was so hard to get off work to do things like get your insurance. And that's why I really like these later hours once a week. So much of our business comes from that."

"I love it," I said. "It's a great idea." Secretly, I was horrified that I would have to spend yet more time away from Iris. Between her sports and school and social schedule, and now my work, I felt like I barely saw her. It was heartbreaking. But, on this particular Friday night, Iris was spending the night with Gabe's daughter Chloe, so she wasn't home anyway. And I was so grateful to have steady work, a paycheck, and a boss who was feeding me clients, that I would never have thought of complaining. I was trying to be very zen, but I did have to take a moment to absolutely panic. The clock was ticking, and I was getting increasingly nervous about Bill's court date. The discovery still hadn't come.

"I'm sorry I can't be here with you tonight," Gabe had said. "But Agnes will be here."

I wanted to roll my eyes. Yeah. Agnes was such a huge help. I might rather be alone.

"That said," Gabe added, "you don't need me. Already." He leaned back, studying me like he was amused. But Gabe had this sense of perpetual amusement about him. In spite of myself, I really, really liked him. He had a good heart, and he was successful because his primary goal was taking the very best care of his clients.

"Charlotte, honest to God, you're the best damn employee I've ever had. I don't deserve you."

"Thanks, Gabe. This opportunity means the world to me. You took a chance on me when no one else would, and I can't ever repay you for that." Gabe was my savior. Well, no, if anyone was my savior, it was Alice. But Gabe was at least my patron saint.

He had tapped his hand on my desk. "Oh, you're repaying me right now."

Gabe got to his feet, and I called, "Have fun tonight! Take care of my daughter!"

"Always," he said as he left.

I had formerly imagined this new world I was inhabiting to require taking potential clients to lunch, visiting their places of business. And, sure, I did do some of that. But I mostly sat right here in my office and waited for people to walk in the door. I'd ask them an extensive number of questions, plug some data into my software, and find out what carrier could offer the best rate and value combination. It really wasn't selling at all. It was just obvious. They had a need; I could fill it. Life insurance and disability were a little more complicated than property and casualty—that was your general car, home, and boat insurance, umbrella policies, etc.—because they required physicals and health histories and had a lot more factors. You're a dentist? Your disability is essentially a whole different product than if you're a teacher. The companies are different, the rules are different.

Anyway, I was a quick learner and I found I really enjoyed protecting people for when the worst happened. And I knew what it was like when the worst happened. If only someone had walked in and handed me a check when it had happened to me, that would have been amazing.

I heard the door chime, and Agnes say, "Can I help you?" in the dullest tone imaginable. I didn't want to get Agnes fired or anything, but for goodness' sake. This woman was the face of our company?

A voice I recognized said, "Yeah, I'm here to take out an errors and omissions policy."

"Mr. Montoya's out," Agnes said. "But the new girl is in the back."

I rolled my eyes. *Really, Agnes? The new girl?* Honestly. I was number one in my MBA program. I could maybe handle selling an errors and omissions policy.

"She any good?" Grace asked. I had to smile.

Agnes lowered her voice and said, "They say she's some kinda mathematical genius." She said it like *math-uh-mat-ee-cal.*

"So, a nerd, then?" Grace whispered back.

I didn't hate that Agnes thought I was a mathematical genius. It almost made up for her previous slights.

"Go on back and see for yourself," Agnes said.

I sat up a little straighter and tried to look extremely busy on my laptop.

"Excuse me," Grace said, tapping on my open door lightly. I didn't expect to see Alice and Julie too. They had been quiet little church mice. And they were holding what appeared to be a garment bag.

"Hello, working girl!" Julie sang. "We're here to visit!"

"Kind of here to visit," Grace said. "I actually do need that errors and omissions policy too."

That made sense. Errors and omissions covered public figures—authors, influencers, etc.—if they got sued for what they posted. It was a little tricky, honestly. I opened a folder on my computer and dragged a file into a new email.

"I just sent you an application," I said. "We can go through it at home because it's complicated."

Julie sat down in one of the drab gray chairs across from my desk, and I eyed Alice. "I'm afraid to even ask what's in the bag."

"Afraid?" she asked so sweetly that I was even more afraid. "Why would you be afraid of a little garment bag?"

I motioned with my hand for her to unzip it. When she did, I gasped. Inside was a low-cut yellow gown, cinched at the waist with a full skirt, trimmed in the most delicate lace.

"And!" Grace said, producing a smaller bag I hadn't even noticed, "the pièce de résistance." She pulled out a fascinator with the most fabulous yellow feathers.

I put my hand to my heart. Belle Epoque at the Beach was, without a doubt, the most fun event of the year in Juniper Shores. Even still, I said, "I see what you're trying to do, but it's a no." I wouldn't, *couldn't* go to my favorite event of the year if I wasn't on the arm of the man who loved me.

"A no!" Julie protested. "I had to beg, borrow, and steal to get our dresses from the theater company."

I rolled my eyes at her. "And I know you hated every minute." My voice dripped with sarcasm. Julie thrived on manipulating people into getting exactly what she wanted. I envied that in a way. I could use a little more of that these days.

"Charlotte, if you will remember," Grace said authoritatively, "Bill's company is the headline sponsor of the event. You have a ton of tickets. We should use them."

I did recall him mentioning that.

"And Merit and Iris are volunteering with their friends," Alice said.

I looked at them skeptically and sighed. "Look, I get it. It's a fun party. But you can't seriously think that I would go out in public when it has only been two weeks since my husband's total and complete humiliation."

Julie reached into her purse and handed me a single piece of copy paper. It took me a few seconds to realize that it was a miniaturized version of our local newspaper's front page. "This is running tomorrow."

The headline read: "BILL SITTERLY MAINTAINS INNOCENCE—AND IS MOMENTS AWAY FROM PROVING IT."

I gasped. The print was too small for me to read, but, well, probably no one else would read it all either. That headline was enough. "Do you think you stretched the truth a little there, Jules?"

She shook her head. "Nope. When I interviewed Bill and Oliver, they seemed very confident. I only used information from their quotes."

I rubbed my temples. "So you're telling me that this will hit everyone's front walks and inboxes tomorrow morning, and I'm supposed to go prance around tomorrow night?"

"Yes," Julie said. "That's exactly what I'm saying."

"Do you know what I've learned from my debacles?" Alice asked. She was a good voice of reason, because who had weathered more scandal than Alice?

"What?" I asked warily.

"People believe that guilty people hide. Innocent people carry on. We are innocent people. I'm tired of hiding away, of not having fun, because of what people will say. They think I killed three husbands. If I can deal with the chatter behind my back, you can too."

Grace nodded. "I haven't been to a single big town function since Troy left. And guess what? It isn't my fault he abandoned his family. I'm not hiding out anymore."

I looked at Julie. She shrugged. "Please. I wouldn't hide out even if I was guilty."

We all laughed.

"Look, Char," Julie said. "This is part of the plan. We put out the article, we go to the town's biggest function and run our mouths, and surely Juniper Shores Socialite will follow suit. We aren't guilty. We aren't criminals. We aren't going to hide."

She said it with so much passion that pride swelled in my chest. It was like when a talented singer hit the perfect high notes in "The Star-Spangled Banner" before a baseball game and you had peanuts and beer and fresh air and just felt so damn lucky to be an American. "God, you give a good pep talk," I said.

"Is that a yes?" Alice asked.

"That's a hell yes," I said.

Alice slumped down in the other customer chair.

"What's the matter with you?" I asked, incredulous. "I thought this is what you wanted!"

"It is," she said wearily. "But now if you're going to go face the public, I have to too."

"Oh!" I said. "Bring Elliott!"

"That will really help," she said sarcastically.

"Why cause a teeny fire when you can burn down the whole damn town?" Julie asked. "Tomorrow night, the mommune comes out in full force."

"We ride at dusk!" Grace said.

I noticed Agnes standing at the door. "I hate to break up the sorority mixer," she said, "but some of us are ready to go home."

"Yes!" I said. "Sorry, Agnes. We're going." She rolled her eyes and walked away, her entire person an expression of her pure exasperation with me.

"She really dazzles, doesn't she?" Grace asked.

I laughed and held out my hand to Alice. "If I'm doing this, you'd better give me that dress."

"Your armor!" Alice said.

"Nope," I said, reaching my arms out to them. "That's all of you."

And as we linked arms and made our way down the hall, I couldn't help but feel like they were. For the first time since Bill's arrest, I didn't feel so alone. And there it was, that proud tightness in my chest again. We were survivors. And tomorrow, there was no question about it: we'd have the whole town talking.

Iris

~~~~~~~~~

Crime Scene

Chloe, Dabney, and I would not be good criminals. For one, the champagne had made us giggly. For two, we hadn't worked through the details of how we'd actually carry out our breaking-and-entering mission. I'd had, like, six sips of champagne *and* was breaking into a house. I was a full-on rebel now. It had only taken one night to convert me to a life of crime. But I wasn't totally sure that breaking into your own house counted as a major crime. Would my mom ground me if she found out? I wasn't sure. But I knew she would ground me for the champagne.

The sand was damp and cool underneath our bare feet as we walked up the beach, the reflection of the moon on the ocean making it bright enough that we could easily find our way.

"Um, guys," I said, realizing that, while it was light, it wasn't quite light enough to see to figure out how to break into the house. "Should we have, like, flashlights or something?"

"Our phones, Iris. Duh," Chloe said.

"Okay, yeah. But our phone flashlights aren't that big," I said.

"Are you trying to get out of a dare?" Dabney asked. "Because that's what it sounds like to me. I feel like there are ramifications for going against the triple dare."

Maybe I *was* trying to get out of it. I could see the house in front of me now, and we turned right to make our way over the sand dune that I knew very, very well. "Maybe we shouldn't do this," I whispered. "We could get in trouble."

"Just think: Golden Goose. Golden Goose."

I couldn't help but laugh.

"It's your own house," Dabney answered. "Plus, we're only kids. We can't be tried in a grown-up court of law." She paused. "Right?" she asked Chloe.

"How on earth would I know? Why don't you ask the daughter of the prison lord?" Chloe said. Then she gasped and put her hand over her mouth. "I'm sorry, Iris. I'm drunk. I didn't mean that."

I couldn't be mad at her for saying something true, even if it did kind of sting. My dad was in jail. My house was locked up with crime scene tape around it. "You're stating the obvious," I said. "But I don't actually know either."

We walked around the perimeter of the pool and up the outdoor steps. I was proud of how super quiet we were being. Well, quiet, that is, until Chloe tripped up the top step and fell into Dabney, who fell into me. Then, somehow, we were all in a pile on the front porch, laughing hysterically. This, I knew, was 10 percent champagne, 90 percent girl giggles that only three best friends really knew how to produce in each other.

"I love you guys," I said.

"Is that the Veuve talking?" Chloe asked, getting up and taking our hands to pull us up too.

"No," I said. "Maybe a little." More honest. "But I really do. You guys could have turned your backs on me and walked away when I was going through a hard time."

"Turned our backs? On you?" Dabney said. "That's so 2008."

We all laughed again.

"For real," Chloe said. "The actions of some man don't get to define us anymore—even if that man is, you know, your dad."

I pulled them both in for a side hug. "Okay," I said, taking a deep breath. "Here goes nothing."

"What now?" Dabney asked. "Do we break a window or something?"

I walked confidently up to the farthest left-hand window in the living room, put my palms flat on the window frame, and pushed with all my might. It slid right up.

"Wow," Chloe said. She was close enough I could see her eye roll. "I'm glad we really stressed about that."

"This window never locked right," I said. "It didn't matter because it wasn't like anyone was going to break in."

"Until now," Dabney said.

"Until now," I agreed, grinning at her.

I was about to climb through the window when Chloe said, "Wait!"

I tensed, ready to start running, but then she added, "You know your house could be, like, ransacked, right?"

I raised my eyebrows at her. "What? Why?"

Dabney nodded knowingly. "Oh yeah. Remember how trashed P. Diddy's house was after that raid?"

I felt a little sick—but it was nice to be prepared.

I climbed through the window and my friends followed me. It was dark, but enough light was shining through the windows that it wasn't too bad. It also smelled . . . weird. Not, like, bad necessarily, but just not like cooking and candles and general "we live here" sort of smells. It was kind of hot and damp. I didn't like it. It made me sad. Still, it was a huge relief to be back in my house. I didn't want to leave. Ever.

We all flipped our flashlights on. We walked through the living room

and dining room, which looked pretty much intact. But that wasn't surprising. They were mostly furniture. In the kitchen, a few drawers and
cabinets were open, and some cleaning stuff was haphazardly on the
floor, but my mom was a stickler for organization, so I felt like the lack
of mess had less to do with the feds taking care of our house and more
to do with the fact that they could see we weren't hiding anything.

We made our way silently up the stairs, and in my room, out of
habit, I clicked the light switch.

"Are you crazy?" Chloe hissed, flipping it back off immediately.

I smacked my hand against my forehead. "Oh my gosh. Sorry.
See? What would I do without you guys?"

"Have these people no respect?" Chloe said, her voice almost shaking. The toy box that was still at the end of my bed had been dumped
out and my beloved stuffed animals were askew. I hadn't slept with
them in years, but still. I picked up Bunny, my favorite, now one-eared
lovey from when I was little, and hugged her to me.

Inside the walk-in closet, I shut the door behind us. *Then* I turned
on the light. "This has to be okay," I said. "It's not like anyone can see
us in here."

"It's pretty much perfect in here," Dabney said. "They must have
gotten bored with your lack of raidable items."

I nodded in agreement as I walked over to my dresses section and
gathered them in my arms, hugging them to me. "My girls. My best
friends."

"Hey!" Chloe protested.

"Shhhh," Dabney said. "She's having a moment with her true loves.
Don't interrupt her."

We all giggled. "Dabs," I said, "you're in charge of shoes. Take
enough that I can get by but not so many that it looks obvious."

She saluted me.

"Chlo, as much as I hate to waste prime duffel bag real estate on them, I mostly need uniforms. And you do jeans too. I'll handle everything else."

We all started rifling through my things quickly and efficiently. More than once I stopped to smell a piece of my clothing. It smelled so good. It smelled like home. So much so that it overwhelmed me, and I had to sit down on the pink plush carpet.

"You okay?" Dabney asked.

I nodded sulkily.

"We should have brought the rest of the champagne," Chloe said. "I assume it's kind of hard to be in your old house trying to grab pieces of the life you left behind—or, I mean, sober, anyway."

I nodded, tears coming to my eyes.

"But here's the thing," Dabney said, "this is just temporary. You're going to be back here before you know it."

"How do you know?" I asked, trying not to cry, clearing the lump in my throat.

"We just know," Chloe said.

I nodded and took a deep breath, trying to be brave, and, for a reason I could not explain, feeling somewhat reassured by her saying that, even though she offered zero explanation. "Okay. It's funny, you know. I spent half the time I was here wanting to be back in New York, and now I wish I could close my eyes and curl up on my own pillow tonight."

Chloe smiled and widened her eyes. "But you can!"

"We can't stay here," I said.

"No, but we can take your pillow!"

That was a really sweet thought.

"Hey, can I get your Miss Dior from your bathroom?" Dabney asked. "I really miss sharing that with you." She made air quotes when she said *sharing*.

"Of course," I said. "Get anything you want. Anything we can carry, that is." I paused. "Chlo, can you be in charge of my pillow?"

"Yup."

"Great." I was having a thought. Julie had said that we should try to help prove that my dad was innocent. I hadn't been able to stop thinking about it. No, I wasn't some total expert in the world of finance, but the premise was pretty easy: we had to find proof that he hadn't stolen that money. "Hey, guys, I'm going to my dad's office really quick."

I opened the door just enough to slip through and closed it behind me, tapping my flashlight icon again. Without Chloe and Dabney, it felt eerie to be here alone in the dark, like a ghost or the boogeyman was going to jump out and grab me at any minute. I took deep breaths and made my way the few steps down the hall into my dad's home office where he worked at least half the time. At work, Dad's desk was always piled with papers and notebooks, files and folders. Here, everything was perfectly tidy on top of his large mahogany desk that ordinarily contained a Mac, a wireless keyboard, and nothing else. Behind the desk sat a matching antique credenza with awards on top. To the right was a small closet that, I knew, held Dad's printer, shelves full of books, and assorted paperwork, perfectly organized. A large leather swivel chair sat behind the desk. My throat gripped when I saw it. Of all the places I could picture my dad, I pictured him here the most. Now the office was basically empty. No computer. But no mess either.

Man, I missed when we all lived here together, when Dad would work from home, when I'd sit on the other side of his desk and do my homework. I picked up a framed photo from Dad's credenza of the three of us at the Rockefeller Center tree lighting in New York. If I could close my eyes and twitch my nose and go back in time, I would do it in a minute.

I missed the man who had raised me, who always came home for dinner and asked me about my day and helped me with my math homework. I missed sitting with my parents in our den watching movies. I missed every simple thing about our life together, and while, sure, so far that ideal family had only been MIA for less time than when I went to camp in the summers, the idea that I didn't know when or if I would get it back hurt the most.

I turned to Dad's credenza and opened the drawers, which were, as I could have predicted, empty. The feds had cleaned out his files, obviously.

I opened my email on my phone and typed in "Dad." An email he'd written to me popped up. *Good luck at your game today. I'll be there as soon as I can! Love you, kiddo.* Tears sprang to my eyes. I knew I had to have this email. I needed to fold it up and put it in my pocket.

I hit the print button. The sound of the printer springing to life made me jump, which was crazy since I was the one who'd started it. I hadn't really expected it to still be there. But a printer was pretty utilitarian. It wasn't like it was storing anything. I opened the door to the closet that held the printer—and then I screamed absolutely bloody murder. It was definitely the loudest scream of my life. I heard Chloe yelling "Iris!" as a man in a mask caught my eye, just for a moment. I don't know how my reflexes were so fast, but, like I had done a bazillion times before, I held my thumb on the picture icon on my phone's lock screen, it popped open, and I started snapping.

I screamed at the top of my lungs again, knowing I was done for. I had broken the rules, and now I was going to get murdered. The man put his hand up to his eyes and dropped something. Probably to strangle me. But he didn't strangle me. He grabbed up the papers lying on the floor and ran past me, toward the stairs.

My fight-or-flight must have been broken because I took the time to bend down and pick up a piece of paper he hadn't grabbed. At a glance I could see that it was a broker statement from one of the mutual funds Dad's company invested with. Well, to be more specific, it was *my* broker statement. Totally ordinary. Why would someone steal that? The creepiest feeling washed over me as I realized that those statements were stored in my room, in my desk, which meant that he had been in there. Dad's office was the closest room to mine, so the robber must have hidden in here when he heard us come in. My whole body turned cold, and I dropped the statement on the desk like I'd been scalded.

Finally, realizing that our lives were in danger, I ran toward my room, calling, "Dabney, Chloe, get out of there! Now!"

My bewildered friends walked toward the hallway. "Come on!" I screamed, panic setting in. "Now!" I sprinted down the stairs and clambered out the window and didn't even look behind me until we were halfway back to Chloe's house.

When I finally stopped, Chloe asked, out of breath, "What is going on?"

"A man," I panted. "In a mask. In Dad's office closet."

Four eyes went wide. "We have to tell someone!" Dabney said.

"Tell them what?" I asked haughtily, regaining my senses. "We broke into the house, and we think someone else broke in too?"

"Again, it's *your* house," Chloe said.

I put my head in my hands. Then I pointed at Dabney. "This is your fault," I said. "You and your stupid triple dares."

"Hey!" she said, holding up a duffel bag. "I love you so much that, even during the panicking and screaming, I got your shoes."

I hugged her. "You're right. I'm sorry. I could have said no."

"That's more like it," she said.

"I even got your pillow," Chloe said.

"You two are good, good friends," I said. "The best."

And here we were, full circle, with me feeling kind of weepy over how much I loved my friends. I pulled my phone out to show them the pictures of the man, zooming in on his features. "I'm pretty good at recognizing people even in masks post-pandemic," Dabney said. "But I don't recognize that guy."

I didn't either.

"Let's tell my parents," Chloe said. "They'll know what to do and then we don't have to tell your mom."

I shook my head. "Nope. Nope. They'll *definitely* tell her. I think we just let it go."

"Iris, someone was in your house!" Dabney said.

"Yeah, but what if it was like some sort of guard or something?"

"A guard, in a mask, in your dad's home office closet?" Chloe asked in a tone that signified I was an idiot.

Okay. Maybe I was an idiot. I shook my head. "Right. That doesn't make a lot of sense." I paused. "But he was taking broker statements, which the feds should have already gotten. Which is why I'm thinking that maybe it was someone with the investigation who left something behind." I bit my lip. "Just let me think about it for a beat, okay? I'll let you know what I decide."

Dabney scrunched her nose. "I mean, maybe Iris is right. We'd be in so much trouble."

Chloe sighed. My duffel suddenly felt heavy, now that my adrenaline had calmed. I was so relieved to reach Chloe's door.

"Back at home, safe and sound," she said.

It was only then that I wondered whether I would ever truly feel safe again.

@junipershoressocialite

Sharing bad behavior and delicious drama in North Carolina's most exclusive coastal zip code. DM with tips, pics, and juicy deets.

SEPTEMBER 7, 5:49 A.M.

26 Posts
9,762 Followers
26 Following

In case you've been hiding under a rock and didn't hear . . . tonight is the night. Juniper Shores' Met Gala. Our Oscars. Our queen Charlotte's debutante ball. Since I was, sadly, not here to keep you abreast of town happenings during last year's ball, a recap:

PIC 1: The mayor's wife debuted not only her new emerald necklace (a birthday gift from her husband) but also her new décolletage (a birthday gift from her surgeon).

PIC 2: Monday's carpool line got a little more awkward when a single mom and divorcé dad, presumably dating, were broken up by aforementioned divorcé's very married mistress announcing to the entire party that she was having an affair with him. And then there were three . . . broken marriages, that is. Jealousy isn't a good color. But it makes for the very best Instagram fodder.

PIC 3: And who could forget two of Juniper Shores' most beautiful, put-together housewives resorting to hair pulling in a particularly heated battle for the live auction trip to the Amangiri? It's okay, ladies, we've forgotten which one of you ripped out the other's extensions with her fingernails. (Well, almost.)

PIC 4: We danced late into the night, underneath the stars, reminiscing about the good times, gossiping about the bad, and, oh yes, our purpose: raising the entire year's budget for the Juniper Shores Arts Council. Ahhhh, what a responsibility and an honor to be a philanthropist. . . .

TNT ('Til Next Tantrum)

JUNIPER SHORES SOCIALITE

Charlotte

Armor

Alice had been right about one thing: this dress *was* a little like armor. Spanxed and corseted into my gown, cleavage high, hair higher, and feathers adorning my head, I felt like I was someone else, like I was play-acting at being a Juniper Shores housewife. And that was 100 percent exactly what I needed to get through what was sure to be a difficult night.

Belle Epoque on the Beach was Bill's favorite event of the year. Well, to be fair, it was most people's favorite event. If you loved a good party, you were pretty much guaranteed to have a great time. If you couldn't be happy here, you couldn't be happy, I remembered as we walked up to the check-in table. Every year when I came to this event, I felt confident, sparkling, alive. But that was because no one could make me feel that way quite like Bill, who would have told me how beautiful I looked, how no costume would be able to match mine. I would feel so loved, so special, that I couldn't help but walk taller.

Tonight was a different story. I didn't want to walk tall; I wanted to duck.

As usual, a large parquet dance floor had been set up on the sand, just a few yards from the ocean. A single tentpole stood in the middle, and from it ran hundreds of strands of bubble lights, creating the feeling that the stars had come down from the sky. Scattered around the perimeter were ten-top round tables and tall cocktail tables overflowing with ranunculus and peonies, alongside crushed-velvet antique couches. Dozens of teenagers—my daughter among them—milled about in period dress, passing hors d'oeuvres, handing out paper fans, and, the most coveted job, wearing shucking belts so that guests could shuck their own fresh oysters. Each of the four sides of the outdoor area held a gilded bar alight with champagne and signature cocktails for easy grabbing, and bartenders waited to serve a full selection of anything else one's heart desired. During this early part of the evening, a massive buffet lined the center of the dance floor, filled with every delicious, delectable offering Juniper Shores could provide, from lobster and fresh sushi to Wagyu beef and caviar, the most beautiful fruit and perfectly roasted vegetables, desserts almost too beautiful to eat, and on and on. At nine on the dot, it would all be swept away and dancing would begin; at midnight, servers would return with trays of tiny sliders and french fries.

I wouldn't make it until midnight. I could already tell. The appraising stares of the crowd would break me before then, because there was no doubt about it: all eyes were on the four of us as we approached the check-in table. "Are you sure you want to be seen with me?" I asked Grace quietly.

"I would never not be proud to be seen with you," she said. My eyes pooled because I knew she meant it, because I would have meant it too, and the mere idea of that stunned me. Being without Bill had felt like torture most days. But I had made friendships here that I never thought I'd get to have. It wasn't even close to an even trade, but it was a very glittery silver lining.

"Okay, ladies," Julie said. "Remember: if you can drop Bill's innocence into a conversation, do it. But don't make it obvious." She fanned herself with her vintage fan. That sweet Elliott had gotten each of us one for the occasion. Even so, Alice had begged off coming here with him on a proper date, and opted to be with us instead. As she'd said, "I'm not going to make my first big night out in years be all about my next victim. I'd rather everyone talk about our cult."

Poor Alice. I was experiencing a little of what it was like to live under a microscope like she had, and it wasn't pleasant. Beside the check-in table—an ornate, gilded Black French antique—sat what I was most excited about: a beautifully constructed eight-foot-tall section of living boxwood hedge that held a single brass bell. When one rang the bell, as Julie did now, a gloved hand appeared with a glass of champagne. But what was woefully missing from the top of the boxwood hedge? The Sitterly Capital logo that was supposed to adorn it, marking my husband's company as the lead sponsor for this event.

I had a moment, one of those we all do inevitably in our lives, where I had to make a decision: Did I confront the chair of the event, Laura Lucas, or did I keep my mouth shut? There had been times when I had been a mouth-shut kind of gal. And then there were ones like tonight, where I was out for vengeance, for blood, and I wasn't going to take one more second of this treatment.

Laura was swathed in green silk and lace that really brought out her eyes, a choker of pearls around her neck that I wanted to snatch off and watch them fall, one by one, to the sand. Which I did not, obviously. Instead, I said casually, offhandedly, "Laura, I thought part of the lead sponsor package for this event was signage on the champagne boxwoods. Was I incorrect?"

I could see Laura having her own moment of debate. She cleared her throat, looking embarrassed, and said, "I'm sorry, Charlotte. I didn't, um, know if . . ."

"You didn't know if her husband would like to recoup his twenty-thousand-dollar investment in your event?" Julie asked snappily.

I shot her a look.

"I didn't know the current status of the company, and to be very frank, I feared that putting out signage might look like a calculated low blow on my behalf."

Julie rolled her eyes and was about to speak, but I touched her arm, very lightly, and she stood down. Because Laura was right. It *would* have looked like she was relishing our fall from grace.

I nodded. "I appreciate that, Laura. I'm not sure if you read today's *Sun*, but Bill is innocent, and all this is being cleared up as we speak. So, yes, the company is very much going to be back in action."

The certainty with which I said that shocked even me. And Laura must have bought it because she turned to her friend and said, "Greta, let's please make sure the Sitterlys' agreed-upon signage gets hung immediately."

Greta nodded, proving that, to her immense credit, Laura had told the truth. There had been a lot of talk about what to do with this sticky situation. The signs had obviously been made. I didn't exactly feel sorry for her, but I did know what it was like to be put in a morally ambiguous position. And, as much as Laura hadn't made things particularly easy for me lately, I knew she appreciated Bill's big fat check. And she would want another one. So she would swallow her pride and fix this. Because what was better than publicly humiliating someone? Being the hero who beat the fundraising goal.

"Thank you so much, Laura." She slipped rhinestone tennis bracelets—quite good ones, in fact—that served as the "tickets" for the evening onto our wrists and said, "I apologize again for the oversight. I will make up for the lost time with an extra mention in the Arts Council newsletter."

"That would be just great." I was going for a charitable tone, but I think it bordered on patronizing, which, honestly, was fine.

"I *loathe* that woman," Grace said into my ear as we walked toward the bar.

"So do I. But, on the bright side, Laura will rehash that exact conversation—Bill's innocence and all—to everyone at this party."

I grabbed a glass of champagne and looked around. I was so caught up in my own mini-drama, I had forgotten to look for my daughter. Her friend Dabney walked by, holding a tray of sweet potato ham biscuits. "You look fabulous," I said. She did. Predictably. Dabney was one of those beautiful, lithe, shiny people that you wanted to hate, but she was just too sweet. And she wasn't just teenager shiny. She was forever shiny, would grow from a lovely girl into a bombshell of a woman. You just knew it. She, Chloe, and Iris had picked out matching dresses in pink, yellow, and blue. Dabney was yellow, Chloe blue, Iris pink. They were the cutest little things. I was so happy for my daughter's supportive friendships. I knew that it was a gift to have a shield from high school girl drama. But I hadn't known until now how very sustaining female friendships could be. I'd never had any quite this good.

"Not as fabulous as you, Mrs. Sitterly. You're the talk of the party."

I laughed, and she put her free hand to her mouth. "I didn't mean it like that!"

I put my hand to her shoulder. "It's fine, sweetheart. Thank you. If you see Iris, tell her to embarrass herself for just a moment and come say hello to her humiliating mother."

Dabney laughed. "Yes, ma'am." She looked at Grace. "You look beautiful too, Mrs. McDonald."

Mrs. McDonald did, indeed, look beautiful.

"Would you like me to tell Merit to come find you?"

"I wouldn't put that on you, Dabney."

She brightened. "Could you please? Any excuse to talk to Merit."

Grace pointed at Dabney. "His head is big enough already, thank you very much. I don't need pretty little things like you fawning over him."

She smiled and turned as a group of partygoers approached for ham biscuits.

"Is that weird?" I asked. "Having girls love your son like that?"

She nodded. "Yeah, like he was all mine and now I have to share him. But I just want him to be happy."

"Don't we all," I said.

At that moment, there was a visible shift in the energy of the party as a very debonaire Elliott Palmer entered the room. Maybe it's dramatic to say a hush fell over the crowd, but, well, it did. Juniper Shores' leading bachelor was back.

"God, I'd forgotten how much I love Belle Epoque," Grace said.

Despite my discomfort, despite my run-in with Laura, I couldn't have agreed more.

@junipershoressocialite

Sharing bad behavior and delicious drama in North Carolina's most exclusive coastal zip code. DM with tips, pics, and juicy deets.

SEPTEMBER 7, 7:30 P.M.
27 Posts
9,767 Followers
28 Following

You didn't hear it from me, but . . .

PIC 1: The Belle Epoque Ball is well underway, and I'll be coming to you all night long with the can't-miss moments from tonight's already *extremely* eventful evening. Tongues are wagging all over town about the group who, until tonight, were something akin to the Four Horsewomen of the Apocalypse. Yes, our mommune mothers came out in force tonight, looking like a million bucks. No, in a town where a million bucks is vacation money, they looked like a *billion*, sauntering in wearing, undoubtedly, the ball's finest costumes, with glowing skin, bright smiles, and perfect hair—beach wind be damned. It's safe to say that all eyes were on these four as they made their way from the check-in table—where they handled a sponsorship snafu with all the grace of the ladies they are. This evening, they are Capote's Swans, and, I'd dare say, Alice is their Babe Paley, ruler of all. With her elbow-length kid gloves, a lavender confection of a gown, and the only tiara I have ever found not to be tacky, laced with fresh blooms, I proclaim her—not to be too cutesy—the belle of the Belle Epoque!

PIC 2: Every queen needs her king, and we are almost positive the actual seas—not just the sea of bodies near the buffet—parted when one Elliott Palmer, clad in the most dashing tux of all, saw Alice Bailey and, for lack of a more refined term, beelined for her. No, it wasn't yet nine. No, the buffet (we need a more elegant word for this culinary work of art!) hadn't been cleared. But, with the string quartet playing a truly moving version of Christina Perri's "A Thousand Years," he scooped up our belle and led her around the dance floor solo. We think it's safe to say that the Black Widow isn't in hiding anymore. In fact, perhaps tonight was her coming-out party.

PIC 3: Word on the street is that our Swans are here on a mission. One of my sources says they are trying to ensnare others in their unhealthy lifestyle and recruit new members of their cult that is an assault on happy families everywhere. If that is true, I'm offended that they, as of yet, have not tried to recruit me. As good as they look tonight, I'd sign up in a skinny second. Ladies, consider this my official RSVP!

PIC 4: Oh, the danger in covering the Belle Epoque is not realizing that the adult drama is way less than half the fun. Our teenagers might be here for service hours, but they are fantastic at also getting caught in the crosshairs. Our senior golden couple—who have made it well over two years together, I might add—are rumored to have called it quits last week. And the passive-aggressive digs at each other are almost too good. No wonder these two are Ivy-bound. They really know how to tear each other down with wit.

PIC 5: This one's for you, Sophie. You'd better hold on to your man. I won't say who, but a freshman with plenty of access to everyone's football hero seems to have caught his eye—and maybe even his hand—a time or two tonight. But we would never, ever stir the pot and say so. Or would we?

TNT ('Til Next Tidbit)
JUNIPER SHORES SOCIALITE

Alice

Enough History

"Elliott, I am going to kill you," I whisper-hissed, stepping away from the party, out onto the sand.

The face that he made was comically horrified. "Never what one wants to hear coming out of the mouth of the Black Widow."

He smiled at me with that smart mouth of his. Oh, and what a beautiful mouth it was.

"I just wanted to let everyone know that I was here with the most gorgeous woman at this ball."

"And you thought dancing on the empty dance floor was the way to achieve that?"

"You could have said no," he said, turning toward me.

I put my hands on his lapels. "I could never, ever say no to you in that tux," I whispered, biting my lip. That was the most utterly true thing I had said today.

He smiled playfully. "Well, now. *That* is a piece of information I will be storing for later."

I took his hand. "I want to show you something."

"Man, this night keeps getting better!" he said.

I laughed as I led him down the shoreline. "You aren't drunk, are you?"

"What? No."

I nodded, hurrying him along past the lights and noise of the busiest part of Juniper Shores, toward the darkness. We turned left into a practically deserted parking lot, and I led him to an old-timey billboard—no lights, no flashing screens—peddling Dollar Beer Night at the Tavern. This was nothing if not a town of inconsistencies, of high highs and low lows, a place where a party that was raising more than a lot of people paid for their houses was beside an Airstream serving slushies.

I bunched up my skirt and put my foot on the first rung of the ladder on the billboard, then looked back at Elliott. Maybe it wasn't my *best* idea to climb in a ball gown. "This is why I wanted to make sure you're sober."

"Wait. We're *climbing* this?"

"Are you scared?"

He smiled. "Doesn't matter. I could never say no to you in that dress."

"I'll remember that for later," I said, starting to climb the ladder that I had scaled dozens if not hundreds of times in my youth.

I was out of breath by the time I reached the top, less from the twenty-foot climb and more from nerves. It had been at least twenty years since I'd been up here. And never once had I brought a man.

I sat, as I had so many times before, and with more care than I'm certain I took as a girl, I scooted out far enough that my legs dangled over the edge. For the first time, I imagined plummeting to my death. Taking care not to tear my skirt, I scooted back and pulled my legs back on the billboard's ledge.

Elliott laughed and sat down beside me. "You know, I think of myself as kind of an adventurous guy. But it has never occurred to me to climb the billboard."

I shrugged. "Well, what can I say? With me, the thrills never cease."

"You can say that again."

I'd give Elliott credit. He was true to his word; he was patient. I'd seen him almost every day this week, and we'd held hands and done a *lot* of talking. And even when the energy was palpable between us, when the air crackled with the electricity we could make together—like it was doing now—he hadn't so much as tried to kiss me.

"So, um, what are we doing up here? Besides missing the party that Bill Sitterly paid two grand apiece for us to attend."

I pulled my knees to my chest, crinoline crunching around me. I pointed off into the distance, where we had a bird's-eye view of the party. The dance floor, the dancers, the food. The music, quieter but still lovely, floated toward us.

"So, you wanted to watch the party instead of attend the party?"

I smiled. "My first job, at fourteen, was right down there, at the Tavern, washing dishes."

Elliott made a face. "Not a good place for a little girl."

I shook my head. "Everyone was really nice to me."

Elliott nodded.

"But I used to come up here sometimes after my shift and watch whatever was going on. The bar scene, happy families getting ice cream, and, once a year, this party. I was a girl with little family and no money and no opportunities that I could see at the time, but I could come up here, and I could watch the rich, fancy people of Juniper Shores dance on that dance floor, and I would dream about being one of them one day."

Elliott stared at me, and I could tell he was really listening.

"And I guess I just think it's funny to realize that all that time I was wishing to be over there"—I pointed to the party—"maybe the best stuff was really happening up here. Because up here, I'm just me. No one is talking about my choices or my checkered past. I think there's an irony in the fact that I used to crave being in those glittering lights, when, really, anonymity was probably better. You know what I mean?"

He nodded. "Alice, they don't get to decide who you are."

"Don't they? I mean, an anonymous Instagram account is now dictating everyone's next moves. These people who say I killed three husbands and am running a cult kind of do shape public perception."

"But public perception isn't truth."

I thought back to Julie and her plan to clear Bill's name. That entire scheme hinged on public perception, and I realized that I was a little jealous that the women under my roof were putting so much effort into fixing Bill's reputation but hadn't considered fixing mine. Although I wasn't wrongfully imprisoned, so perhaps that was selfish.

"Sometimes I think about going somewhere new," I said, sighing. "But then, even still, even now, I can come back to the top of this billboard and suddenly be a kid again. There's something about a place with your history, that knows all your secrets, that's kind of hard to move on from."

Elliott took my hand and kissed it. "You don't have to explain the lure of history to me. I spend my days engrossed in it." He cleared his throat. "I came back here for it. If you can consider you and me a year ago history."

Below us, I could see, under the glow of the string lights, the massive food table being disassembled, the stage in the center of the dance floor being erected, the band beginning to come in. That was one of the coolest parts of Belle Epoque. The band was in the middle, not on the end, so wherever you were, you were in the action. "Enough history," I said. "Let's go dance."

Elliott smiled. "I thought you'd never ask." I moved to get up, but he said, "Hey, thanks for sharing your special spot with me."

I nodded. "You're the only man I've ever brought up here." I paused. "What I'm saying is, don't screw it up."

He laughed. "I absolutely will not."

Elliott stood, so dapper in his tux, his bow tie ever so slightly askew from the climb. He took my hands in his and pulled me up. As I smoothed my dress, he never took his eyes off me. And I felt, quite simply, loved. Admired. Adored. How was that even possible? How could this man just look the other way, ignore all the things said about me, and love me anyway?

He ran his index finger down the side of my neck, along my collarbone, leaving chill bumps in its wake. I took a step closer to him, closing the small gap between us. "You really don't care what they say about me?"

"I know you, Alice." He stooped down so we were eye level. And he repeated, "I *know* you."

The deepest calm settled around my chest, my stomach, the parts of me that always felt a little off-kilter.

"Can I be honest about something?"

"Always."

"Elliott, I underestimated you. I mean, I loved you. And I believed you loved me. But I thought you were kind of a good-time guy. I didn't believe you could handle the messy parts of me, the dark parts, the scary parts that I think we both need to face will never fully heal."

He nodded. "That's why I knew I had to come back. Because I realized that you have been through so much that just assuming you knew certain things—like that I was never going to leave you, that I didn't need you to take care of me—wasn't going to cut it. I needed to say those things out loud."

Now he had. Several times, in fact.

He put his finger under my chin. "And I need to tell you out loud, Alice, that I can't explain it. I don't know why or how except for destiny and magic, but I love you in a way that feels like breathing, in a way that I cannot stop, even when I try."

In that moment, on top of that billboard, in the dark, with the music of the Belle Epoque orchestra floating up and encircling us, I finally decided to let myself fall—into Elliott. Not off the billboard, to be clear. As he slipped his arms around my waist, I lifted my head, just a little, and let myself melt back into the kiss that I had missed for so long, the one that I had dreamed about. I let myself savor the way his lips, plump and soft, felt on mine, the way his hand felt in my hair.

It wasn't a first kiss. Not really. But in some ways, it was. Because it was my first kiss with Elliott where I knew that I was willing to change my life for him, that I was willing to move into this next step together, that I was willing to set aside my fear and my pain and the routines that felt like they were saving me to create something that might set me free in a way I had never expected.

I would let go. I would take the leap. Because, as Elliott had reassured me dozens of times this week, he was man enough to catch me if I fell.

Iris

~~~~~~~~

Golden Boy

"Chloe, you have got to quit drinking the wine! People are going to notice!" I scolded, as firmly yet quietly as possible. Out in the party area, everything was elegant and calm. In our staging tent, things were utter chaos. The real catering staff was buzzing about, not even trying to hide their disdain for the high schoolers.

The chef was shouting orders. Pans were sizzling, plates were clanking, everyone was tense. This chaotic scene made it perfectly possible for several of my classmates to sneak wine without anyone being the wiser. I didn't care if most of them got in trouble. But I needed Chloe. She couldn't get suspended.

"Oh, relax," she said. "Don't you have mini crab cakes to serve?"

"You do now," said Ben, looking oh so very handsome in his tuxedo. He handed me a tray. "Hot out of the pan. You should sneak one before you take them out." No wonder the real catering staff hated us. We were super unprofessional. We ate the food, we drank the wine, and we viewed being here as a fun and glamorous way to spend a Saturday night.

Speaking of high schoolers who made Leo in his *Great Gatsby* tux seem average, Merit walked over, wearing the coveted oyster shucking belt. Of course. Because Merit was the golden boy. If there was a perk to get, he got it. I shuddered and said, "How many old ladies have made inappropriate remarks to you so far tonight?"

He looked up at the sky. "Uh, the numbers don't reach high enough."

"The challenges of being Merit McDonald," Ben said. I looked for the joking in his voice, but there wasn't much.

Merit didn't respond. "Okay, well, I'm going to get back out there. See if I can get any dollars in my belt."

He winked at me, and I knew I blushed. I hated how much I liked him, how hard my heart raced when he was around. But there was nothing I could do to change the laws of chemistry.

I ventured out with my tray of crab cakes, making my way toward a cluster of men who seemed ever so slightly overserved. I was about to insert myself and say "Crab cake?" when I heard one of them say, "Laura says Sitterly claims he's innocent."

And another said, "Please. Wouldn't you say you were innocent too?"

A third added, "That son of a bitch lost almost a half a million dollars of my money. He'd better hope he stays in jail."

I felt frozen, cold inside, and, most of all, invisible. Here they were talking about *my* father, and they didn't even notice me.

I couldn't help myself. I should have walked away, but instead I said, as calmly as I could muster: "He *is* innocent." I looked at one of the men whose back had been to me, recognizing him as he turned. "I would think that maybe our *judge* should realize that people are innocent until proven guilty."

He chuckled and said, shrugging a little, "Oh, honey, if you believe that man is innocent, you're even dumber than you look."

It was like being slapped. Tears sprang to my eyes, and I almost dropped my tray but didn't, thank goodness. As I stood there, stunned, I registered one of the men saying, "Tommy, for God's sake. She's a child."

And another one, who I thought was Paul Lucas, said, "That's Bill's *daughter*, Tommy."

As I turned away, the judge—Tommy, I guess—said, "I'm sorry, honey. I didn't mean—"

I don't know if it was the cruelness of the comment, his thinking I was dumb, their saying those things about my dad or, maybe worst of all, the idea that I had to face the fact: What if Dad was lying? What if he *was* guilty, and he was just saying he was innocent? Whatever the case, I burst into tears as I made my way back into the tent.

Ben grabbed my arm as I passed. "Iris! What's wrong?"

I just shook my head, trying to get myself together. This was mortifying. As I took deep breaths, Merit entered the staging tent and ran over to me. "Iris! What happened?"

I looked from Ben to Merit and pointed outside, "The *judge* of all people told me that if I believed my dad was innocent, I was dumber than I looked."

Ben said soothingly, "Iris, you know you aren't dumb. And you look beautiful."

Merit took off his jacket and rolled up his sleeves in a way I found unsettling. Ben was still talking, trying to calm me, when Merit started walking. "Merit," I said, following him, leaving Ben midsentence. He was walking fast and with purpose. "Merit!" I said, trying to grab his shirt. "Leave this alone. It's fine. I'm fine. Don't worry."

Merit was too quick and too focused, and I felt like I was in a dream, outside of myself, when Merit said, "Hey, Judge Andrews." The judge turned, and I saw his eyes change the moment before Merit reared back and punched him in the face.

"Oh my God. Merit!" I screamed. The judge stumbled back into his crew who, fortunately, caught him, lest he be splayed on the ground.

One of the security officers had Merit in his grip as Merit said, "Maybe you should find something better to do with your time than insult teenage girls."

The judge stood up, and as the officer started to pull Merit away, he said, "Wait. Let him go."

The officer said, "Are you sure, Judge?"

He nodded. "Are you insane? We face Howard High next week. We can't win without Merit McDonald."

The security officer gave him a once-over. "Oh, you *are* Merit McDonald." He let him go so quickly Merit's arm flopped to his side. "Don't want to injure that cannon," he said, rubbing Merit's bicep in a way that, honestly, bordered on creepy.

Merit smoothed his shirt. "I'm sorry, Judge. I shouldn't have—"

The judge put his hand up. "No harm done. I deserved it. I'm sorry, young lady. You have a gallant boyfriend to stand up for you."

All of a sudden Sophie appeared, and right in my face, at a decibel level I have only heard from injured animals on TV, screamed, "HE IS NOT HER BOYFRIEND." Then she stomped her foot and walked away.

The judge patted Merit on the shoulder. "Good luck with that one, son."

In spite of myself, I laughed. Mom and Grace came running toward us, the news obviously having made it to their corner of the party.

"Oh my gosh, Tommy," Grace said, in a tone that was both horrified and flirtatious at the same time. It was a real skill to strike that tone, something I would practice later in the mirror. "I am so sorry that my son has"—she looked pointedly at Merit—"lost his mind. Are you okay?" She practically purred the last part.

The middle-aged, portly man stood up taller and rubbed his lapels. "Took a punch from the best quarterback this town has ever seen and didn't even lose my balance."

Oh, Lord. He was for real flirting with her. She didn't seem to notice.

Instead, she looked at us and said, "Car. Now."

"Both of you," Mom chimed in.

We were in big, fat, huge trouble. But I was so happy. I squeezed Merit's hand. He squeezed mine back. He had stood up for me; he had punched a judge for me. The lights twinkling overhead, the smell of the salt air, the floating melody of the orchestra, and Merit's hand in mine . . . I was grounded forever and ever, for sure. But this was still the most perfect moment of my entire life.

@junipershoressocialite

Sharing bad behavior and delicious drama in North Carolina's most exclusive coastal zip code. DM with tips, pics, and juicy deets.

SEPTEMBER 7, 10:40 P.M.
28 Posts
9,801 Followers
29 Following

You didn't hear it from me, but . . .

PIC 1: Alice Bailey wasn't the only one coming out tonight. . . . The newly divorced owner of everyone's favorite Juniper Shores bar is here looking fit and fabulous—with a new *man* on his arm. More on that later.

PIC 2: Let's cut to the chase: The punch heard round the world will go down in history as the most epic moment ever to take place at Belle Epoque on the Beach. And we aren't surprised. Is there *anything* Merit McDonald can't win? A state championship. A battle with the town's judge. The heart of every girl in town?

PIC 3: Despite that, though, the crown for biggest scene at Belle Epoque goes to . . . drumroll please . . . Sophie Parker for her version of crazy high school girl obsessed with her boyfriend! Sophie, darling, you're better than that. And, if we're being honest, you should be a little bit glad that Iris Sitterly didn't punch *you*. (She's learned things in prison, you know.)

We will be back with more bits and pieces from Juniper Shores' most fabulous night. Because what good is a party without the recap after?

TNT ('Til Next Teen Drama)
JUNIPER SHORES SOCIALITE

Charlotte

#freebill

I drove Grace, Merit, and Iris home, and we texted Elliott to ask him to please make sure Julie got home. We figured he didn't need to be reminded to get Alice home safely. The party was only a four-minute drive from the house, but it felt much longer since we rode in total silence.

Merit was on his phone, which seemed like a potentially unsafe choice since his mother was clearly on the warpath. But from what I could tell from my glimpses in the rearview mirror, Merit didn't seem particularly contrite. He just sat there texting, while Iris watched him, clearly trying to catch his eye. She was trying to get her story straight, that was for sure. But what did Iris have to do with any of this? I wanted to ask. Or maybe just turn on the radio. But Grace's face was stone-cold, staring straight ahead, and even though I knew she wasn't mad at *me*, I didn't want to poke the bear.

She got out of the car and stalked up the stairs. We trailed in after her, and she closed the door and locked it behind us, which was unsettling. "Sit down," Grace said. "All of you."

"Me too?" I squeaked.

"Yes. I need moral mom support."

Iris and Merit sat down in their normal seats at the dining room table. Grace and I sat across from them. Grace crossed her arms on the table and sighed. "Merit, on the way home, I was thinking about how you really are a model son. You make great grades and you're a star athlete, and I know that you go to great lengths to not cause me extra grief or trouble. I know that. I understand that you cannot be perfect all the time. But please tell me why you felt that punching a judge in the face was a good way to rebel."

Merit seemed pale. And it interested me that Grace said he went to great lengths to be a model son. That was a good quality, of course. But the statement seemed to run deeper than that.

"It was my fault!" Iris interrupted before Merit could speak.

"Great," I said under my breath. I reminded myself that she was going through so much. I reminded myself that, as the way she'd climbed into bed with me last week proved, so much of her was still just a soft, sweet, scared little girl.

Grace smiled. "Iris, sweetheart, I appreciate that. I do. But Merit doesn't need you to take up for him." She looked at her son again.

"No, Grace, I mean it," Iris said. "The judge was saying that Dad was guilty and that if I didn't believe that I was dumb. Or I looked dumb, or—"

"You were even dumber than you looked," Merit said.

"Well, thank you," Iris said, smirking. "What a helpful time to chime in."

My face was getting hot, and I could feel my heart pounding. "I'm sorry. He *said* that to you?"

"He was just drunk, Mom. He apologized."

"I don't care!" I protested. "There is no excuse for a grown man saying anything like that to you!" I stood up from the table, enraged. *No one* talked to my little girl like that.

Grace put her hand on my arm. "I'm mad too, Charlotte, but I think it's fair to say that Merit settled the score."

"No! We should turn him in! Get him suspended!" Even as I said it, I knew it was idiotic. Maybe somewhere else that would be an argument. But in a town this small—and in regard to a man that beloved—I would somehow end up being the one who got punished.

Grace just patted my arm, a little sympathetically. To console myself, I thought of what people must be saying about that insufferably proud man's fall from grace at the hands of a teenager. I sat back down.

"Merit," Grace said calmly. "There is never any excuse for violence—"

"But, Grace!" Iris interrupted.

Grace put her hand up. "—but in this specific case, I'm glad you punched him. I wish you'd knocked him the hell out."

Merit smiled but still said nothing.

"So, are we grounded?" Iris asked.

"I can't think of why you would be," Grace said. "But if you can think of a reason, please feel free to fill us in."

Merit got up and kissed Grace's cheek. "Thanks, Mom."

"Sit back down, please," she said.

Merit looked concerned, but then Grace said, "I need more details about Sophie's tantrum." She grinned, and we all started laughing.

"The best part of any good party," I said, "is unpacking all the details afterward. So settle in. In fact, I'll get us some snacks."

But before I could, I heard the doorknob turn and then a key scratching in the lock, and Julie burst through. "You guys!" she said. "I think we did it! I mean, at least we did something."

"What do you mean?" I asked.

Julie bounded over to us. "Check out Juniper Shores Socialite."

I gasped as she handed me her phone. On the screen was a red square and, inside, the hashtag *#freebill*. It might not bring Bill home. But I could feel the tide starting to turn.

@junipershoressocialite

Sharing bad behavior and delicious drama in North Carolina's most exclusive coastal zip code. DM with tips, pics, and juicy deets.

SEPTEMBER 7, 11:11 P.M.
29 Posts
9,962 Followers
29 Following

Yes, yes, I know: You're here for the party. So are we. Serious is not what we do here. But every now and then, every good socialite needs to stand up for what she believes in. After overhearing more than a few bits and pieces of conversation tonight at Belle Epoque on the Beach and reading Julie Dartmouth's stirring interviews in this morning's *Sun*, it comes to our attention that Juniper Shores' own Bill Sitterly might just be unjustly incarcerated—at least for now.

Look, fam, in 2021, we freed Britney. In 1993, we freed Willy. This year, if you ask me, we need to band together to free Bill. So, join me, join me, wherever you are, in taking a stand for a man who, sure, yeah, may be guilty, but he at least deserves the dignity of house arrest until we know for sure. I'll leave you with this: If Bernie got to serve time at home, shouldn't Bill?

TNT ('Til Next Trial)
JUNIPER SHORES SOCIALITE

~~~~~~~~~~

Lucky Breaks

Six days had passed since Belle Epoque, and #freebill was really taking off. Well, around here, at least. Everywhere we went, people stopped Charlotte to ask what they could do, how they could help, if it was true that Bill had been framed. And that was great. But she was still incredibly anxious about what evidence could be used against him. Tonight we had talked her into getting out of the house, getting away from the phone and computer, and forgetting all her troubles with some good old-fashioned Friday night lights.

I looked around at the familiar scene, sitting in the bleachers at Juniper Shores Prep, cheering for the Marlins. How many nights had I sat in these stands? I couldn't even begin to count. Two rows in front of me sat a little girl with blue-and-white ribbons in her pigtails. Her grandmother reached over to hand her a box of Milk Duds, and I smiled, thinking of my darling departed Mina, the aunt I barely knew who, after my mother died and my father was incarcerated for involuntary manslaughter, rescued me. And I do mean that literally. Mina was sixty-four years old, my mom's oldest sister, nearly twenty years her senior, the day I entered her quiet, calm, organized home. I was a terrified little girl of ten who had lost her beloved mother to a car crash, her father to prison, her predictable-if-sometimes-annoying siblings, her home, her everything all in one fell swoop.

I think I knew from the first day with Mina that I was lucky. I knew that not every kid with no parents got to live in a pink bedroom with sheets that smelled like flowers and with a kind woman who cooked amazing food and told great stories. Mina never tried to be my mother. She only tried to take care of me, to love me, to help me love myself. She believed she could only take on one child and, since I was the youngest, since I would be displaced for the longest amount of time, she chose me. I couldn't have known then that my siblings would spend the rest of their lives resenting me for that; I couldn't have known what a wedge it would drive between us.

Even so, I would have chosen Mina. She gave me—against all odds—a wonderful childhood.

I don't know if it was conscious, but I think that's why I knew, when Julie was in trouble, when my niece was down and out like I had once been, that I had to take her in. Mina had rescued me; I would rescue Julie. I had spent every day since trying to be like Mina, trying to be there for the kids and adults alike at the mommune, to support them and make them feel like they had someone. And, in a lot of ways, the mommune was my way of re-creating what I loved most about my childhood: the delicious chaos of a huge family. I was never happier than when kids were running through my house, food cooking, music playing, people laughing.

Well, never happier than in moments like these when I jumped to my feet and cheered as Merit snapped the perfect pass to number 44, who ran right into the end zone with it. Touchdown, Marlins! Beside me, Audrey, Brenna, and Jamie stood up and waved their pom-poms in their "mini Marlins" uniforms. These were sold as a fundraiser for the school, and no little girl in Juniper Shores could be without one.

That was one of my favorite charitable acts, buying uniforms for little girls who couldn't afford them so they could live out their cheerleader dreams. I had cheered for this team many moons ago. Sometimes it felt impossible that I wasn't cheering for them now. Well, in a car-wash skirt and crop top, I mean. I would always, always be cheering for them. School events, like church, allowed me to be the happiest, most relaxed version of myself. For a couple of hours, I was that girl under Mina's protective watch again, not the woman who had lost so much.

Grace and Charlotte were to my left, and Grace shouted, "That's my boy!" as she and Charlotte high-fived.

Iris and Emma were off in other parts of the stadium with their friends, obviously. They couldn't possibly be seen with the likes of us. I remembered being that age, only I never had the feeling of mortification over my parents. I only wished that mine were there to embarrass me.

All of a sudden, on the other side of the stadium, much too far away for my sight to be accurate, I spotted a man who looked just like Jeremy. Or, well, what Jeremy would look like eighteen years later, if he had lived. I gasped out loud, and Charlotte looped her arm around mine. "Are you okay?" she murmured.

"Sorry," I whispered. "I have this thing . . ." I realized I had never said this out loud to anyone, and now I wondered if I should. I knew how information could become a weapon, even in the hands of people who claimed to love you.

"What thing?" she asked.

I was quiet for a moment. When I scanned the opposite bleachers, the Jeremy look-alike was nowhere to be found.

"You can tell me, Alice," she said. "Believe me, if we're having a secret-off, you know more of mine."

I sighed. "This is going to sound crazy, but ever since Jeremy died, I have seen him everywhere. For eighteen years, everywhere I go, some poor stranger becomes Jeremy."

She looked at me dully. "That's your big secret? You see your dead husband in crowds? Alice, that must be the most common thing in the world."

"It is?"

She laughed. "Yes! It is!"

I felt a little better. "I know he's dead. I cashed the insurance check."

As soon as I said that, I wished I hadn't. Wasn't one of the rumors about me that I had killed him for the insurance money? But Charlotte said, "They don't give out those checks unless they are damn sure you're dead. Believe the brand-new insurance guru on that one."

We both laughed, which was a little macabre. But you had to laugh or you'd cry.

The crowd cheered again, and I looked up to see a kick sailing through the goalposts. Merit's friend Alex was a senior who I thought was a particularly good influence. He complained that kicker was the only position his mother would let him play because she didn't want him to get hurt. But, funny thing, as much as he didn't want that position, he was being recruited by top schools in both the Southeastern and Atlantic Coast conferences. Moms can be pretty smart sometimes.

Charlotte put her arm around me. "Do you know what I think?"

I shook my head.

"I've always thought that those little glimpses were God winks, reminders from the other side that the people we love are still with us. I bet Jeremy is always watching over you because he wants you to be happy."

"Is he? Or is he pissed and killing off my other husbands?"

We both laughed again, the light mood returning to the evening.

"Thank you, Charlotte," I said. "Sometimes it does help to talk about these things."

"I'm always here," she said.

"I know." It shocked me that I meant it. I loved Julie and Grace with all my heart, but they needed me in a way that Charlotte didn't. I felt like I couldn't confide in them because they had so much else to worry about. Charlotte had a confidence about her, even during this terrible time, that made me know she was someone who could be relied on. I think that's why I felt I could open up to her. It was nice, after so many years of hiding so many parts of myself, to feel like I had a true friend.

I heard Julie, from the other end of the girls, yell, "Elliott! We're over here!"

He caught my eye and smiled; even from a distance, he made my heart race, my mouth go dry, my palms sweat. And suddenly I realized I didn't want to be in a crowded stadium with him. I wanted to be very much alone.

Grace leaned over. "I still can't believe you even pretended to try to break up with him. That man is a god."

"He's real, too," Charlotte said, elbowing me.

"What?" Grace asked. It was so loud in the stadium she couldn't have overheard our earlier conversation, despite her proximity.

"I'm just being silly," Charlotte said as Elliott reached us and leaned down to kiss me for the whole world to see, his hands full of snacks.

"You'd better be careful," I said. "You'll be getting calls tomorrow about consorting with the Black Widow."

He laughed and kissed me again. "Don't care," he said. "I still hold the Juniper Shores Prep bench press record. You can't off me. Too strong." I put my hand on his arm. He was very, very strong.

Charlotte added, "Plus, how many people could even be left to call him after the flurry I'm sure he encountered after Belle Epoque."

Elliott nodded. "She's right. There can't be anyone left in town." He winked at me.

I laughed, and Elliott handed out popcorn and candy to all of us.

"You know the way to our hearts!" Julie said.

"Especially mine," I whispered. We settled onto the hard ribbed metal of the bleachers, and Elliott took my hand. Just the feel of it caused goose bumps on my arm, heat in my body. He was being so patient with me. I scooted closer to him, realizing that maybe I was losing mine.

"Elliott!" Brenna called. She had met him several times at the house, and the girls all loved him. It was hard not to. "Open your mouth, and I'm going to see if I can throw popcorn in it!"

"Oh yes!" he said.

From beyond her, Julie reminded them, "Now, girls, this is only a grown-up game. It's a choking hazard."

I would be prepared to do the Heimlich. All I needed was for Elliott to choke to death beside me on the bleachers. Elliott opened his mouth, Brenna threw the piece of popcorn, he moved his head just in time, and our whole little section cheered as he caught it. People looked at us strangely because nothing exciting was happening in the game. But we were in our own little world. I liked how it felt, how it sounded. I liked having Elliott as a part of it. It made me sad that, one day in the future, I would have to choose between this man I loved and these women and their children who felt like my family.

Elliott leaned over and kissed my cheek, and for a moment I stopped worrying. Merit threw another touchdown pass, and we were on our feet again, cheering. This, I felt in my very bones, was what Friday nights were made for. Friends, fun, football. And popcorn, always popcorn.

Iris

~~~~~~~~~~~~

The Password

"I keep thinking I see him everywhere," I told Chloe. Chloe, Dabney, and I were sitting in the row of bleachers right in front of Greg, Ben, and their incredibly annoying posse of friends, and behind Emma and her cute little seventh-grade group of girls. I was glad Emma and I would be in high school together. Being a freshman could be tough between the senior boys excited for fresh meat (some were nice, some were not, and you needed an older girl to tell you the difference) and the older girls who were mad that you had stolen their social standing as cute new girl on the block.

Emma was adorable now, but you could tell that once she lost the braces and the babyish roundness to her face, she was going to be a knockout. I'd probably be jealous. But I'd still look out for her.

"Who?" Dabney asked.

"The man in the closet," I whispered.

"We could barely see him in the photos," Chloe said.

"Well, I know, but the more I think about it, I remember this, like, wavy brown hair with a little bit of gray in it and his eyes were strangely round. And very green." I paused. "I think. I don't know. They kind of glinted at me, and they seemed green, but they might not have been."

Chloe rolled her eyes at Dabney. "With information like that, we should have gone straight to the police."

"So basically, every middle-aged man looks like him?" Dabney asked me, shooting a *you're being a bitch* look at Chloe.

I nodded. "Exactly."

"I still think we should tell my parents," Chloe said, slurping her soda. Chloe was funny because she could look so grown-up with a glass of champagne and practically ten years old with a paper Pepsi cup with a straw.

Maybe she was right. But I hated getting in trouble. And I was afraid that was the only thing that would come from telling the adults.

I glanced down at the field—the football was really secondary in this social outing—just as Merit snapped a pass. My heart dropped. He was so hot. And there was freaking Sophie cheering her heart out for him in a skirt so short you could literally see her butt cheeks.

"Hey," Ben said, leaning over behind me. "Want some Whoppers?"

Whoppers were my favorite candy. "You'd share with me?" I put my hand to my heart. "Oh, Ben, what a gentleman."

He rolled his eyes. "Only because I got the king-sized pack."

"Hey, Chlo," Greg said. "Want to go walk around for a minute?"

Dabney and I both glared at her because that was totally code for *make out behind the field house*. But she jumped up and said, "Sure! I'd love to!"

Dabney and I rolled our eyes at each other as they disappeared. Chloe had suggested that maybe we were jealous she had a boyfriend. Maybe we were. But, as Merit faked a pass, tucked the ball under his arm, and ran down toward the end zone, I knew that I wasn't jealous that *Greg* was her boyfriend one little bit. Because I only had eyes for one boy. And he thought I was his sister. So, cool. Right on track.

Everyone was on their feet cheering, "Mer-it! Mer-it! Mer-it!" He was about to score when a huge linebacker came out of nowhere and pummeled him to the ground.

It was always rough to watch boys get tackled like that, but when it was Merit, it was like I actually felt the shock in my whole body.

"Um, he's not getting up," Ben said.

Before I could even register that Merit was lying flat on his back, I felt myself running down the concrete steps and onto the field, which was strictly forbidden. What was I doing? I looked like a total idiot! I wasn't his girlfriend. I wasn't his sister. I was capable of having all these very rational thoughts while in a full-out sprint across the field, where the hundreds of people in the stadium could see me. Those thoughts just weren't strong enough to supersede the thought that I HAD TO GET TO HIM. Right now. Stupid Sophie beat me to it. But I knelt on the other side of him. Coaches and players were swarming. Merit looked around and said, "Iris." I couldn't help but look up at Sophie, who scowled at me. Things had been, um, *tense* between us since Belle Epoque. I'd mostly tried to avoid her.

Sophie said, "I'm right here, baby," as if he'd said *her* name, which he very clearly hadn't.

"Guys," he said in his sure, steady Merit voice. "I am totally fine. Just got the wind knocked out of me. If you could give me, like, two inches of space, I'd love to get up now."

Grace, from behind me, cried, "Merit!" and the seas parted. Mom trumps all.

He sat up and smiled. "I'm fine, Mom. I promise."

She was crying. "You promised me that if you were quarterback you wouldn't get hurt! You said you wouldn't get tackled! So what would you call that if not a tackle?"

Coach Bradford put an arm around her and said, "I think he's just fine, Mrs. McDonald, but the team doctor will get him all checked out in the field house. I promise you."

"Well, I am going with him," Grace said.

"Me too!" Sophie chimed in, getting up to walk beside the coach and Grace.

Sitting up on the field now, Merit looked over at me and smiled and rolled his eyes.

"You're okay?" I whispered.

"Yeah. The not-breathing for a second was kind of scary, but I'm okay."

"Promise?" I asked.

"Promise." He paused. "Hey, you're pretty fast when you want to be. Have you considered trying out for the football team?"

I smiled, half basking in the glow of his attention and half freaking out that he had seen how I broke Olympic speed records to get to him. But he had said my name, only mine, in his blacked-out, oxygen-lost moments. That had to mean something, didn't it? "I wouldn't want to show you up," I said. "I know how important this quarterback thing is to you."

"And you ran to me so quickly because . . ."

"Because I was nervous my surf lessons might get canceled," I said smoothly.

Merit laughed.

"Okay, big guy," said Dr. Montgomery, whom I'd seen a couple years ago for a sprained ankle. "Let's get you checked out."

Two of Juniper Shores' biggest football players helped Merit up, and he put his arms around their shoulders. The crowd went wild. It was only then that I noticed both teams' players were down on one knee. They all clapped as Merit got up.

"Well, this is embarrassing," he said. "And, hey, could you please keep Mom and Sophie from coming into the field house."

I shrugged. "Come on, Merit. I'll do my best, but we both know that might be impossible."

I walked over to Grace, unable to resist turning to look at Merit one more time. "Hey," I said, "I think he's okay. He doesn't really want anyone in the field house."

Ignoring me, Grace turned and made a beeline for the field house anyway.

"What are you, like, his spokesperson . . ." Sophie gave me the up-and-down, then added, ". . . *freshman.*" If she was mad about his saying my name, not hers, she wasn't hiding it well.

I put my hands up. "Just passing along a message."

Two other cheerleaders ran up beside her. "Yeah, and that's *all* you'll do with him, if you get my drift," Sophie said.

Great. Just what I needed. To be on the entire cheerleading squad's hit list.

"That's practically all *you* do with him," said Franklin, one of the girls.

Sophie shot her a look.

"What?" the other cheerleader asked.

"Never mind," Sophie said. "I'm going to go check on my *boyfriend.*"

She said the word with special emphasis in my direction, as if half my thoughts weren't centered on the fact that he was her boyfriend. Please. I was aware.

I was humiliated to have to walk all the way around the perimeter of the field and back to my seat as the players lined up again. As if I wasn't feeling self-conscious enough, Dabney was waiting to say, "Smooth," when I got to the bleachers.

"Is he okay?" one of Ben's friends asked. I couldn't help but notice that Ben was gone.

"Yeah," I said. "I think so. They're checking him out now."

I sat down and whispered breathlessly to Dabney, "Sophie and I were on either side of him when he was kind of waking up, and he said *Iris*." I said my own name like it was the password that unlocked the door to a magical kingdom.

Dabney and I both squealed. "He's totally going to dump her for you!" she whisper-shrieked.

Chloe reappeared, hair mussed and lips red. "What did I miss?"

Dabney and I rolled our eyes at each other. "Subtle, Chloe," Dabney said. "You can barely tell you've been making out."

"Oh, good," Chloe said, missing the sarcasm.

"What you missed is that Merit loves our girl, not Sophie."

"What?" she asked breathlessly.

I shook my head. "That's a serious overexaggeration." But was it? As Dabney and Chloe chattered about what had just transpired, I thought of Merit, of the way he looked at me when he opened his eyes. I wasn't reading into that, was I? It had been real. We had definitely had a moment. And I couldn't wait to get home and find out if maybe, just maybe, we could have another one.

Greatest Hits

"I feel guilty for not going to visit Bill today," I said to Alice as I helped her set the table.

"You went yesterday, Charlotte," Grace said. "You have a job and a child to raise. You're doing your best."

She had a point. Even still, that longing I was used to now, that felt like a part of me, swamped me. What I wouldn't give to be back in my house with my husband. Or, well, anywhere with my husband for that matter. Anywhere but jail, that is.

It was so incredibly frustrating. Everyone seemed to be Team Bill and public perception was shifting in a way that I did think could be helpful for us. I just wanted it to be helpful *faster*.

Julie walked down the steps, groaning, her three clean little ones trailing behind her.

At that exact moment, there was a knock at the door. Her ex, Houston, very rarely showed up when it was his time with the kids. She never even told them anymore when he was supposed to come. But it appeared that tonight was the exception to the rule. Alice crowed over how fresh and clean the girls were as Julie opened the door and said, "Only three hours late. Not bad."

"Why do you always have to start with me, Jules? Seriously," he said. "I was working overtime so I can afford to pay you. Isn't that what you want? Child support?"

Julie put her hand to her heart. "Oh, yes. When I was a little girl all I dreamed of was that I would find a wonderful man and bear his three children so that maybe one day he could pay me child support!"

Brenna was watching her parents, so I went to her, scooped her up, and said, "Mommy and Daddy, I think Miss Brenna is all ready!"

They got the hint and were suddenly all smiles. "Who wants Chick-fil-A?" Houston asked with top-dad enthusiasm.

"I do! I do!" they said in unison.

I laughed as Grace visibly shuddered.

"Remember that Mommy has the girls all nice and clean, so maybe no play place tonight," she said, smiling through gritted teeth.

Houston rolled his eyes but said nothing. He picked Audrey up and kissed her cheek. "All right, princesses. Let's go get some dinner!"

"Can we get ice cream, Daddy?" Jamie asked as they walked out the door.

"Of course!" he said. "It wouldn't be Daddy night without ice cream."

Julie shut the door, leaned against it, sighed deeply, and said, "It must be so great to come pick up three clean children, do all the fun things with them, and then drop them off, exhausted, sugar-laden, and overstimulated from too much TV."

Grace walked away from the kitchen to hug her. "No, it's not. Because you get the real stuff, the good stuff, the pride of knowing that you are parenting three gorgeous girls to the best of your ability and helping them grow into strong, healthy, well-adjusted adults. He doesn't get to have that."

Julie nodded resolutely. "You know what? You're right. You're totally right."

Grace looked up at the oven. "Dinner won't be ready for another thirty-six minutes."

Alice had already pulled a bottle of rosé out of the fridge. We followed her to the porch and sat down in the comfy chairs, looking out over the ocean. She handed me the first glass of wine. "I think you're doing great, Charlotte," she said.

"I think the plan is working," Julie added.

I nodded. "I definitely think people are at least skeptical about Bill's guilt, which is good. But I was kind of hoping something bigger would have happened by now."

"I know, sweetie," Alice said. "So were we."

"But good things come to those who wait?" Grace asked skeptically.

"Worked for Alice," I said, grinning at her, trying to change the subject.

She smiled but didn't say anything. Juniper Shores Socialite had had a ball discussing Alice and Elliott's potential marriage timeline this week. But I couldn't read Alice's take on the situation, and I didn't want to pry.

"What about you two?" I asked. "Any loves on the horizon?"

Grace scrunched her nose. "I am sadly, pathetically, awfully hung up on my not-quite-ex. I can't move on from him, and I know I should be able to, but there's this part of me that clings to the shred of hope that he was having a midlife crisis, he'll come to his senses, and I'll get my family back. So, if a man so much as smiles in my general direction, I practically snarl at him."

I laughed, and Alice said, "She's not kidding."

"What about you, Jules?"

"Oh, after Houston, what man could possibly live up to my expectations?" she asked dryly.

"So that thing on Juniper Shores Socialite about you getting back together with him . . ." I started.

She groaned. "Totally, completely false." She paused. "But, seriously, I think I'd like to find someone, but I don't have time to date."

"We would all chip in more with the girls!" I said. They were adorable, and the more Iris's social life and activities took over, the less time I got with her.

Julie shook her head. "No, no. You guys are rock stars. I think, deep down, I just can't imagine someone taking me on with these three tiny children."

"That is an awful thing to say!" Grace said. "You are a catch! Any man would be lucky to snap you up."

Alice and I nodded in agreement.

"Nice cheerleading," Julie said, "but I think we know that this presents a lot of added challenges. So, unless someone falls into my lap, I am ignoring that part of my life."

There was such a lightness about now, despite the heaviness of some of our circumstances. Maybe it was the constant, soothing rhythm of the tide rolling in and out. Maybe it was the gentle noise of cicadas humming and grasshoppers singing, the way it always made me feel so at peace.

The sound of the porch doorknob turning silenced us all. My beautiful girl walked through the door.

"Hi, sweetheart!" I said, pulling her onto my lap.

"Hi, Mama," she said.

I kissed her cheek. "How was soccer?"

"It was good."

"Did you spy for me?" Grace asked. "Did Merit really sit out at football?"

She nodded. "He did. I walked down there with him and made Coach promise me that he wouldn't let him play."

I squeezed her to me.

"What a good little mother you are," Grace said.

"Now that I have you . . ." I said, deciding to bring up something I had noticed a few days ago but hadn't gotten around to mentioning. "How exactly, might I ask, did you manage to get the clothes and shoes you've been casually pulling out and hoping I won't notice?"

Iris made her telltale face, the one she makes when she's considering whether she's going to lie or tell the truth.

"Iris . . ." I said. "I will know if you're lying."

She sighed. "Chloe and Dabney have been letting me borrow things."

I raised my eyebrows at her questioningly.

"What? You know we like to have all the same clothes."

That was true. I was about to ask more when she said, "Oh! I forgot! Oliver is out in his car and needs to talk to you."

I texted him. *Come on in!*

"How are things looking for Wednesday?" Alice asked. "Do you think you're going to beat Central?"

"For sure," Iris said. "We're really looking strong."

Oliver opened the porch door and said, "Uh, hi, everyone."

I patted Iris's leg. "Why don't you go up and get your shower."

"Because I stink, or because you don't want me to be here for whatever Oliver is about to say?"

"A little of both."

She smirked as she got up and left.

Oliver gestured to me. "Should we, um . . ."

I shrugged, pointing toward the open rocking chair. "Why don't you sit with us. I'll tell them whatever you're about to say anyway."

"Everyone in the beach house is family, and there aren't secrets among family," Julie added, winking at me.

Oliver looked confused as I said, "Beach house rules."

"In that case, hi, I'm Oliver. I know Julie already, of course, from our story."

Grace and Alice introduced themselves. Oliver turned toward the ocean and said, "What a spectacular view," and Julie mouthed to me, *He is hot.*

I had to keep myself from laughing out loud. "Have you come bearing good news?" I asked. The raw hope in my voice embarrassed me.

"Potentially good news," he said. "With all the hubbub around town about free Bill and whatnot, I've gotten some information that makes me feel like we could file a motion for bond reconsideration once I get discovery to use to my advantage too."

Alice, Grace, and I looked blank, while Julie gasped and leaned forward. "Do you think the prosecutor will reconsider?" Then she looked at us. "House arrest," she said. "He's trying to get him out on bond."

"Ohhhh," we all said.

"Are you asking as a reporter or an interested friend?" Oliver asked, a touch of flirtation in his voice.

"Can't I be both?" she asked.

Grace and I shared a look. I was, obviously, more interested in my husband's prospects, but they were flirting, and it was noticeable.

"Not right now," he said.

"We're going to have him out of there in no time," Julie said, obviously noticing the panic on my face. "So this is just a piece of the puzzle." She nodded resolutely.

I nodded back less resolutely. My heart began to ache for the man who was always by my side, always cheering me on. I wanted to do more. I wanted to help. I wanted to *save* him. But with no access to his client files, with no knowledge of the evidence against him, there wasn't much I could do but wait.

"Can I get you a drink?" Julie asked Oliver.

He smiled. "I can't think why not."

I almost laughed out loud. She had just asked for a man to fall into her lap. Now if only a huge piece of evidence would fall into mine.

Alice

~~~~~~~~~

Bad Juju

Sometimes I wondered what would have happened with my husbands had they not died. If Glen hadn't been killed in a car crash on the way to his knee surgery pre-op, would we be watching a movie with our kids and dog right now? If Walter hadn't fallen off that ladder, would we be on the beach hunting for shells? Would we be happy? Sometimes, listening to the stories of my fellow mommune members, I wasn't so sure. With all the lying and cheating and deception that went on, would any of my loves have lasted?

Maybe it was naïve, but I always came back to Jeremy. I always believed that we would have been the ones to make it forever; we would have been the ones to fight through the hardest times and make it to the other side. But I never had the chance to find out. And that was what I couldn't move past. Or maybe I didn't want to move past it. Was that why I stayed here in this house, pouring salt in the wound?

The first time Jeremy ever brought me to Juniper Shores, twenty-five years ago, we had walked by this house that has been mine for years now. "Babe, one day you and I are going to live in this house," he said. "It's going to be all ours."

I knew that was why I had convinced Walter to buy it, pooling his resources with the insurance money I had saved from Jeremy. Sure, it was a ridiculously large home for two people. But as a bed-and-breakfast, it was perfect. We had our own private suite upstairs, on the front of the house, and the rest was set up ideally for couples or families looking for a beach getaway. I had told Walter it was my dream to run a bed-and-breakfast. But that wasn't wholly true. It had been my dream to live in this house with Jeremy. It was as if, by buying it finally, I had made good on our promise; I had carried out our dream.

Only now, as I drove alone through town, I realized that one person couldn't make another's dreams come true. Not completely, anyway. And certainly not when the other person was dead.

I walked to Elliott's front door. For months after he left town, I would ride by to see if a FOR SALE sign had appeared in the yard. It never had. And so maybe a tiny bit of me had always been clinging to the hope that he would come back home. Now that he had, my body felt jittery, tingling, alive with the mere thought of being in his arms. I was a forty-five-year-old woman, for heaven's sake. But he made me feel like some hormone-addled schoolgirl. I was here to have a serious talk with him, I reminded my pounding heart.

But then the front door flew open before I even knocked. And I don't know if it was me or him or some law of physics or chemistry or nature, but the moment I saw that man, my mouth found his, and his hands were underneath my dress, which I *knew* was too short, where he could grasp perfectly to pull me into him. Then his mouth was in the hollow of my throat and my hands were in the waistband of his jeans, and I couldn't even have told you what talking was, much less have done it. Elliott lifted me in the air, and I wrapped my legs around him, my arms around him, my mouth on his mouth. I felt so small and safe in his arms, like I was floating on air, until I came down, soft and slow, on the thick comforter on his bed. I was thrumming with what would come next, grasping for it. Every look, every touch these past couple of weeks had been foreshadowing this exact moment that I realized I couldn't wait one more second for.

I pulled Elliott's T-shirt over his head greedily. But he, now shirtless and gorgeous, unbuttoned the top button of my dress, kissing the skin underneath it. Then the second button. Then the third. It was slow and languid, and every time he touched me, I felt like I might burst into flame. He sat back, staring at every inch of me like I was the only woman he had ever seen, like my skin was fresh and young and perfect, like I was new, untouched.

"I love you," he said firmly, seriously. "I mean it."

I nodded, pulling him to me, wrapping my arms around his strong, smooth back. "I love you too," I said, in his ear, so he would know I meant it.

I was reminded that three husbands and several serious boyfriends later, Elliott and I together were some sort of metaphysical poetry. I lost myself in him, forgot I was tethered to the earth for minutes at a time. It didn't hurt that he was in his physical prime, perfectly fit and toned, filled out and weathered enough to look like a real man. But it was more than that. We had a connection that I could no longer deny, a connection that would force me to make some tough decisions.

Afterward he got up to shower, and I stretched my arms long in Elliott's bed. I was usually a stickler for white sheets, but, when we were together a year ago, I had come to love his plaid ones, worn soft and thin from washing. I loved looking out the picture window in his sparse bedroom, seeing his boat docked in the canal right out front.

Now freshly shaven, Elliott got back into bed and wrapped himself around me smelling of Colgate and Old Spice. The Original, of course. "Gosh," he said into my ear, "wouldn't it be great if we could wake up like this every morning?"

I turned to kiss him. "I don't know," I said sleepily, my body so relaxed I wondered how I would possibly go on with my day. "Would it? Or would I become old hat and you would get sick of me?"

He kissed my neck and my shoulder and my elbow. "Never, ever, ever, ever could I get sick of you. You are the most intoxicatingly fascinating woman I have ever known. There is never enough you for me."

That made me smile. I wondered if all my losses had made me too closed off. On the contrary, it seemed I had shared just enough with this hot, hot antiques dealer with chiseled abs, more stories than O. Henry, and a kind heart. He was perfect. If I was ever going to get married again . . . But no. Nope. I would never get married again. I loved Elliott, so it was my job to keep him safe. Even from me. Yes, I was back in his bed. But it wasn't my boyfriends who died; it was my husbands. So as long as I wasn't walking down the aisle toward him, I reasoned, things would be okay.

"Aren't you supposed to be on your way to that estate auction right now?"

"I need to leave in five," he said. "But I wish you'd come with me. Isn't antiquing with her boyfriend every woman's dream?"

"Anywhere you are sounds like a dream," I said. "I wish I could go with you." I looked over at the old white Sony clock radio on his nightstand that he had pulled out of a box of things from college after his divorce. "But I need to be home. I don't think Julie could manage without me there for the girls, and Charlotte has a new job, and I promised I'd help with shuffling Iris around to practices so she wouldn't have to worry. And, of course, there's bath time and mounds of laundry and . . ." I trailed off, leaning over to kiss him. He ran his fingers up and down my bare stomach and I said, "Maybe you could just stay right here?"

"Maybe you could," he whispered. Elliott pulled away, sat up, and studied me as if he was debating something.

"What?" I asked.

"It's just . . . well . . ." He hesitated, and I knew what he was going to say.

"I'm ready to move on," I said, cutting him off, saying what was in my heart.

His eyes widened.

"No! No!" I amended. "Not from you! *To* you."

He put his hand to his heart. "Well, that's a relief. Geez, Alice. You sure know how to make a man panic. So does this mean that we get to have the talk now?" he asked, grinning at me.

"Let's do."

He studied me for a moment, as if unsure how much to say.

"You aren't going to scare me away," I said, meaning it. "Elliott, I haven't felt like this since . . ." I paused and looked out the window over the water. I was going to say "since Jeremy," but I didn't think that was even accurate. I was so young with Jeremy, everything was so rose-colored. "Well, I haven't felt like this ever. I haven't fallen like this in my entire life."

He smiled at me. "Well, good. If you aren't scared . . ." He paused.

I laughed and motioned for him to continue. "If I'm not scared . . ."

"I want us to live together. I want to be with you for real."

I took a deep breath. I'd had a feeling that was coming. The obvious next thing to say was: "Elliott, you've been back in town for a minute. Don't you think we're moving kind of fast?"

But I knew the answer even before he said, "Al, we were right here last year before you unceremoniously dumped me." He grinned and winked at me. "Moving in was the obvious next step. And I know I haven't been back long, but nothing has changed. I don't feel like we're starting over."

"Me neither," I whispered. "But the moving thing could be a little tricky. . . ."

"If you just didn't have all these hangers-on. . . ."

I laughed and swatted his arm. "Don't call them that! They are my family. I love them."

"Some of them are your family," he said.

"No. All of them are my family."

"Fine," he said. "They're your family. But what about me?"

"You are my love," I said. I thought about that beautiful house on the beach, the one I had redone with such tender care, looked after because in some weird way I was convinced that, if I could just make that house good enough, it would bring Jeremy back to me. But Jeremy was dead. The dream was dead. And it had taken me years to realize that. I was scared by how certain I felt, but I knew it was true when I said, "I think I have to leave that house."

Elliott scrunched his nose. "Bad juju?"

"Something like that." I knew he was thinking about Walter, about his death-by-ladder. But it wasn't Walter who haunted me in that house. It was Jeremy. And I knew a part of me didn't *want* to let him go. Because if I did, then it was really over. I chastised myself constantly for harping on something that had happened eighteen years ago. Was it even normal to hold on to a love so tightly for so long?

"So do you want to move in here?" he asked.

Elliott's house was fine. It was small and masculine, and his boat was right there. I had had a change in my financial situation as of late that would have made selling my house and moving into his the most feasible option. But I couldn't very well kick everyone else out just because I had moved on.

"A fresh start?" I asked.

He smiled. "Sure. I'll start looking. You do the same."

I nodded. "But, Elliott, I can't put a timeline on this. I have to let

Julie, Grace, and Charlotte know and give them plenty of time to make a new plan."

"Sure," he said. "I get that. I can't imagine that we'll find the perfect house right away anyway."

Was I really doing this again? Mingling finances and lives with another man? Leaving the safety of the mommune? Was I ready for all that? Maybe I was and maybe I wasn't. But I reasoned that I'd never know unless I tried.

I didn't want Elliott to leave. But he had a job and a life, and he needed to get to it. "You're going to be late!" I piped up, trying to sound sunny. "I'll walk out with you."

"Stay as long as you like," he said.

He kissed me, long and deep and sweet. "One day," he said, "I'm going to sweep you off your feet. I'm going to whisk you away to a lavender field in Provence and keep you all to myself."

"That sounds lovely."

"I see you there," he said. "When I close my eyes and I picture you, that gorgeous dark hair of yours is blowing in the wind in a field of lavender."

I kissed him again. That wife of his was a fool. Who would cheat on a man like this?

I drove back to the mommune in a love-soaked haze. I knew a life with Elliott was what I wanted, but I was responsible for so many people; so many lives were tied up with mine. I couldn't just leave them. And I wanted a life with them too. It was impossible to have both.

I walked up the steps and through the house to the front porch. I stood there, watching the waves roll to the shore. Then I closed my eyes and took a deep breath. And I wasn't even a little surprised to find that when I inhaled, I no longer tasted salt air. All I could smell was lavender.

Iris

~~~~~~~~~~

Territorial

The best thing about the phone beside my bed in the mommune was that I could use it to call any room in the house. The little girls thought it was the most fun thing ever when I called their bunk room. I was procrastinating on writing a paper and had a few minutes before Merit was going to take me to see my dad, so I decided to make their day a little brighter.

I picked up the receiver, waiting for the dial tone. It took me a second to register that I wasn't hearing the beep. Instead, I heard Alice. I wouldn't have purposely listened because I liked Alice, but, come on. What did a middle-aged woman have to talk about that could be interesting anyway? But then I heard, "I can't believe we've already found two houses we like online."

"I know," a voice I recognized as Elliott's said back. "And it's such a crazy market. I have to think that means this is meant to be."

"Let's not get ahead of ourselves, though," Alice said. "Remember, it's not like I'm just going to tell them all to leave."

My stomach gripped. Oh my gosh. Were Mom and I part of "them all"? If we were, where would we go?

Elliott said, "We haven't considered that I could just move in with you and three other families." They both laughed.

Alice sighed. "No. I want to move in with you. I really do. It's just that thinking of leaving them hurts."

My eyes widened. Alice was going to move in with her boyfriend? But she was, like, our leader. Plus, it wasn't like we could all stay at Alice's without her. I panicked. I didn't want to leave this house. I didn't want to leave Grace and Julie and Emma and Brenna and Jamie and Audrey and, maybe most of all, Merit. I loved this weird, crazy life we'd made together.

Although I had to hold on to the hope that Dad would be home and we'd be out of here soon anyway, right? Sure, there was no doubt that, in our current situation, Mom and I felt stronger as a part of the mommune. But this was a small stopover for us no matter what happened. And what about Alice? Didn't I owe it to her to want her to be happy?

"I want to make a life together, Elliott. I swear I do. And I do want to live with you. I'm just trying to figure out how to make it all work."

Merit's voice calling "Iris!" made me hang up the phone quickly, which was dumb. For all he knew, I was making a call, not listening to one.

He looked at me suspiciously. "Whatcha doing?"

"Oh, um, I was going to call the girls. They like it."

"And they didn't answer so you furiously slammed the phone down?"

I smiled in a way that I hoped was so cute he forgot I was being sketchy. "Thanks for driving me," I said, hopping off the bed and slipping my shoes on.

"Uh-huh," he said. "Smooth transition there." He paused. "Look, Iris, are you sure you should be going to see your dad alone?"

I peered at him. "Asks the boy who got us burner phones?"

"I know, but that's different. This is jail. It's not safe. A burner phone isn't going to, like, shank you in the prison yard."

"I don't know what any of that means," I said as he followed me down the steps.

"Well, I don't either, but I also don't want to find out."

"But see, I'm not going alone. I'm going with you."

"Going where?" Alice asked from the bottom of the steps. Whoa. How did she beat me downstairs? She was fast. Like sneaky fast. She must have gotten off that phone call really quickly.

"Chloe's house," Merit and I said simultaneously, as we'd discussed earlier.

"*You* are going to Chloe's house?" Alice asked him.

She had mad mom skills.

"Sophie's going to be there," I whispered to Alice.

I wasn't sure if she bought our lie, but she stopped her questioning. Plus, *she* was the one lying. Would she really leave? And if so, then what?

"We'll be home in time for dinner!" I said in a singsong voice as we headed out.

Merit shot me a *smooth* look. Okay, maybe I had oversold it.

We got in Merit's car, and he was quiet for a minute. "I'm going in with you," he said with finality.

"You can't come in with me. You have to be on the list, and you aren't on the list."

"So, I'll get on the list," he said, flipping the dial on the radio and turning it up.

"It takes, like, a while."

He looked over at me, exasperated. "There are a lot of rules in jail."

"Yeah. I think that's kind of the point."

He did his laugh where the breath came out of his nose, the one that made me fall in love with him just a little bit every time.

"So, uh, how's Sophie?" I asked. I was going for casual, but it came out high-pitched and borderline desperate. I was pathetic.

"Oh, you mean my GIRLFRIEND?" He yelled the last word.

"The very one."

"She's, uh, maybe somewhat threatened by you."

"Who wouldn't be?" I asked coyly, flipping my hair.

We both laughed.

"I like Sophie, but it's kind of a lot," he said. "She's very territorial."

"You don't say."

"Juniper Shores Socialite isn't helping matters much," Merit said. "In fact, I kind of think she's the root of all our problems—which I keep telling Sophie. I mean, if you trust an anonymous Instagram account more than your own boyfriend, we've got bigger issues, right?"

I nodded. That was a good point. The amount we all trusted said Instagram account was concerning. "Who do you think it is?" I asked.

"Who do *you* think it is?"

"I really thought it was someone in our house, but now I'm not so sure," I said.

Merit laughed. "Like my mom?"

"No. Your mom's too classy. Maybe Julie? Not Alice, because Juniper Shores Socialite is obsessed with talking crap about Alice."

"But you don't think it's someone in our house now?"

I thought for a minute. "No. I think it's someone kind of obsessed with our house. Maybe Laura Lucas. Or Chloe's mom."

Merit nodded. "Chloe's mom seems like she has a lot of time on her hands." He paused, then perked up. "Oh! And she is so up in Chloe's business. She knows everything going on at the high school too."

I nodded. "I think that's what stumps me."

Merit gasped. "Wait! She always says 'we.' What if it's, like, a mother-daughter duo!"

My jaw dropped. "Yes! I think you're totally right." I thought for a long moment. "But I really don't think Chloe would have let her mom talk junk about my dad like that."

"Maybe not," Merit agreed. "But people will do crazy things when they're getting attention for it."

We pulled up in front of the white concrete building that I knew a little too well now, and my stomach turned. I'd been so distracted, I'd forgotten that I was coming to jail.

"I'll be right here," Merit said.

"I'll be quick." He looked kind of, I don't know, stricken or something, so I said, "I promise I'll be fine. My dad will be there to take care of me."

"Yeah, that makes me feel a lot better," he said under his breath.

The way he said it made me feel wistful. Because I wanted Merit to want to take care of me. I wanted him to be the one keeping me safe and guarding my heart. I took a moment to appreciate the way his hair brushed across his forehead. That Sophie was so lucky, and she didn't even know it.

"It's fine," I said.

"It's fine, it's all fine, everything's fine," Merit said back, smiling. When I didn't move, he added, "Hurry up! I'm not hanging around prison for fun."

I had called ahead, so Dad was waiting in his normal spot, on the couch by the window in the visiting room. "Hey, kiddo," he said. "I'm surprised Mom let you come by yourself."

"Uh-huh."

He gave me his sideways dad-look. "Iris. Does your mother know you're here?"

It wasn't like I could flat-out lie. It wasn't like he wouldn't tell her. "Well, I probably mentioned it to her. But she might have been busy when I did."

"Uh-huh."

"So, like, maybe don't bring it up."

"Iris . . ."

"Dad! Mom couldn't come today, and I wanted to see you! Don't you want to see me?"

He took my hand. "Of course I want to see you, sweetie. But I want you to be safe."

"Merit came with me," I said. "He'll keep me safe." Everything inside of me melted like hot liquid when I said that.

Dad sighed. "Well, you're here. So, tell me what's going on."

I filled him in on all the details of Belle Epoque on the Beach that I hadn't told him yet in our quick phone calls—except for the judge part, which would needlessly hurt his feelings.

"Man, I hated to miss that," he said. "Your mother is always the most beautiful woman there."

In my normal life, I would have rolled my eyes. Now they filled with tears. There's nothing like a huge crisis to put things in perspective. "Dad, the best part of all of it is that a lot of people really believe you're innocent now." I paused. "How is Oliver coming on proving that?"

"Well, it's interesting, kiddo. Since the evidence hasn't come in yet, we don't have much to go on. But we have reason to believe the feds think other parties are involved. When we know who they are, that will help."

"So, like, who would you think it was?" I asked casually. "If you had to guess." This was a question that would have tipped my mom off instantly. Dad just said, "You know, honey, I don't know." He paused. "The only thing I can think of that was weird recently is that we had some statements with some errors in them from the Capstone Fund. But they were very small, and the money was all there so . . ."

"The Capstone Fund," I repeated, trying to remember it.

"Yeah. And they mentioned my being a flight risk, so we have to think someone overseas is being investigated. If I had to guess, maybe the Artemis Fund? Maybe the Mallick? But this is all based on my sitting here thinking. Nothing factual."

None of that meant anything to me, of course. I mean, I recognized the names from my limited internship experience. But that was about it.

Dad smiled. "Are you thinking of following in Dad's footsteps?"

He looked so proud that I couldn't bear to say what I was thinking: *After this? Um, hell no.* So I just shrugged. "Maybe. You know I always loved my internships."

"You know, honey, this business is all about relationships. I know the guys at all these funds. Hell, I've worked with the Capstone Fund for easily ten or twelve years. Sometimes I just email or call Dan— that's the guy who started it—and we chat and cut up, and a small mistake here or there isn't unheard of. It happens."

"Or maybe he stole the money?" I asked.

He shrugged and said, "I can't imagine that Dan . . ." He stopped and a look crossed his face, and I could tell he was finally starting to get suspicious. Dad leaned over and patted my leg. "Sweetheart, this isn't your problem. Oliver will figure this all out. Because I'm not guilty. Okay?"

It wasn't okay. I wanted to do something. I was about to say more, but Oliver walked in, looking like he was on a mission. "Oh, hi, Iris."

"Hi, Oliver."

"I hate to cut your visit short, but . . ."

I shook my head. "It's okay. Merit is waiting for me, and there's nothing to cut short because I was never here."

He smirked at me. "Uh-huh."

"Are you picking up what I'm putting down, Oliver?"

"Oh, I'm picking it up," he said.

I thought back to that man in our house, to the paper he'd dropped. It hadn't occurred to me until right now that it could be important. What if those statements were a clue? And who's to say that man hadn't gone back to the house later to get the one he dropped or look for more of them? It wasn't any more secure than the night I sneaked in with Dabney and Chloe. Maybe I would tell Oliver. Later. Not in front of Dad. He would just worry. Or, well . . . Chloe, Dabney, and I had made pretty good detectives so far. Maybe we could handle this.

I kissed Dad goodbye. "I love you," I said.

"I love you too, honey."

I pointed to Oliver. "Work faster."

He smiled at me. "I hope we have some really good news soon."

At that happy thought, I bounded back out to the parking lot. "What are you so excited about?" Merit asked when I got in the car.

"It's just always good to see my dad," I said. "I miss him, you know?"

Merit gave me a withering look.

"Of course you know," I said. "Your dad is in Tokyo."

"He wants Emma and me to come for spring break, but I don't know that I really want to fly with my twelve-year-old sister to Tokyo. It seems like a lot of responsibility."

"Your mom wouldn't fly with you?"

Merit pulled out of the parking spot and then looked out the windshield, taking a long time to answer. "Mom can't be around Dad," he said. "I can't go back to that."

"Back to what?"

"Never mind," he said. "Well, as promised, you were very fast. Did anyone threaten you while you were in there?"

"Ha-ha," I said. "I didn't even see anyone else."

"Maybe you should consider wearing a longer skirt next time you visit." He gave me a scolding look, and excitement that he had noticed my skirt length zipped through me.

"Maybe you should mind your own business," I said.

"I will start minding my own business when you quit needing my Uber services." Merit squeezed my shoulder, his hand lingering.

I thought back to Sophie, to her friend implying that she and Merit basically just talked. And I had the fabulous thought that that was because he didn't love her. He loved me. Now all that was left to do was figure out a way to make him confess.

Crystal Clear

Work had been so busy today that I had barely had time to obsess about the fact that, this close to Bill's first pretrial conference, discovery should be coming in any minute. Oliver had texted me earlier: *Nothing yet.*

Yet somehow, between setting up a group disability policy for a doctor's office, quoting a huge car dealership's health insurance, lunch with Gabe and the owner of three hundred apartments we were trying to woo, and an afternoon of playing catch-up on emails and a few walk-ins, I had managed to check out something I was avoiding. It was just a chat room, one of those simple things that I had come across while—dangerously—googling "Bill Sitterly." And sure, I had found furious messages from multi-multimillionaires who had lost one of their millions. But I also found notes from retired couples who had given Bill their entire retirement and lost everything. Men going back to work as greeters at Walmart. Women going back to doing hair despite the arthritis crippling their fingers.

It was a horrible feeling. I thought about Alice, about how she'd seen me in the bank that day, and wanted to help. And I suddenly got the feeling that I wanted to help too. Maybe it wasn't my responsibility, necessarily, to give these people back what they had lost. But I began to feel that way.

I was trying to shake the heaviness I felt on my drive home, the thoughts running through my head that I did not want to have. The town was aflutter with the idea that Bill was innocent. But was it enough? What if he went to jail anyway? What if he had been framed so well that he took the fall for something he didn't do? And, worst of all, what if he was lying to me? What if he was guilty? I had been so great at pushing those thoughts away that they took my breath away as they all flooded in now.

If that was the case, I would never get my money back. Never get my house back. Iris and I would really, truly have to start over. And, while my job at Montoya & Sons was getting us by, if I had to make a full-on fresh start, it had to be in New York where everyone wasn't talking about my family. I didn't want Iris to have to leave her friends. But it was the only way. I could get a job with Bradley, make a new start for us, pay those people back—at least the ones who had lost everything. I probably couldn't fix everyone's problems, but I could fix some.

I would say it was a weird or coincidental time for Bradley to call, but wasn't that what life was like? You thought of someone, and they appeared in line behind you in the grocery store. You wanted to go on a trip to the Caribbean, and suddenly all you saw was pictures of boats in clear water. (Side note: I desperately missed being the person planning those vacations.)

I hit the phone button on my steering wheel—I would never again take having my own car for granted—and said, "Well, hello. Have you called to beg me to come work for you?"

I don't know how I pulled off such a cocky tone when I was feeling so low.

He laughed. "Something like that."

"Seriously?" This could be an answered prayer.

"I'm really calling to ask you if you've heard of the Capstone Fund."

I racked my brain. "Is that Dan Isaacs's fund?"

"Yeah."

"I mean, yeah. I've heard of it, but I'm not, like, up to date on it or anything."

"Do you know if Bill invested with Dan?"

I blew out my breath, trying to exhale the butterflies filling my stomach. They were in-between butterflies, butterflies of thinking something either really great or really horrible is coming next and not being sure which. "I honestly don't know, Bradley. But I know he and Dan are friends, so I would think it's highly possible. Why?"

Please be good news. Please be good news.

"Look," he said, "I don't even know if this is true. But I've heard rumblings today that the SEC has launched an investigation into them."

"But, like, a secret investigation?"

"For now, yeah. But I'm just wondering if Bill was caught up with them if there are dots to connect there."

Please, Lord, let this be their fault and not his.

Bill had already called me today, using twenty of his phone minutes instead of ten. So I couldn't be sure if he would call tomorrow. I needed to ask him, but I didn't know when that would happen. There was no way I could go see him tomorrow either. My day was slammed and, as much as I missed my husband, I couldn't risk losing this job. So, at the stoplight, I texted Oliver: *Capstone Fund.*

"I so, so hope you're right, Bradley. I'll get his attorney to look into it."

"Okay, but this did not come from me. I shouldn't even know about this."

"Of course," I said. "And I am so appreciative of you putting your-self on the line for me like this."

"For you," he said. "Not Sitterly. I still can't stand him, to be clear."

I smiled. "Crystal clear."

"Oh, and, Char?"

"Yeah."

"I'm calling to tell you that I've asked around, and if you still need a job, I think I can give you one."

"I'm sorry. What? Really?"

"Yeah. No one thinks you had anything to do with this." He cleared his throat. "Charlotte, you didn't, did you?"

I laughed incredulously. "Bradley! *Bill* didn't even have anything to do with this. I'm so out of the game, I don't even know if he's in-vesting in Capstone. No. I had nothing to do with this!" I instantly re-gretted saying how far out of the game I was. But, well, he knew that.

"I had to ask." He paused. "Look, just keep me posted. Come up here, interview, meet the office staff."

My eyes filled with hot tears of gratitude and stress and horror. Gratitude that he would help me. Stress that I might actually have to do this. And horror that I might have to live for years without Bill. On the bright side, I did know that, if he had to stay in jail, they would likely relocate him to New York if I moved. My stomach began to hurt. How was that the bright side?

"Thank you. Seriously. I'll call you next week."

"I'll keep you updated if I hear anything between now and then."

I hung up the phone as I pulled into the driveway. I wiped my eyes and took a deep breath. I had so much to process, so much to figure out. But for now, it was my week to do laundry. So I walked upstairs hoping to find my daughter. I wanted a big hug—and maybe a little help with the folding.

Alice

~~~~~~~

A Button

My sister can make me absolutely crazy. In fact, I would say that she is the only person in all the world who has that specific effect on me. I love her. I *do*. I would walk through fire for her. And she gave me my favorite person in the world, my niece Julie. But she's just so darn competitive with me. While I'd like to rise above, while I prepare myself to *just freaking be the bigger person*, Delia always finds a button. She always pushes it, leans on it until she cannot lean any harder.

So when she sauntered in the back door of my house and called, "Yoo-hoo! Al-ice!" my heart rose all the way into my throat. Because of all the things I hated, I hated surprises the very most. I've never liked them, not since I was a kid. And then the dead husbands didn't help matters much. Delia knew that very, very well.

I was in the laundry room, folding clothes with Charlotte, who noticed my expression immediately. "Who is that?" she whispered.

I was frozen to my spot, powerless to move. "My sister," I whispered.

"Oh, good?" Charlotte asked. Definitely a question.

"God, grant me the serenity," I said out loud as I heard Brenna say tentatively, "Nana?"

I walked out the laundry room door. "Del!" I squealed with an enthusiasm that, once I saw her, I began to feel. Of all my siblings, Delia was the only one I really kept in touch with. I had tried, at various times throughout the years, to reconnect with all four of them, to gather us together, either alone or with our families. But things always seemed to fall apart at the end. And, really, I knew why. We were strangers now. I hadn't lived with them since I was ten years old, and the resentment over the "good deal" I'd been handed in the wake of our shared tragedy didn't help much. Although I sometimes wanted to point out to my brother Daniel that he'd only had to live in foster care for six months, to my sisters Delia and Emily that they had at least gotten to live together. But I never did. We never got into anything real. Instead, we spent half our time making small talk, getting filled in on parts of each other's lives we should already have known.

"Al!" Delia said, kissing me on both cheeks and hugging me enthusiastically. She looked around the open floor plan of my gorgeous waterfront home and said, "So I see you've stuck with those oystershell countertops. Such a bold look."

And so it began. Charlotte put a forceful hand on the small of my back, seemingly to hold me up. I appreciated it.

Julie was trotting down the steps and stopped abruptly. "Mom? What are you doing here?"

"Can't I come visit my favorite daughter and granddaughters?"

Julie was Delia's only daughter, but my sister was the kind of woman who would choose a favorite and then tell all her children who that was—and, more to point, who it wasn't.

I looked over at Grace, who wiped her hands on her kitchen towel as we walked from the hallway toward her. "Hi," she said with a wave. "I'm Grace. I'm a friend of Julie's."

"Ah, yes," Delia said wistfully. "Another castaway on Alice's shipwreck."

Grace didn't take the bait. "Are you staying for dinner? I'd be happy to set another plate."

Delia lit up. "Oh, that would be lovely. Just lovely. Thank you for offering, Grace." She shot me a look that said, *At least someone did.*

But, see, I hadn't offered because I didn't want her to stay. I had decided, after losing my nerve many times, that tonight I was going to sit down with this little family of mine and tell them that I was planning to move in with Elliott. That they could take all the time they needed. That there was no rush. If it took months or even years, we could wait. We would work it out. I was so happy to move in with him. But I was so sad—and, quite frankly, a little terrified—to be moving in a different direction. I had succeeded at mommune life. I couldn't say the same for couple life.

"Grace!" Charlotte said in a high-pitched voice. "Why don't we open some wine for Julie's mother?"

Julie's mother didn't need wine. Julie's mother got even worse when wine was involved. That said, *I* desperately needed wine. And I thought it might be better for me to have something to calm me down, even if it amplified her.

"I'll bring it to the porch," I said. "Give you and Julie a little time to catch up."

"Yes," Delia said. "Thank you. It will be nice to have a little time with *my* daughter."

Julie shot me a conciliatory smile as she closed the porch door behind them.

"She's always reminding me Julie is *her* daughter. *Her* daughter," I said, feeling myself getting worked up. "Where was she when *her* daughter and *her* grandchildren were living in that disgusting roach-infested apartment with water stains all over the ceiling? Where was she when *her* grandchildren were wearing too-small shoes because

Julie had no savings, a new reporting job, and couldn't afford groceries, rent, *and* shoes?"

Grace silently handed me a glass of wine, while Charlotte perched on a stool and watched me sympathetically. This was the best part about a house of women. They understood when you simply wanted to vent. "I'll take wine out to Delia," Grace whispered.

Jamie tore into the kitchen. "Anally! We're going to do a show for Nana!" She was wearing a sparkly pink tutu over her school uniform and a pair of red *Wizard of Oz* slippers, and my heart swelled. When the girls moved in, they were too little to say, "Aunt Alice." Instead, it came out "Anally," and the nickname had stuck.

"Yay!" I said, gathering all my enthusiasm. I pulled her to me, and my heart hurt with how much I loved her.

I thought again of that night I found out my mother had died—in a sea of glass and gasoline. The night my father fled the scene of a crime of his making with a bottle of brandy and never came back. When I was not much older than Jamie, I knew the terror of being all alone in the world, of having no one to help you or care about you or save you. I could conjure that feeling in an instant. It could well up in me with no warning at all. I was so grateful that I could give her a chance to live a different life, have a different story. I was so grateful that I wasn't that little girl anymore. I had all these people around me to love me. I had this family I had built for myself. Yes, I had lost three men I had loved too, but I wasn't alone. *You aren't alone*, I reminded myself, calming myself down, backing away from the ledge of my biggest fear.

"You are going to be absolutely magnificent! I can't wait to see the show!" I told Jamie.

Audrey skittered in behind her in her *Beauty and the Beast* gown, a yellow confection of cheap tulle and thickly applied glitter. Brenna trailed in last in all black.

"And who are you?" Charlotte asked.

"I'm the director," Brenna said importantly. "So I need to blend in."

We all cracked up as she said, "Come on, Audrey," and the three sisters made their way to the porch.

"They are really something else," Grace said. She paused, taking a sip of wine. "So, why do we think your sister is here?" She raised her eyebrow at me.

"Oh, she needs money," I said offhandedly. That's usually why she showed up. And that was her excuse for not being able to take in her daughter and grandchildren. And for years and years, I'd been able to give it to her. But circumstances had changed for me, at least for now. I couldn't be her money tree. I was strongly considering going back to work at the school—if they would have me, that is. But they had openings, and I'd left them on positive terms. *It's not you, it's me* was true for once. It wasn't great money, but it was enough to get me by. But, more than the money, I felt like I was ready. I missed the children and the sense of community. I missed feeling like I was making an impact. And if I wasn't going to be at the mommune, I needed something to occupy my time.

"Nice," Charlotte said. "Well, I guess if you know what to expect, you'll never be disappointed."

I smiled at her and patted her hand. "Listen to me going on and on. How are things with Bill?"

She sighed. "He's hanging in there, but, you guys . . . I know Bill is innocent, but what if he gets convicted anyway? It happens all the time."

The thought made my stomach turn.

"That's not going to happen," I said firmly. But we both knew that happy thoughts weren't going to fix this.

"Not only might I really need to start a new life for us, but there are people who lost their entire savings in this debacle. Even if it isn't Bill's fault, I think we should try to pay them back. The idea of old couples losing their whole retirement makes me feel ill."

"I know, sweetie, but it's not your fault," Grace said as she removed the plates from the cabinet.

We each took a stack and, as we began setting the table, Charlotte said, "I wanted to wait and tell you this at a better time, when we were all together, but I do have a job offer on the table in New York. If the worst happens, Iris and I are going to need a fresh start. And if we get one, so should everyone else. I want to be able to pay everyone back."

My head snapped up when she said that. Well, she had beat me to the punch. We couldn't both announce we were leaving. "But how would you even do that? Aren't the fraud victims' names protected for their privacy?"

She nodded. "Well, yeah. But I'm sure I could figure it out."

I hadn't realized this was how Charlotte felt. "Honey, I think that's so kind of you, but I'm not sure that spending your life paying penance for something you didn't do is going to help anything at all."

But didn't I understand that? Wasn't that what I had been doing too? Trying to atone for sins that weren't mine to begin with? Trying to somehow right my karmic ship so that these horrible things wouldn't keep happening to me?

"So you really think you'll go back to New York?" Grace asked.

Charlotte looked down at her feet. "If things don't get better soon, I think I'm going to have to."

The idea of them leaving swamped me with grief. "Oh, Charlotte. We would miss you so much!" I meant that. I did. But also, in the back of my mind, I knew it was crazy. I was *moving*. I needed them to go. But the reality of it was crashing down around me.

She smiled. "I will miss you all terribly. But I think it's the right thing."

"But is it the right thing for your daughter?" I asked, suddenly feeling incensed.

Charlotte looked puzzled, and I realized I had been too forceful with her. I tried to never raise my voice, never get upset. "I'm sorry," I said. "This is the Delia effect. She isn't even in the room and she's irritating me." And I was *leaving*. It wasn't like I could keep Iris. What was wrong with me?

Charlotte nodded. "Iris isn't going to be happy," she said. "She loves it here. But New York is her home too, so I think she'll adjust."

Grace walked over and hugged her. "I'm so proud of you."

They both looked at me. I knew this was the moment that I was supposed to say something heartfelt. But I couldn't quite muster it. Because I didn't mean it. I didn't want her to leave, and I needed to do some work to figure out why. Was I less ready than I thought to move in with Elliott? No. I knew I was ready. I just wanted both. Life with Elliott, and the mommune. But that wasn't reality.

Fortunately, I was saved from too much soul-searching by Julie opening the porch door and saying, "The show was marvelous! And we have some hungry, hungry dancers!"

"Oh, I know it was amazing!" I said. "We'll have to catch an encore performance!"

I finished setting the table while everyone filed in to sit down. Merit, Emma, Iris, and her friend Ben arrived, and I couldn't help but smile at the little group of them. Iris pining over Merit, Ben pining over Iris, Emma just wanting to do anything and everything that Iris did.

I realized we didn't have enough seats at the same time Ben did. "I'm so sorry!" he said. "I can go home for dinner."

"No, no! Don't be ridiculous," I said, scooting over the chair at the head of the table and sliding another one in beside it. "We were expecting you. I promise."

My sister glared at me. "What she means to say is that her perfect table is ruined because she wasn't expecting *me*."

I knew better than to fire back at her. I was trained in the art of letting things slide. But I was flustered and frazzled by Charlotte's news. Which was ridiculous because the bottom line was that *I* was planning to leave too. It was all hitting me at once. That sadness and frustration hadn't left me any room to deal with my sister. "Well, no, Delia, I wasn't expecting you. Since you didn't tell me you were coming."

Much to my surprise, she didn't respond. Grace carried several trays to the table. "Cauliflower tacos with cashew crema!" she announced. We all clapped, as we did most nights, because Grace's creations were always masterpieces.

"My favorite!" Brenna squealed.

Delia was studying the trays critically. "Where's the meat?"

"Oh, Grace is a vegan chef," Julie said. "And she makes us the most extraordinary meals."

"You won't believe how good they are," chimed in that sweet Ben, who to my knowledge had never once eaten Grace's cooking.

Delia shook her head. "That isn't healthy for the children. Not one bit."

She was being so incredibly rude. Even if she felt that way, she shouldn't have said it in front of Grace.

"Just another reason I'm glad you and the girls are coming home to live with me, Jules," Delia said importantly.

All eyes were on Julie. You could have heard a pin drop. Julie was leaving. Charlotte was leaving. That deep, longing ache took hold again. *You're all alone, Alice. You're all alone.*

But then I thought of Elliott, of the life we were going to build together. The thought of him soothed me—until I remembered that, like every other man I'd ever loved, he could be gone in an instant.

Charlotte
~~~~~~~~~

Next Chapter

I've never seen a bomb erupt in real life. Only on television. It's at once horrifying and awe-inspiring the way the explosion starts at a center point and bursts in circles around it, leaving nothing in its wake untouched. That was how it was at this dinner table. Delia had dropped an atom bomb. Grace dropped the radishes, the dish shattering on the hardwood floor, the healthy and beautiful taco garnish scattering.

I hopped up to help her clean it up, wishing desperately that my daughter and I weren't here to get entangled in whatever family drama was about to ensue, and practically feeling her embarrassment at having Ben witness this.

Grace seemed frozen to her spot, crouched behind Julie, as I scrambled to pick up the largest glass shards first. "You're moving out?" she whispered to Julie. "You didn't even tell me." Her unspoken question seemed to be, *And what am I supposed to do now?*

I couldn't blame her. Even though I had shared my tentative plan to move back to New York, I didn't have a timeline for it yet. I certainly wasn't ready to walk out the door tomorrow or anything. What if Alice decided that, with her niece gone, the mommune was a thing of the past? The idea of going back home without Bill still unnerved me. But Iris and I might not have a choice.

"Mom!" Julie scolded. "I told you I would tell them at the right time."

Delia didn't respond.

"How could you do this to me?" Alice exploded.

I jolted up from the floor to look at her. I had never ever seen her lose her cool until tonight. But I knew that certain people were triggering for even the calmest of us.

Part of me wanted to grab the children and run. Another part wanted to watch this play out. And the last part of me knew that I couldn't do either because I had to get the glass off the floor. I tried to be as inconspicuous as possible as I walked to the pantry to retrieve the broom.

It was close enough that I caught Julie saying, "Aunt Alice, I am so incredibly grateful for your immense, total, unimaginable generosity. I just felt that I had long overstayed my welcome."

"Julie, what did I do to make you feel that way?" Alice asked, her eyes filling with tears.

I turned to see always-strong Julie shrinking. "Nothing, nothing," she stuttered. "But when I moved in three years ago, I think we both thought it would be for a few months. I . . ." She trailed off, looking down at her hands and, it appeared, trying not to cry. "I wanted to give you your life back."

Alice's eyes were glued to Julie. "I cannot imagine my life without you," she said. "All I have ever wanted is to care for your family like you were my own."

"But that's the problem," Delia said in a tone that made me want to drop the broom I was wielding and smack her. "As I continue to remind you: she is not your daughter."

I'd just turned to empty the dustpan into the trash when Alice said, "Oh, just shut up, Delia."

Brenna gasped. "We don't say shut up in this house!"

That was when Grace finally unfroze and sprang into action. She walked over to the three little girls and, taking Audrey's and Jamie's hands, whispered, "I've been dying to finish that puzzle in the bunk room."

"Yes!" Jamie said.

"But what about my tacos?" Brenna whined.

"I'll bring you a special plate in there," I said.

"We aren't allowed to eat in the bunk room," Jamie said.

"I think it will be okay maybe just this once," I whispered.

They looked up at Grace, who nodded in confirmation.

"Hooray! Tacos in the bunk room!" Brenna shouted.

"Hooray!" Audrey parroted, and they all trooped down the hall.

If I had to guess, neither Delia nor Alice nor Julie was even aware of what was going on around them. Delia said, "Oh, there she is. The kumbaya-singing, house-opening Alice has finally cracked."

My first thought was, *What an odious human.* But then it washed over me what I had done. I had moved into a house with a bunch of people I didn't know at all. I had put my daughter in harm's way. Or potentially, anyway. Yes, we had heard rumblings about Alice, but didn't people love to gossip? Especially in a small town? And couldn't people change? Alice had had a very difficult life. She couldn't always be a perfectly poised lady.

I was trying to catch Iris's eye, to indicate that she, Ben, Merit, and Emma needed to get out of here. But I could intuit in that way a mother can that every single one of them was ignoring me. Who could blame them? This was better than reality TV. If it wasn't happening to my friends, obviously.

"I just don't understand," Alice said, fixed on Julie.

Julie's face was red. "Alice, I mean it, I don't want to leave. I just thought it was time for your next chapter."

Alice smiled sadly down at her hands, and Julie picked up: "I see you with Elliott. You can't let him go again for us."

Alice nodded and looked as if she were about to speak. But then Delia said, "Plus, it's high time that my daughter and my grandchildren were with me."

"Delia, what about when she was practically poverty-stricken? Was it not time then?" Alice asked. She stopped, and I saw something dawn on her. She laughed. "Oh, I see. Now that Julie can help out with the bills, you want them to be with you." She looked at Julie. "If you want to be on your own, fine. Be on your own. But do not let her take what you have worked so hard to build back up. I mean it, Julie."

Julie looked like she was holding her breath, her head swiveling from her mother to her aunt and back again.

Alice put her head in her hands. "I'm sorry," she said. "I'm so sorry. I don't want you to feel stuck in the middle of our problems." She took a deep breath. "If you want to go with your mother, then that's fine. You know I get scared about being alone and—"

"You aren't going to be alone," Julie said.

"Well, with Charlotte and Iris moving back to New York and—" Alice gasped, clasping her hand over her mouth.

My jaw dropped.

Suddenly, all the eyes in the room I couldn't get to look at me before were now laser-focused. Iris jumped up from the table. "What? Is that true?"

I let out a deep sigh. "Honey, nothing is decided yet. But obviously our future is looking a little different, and I have to think about what's best for the two of us."

"Fine. Then I'll go live with Dad."

"In jail?" I asked. Maybe not the right thing to say to a volatile teenager, but honest to God.

Iris's face turned red. "Mom, I love it here and I don't want to leave. I don't want to go back to New York!"

I knew she wouldn't want to leave, but she hadn't wanted to leave New York either, so I figured a part of her would be happy. Then again, this wasn't exactly the perfect way for her to find out about my plans. *Thanks, Alice. Really.*

Before I could respond, Iris said in a strained, devastated voice, somewhere between screaming and crying, "And it's not like I can stay here because Alice is moving in with Elliott!"

Everyone swiveled to look at Alice.

"What?" Julie asked.

"Honey, we can talk about this later," I said to Iris.

But before the sentence was even out of my mouth, Iris was flying out the porch door. Ben scrambled out of his chair to follow her.

"I'm so sorry," Alice said to me, her hand on her forehead. "It just flew out of my mouth. I am such an idiot."

Delia chimed in, "Making a big deal about my daughter leaving when you're the one leaving her."

Alice took a deep breath, and I could see her returning to herself. "Del," she said, "I would never leave her. I'll give her all the time she needs. But Julie is right. I love Elliott, and I do want a future with him."

"I sensed that, Alice. And I want you to be happy," Julie said.

Delia rolled her eyes, and I was shocked at how much hatred I was able to find for a woman I didn't really even know.

But I was also gobsmacked about Alice and Elliott. I couldn't unpack that right now though. "I'm going to go check on Iris," I said.

Merit stood up. "No, no. Let me. I think that might go over better."

I had been worried about them being under the same roof, but gosh, what a good kid that Merit had turned out to be. He was so mature, so wise beyond his years. He took care of everyone in this house like it was his job. And he was just a kid, something I had to remind myself of.

"I'm right here if you need me. Okay?"

He nodded. "Okay. But she'll be fine. She just needs time to cool off."

Emma looked up and said, "You know, Mom isn't that great at puzzles. I think I should go help."

Smart girl. This wasn't my drama around this table, and I had inserted myself way too far into the fire already. I'd gotten burned, too.

"You know, I think I'd better take those tacos in there."

I gathered the plates and left the other women behind. Voices rose around the table again, but I didn't really care what they were saying anymore. All I could think about was my child, out there on that beach, hating me with all her heart.

I knew part of this was regular teen girl stuff, but she had also been through so much these past few weeks. I wished we could rewind to those simple days when it was just the three of us around the table. I wanted to hold on to the hope that we would get there; I wanted to believe that a miracle would happen for our family. But I had to be practical. I had to prepare for our future too. And whatever happened with the mommune, my realest future, my top priority, was my daughter.

Grown-Up Stuff

I'm just going to stay here with Chloe. Her parents probably won't even notice I'm there, I thought as I ran, barefoot, down the rough wooden steps. I had pulled more than a few splinters out of the little kids' feet from these steps. I knew I should be more careful. But all I could think about was getting away. I ran as fast as I could through the sand and over the dune, not looking where I was going, ignoring the threat of sandspurs and ghost crabs. "Iris!" Ben was calling behind me. "Iris, wait!"

But I didn't stop until I reached the shoreline, until my feet, still running at top speed, splashed through the tiny waves. My pulse was pounding in my ears, my heart thumping.

"Geez, you're fast," Ben said, out of breath too.

I tried to half-smile at him, but it didn't quite take.

"That was, um, a lot," Ben said.

"You think?"

He put his arm around my shoulders. "I don't want you to go."

I looked up at him. "Well, do you think I want to go?"

I *really* didn't, which kind of stunned me. How many times had I complained about how small it was here? About how I wanted to go back to the city with all its things to do and my original friends? I'd wanted to go back to my school. But now, at the mommune, I felt like I had a place. I felt like I was home.

"And what does this even mean? Is my mom just giving up on my dad? We've made it so far and—" I stopped abruptly.

"What?" Ben asked.

"I just have to prove my dad is innocent."

Ben squeezed my shoulder. "Iris, I love this about you, but I don't think that's really your responsibility."

I shot him a look and he said, "Or maybe you'll be the one to save the day. If anyone can, it's you."

"Better answer," I said. We both smiled.

"Well, maybe you won't have to go," Ben said. "Maybe your mom won't do it because she sees how unhappy you are."

I shook my head. "I mean, she's right, you know? It's totally possible that Dad could go to jail for a crime he did not commit. And we can't stay here then. Sure, it was kind of cool to be here where everyone knew us and thought we were a big deal. But if he's in jail, we need to be in a place where we can blend in a little better."

Ben turned to me, taking my elbows in his hands. And my heart started pounding again. I was suddenly very aware of the cicadas humming, of the silvery moon over the ocean, of the sea oats waving in the breeze. All my senses were on high alert. Something was happening here.

"I don't want you to leave," Ben said quietly.

I couldn't make eye contact with him. Because, oh my gosh, did Ben *like me*? Did he want to be more than best friends? Did I? Sure, there'd been moments, plenty of them, when I wondered what it would be like to kiss him, to hold his hand. And, yes, his proximity was making my heart beat out of my chest. But I was sure that whatever was about to happen would guarantee that I lost my best friend. If I told him I didn't like him like that, and he liked me like that, then we could never go back to just being friends. And if he tried to kiss me, and I didn't kiss him back, our friendship was over. And if he kissed me and I kissed him back and I liked it, wouldn't we just eventually break up and I'd lose him anyway? It was truly shocking how many thoughts a person could have in the span of a split second.

"Iris, there's something I've been wanting to tell you," he said.

Oh no, oh no, oh no. How did I make this stop? There was a slight, teeny chance, I was now realizing, that maybe I liked Ben too. But I couldn't handle losing my best friend right now. But if I stopped him from saying what he wanted to say, wouldn't that be nearly as bad?

"Hey," Merit said, out of breath, running up to us, resting his hands on his knees and panting. There was a little bit of sweat breaking through his T-shirt. He straightened up and brushed his hair out of his eyes, and it was like angels started singing and the moon was only shining on him. Yes, I might like Ben. But no one on earth was Merit. "Iris, you can't just run out like that."

Ben was staring at Merit so intently that I wondered if he was trying to incinerate him.

"Hey, man," Merit said, putting his hand on Ben's shoulder. "Can we have a minute?"

Ben dropped my elbows and looked at me. I knew there was more going on here than met the eye. Ben was asking: *Him or me?*

"Sorry about all this," I said as lightly as I could muster. "Bet you won't come here for dinner again! I'll call you later, okay?"

It sounded awkward, and only someone who knew him as well as I did would have noticed how Ben's face fell, how I'd just answered the question lingering between us. I had basically said: *Merit. I choose Merit.*

It was crazy, because I knew Merit didn't choose me. But as my mom always said, the heart wants what it wants; I don't make the rules.

I watched Ben trudge up the sand toward the house. Merit sat down and patted for me to sit beside him. I did, so close that our hips were nearly touching.

He turned his head to me; I could see literally up his nose. It was clean, thank goodness. Although maybe it would have helped if he'd had a huge booger hanging out. But I think I still would have found him totally irresistible.

"Iris, do you know how lucky you are to have a mom like yours?"

I was taken aback. "Um, that was definitely not what I thought you were going to say."

"Well, that's what I am saying. I know we're kind of just kids. But also, we're old enough to know that our parents are real people, and these things affect them in a huge way. Maybe even more than us."

"I've lost you," I said.

"Look. You have your whole life ahead of you. You'll go to college, and fall in love, and get married, and start a family—or not. I mean, whatever you want to do. I'm just saying, for example. But your mom has done all that and lost all of it." He paused. "All of it but you."

A knot formed low in my stomach, which was much less pleasant than the nice butterflies I'd had there for Merit earlier. "Okay, sure. Whatever. But I don't want to move to New York. I want to stay here."

"I want you to stay here too," Merit said. That brought the butterflies back. "But you don't need the mommune. You don't *need* to be here. And you should take a lot of comfort in that."

"Well, you don't *need* the mommune either," I said.

He shook his head and turned away from me, looking out over the water.

"What?" I asked. "You have a rich dad who sends you all the money you need and a mom who's like Betty Crocker with a blog."

He made that little snorting sound out of his nose that I loved. "Maybe now," he said.

"What does that mean?" I asked.

"Nothing. Never mind."

Curiosity rose in me. Why *was* Grace here? Her kids were half grown and she had plenty of money. I mean, the mommune was fun and all, but didn't it kind of have an expiration date? "Merit, come on. We live in the same freaking house. You can't just brush me off and pretend nothing's happening."

He turned toward me again, examining my face, as if trying to decide something. Then he looked back at the water, picking up little fingerfuls of sand and letting them dribble back onto the beach. "My mom wasn't good after my dad left. She just . . . I don't know, couldn't get out of bed, couldn't take care of us. If it wasn't for Julie . . ." He shook his head, and I realized his eyes were shining.

He looked at me again. "Look, my whole life right now is about making sure my mom doesn't get upset. Because when she gets upset, she hides. She becomes someone else. So my whole job and Emma's whole job is to make sure she's okay."

"Merit, that is so much pressure." Guilt swamped me. Here I was bitching about moving to New York, and Merit was dealing with, like, real, heavy, grown-up stuff. "So that's how you got to the mommune then?"

He nodded. "Julie finally took Emma and me. It was months before she convinced my mom to move in too. Julie and Alice just kind of took care of us all that time. It was awful, but I know we're lucky. We had this awesome place to go. And my mom is good now. She's better."

I shook my head. "Gosh, Merit. How do you do everything you do and have all that on you? I mean, you have good grades, you're the star quarterback . . ." I trailed off.

He shrugged. "I know this sounds crazy, but for a while I think I thought if I could just be good enough, just be the best, that maybe my dad would come back and then my mom would be happy."

Sadness washed over me. Who would have imagined that Juniper Shores Prep's golden boy was carrying the weight of the world on his shoulders?

"I realize now that that isn't going to happen. But I still want to keep things perfect for my mom, just in case. I worry about her all the time."

I patted his arm. "I guess I don't worry about my mom enough."

He shrugged. "It's not your job. It's not mine either. But here we are."

"Being a good person is complicated," I said, sighing heavily, somewhere between serious and joking.

Merit put his hand on my arm. "You are a good person. The best person."

There they were again. Those explosive butterflies. Merit's perfect, beautiful face was inches from mine. And I felt like he was testing the waters. He had said my name when he was hurt on the field. He had punched a judge for me. Those things had to mean something. I'm not impulsive by nature, so I don't know what made me do it. But I leaned in and put my lips on his. I shifted my body toward him, putting my hand on the back of his neck. For a second or two, he kissed me back, and I felt like I was in heaven. So *this* was kissing. Not bad.

But then he pulled away and said, "Iris," in a tone, with an expression on his face that made mine blazing hot. I had totally misread this. I jumped up, saying, "Oh my God. I'm so sorry." Now, instead of running from the house, I was running toward it.

"Iris, stop!" Merit called.

I did not, but, unlike Ben, Merit was way faster than I was. He grabbed my arm. "Stop it right now," he said.

"I'm such an idiot," I said, humiliation coursing through every cell.

"No, you aren't."

"Of course I am. You have this super-hot older girlfriend, and even if you didn't, you wouldn't be into me. I'm just this little kid to you and—"

He put his palm to my mouth. "Stop talking."

It should have been rude, but it wasn't. It was Merit. It was soft and gentle and kind and made tears spring to my eyes.

"You are perfect," he said, his hand still on my mouth. "It's just that . . ." He paused for a second, then took a deep breath. "I'm going to say something, and I think it's going to shock you."

He stopped again, as if deciding, then dropped his hand from my mouth.

"Iris, can you keep a secret?"

I could feel my eyes widen, and my mind was racing. What could the secret possibly be? I nodded and whispered, "Duh. Beach house rules," trying to sound cool even though I didn't feel it.

Merit took a deep breath, then blurted out, "I'm gay." He said it like he was trying on a sweater, and he wasn't sure if the sweater fit and maybe he was going to send it back.

I rolled my eyes. "Please. You don't have to go that far. You don't have to lie. You can just not like me. I'll live through it." I looked up toward the sky. "I think."

He shook his head, and I was filled with curiosity again. "No, I mean it. I've never said it out loud, but I've known for a long time."

My mind flipped back to Sophie's dumb friend insinuating that Merit wouldn't have sex with her.

"Ohhhhhh," I said. And then, "Wait. Really? You're the star quarterback."

He laughed. "Yeah. That doesn't necessarily preclude me from being gay. I mean, in my limited experience."

"Whoa." I didn't know how to feel. A little relieved, honestly, that I hadn't made a total idiot out of myself. A little let down that the boy I thought was my great love could never love me back. But, most of all, proud that he had confided in me.

"So, your mom doesn't know?"

He shook his head. "And, Iris, you may not tell your mom or Alice or anyone. I just trusted you with my biggest secret, and I do mean *trusted*. I will not be telling anyone else for a long, long time."

"But why?" I asked. "They would all be fine with it."

"Maybe," he said. "Maybe not. But I can't risk that they won't be and that my mom spirals again. Especially now if it's true that Alice is moving in with Elliott and everything else is changing too." He put his hands to my shoulders and looked me squarely in the eye. "I can't move to Tokyo, Iris. I just can't."

We both laughed. I crossed my heart and said, "Your secret is safe with me." I paused. "But . . . you know I'm kind of a pain in the ass. So we will revisit telling other people later."

He laughed. "I wouldn't expect anything less." Then he groaned.

"What?"

"Please, please tell me that wasn't your first kiss?"

I debated. Did I lie? But, I mean, he'd just *come out to me*. I scrunched my nose.

"Oh, Iris. I'm so sorry. That is awful."

For a moment, I did feel deflated. But then I rallied. "Nope. It's not bad. Because my first kiss was with the hottest junior guy in the school. I don't ever have to mention the rest."

"Good spin. I like it." He paused. "Plus, I mean, it was kind of a good kiss, right?"

"It was a good kiss," I agreed.

"If I was into girls, I would have been into it."

I paused and gasped. "Wait. Is there a *guy*? Do you like someone?"

He raised his eyebrows at me, and I gasped again. "There is! There's a guy!"

"He doesn't know I like him, and I wouldn't, like, cheat on Sophie. But you know Chris from my third-period English class?"

My eyes went wide. "No way. *He's* gay? How do I not know this? Does he like you too?"

Merit paused and put his hands lightly to his chest as if to say, *Who wouldn't like this?*

"Right. You're Merit McDonald. Even a straight man would be attracted to you."

Merit laughed and put his arm around me, and we started walking toward the house.

"Wait, so that's all I get? No details?"

"That's a lot for one night, I think."

I put my arm around his waist, my heart swelling with pride. "Wow. I'm so honored that you told me. Why me?"

He shrugged. "I've been wanting to tell someone for a long time, and I guess I knew that you wouldn't judge me and that you could keep a secret." He looked down at me. "Plus, I didn't want you to feel bad like I didn't like you." He sighed. "Thanks, really, for being so great about that. You made it so easy."

I leaned my head against his shoulder. "Okay. Well, I guess I'll have to find another great love. You and I will just have to be best friends." I stopped and squealed. "We can be like Will and Grace. We can live together and—"

"We do live together, psycho." He paused. "And, um, I don't know if you've found your great love. But I feel pretty sure your great love has found you. . . ."

I was puzzled for less than a second. Ben. "You think?" I asked.

"Any guy who wouldn't leave you alone after that dinner deserves some sort of medal of honor," he said. "Yeah, I'd say he's pretty much in love with you."

I bit my lip as we walked over the dune. "Damn," I said. "If I admit I like him, I'm losing my best friend."

"Nah. You just got a new one. Remember?"

That made me feel so much better. And for the first time, when I thought of Ben, I let myself realize that his crush wasn't one-sided. I *did* like him. And maybe that wasn't something to be afraid of. From the dune, the lights inside the mommune sparkled and shone, and you couldn't help but wonder about the people who lived inside. No, not the people. The family. We might be dysfunctional, but, in this short period of time, we'd become one. I felt happy and lucky and warm inside. I didn't want to leave. It broke my heart. But on a night as beautiful and clear as tonight, I couldn't help but be filled with the hope—no, the *knowing*—that everything was going to be okay.

@junipershoressocialite

Sharing bad behavior and delicious drama in North Carolina's most exclusive coastal zip code. DM with tips, pics, and juicy deets.

SEPTEMBER 17, 7:50 A.M.
33 Posts
10,444 Followers
31 Following

You didn't hear it from me, but . . .

PIC 1: This town really knows how to take up a cause. I've been told that the cries of #freebill heard all throughout town have really helped fortify the Sitterly family. Let's keep it going. Light your prayer candles, wear your crystals, spread a little sage. Goodness gracious, we sure do love it when this town comes together.

PIC 2: But let's be super honest: we also love it when this town falls apart. Speaking of falling apart . . . Could it be real? Could it be true? Are our beloved mommune members parting ways just days after their epic night out at Belle Epoque? A little birdie told us that one Julie Dartmouth is leaving to take care of *her* mommy. Where is Grace without Julie? And can stand-by-her-man Charlotte continue to stand in Juniper Shores without the mommune?

PIC 3: There's one person this might be good news for: Elliott, our man, with Alice's time freeing up, make your move! Pin her down . . . at your own risk. (Sure, we're #teamalice these days, but, come on . . . three dead husbands? Not a coincidence.)

PIC 4: Sophie Parker and Merit McDonald were all smiles at the Car Wash for a Cure last week. We're happy to report (okay, happy*ish*) that the trouble in paradise seems to have passed.

PIC 5: Well, we've always suspected that Iris Sitterly's BFF Ben Aldridge was somewhere on the continuum between crushing on and totally in love with the New York City import. But maybe we were wrong about all that. He's been spotted on more than one occasion with fellow freshman Lily Woods. Could a fall homecoming invite be far behind?

PIC 6: We're expecting a little extra partying this Saturday night after our seniors roll in to take their SAT one final time before sending out their college applications. We sure will miss this rowdy and beautiful bunch when they flee for the Ivys. As the great philosophers say: we hate to see them go, but we love to watch them leave.

TNT ('Til Next Test)

JUNIPER SHORES SOCIALITE

Vengeance

We all left that morning without speaking. That was a first, and I didn't like it, but I couldn't face everyone. I knew from experience that wasn't a good strategy. What if it was the last time I ever saw them? But I was embarrassed about my behavior. Why, why, why did I let my sister get to me like that? And, furthermore, why had I come so unglued at the idea of Julie leaving? If I had just told them the truth about Elliott right away, this all would have been better. We were house hunting, for heaven's sake. We had already looked at a cedar shake house three doors down from my current one, right on the beach, that was much smaller but perfectly appointed. I was obsessed. But Elliott had fallen in love with a sound-front white clapboard historic home with a slip for his beloved boat. We would probably choose one of them because they were both so great. Either way, Julie moving out was a solution to a problem for me.

I think I knew—but didn't want to admit—that it upset me so much because Julie was choosing Delia over me. Which was childish: Delia was Julie's *mother*. But there was no doubt that, of the five of us, Delia had been Daddy's favorite, which as a child I always felt really deeply. I was always trying to be the best for him, have his beer for him when he got home and his slippers by the door, so he would love me too. But he was always Delia's. Sure, as a forty-five-year-old woman, I could see that being the favorite of an abusive alcoholic was no great shakes. But that latent trauma is hard to overcome. And it had made me act ridiculous last night.

I sighed as I walked through the door of the church that always felt like it saved me from myself, and picked up the morning prayer bulletin that listed the relevant prayer book pages and provided the readings for the day.

Morning prayer was usually attended by maybe five or six parishioners—so few, in fact, that I always wondered how Father Matthew could justify it. But there was something soothing about the emptiness too. It was the exact opposite of the jubilant Sunday mornings where I got to sing and feel wrapped in the loving embrace of promises I couldn't see but believed all the same. Even after what I had been through, I believed them.

I sat down in my usual pew, the front row of the back section of the church. It was far away from the priest in these smaller services, but I liked it here, the sun streaming through the stained glass windows all around me. I felt safe here. I couldn't say that about many places.

Bonnie slid in beside me and patted my knee. "How you doing, sweetie?"

I scrunched my nose. "Honestly . . . I let my sister get to me last night, and I was not my best self," I whispered.

"We can't always be," she whispered back. "We're all just doing the best we can."

Leslie slid in beside Bonnie, looking flushed. As Father Matthew emerged from the side door and approached the sanctuary, she grinned at him like he held the key to her salvation. To my shock, he smiled back at her.

"Leslie, you dog!" I whispered. "Is your little plan working?"

She winked at me and pretended to shine her nails on the lapel of her jacket. Bonnie, Leslie, and I laughed quietly.

My phone buzzed in my purse; ordinarily I wouldn't have looked at it in church, but I was hoping it was something from Julie or Charlotte or Grace. Something that would build a bridge for us to walk over. Because I didn't know how to recover from last night. I clicked the text message notification and then the link inside it. The header on the webpage said: *The Capstone Fund.* Underneath were pictures and descriptions. I was confused.

I switched back to the text message box, where I saw this was from someone named Bradley. His message said: *This is the fund I was telling you about. Thoughts?*

It hit me that this wasn't my phone. It was Charlotte's. Shoot. I needed to get this to her. I knew I shouldn't, but I opened that webpage again; this must be where Charlotte was going to be working.

The top picture was a man who looked vaguely familiar. I spotted his name: *Daniel Isaacs.* I gasped and clicked the phone screen off as if he were going to come through it and get me.

"What's wrong?" Bonnie asked.

As if scolding us, Father Matthew cleared his throat and said, "Let us begin on page seventy-five in the Book of Common Prayer."

I opened my book, but I wasn't listening. I was thinking about that man's face. His name. Why someone was sending his information to Charlotte. My face felt hot. I couldn't quite put two and two together, but I knew that something was wrong here. I wanted to leave, but I didn't know what my next move would be. I was going to have to admit to Charlotte that I had looked at this. I needed answers.

But didn't Charlotte need them too? I thought about the ways in which I had lied to her, at least by omission. It wasn't right, and I knew I needed absolution. I knew I needed to tell her the truth. And I needed to apologize to Julie for questioning her decisions, which she, as a grown woman, had absolute authority over. I was only trying to help them, all of them. Could they see that? Would Charlotte see that? And, really, didn't I have some forgiving of my own to do? Weren't there a number of things—one in particular—that I was holding in my heart that weren't serving me?

I knew that holding grudges was like drinking poison and expecting the other person to die. I didn't want to drink poison, but I wanted what was right.

My mind shifted back to the present as the priest said, "Vengeance is mine."

I looked down at the bulletin. Had he really just said that? I scanned the reading. Yes, it appeared that he had.

Vengeance. I didn't think of myself as a vindictive person, but as I read ahead of Father Matthew, I felt antsy. I rolled the bulletin and put it in my purse, already imagining where I would hang this quote on my mirror. A lesson, a reminder when things got rough.

I felt rude leaving in the middle of the service, but I needed to be outside. I needed to talk to Charlotte. I needed to talk to Iris. I needed to get to the bottom of what I had just seen on that phone screen. I tapped Bonnie's arm and gestured to the door, mouthing, *I have to run.*

She looked concerned as I slid out. I took a deep breath as I stepped outside onto the brick walk, surrounded by azalea bushes, oak trees, and a weeping willow that had to be hundreds of years old. The way the light filtered through the canopy of old branches above me was one of my favorite things about this church. It felt like God was everywhere here, like you could smell him, see him, reach out and touch him.

I stood for a minute or so, savoring the warmth of the sun on my face and body, thinking about where I went next. Home. And then where? I had so many scores to settle today. What would I choose first? Worry welled in my chest. Was Charlotte hiding something from me? Was she in cahoots with a man who was the most painful part of an undeniably painful past?

As I walked to the car, I had the most uncomfortable feeling that someone was following me. The town streets were busy and crowded, so what made me think that? This was the price I paid for a life of trauma, of loneliness, of being left. Anxiety crept up on me at the oddest moments.

I tried to shake off the feeling. This was part of why I loved having a full house so much. I felt safe. Then again, more people came with more baggage, more scars, more risk. Maybe more than I had even considered. Yet as I drove through town, I felt like if I could just get home, all of these bad feelings would go away. If I had learned anything from years of living by the ocean, it was that even my biggest problems could—eventually—be washed away by the tide.

Charlotte

Gambling

I was surprised to see Oliver waiting for me in the parking lot of Montoya & Sons. I had dropped Iris—who still wasn't speaking to me—at school this morning, feeling somewhat uneasy about everything that had transpired last night. I knew that Alice breaking my news about New York was a mistake in a moment of passion, and that really I was to blame. I should have told Iris before saying anything to Alice. But Alice should have told us about Elliott. And Julie should have told us about her mother. I knew it was crazy to blame them for keeping secrets when I was keeping my own. I think, most of all, I felt unsteady today knowing that the place that had been my respite was falling apart.

Fortunately, throughout the course of my breakfast meeting with a client, I had managed to put all that behind me. Alice and I would talk it out. She'd told me how crazy her sister made her. It was all fine. We all had things to be embarrassed about.

Oliver walked over to my car, and I moved the book and makeup bag Iris had left so he could climb into the passenger seat.

"I just wanted to tell you that I'm going to be really busy for a couple of days." He sighed. "Discovery came in."

I felt my face scrunch. "Is everything okay?"

He nodded. "Sure. Fine. They are just burying me in boxes."

"Can I help?"

He smiled. "That's nice, but no." He paused. "I have a couple of interns who will help me."

Tears filled my eyes. This was it. The moment we had been waiting for. Do or die. Oliver had to find enough holes in the prosecution's evidence to get this thing dropped once and for all.

"Hey," I asked, just thinking of something. "Did you invest money with Bill?"

"Well, sure," he said.

"So you trust him?"

"Sure. Yeah, I trust him. And it's that trust and confidence that is going to lead me to the exact thing I need to get him out of this mess."

I desperately, desperately hoped that was true. Oliver's phone rang, and he looked down, then silenced it. "Hey, I need to run," he said.

As he opened the door, I said, "Hey, Oliver?"

"Yeah?"

"Could I have a list of the clients who lost money?"

He paused for a moment, and I could see him deciding, so I pressed. "Oliver, Bill and I are married. It's not like this is confidential from *me*."

He nodded. "I guess I don't really see why not." He paused. "But, Charlotte, I don't see how that's going to do you any good."

"I just need something to focus on. I'm especially worried about those people who gave him literally all their money. I mean, can you imagine? You give your whole retirement to Bill, and then—*poof!*—it's gone?"

He shook his head. "It's a damn shame. But it isn't Bill's fault."

"I know, but I just . . . I don't know. I feel like I could help."

"Okay," Oliver said. "If that's what you want to do then I'll support you."

"Oh! Oliver! The Capstone Fund." I filled him in on what Bradley had told me, and his eyebrows raised in a way that I recognized.

"You already knew," I said.

He winked at me. "I need to get started on getting your husband out of jail." Oliver's phone rang again, and he silenced it again as he turned away. "I'll email you the list when I can get it all together."

The list. Of people I would pay back. With my job in New York. I was suddenly swamped by sadness. What if it was months or even years before I was back under the same roof as my husband?

Sonja, our mail carrier, called, "Hey, Charlotte!" breaking me out of that awful thought.

"Hi!" I called back, shading my eyes, walking toward her through the parking lot. She handed me a fat stack of mail. "Thanks," I said.

She waved and was off, just as I noticed that the letter on the tippy top was for me. And it was addressed in handwriting I adored. I used to tell Bill how romantic I thought it would be to write love letters back and forth. How I wished I could take that back now. I didn't want to write our love story; I wanted to live it. I slid my finger under the seal and, right there on the sidewalk, started reading, as if it were a dessert I couldn't wait one more second to dive into.

Hello, my love,

Well, it has taken me all this time to save up enough to buy a stamp, paper, *and* an envelope. But I persevered and here we are. (Side note: how men manage to form prison relationships, afford the stationery to write back and forth, and marry when they are released, I'll never know.)

I don't know if I would properly call this a love letter—you know I'm not great at these things—but it is most certainly a thank-you letter. Thank you for loving me through all this hell. Thank you for believing in me and fighting for me even on the dark days. I wouldn't have made it through this ordeal without you, and every night, as I fall asleep, I imagine that I am holding you in my arms, like I used to, like I often took for granted. I will never take you for granted again. Or Iris. Or our wonderful life. We really do have it all, and I'm not sure I even realized it.

I love you more than words can say, and I am doing everything I can to get out of here and back to you, soon. So very soon. You are the world's greatest wife, and what I did to deserve you, I'll never know. But I'll spend the rest of my life reminding you how cherished you are. I promise.

All my love,
Bill

I wiped my eyes and put the letter back in the envelope, knowing that I would read it again and again and again. I wished briefly that Bill had saved his money for a tuna packet, but no. I needed this today. Even from inside, he was still taking care of me. And today, now, I would go into work, hold my head high, support our family, and take care of Bill the only way I could at the moment. Until he was back home with me again. Any day now, I hoped.

As I walked into Montoya & Sons, I realized I would miss the fluorescent lights and weird smell, the dingy carpet, and Gabe. And, yes, even Agnes. I was so grateful for them. They had stood by me and helped me when others turned their backs. And it surprised me how much I hoped, deep in my heart, that I got to stay.

Men 101

Ben was one of the only people in the world that I pretty much never felt awkward around. I mean, he was my best friend. He knew me better than anyone, so I never had to sit around and wonder if what I said was weird or if he took something the wrong way. And part of that was the beauty of guy friends in general. They didn't jump to being offended. They tended to give you the benefit of the doubt. So that was why, even when everything was falling apart, even when the world felt like it had turned against me, I thought of him, I wanted to run to him. Ben was my safe place; Ben never let me down. And I had realized in my exhausted, devastated haze: That meant something. That was *everything*. And I needed to let him know how much it meant to have someone who was always there for me.

Or, well, that was what I'd thought. That might not necessarily be the case today. Usually Ben met me outside, but I didn't see him this morning. So I stalked through the halls, avoiding the swarms of teenage bodies, and found him at his locker, outside his homeroom, talking to Lily Woods. She was flipping her hair, and I was surprised to find that I was suddenly, intensely jealous. Was Juniper Shores

Socialite right about them? Ugh. What if he asked her to homecoming? The idea made me nauseated.

I had woken up this morning feeling like I wanted to give things with Ben a shot. Yes, I was worried about losing our friendship. But maybe that wasn't a good enough reason to not see how things went between us. Plus, even though he hadn't come out and said he liked me, he kind of had. I mean, things were going to be weird between us now regardless. The fact that he hadn't waited for me outside this morning? Exhibit A.

"Hey," I said, coming up to the two of them. Lily was giggling, and her braces were hot pink and her uniform blouse was, in my opinion, so tight it made her look super desperate. It would have made me feel slightly better if she weren't totally rocking it.

"Hi, Iris!" she said.

"A Lily and an Iris," Ben said, smiling at her but definitely not me. Gag.

"Yeah. Flower names must have been in the year we were born," I said, aiming for a bored tone but sounding maybe a little shrill.

If Ben noticed, he didn't let on, because he didn't. Even. Look. At. Me.

"See you around," Lily said flirtatiously, giving him this little wave.

"Can't wait," he replied.

Can't wait? Fine. Be that way. Cool. I took back all the thoughts I'd had this morning about telling him I liked him.

Ben finally turned to me like it was paining him, and leaned his back against his locker dramatically like he was creating the maximum space between us.

"So, last night was crazy, huh?" I ventured.

"Yeah. I guess," Ben said. "Is that, like, your norm?"

He didn't seem worried for me or any of the usual friend things.

He almost seemed annoyed, like I had somehow caught him and trapped him in this with me. "No, Ben, it isn't the norm," I said. Now I was annoyed. "It's usually really fun. We, like, laugh a lot and stuff." He wasn't smiling at all, and I suddenly felt warm. "Is it hot in here?"

Normally he would have made a joke about me being hot, but instead he said, "Maybe you're getting Covid."

"Thanks." I smirked. "That's really helpful." Then I couldn't help myself. "What's with you? I know it was a weird night, but it was weird for me too. It's not my fault all the adults were acting like lunatics. And, if you'll remember, it was kind of traumatic on my end. It's not like I want to leave."

"You don't want to leave Merit," he said like he didn't care.

Fine. If he was going to be a jerk, then so was I. "No," I said. "I don't want to leave Merit. Or Emma. Or Brenna, Audrey, Jamie, Grace, Alice, or Julie." I looked at him pointedly, raised my voice, and said, "And up until this moment, I didn't want to leave *you!*"

Then I spun around and headed toward my history class, grateful that Ben and I didn't have it together. But *Lily* was in my class. I'd had basically no opinion about Lily until five minutes ago. And now I loathed her and her hot pink braces and her little streaks of gold fairy hair.

"Hello, Miss Sitterly," Mr. Baldwin, the history teacher, said. He was probably like my mom's age, not that old, but he wore these sweaters with leather patches on the elbows and horn-rimmed glasses and had this accent like he had been born in a movie about the South in the early 1900s.

"Hello, Mr. Baldwin," I said, dropping my heavy backpack with a thud and slumping down into a desk in the front row.

"Are you all right, Miss Sitterly?" he asked.

"Well, Ben said I looked like I was getting Covid, so maybe not."

"Oh my God! You have Covid!" piped up Annabelle, this really annoying girl beside me who looked like she was ten.

I rolled my eyes. "No, Annabelle. I obviously wouldn't come infect our entire class like some self-centered abomination."

She looked relieved.

"If you need to visit the nurse or the counselor, you have my permission," Mr. Baldwin said.

"I feel fine," I sulked. He probably thought I was having my period and needed to be examined by a woman. *Men.* I hated all of them today.

We were studying the Spanish flu outbreak during World War I, which was, honestly, not a super upbeat topic. Not helping my mood. And I noticed Annabelle scooting farther away from me, so it was obviously giving her Covid paranoia too.

I wanted to get out of here. It would be easy enough to fake being sick, but between classes I realized I didn't have my phone, and I couldn't call my mom. I went to meet up with Ben by our lockers, where we normally did, so I could call Mom from his phone, but he wasn't there. Maybe he was avoiding me. Maybe I was being paranoid. Then something hit me: *You're going to miss Merit.* That's what Ben had said. I gasped, standing there in the hallway. He had seen me kiss Merit. *That* was why he was so mad. He thought Merit and I were a thing now. The simplest thing would be to tell him the truth, that I'd had a crush on Merit and he had rejected me. But, come on, Men 101. They don't want you when they think no one else wants you.

I had to get to the third floor, where Merit's next class was. I couldn't be in love with him anymore, but he could still drive me around. Or maybe I could be in love with him as long as I was honest with myself that he would never love me back? I had a friend in New

York who was determined she was going to turn this guy straight, but that didn't seem to work really well, so I was going to let that be. Merit and I were friends. And housemates. And he was my chauffeur. And that was it.

I was super out of breath by the time I ran up a couple of flights of stairs to find him. "Merit," I gasped. "I need you to take me home." I took a deep breath.

"Now?"

"Yes. Now."

He shook his head. "Um, no."

"Please?" I whined. "I'm having a bad day, and I want to get out of here." The look on his face told me that wasn't compelling enough. "I thought you loved me, and we were best friends and mommune siblings."

He rolled his eyes. "I punched a *judge* for you, Iris. I've done my part."

I glared at him. "Merit, I'm trying to put my *family* back together. I would think if anyone in the world would understand that, it would be you."

"I care about your family, Iris, but I have mandatory football practice. If I get caught skipping school I can't go, and then I can't play on Friday."

The warning bell rang, meaning I had two minutes to get all the way to the first floor and into the A hallway. No way I was going to make it to my next class on time. I had one last shot. "Merit, Dad mentioned something last time I saw him, and I want to see if I can sneak into his office to dig around a little."

He raised his eyebrow. "Fine."

"Wait, seriously?"

He started walking.

"You won't just skip school, but you'll commit, like, a felony with me?"

"I have to."

"And why is that?"

"Because no one is going to arrest *me* two days before the West game." He stopped and gave me a once-over. "You'd be in juvie for sure."

As I followed Merit out into the parking lot, the sun on my face feeling like freedom, I realized something: I'd lied to bust out of here. But now I was going to have to follow through. I stood up straighter and took a deep breath. I was going to be a hero today. Merit and I were going to save my dad.

Sharing bad behavior and delicious drama in North Carolina's most exclusive coastal zip code. DM with tips, pics, and juicy deets.

SEPTEMBER 17, 11:18 A.M.
34 Posts
10,516 Followers
32 Following

You didn't hear it from me, but . . .

PIC 1: What will-they/won't-they couple was seen skipping school together? None other than Merit McDonald and Iris Sitterly. Cover your ears, folks. This will be the Sophie scream heard round the world.

PIC 2: Word on the street is that it's getting close to judgment day. Bill Sitterly's trial is forthcoming, and, well, inquiring minds want to know: Does the prosecution have enough dirt . . . uh . . . we mean *evidence* to keep him? Or will our cries of #freebill finally be heard?! (If there was ever a place for an interrobang, this is it.)

PIC 3: We heard it from a friend who heard it from a friend who heard it from a friend that . . . Elliott P. has hired a realtor?! Is he selling his house and moving into the mommune with the other families? Is Alice moving out? Is this the end of the mommune as we know it? If so, we do *not* feel fine.

PIC 4: Maybe most important of all, has anyone else heard that running back Paul Hartford got ISS? *For pantsing someone in PE?* And now he can't play on Friday? Principal Windsor, *come on*. That's a prank, not a crime. Let the boy play! We can't get that West win without him!

TNT ('Til Next Touchdown)

JUNIPER SHORES SOCIALITE

Charlotte

~~~~~~~~

Approved Person

All day I'd had this weird, unavoidable feeling that things were just *off*. Of course they were. My husband was in jail. The discovery had come in. To top it off, I was still feeling a little weird about everything that had gone down at the mommune last night. And how Oliver said he'd be out of touch for a few days. And the heaviness of thinking about the potential New York move and what that could mean. And, of course, I hated when my daughter was mad at me. I was very much of the school of thought that I was her mother and not her best friend, but still. I liked it when she was happy. Anyway, anxiety increases anxiety, right?

I went to get my phone between clients to text her. I wouldn't apologize necessarily. Not yet. I'd go with something sort of neutral. Maybe, *Want to grab burgers tonight after practice?* Something that would make her happy (because it wasn't vegan!) but not suggest that I was sucking up. I rustled around in my bag for a minute before it hit me: I had left my phone at home. I looked at the time in the corner of my computer screen. I had twenty minutes until my next client. I could probably make it. If I was really efficient, maybe I could even grab a coffee too.

As I drove, I thought about the day in the bank when Alice had taken me back to the house, when she'd asked us to live with her. What if I had said no? Would we have been better off? But no. Look at all the good that had come from that one chance meeting. I had made three friends who'd changed my life, and Iris and I had had a place to lick our wounds while we got back on our feet. One bad dinner wasn't going to make me second-guess everything.

I ran up the back steps to the mommune and flung the door open, calling, "Alice! Grace! Julie!" No answer. I grabbed the leather pouch on the hall table where we stowed our phones. My phone wasn't there— but Iris's was. Along with another one that I thought was potentially Alice's, but I wasn't positive. That was weird. Maybe she had accidentally taken mine. "Shit!" I said out loud. "I knew I shouldn't have given in to that dumb rule."

I ran up the stairs into Alice's room. "Alice!" No one answered. I looked around and peeked out on the porch. No Alice. Where *was* she?

As I glanced around her room, scanning the surfaces to make sure my phone hadn't somehow gotten up here, something caught my eye: a church bulletin stuck in the mirror above the dresser. A line had been highlighted: *Vengeance is mine.*

Vengeance. Good Lord. That was creepy. Was Alice *that* mad at her sister?

I shook my head, snapping myself out of it. Alice was always leaving her church bulletins around. She never missed a service, it seemed, and she often highlighted passages that spoke to her. This wasn't new.

I was shocked at how completely helpless I felt without my phone. I had lived my first fifteen years without one just fine. And I really hated that Iris didn't have hers. I liked knowing that I could reach her.

I ran into my room to grab my laptop. I could at least text from that.

I composed a text to Iris (who I knew didn't have her phone), Merit, and Emma: *Hey, kiddos. My phone is MIA and Iris's is at the house. I'll take my laptop to work so you can text if you need me, but call me at work when you get home!*

I copied and pasted the same text to myself just in case Iris had my phone.

I glanced at my texts quickly in the iMessage icon on my laptop, noticing one from Bradley. It wasn't highlighted as unread, but I knew I hadn't seen it. I opened the link to the Capstone Fund and glanced through their directors. I didn't know any of them. I mean, I recognized Dan Isaacs from Bill talking about him, but that was it. As I was reading his bio, an email notification from Oliver popped up in the right-hand corner of the screen.

I clicked down to my email. The body said: Client list and amounts. Oliver's email signature was underneath.

As soon as I opened the file, my heart started racing. I hated seeing these names in black and white, knowing that these people's lives had been ruined—or at least changed. I knew how that felt. Then I gasped. I looked away from the screen, and then back down. This couldn't be right. She would have told me, wouldn't she? We couldn't have gone this long in our relationship with a secret this big. I felt light-headed, swimmy, my mind careening up hills and around curves. Maybe it was a coincidence. Maybe I was seeing things. I looked down at my screen again, and there it was, in bold black type.

Bailey, Alice, Juniper Shores, NC

"What?" I said quietly, out loud. "This can't be true."

I wasn't even sure why, but between my missing phone and the "vengeance is mine" verse in her room and this news that surely ought to have come up over the past couple of weeks, my chest started to feel tight. Was the vengeance against *us*?

For now, I had to set all that aside. I had a client meeting in eight minutes, and it would take me six to get back to the office. I picked up my laptop and walked down the stairs and out the door, feeling, for the moment, grateful to get out of this house. As I got in the car, I questioned why Alice wouldn't have told me about this. And that made me wonder if Iris and me coming to live here wasn't a coincidence at all.

Iris

~~~~~~~~

Half-Day

"So, where exactly are we going?" Merit asked.

"Do you know where my dad's office is? Beside Trader Joe's?"

Merit eyed me. "Is this just a ploy to get you that weird flavored popcorn you like?"

"It isn't weird!" I protested. "And if I didn't know you were gay, I would think that remembering that little tidbit meant you loved me."

As we neared my dad's office, I said, "Go around the back so no one will see us." When we did, I immediately recognized the car parked there—and the man inside it.

Oliver rolled his window down, giving me a scolding look. I tried not to look sheepish in return. "Hey, Oliver," I said casually. "Just doing a Trader Joe's run."

"Uh-huh," he said. "You know you can't go in there. There isn't anything important left inside anyway."

I sighed. "I know. I *know*. I just keep thinking that if I can get in there and look around, I could find *something*." I paused. "Wait. If we can't go in, what are you doing here?"

He smiled. "I keep thinking the same thing you're thinking—even though I well know that illegally obtained evidence is inadmissible in court."

I did *not* know that.

Oliver looked around. "Hey, Iris. I wanted to tell your mom that I got your locks changed, but I can't get her on the phone."

I eyed him. "Wait. Our locks changed? So, does that mean we can go home?" I felt excitement rising into my throat.

"Oh, um," Oliver stuttered. I could see him realizing that he'd stepped in something. I just wasn't quite sure what it was.

"Oliver . . ."

"Well, technically, yes, but I don't think I was supposed to—"

I let out a Sophie-level squeal. That was actually a new term around school. I jumped out of the car and hugged Oliver as best I could through the window. "You are my favorite person in the entire world!"

He patted himself on the back. "I know. I know."

"So I can go, like, now?"

Oliver looked at me sternly. "Iris, you may not go without your mother. Do you understand me? She gets to make the decision about when you go home."

"But—" I started to protest.

Oliver looked at the clock on his dash. "It's eleven forty-five. Shouldn't you two be in school?"

"Half-day," Merit and I said simultaneously.

Oliver made a skeptical grunting sound.

"Thank you, Oliver! I'm so excited!"

I got back in the car, and Merit muttered, "So, I assume we aren't going to tell your mom, but that we are going to your house right now."

I patted his shoulder and whispered, "It's like we have one mind."

Merit sighed. "Well, on the bright side, there's very little chance I'll be arrested."

"Never say never," I said. "The day is young."

Walking into my own house—with my own key instead of breaking in through the window—was like Christmas Day and getting invited to prom by a senior and the day the little crispy chocolate Cadbury eggs hit the drugstores all at once. Merit and I stood in the entrance hall, staring through the paneled living room and dining room and all the way to the beach. I inhaled deeply. So, no, it didn't smell like my house after being closed up for so long. But it was my house. I was home. I tried not to let the thought of what Alice had said at dinner last night ruin my moment. And I *really* tried to block out the thought that some creepy potential convict slash murderer had been in here. Even still, I shivered.

"You okay?" Merit asked.

I nodded, but I was kind of lying. I was scared. Did I even want to live here now?

"Glad they changed the locks," I said.

Merit was really still. He seemed scared too, which bugged me. I needed him to be my rock. "Can we go back to school now?" he whispered.

"No," I whispered back. I walked up the stairs, into my dad's office.

The lone broker's statement that the man in the mask had dropped that night was still sitting on the edge of the desk. I picked it up, and my heart started pounding in my chest. Dad had mentioned Artemis, Mallick, and Capstone. And this statement, *my* statement, here in my hand, was from the Capstone Fund. That had to mean something.

I walked with purpose toward my room and opened the drawer on the side of my desk that—much to my relief—still contained four file folders. One was marked *Report Cards,* one said *Iris Statements,* the third was *Homecoming Looks,* and the last said *Vision Board.* That was for the things I cut out from magazines that inspired me and saved to put on my huge corkboard over my desk when I had time in my very busy schedule.

The folder that I was most interested in was the statements one. Dad gave me my broker statement and my personal statement every single month, and part of our deal was that I had to go through them to see where my money was going and get a feel for his end of the job. I might or might not have followed through on my end of the bargain. Which was why I put the statements I hadn't actually looked at in the *Homecoming Looks* folder, and only kept the ones I'd reviewed and highlighted in *Iris Statements.* I didn't think Dad would ever look, but better safe than sorry. Free money was amazing, and I didn't want to stop the gravy train.

"What are we doing?" Merit asked.

The *Iris Statements* folder was empty. "Oh my gosh," I said. "It's empty! That guy, whoever he was, was stealing my statements!"

"What guy?"

I felt too crazed to answer. Lucky for me—and unlucky for the burglar—most of the good stuff wasn't filed in the right place anyway.

"Here," I said, handing Merit a stack of personal statements from my *Homecoming Looks* folder. "See if you can find any from the Capstone Fund."

He sat down on my bed. "Yeah. Here's one."

"Put them in a separate pile."

He rolled his eyes and sighed, and I got to work on the broker's statements, sorting on my end too.

"Okay," I said. "So, like, on my July statement, what is the total for the Capstone Fund?"

"It says $716.25."

I looked down at the broker's statement from July. "Damn," I said, "$716.25."

"Why 'damn'? What are we looking for?"

"Um. I have no idea."

We both burst out laughing.

"Okay," he said, "here's June." I found my corresponding June statement as Merit said, "Fifteen shares, $723.15."

I stopped and looked up at him. "Wait. What did you say?"

"Fifteen shares, $723.15."

I looked down at the paper in my hand. "The broker's statement says 12.75 shares at $723.15."

"Okay," he said. "A typo maybe?"

I couldn't answer him. My mind was holding on to all these different thoughts and remembering my dad saying that some of the Capstone Fund's statements were off. Something was happening here. I just wasn't sure what it was yet.

"Look at, like, December of last year."

He rifled through his papers, and I rifled through mine.

"Ten shares at $436.70," he said.

I gasped and looked up at him. "Mine says 8.5 shares at $436.70."

"So what does that mean?" he asked.

I still didn't know. I motioned at him. "I don't have my phone. I need yours!" I did a quick Google search of the correct price per share of the Capstone Fund from June, and from December. Then I started talking out loud. "Okay. So, basically, what is coming on the investor statements from the Capstone Fund is correct. The share price and the share number reflect each other. But on the broker-facing side, the total is the same, but the number of shares is . . . well, it's less." I gasped again. "That's why that guy was stealing my statements!"

I felt wild and panicked and thrilled all at once. "You have to take me back to the mommune to get my phone. I have to get Oliver."

Merit nodded and gripped my forearm. "Iris, I don't totally understand what's happening here, but you have to calm down a little—or at least explain it to me."

"The Capstone Fund was the one forging client statements, not my dad. And I'm pretty sure I just proved it."

Alice

~~~~~~~~~~

Backfired

I don't know when the anxiety started, exactly. It certainly intensified after Jeremy died. I'd wake up in the night, sweating, panting after having dreams of trying to save him, of that moment he stepped onto the gondola to go up the mountain, the last minute I ever saw him. What if I had kissed him goodbye one more time, and he had missed the ride? What if, instead of veering left at the top of the mountain, he had veered right? Had he fallen? Hit his head? Died right away? Had he screamed for help, suffered, suffocated? I always felt like that was closure I needed, but, then again, maybe knowing would only have made it worse.

That said, this feeling of being followed wasn't a new one, I thought as I walked down the beach, trying to clear my head. Neither was the idea that every time I went to church, every time I did a good deed, I was working off a little bit of my sin. Or, in a larger sense, that maybe I was making people see that all those things they said about me weren't true. I often wondered: If they knew just how much it hurt, would they continue?

If I looked deep down, maybe that was the impetus for starting the mommune. Certainly, I did want to help my niece and her kids. And

I wanted to help sweet Merit and Emma. But I also wanted the town to see how kind I was, how giving, that I hadn't killed my husbands for their insurance money or whatever they thought. How could a woman who opened her home to people in need do that?

But then, of course, that had backfired. And rumors about the sinister things going on within our four walls started.

I climbed the steps from the beach and opened the door. I put Charlotte's phone back in our storage spot and grabbed my own.

"Hello!" I called as I walked inside. No answer. Grace must be at the grocery store. She went to the grocery store every day. I was a make-a-list-and-go-once-and-get-it-over-with kind of shopper—well, back when I used to do the shopping. I guessed that was another thing I'd have to get used to doing on my own again.

I went upstairs and walked into my bedroom, glancing at the church bulletin in the corner of my mirror. Today had soothed me. When people found out, when people knew I had not retaliated against Bill when I found out that he had stolen more than half of my last husband's money, the money I had invested with him—no, the money I had *begged* to invest with him—surely they would see how giving I was and it would clear my name. Bill was a New York broker with a big reputation. He was notoriously hard to get in with, so when he called saying that someone I was certain I didn't actually know had suggested he call me, I had jumped at the chance to become one of his only Juniper Shores clients; I had even boasted about it to friends. I had felt so proud that the famous Bill Sitterly had deemed me worthy of his skills.

Man, that had backfired. But I had done nothing. I had remained calm in the face of losing what was most of my retirement. Not only that, but I had taken in Bill's wife and child. Surely people would see that, and I would be vindicated. I couldn't wait for that day.

I put my shoes in my closet, trying to ignore what I had seen on Charlotte's phone. It wasn't like I didn't know my first father-in-law had a hedge fund. It wasn't like every now and then I didn't google Jeremy's parents to see what was going on in their lives. Over the years, they had started a scholarship in Jeremy's name, named a tennis court for him at a park, had a tree lit at the hospital in his honor. Never once had they invited me to celebrate and remember him. That hurt almost as much as losing him. Why had they just abandoned me?

But what I couldn't figure out now was why someone had sent Charlotte Dan's fund information. Did they know each other? And, if so, did Dan know Charlotte was living with me? Was Dan up to something? I decided that I needed to put those thoughts aside. Grace had offered, but maybe I would go pick the little girls up from school. Nothing brightened my day quite like their three cheerful voices chittering and chattering about every detail of their days.

As I came down the stairs, anxious to text Grace to tell her, I heard a knock on the back door. I didn't even think; I just opened it, wide and fast and free like the world had never hurt me, like I'd never been a victim, like I'd never been tricked or taken advantage of. I was used to the safety of all these people under one roof; I was used to knowing that I had somewhere to turn.

Did I recognize the man at the door instantly? I'm honestly not sure. But what I do know for certain is that, the minute I saw him, the world went black.

I don't know how long it was before I realized that I was on the floor, how long it was before I willed myself to scream. But I trusted him, didn't I? Was I sick? Was I dead? I had a vague notion that a man's hands were trying to lift me up.

But that could just be the dreams again. Some days I had to stay in that other world to get by. Some days I had to tell myself lies to get out of bed. When you live like that, sometimes it's hard to know what's just another figment of your imagination and what's the truth.

"Alice," a voice I would have known anywhere said. It was gravelly and deep with a touch of Southern drawl. It was a voice I heard often in my dreams. But right now, for some reason, I didn't want to sink into it, didn't want to stay with it.

"Please wake up, please wake up, please wake up," I said three times out loud, as if I were Dorothy in *The Wizard of Oz*. If that didn't work, maybe I should try *There's no place like home* next. I was looking up at the ceiling, trying to avoid the face that was so close to mine, the minty breath, the scent of salt and musk that I remembered somewhere deep in the recesses of my mind. Because this wasn't real. It couldn't be real.

"Alice, you're awake. You have to believe me. You are awake already. I know it must be kind of a shock, but this is happening."

I shook my head back and forth, my skull pressing into the hardwood. "It's not happening because you are dead!" I screeched the word *dead* a little louder than I meant to. I searched my mind for explanations. One thing was clear: Jeremy wasn't alive. So, either I was asleep, *I* was dead, or this was an impersonator who looked a lot like him.

But as he pulled me into a sitting position, he said, "You did it, Al. You bought our house. I can't believe it." He put his hand over his heart. I had never told anyone that we had dreamed of buying this house together.

As he pulled me into him, as I felt my body go limp with fear and dread and maybe a little relief, I knew it was him. Every cell in my body recognized that this was Jeremy, my love, my husband, the one I had pined for every day for eighteen years. "I love you," he said in my ear. I realized he was crying. "I've loved you all this time, and I've been counting down the moments until I could come back here to get you."

"Jeremy," I whispered, breathing him in. I closed my eyes to savor the smell of him, the feel of him, his beating heart, his living body. Maybe I couldn't reconcile what was happening, but all the same, tears of relief poured down my face. This was obviously a dream, but it was a good one; it was a dream I wanted to stay inside of.

I grasped his shirtsleeves, balling them in my hands, trying to figure out whether he was actually flesh and blood and here.

I pulled away. This was completely inexplicable. I was torn because I wanted to relish the feel of him, the sound of him, but I needed answers. It was too much to handle. "I don't understand. You died. In an avalanche. I was there. I was at your funeral. I have cried and mourned you for eighteen years." I paused. "Your mother and I send each other flowers every year on the day of your death and your birthday. You are dead, Jeremy."

He shook his head. "Oh, Mom. So dramatic."

It wasn't dramatic for a mother to remember her son's birth and death days. Finding my strength, feeling like I needed to be in a position of power, I stood up, still weak and woozy. Weak and woozy but undeniably awake. It wasn't dramatic for a mother to do that unless . . . "Your mother knew you were alive." Not a question.

He stood up too and tried to pull me back to him, but I pushed away. He scratched his chin. "Well, baby, see, I was in a little bit of trouble. I got mixed up in some bad deals with some bad guys, and this was the only way we could figure to get me out of it. You understand."

I was aghast. "I what? No, I'm sorry. I do not *understand*." I paused, thinking. "Jeremy, that avalanche was real. Other people died in it."

I hated how gleeful he looked. "I know! I couldn't have planned it any better. We weren't planning for me to disappear that day, but it was the perfect out." He hesitated. "Look," he said, "I will explain everything later. But for right now, we need to go. I have a plan. We can restart our lives together."

Now I was really confused. "What are you talking about?"

He put his hand to his forehead. "Sorry. I'm just so excited to see you that I'm jumping all over the place." He wrapped me in his arms again and planted a kiss on my lips. I was so unsuspecting that I let him. "There's so much to do, Al. We can get our life back."

We can get our life back. The idea was so tempting. For the briefest second, I could pretend that we were picking up where we left off, that I was a new bride, and I was finally going to get my happily-ever-after with the man I had fallen head over heels for when I was just a girl. So, no, maybe he hadn't exactly been the man I thought he was. But who was when you got right down to it? Weren't we all different from what we seemed?

Even in my haze, I thought of Elliott. Thinking of him gave me pause. I wasn't in a rational enough head space to think clearly about what Jeremy being alive meant for me, for our future, for what came next. But rational or no, I did have the feeling that I didn't want to be apart from Elliott. Then again, if Jeremy was really back, wouldn't I have to at least try to make things work with him? I was so confused. *And surely I'm dreaming. Right?*

Jeremy took my hand and led me over to the dining room table. We both sat down. He looked around and said, "Wow. You really did it, babe. I just wish we could stay here."

I took a deep breath. *Focus, Alice.* It was starting to occur to me that a man who had faked his death and had obviously been in hiding for nearly two decades was maybe not *stable.* Not even stable-ish. I needed to get him out of here—but my curiosity got the better of me. And, even more than that, I had pined for this man for most of my adult life. I loved him. Even if I wanted to, I couldn't just walk away now.

"And why can't we stay here?"

"Well, we're going to have to leave the country." He did this little half-snort. "I'm technically dead, if you hadn't heard."

"Where will we go?" I asked. I obviously wasn't going *anywhere* with him. But as it was sinking in that he was actually here, I was beginning to be afraid of him. I needed to keep him here. Someone would come home eventually. Someone could help. If I got in a car with him . . .

"Panama," he said. "We'll eventually get you a new identity, but you're fine for now."

He said it like this was just so ordinary, like I was going to say, *Sure, honey, I'd love to hop a plane to another country and change my identity.* Well, if he'd been doing this for the past two decades, maybe it did feel ordinary to him. The thought sent a shiver up my spine. I had to stall. I couldn't leave this house with him. Who knew what he was capable of?

"So where have you been all this time?" I asked as breezily as I could muster. "Panama?"

"Panama for a bit, the Caymans, Brazil." He paused. "It worked pretty well because I was able to get a new identity—passport, the works—and manage offshore accounts for my dad."

That was when the nausea set in. Dan Isaacs and Capstone and Charlotte and Bill were swirling around in my head. Jeremy was the missing connector here. I just couldn't figure out exactly how.

"Have you been home to Juniper Shores at all?"

"I've been back now and then, yeah. Mostly because I was dying to see you."

Recognition washed over me. "So I'm not crazy! I *have* been seeing you!"

He laughed and reached out for my hand. I wanted to snatch it away, but I couldn't quite say why. Hadn't I dreamed that this impossibility was somehow possible? And now, here we were. "Sorry about that." He grimaced. "I'm not going to sugarcoat it, Al. Seeing you with other men hurt."

I squinted at him. I wanted to say, *I planned your funeral*, but I didn't want to get off track. "So you've been working for your dad?" I asked like we were estranged lovers just catching up.

"Yeah. But, well . . ." He bit his lip.

And suddenly, a switch flipped inside me. Whoever this man was, he wasn't that kind, sandy-haired kid I'd fallen in love with. Maybe he never had been what he seemed. But a couple of decades and a lot of life experience had lent me the clarity to see that whatever was going on here wasn't okay. And I needed to know every detail of it.

This was a part I had to play. I reached out and took his hand. "Jerbear, you can tell me anything. You know that. I'm your safe place."

I used to say this to him when we were kids, when we were just starting out. The words soured in my mouth now. I was trying not to be sick.

"Well, I might be in a little trouble, babe. And I need to get out of here before my dad finds out."

That was when I knew for sure: whatever Bill Sitterly was in prison for was actually Jeremy's fault. All the threads of my life were joining together, crossing. The patterns were repeating, the layers folding in on themselves. Somehow, even though I thought I'd moved so far past Jeremy and that life, he was back here. He was, quite possibly, responsible for this new chapter. I didn't know how to fix it, how to make it right. So for now, I would ask as many questions as I could. I would remember every detail. And I might just free Bill after all.

Overeager

I grabbed my backpack out of Merit's back seat. "Thanks, buddy!" I said, flashing a grin at him. "Now go back to school so you can practice, and we can beat West!"

"You know, you could come back with me. Potentially save yourself from in-school suspension?"

Nervous butterflies invaded my stomach. I'd never even gotten detention before, much less ISS. But I needed my phone; I needed to call Oliver. If ISS was the trade-off for saving my dad, well then, I would get it a million times over. I waved Merit off and turned toward the house.

The garage door was open, so instead of going up the outside steps, I walked inside and in the back door of the bottom floor, which had a little half bath and a full mudroom. I was in a huge hurry, sure. But I also had to pee.

But voices from upstairs distracted me. I walked quietly up the first leg of the zigzag stairway and stopped on the landing where I could see Alice, at the head of the table, sitting with a man. They both had their backs to me.

I heard Alice say, "And how does all that relate to Bill Sitterly?"

My eyes popped open wide, and I barely managed to stifle my gasp. I crouched down on the landing, where I knew from lots of hide-and-seek with the girls that they wouldn't be able to see me from the table.

"Well, because they were mostly his clients who I was, well . . ."

"Stealing from?" Alice asked.

"No, no, no. Not at all," the man said.

Shit. Shit. Shit. My phone was up there. I didn't know what this was, but I needed to be recording it. Who was this man? And was Alice in on whatever this was? I could try to write down what he was saying. That would be better than nothing. As I stuck my finger between the two zippers in the top of my backpack and started easing one down silently, it hit me: my burner phone! I had a burner phone! I could record this!

I dug around as quietly as possible. The man was saying, "My intention was never to steal from them. And that was the beauty of the situation."

I grabbed the phone and hit record just as he said, "See, they would invest in a share of Capstone. I would move nine-tenths into the actual fund and one-tenth into my shadow account." He paused. "I was buying options to mirror the return of the Capstone Fund, but actually making *more* than the fund. So the clients were getting their fair share, and I was pocketing the difference."

I scrunched my nose. What, now? I was glad I wasn't taking notes because this sounded complicated, and I wasn't sure I would get it right.

"Okay," Alice said. "So the clients were actually making what they were supposed to make, but you were kind of skimming off the top?"

"Exactly," he said. "So it wasn't stealing."

"Sure," she said. "Definitely not stealing."

I rolled my eyes and shifted just a little. Squatting on the landing behind the stair post wasn't exactly comfortable.

"I created an algorithm to mirror the returns, and it worked ninety-eight percent of the time. And who was going to notice the two percent? As it turns out, no one. Not for, like, ten years."

"So you were making a lot of money off of this?" Alice asked.

My thoughts exactly. I realized that we were in the middle of an all-out confession here. Yeah, my phone was recording, but this might be a good time to get the police involved. I opened a message over the recorder and typed in my mom's number. She had messaged Merit that she didn't have her phone, but I knew her iMessage was probably up. At least, I hoped. *Mom!!! Call 911 to the mommune right now!!*

Then I clicked back to the voice recorder. Still on. We were good.

"Over the ten years, I was saving every single month in the hopes that one day I'd have enough to come here, sweep you off your feet, and get you to run away with me."

Um. Plot twist. What? My heart started beating really fast. This was someone who loved Alice? And if so, what did that mean about her involvement?

She put her hand on his. "That is so sweet."

Um. No. Framing my dad is not sweet at all.

"Wait," Alice said, "so are *you* the one who recommended Bill call me to invest with him?"

"Yes!" This man, whoever he was, sounded so enthusiastic. "Then that way I could make us extra money off of our money."

Our money. Huh.

"Everything was going great with the plan, but I got a little over-eager because, well, I was getting really good at beating the fund's return, so I started taking a little more and a little more. Twelve percent, fifteen percent."

I thought back to my math. I didn't have the full picture yet, but that was what was happening in my account!

"Then these strange economic conditions exposed my algorithms and, well, I lost a lot. A whole lot. Enough that I couldn't fake it anymore."

Alice leaned in and said, so sweetly, "So what did you do then, sweetheart?"

He smiled at her in a way that turned my stomach. Who *was* this man? And what about Elliott? A very uncomfortable feeling washed over me.

"I had always forged the client statements, obviously. So when the accounts lost money, it wasn't like the clients were going to call my dad or someone at Capstone. They were going to call the broker."

"Like Bill Sitterly?"

"Exactly."

"Okay, right. But wouldn't it be easy to figure out that all this led to you?"

"Eventually," he said. "But I was the whistleblower. I called the SEC about Bill Sitterly, and, for the moment, they have enough evidence that it at least looks like he was the one who stole the money." He cleared his throat. "Which is why we need to go now, Al. We have to leave the country before they start digging deeper and realize it wasn't Bill after all."

She nodded sincerely. "But, why, sweetheart? It seems to me that you covered your tracks. Let's just stay here and let Bill pay for your crimes."

My jaw dropped. Who *was* this woman? I didn't know Alice Bailey at all. The man turned his head toward her fully, and I realized something: I might not have known Alice but I knew that man. I tapped over to my photos to compare. Sure, I couldn't see his whole face. But that wavy hair, those green eyes, the crease in his forehead—that was the man in my house. I was sure of it.

He sighed deeply. "I had been doing this for so long that I got a little sloppy. I forgot to forge a few of the broker's statements and put the real number of shares the clients were purchasing on there." He paused. "It wasn't a huge deal. Dad and Bill have worked together for so long, no one ever checked—or, well, the time or two Bill noticed, it was easy to shrug it off. Although I accidentally did it to his daughter's account a few times. I guess he didn't notice those."

"Iris!" Alice said.

He nodded. "Yeah, I guess. After the raid at his office, I broke into his home office to find the broker statements, go through and figure out which ones I needed to fix. But his computer was already gone. I don't know what made me even look in the girl's room, but jackpot!" He paused. "Even so, if the SEC has copies of those statements, they'll figure it out. Probably, anyway. So that's why we have to go."

I wished I could text Oliver, but I didn't have his number saved in my burner phone, and I didn't have it memorized.

I was getting really uncomfortable from all this squatting, and I still had to pee, but I was so afraid if I made a sound, I would give myself away. Plus, I was *furious* at Alice. Just let my dad rot in jail? For something he didn't do?

My heart was beating wildly because I had a recorded confession. This would save my dad. I knew it would. So now I had to figure out how to get out of here as quietly as possible. Before I could, the door beside Alice flew open. My mom appeared, screaming "Iris!" And all my worries about a discreet getaway suddenly disappeared. Mom had arrived. She would take it from here.

Be My Guest

Call 911 is probably the worst text you could get from your child. It's at least in the top ten. Poor Addie Walker, one of Juniper Shores' most lauded matriarchs, was sitting across from me discussing which pieces of jewelry she had gifted to her children and therefore no longer needed to keep on her insurance policy, when Iris's text dinged to my laptop.

I picked up the office phone and said, "I'm so sorry, Mrs. Walker! We're going to have to do this later," while dialing 911.

When calling 911, one should know one's emergency when asked. I did not. In fact, I didn't even know the number that had texted me. But I wasn't going to wait to find out if it was some sort of unfunny hoax. "I need police to Four Twenty-Seven Ocean Avenue right away. Hurry, please!"

And then I hung up and, grabbing my purse in one swift motion, threw my pumps to the floor and ran out the door as fast as my bare feet would carry me. I was so panicked I felt light-headed and, for sure, should not have been driving. I laid on my horn, ran a stoplight, and drove a solid twenty miles an hour over the speed limit the entire way home. I had to get to Iris.

A car I didn't recognize pulled into the driveway right behind me, but I didn't wait to see who it was. I ran up the stairs, threw open the door, and screamed, "Iris!"

"I'm here, Mom!" she called, her head popping up from the downstairs landing. I ran to her, threw my arms around her, and covered her in kisses. "Are you okay? What is going on?"

Before she had time to explain, there was a knock on the already open door, and a voice behind me said, "FBI."

My stomach flipped as I turned to look at the man who had spoken. What in the world could be happening *now*? It was only then that I noticed Alice sitting at the dining room table with a man who was now scrambling up from his seat.

"Jeremy Isaacs," the agent said, holding up his FBI badge, "you're under arrest."

I had no idea who this person was, but even without knowing him, I could read his face. *Try to run? Stay and face the music?* As if on cue, sirens rang out from what sounded like both ends of the street.

"Son," the agent said, "let's do this the dignified way."

Jeremy looked at Alice. "I love you. I'm so sorry. We were so close to being together again."

Alice looked mystified.

A group of firefighters—our town's first responders—came to the door as the FBI agent was saying, "You have the right to remain silent . . ."

"Are we okay here?" one asked.

I looked at Iris. "Are we okay here?"

She nodded, and Alice ran over to hug her. Iris pushed her away. "No way. You were just going to let my dad rot in jail? Take the fall?"

I felt my brow furrow.

"Iris, oh my gosh, no!" Alice exclaimed. "I was saying anything

I could to get Jeremy to talk. I was trying to memorize every single thing he said so that I could tell the FBI and get your dad out."

Iris raised one eyebrow at Alice. "Are you sure?"

"Honey, yes. I was playing a part." She paused. "I have been through a lot in my life, and that was the scariest thing yet. The man *faked* his death. No, I was definitely not planning to run off to Panama with him. I was trying to stall because I was afraid if he got me in his car, he'd kill me."

Before Iris could say anything else, another FBI agent strode through the door.

"Ms. Bailey, we're going to need to ask you some questions."

She nodded. "That's fine. I will try to tell you what he told me, but I can promise you on my life I thought that man was dead."

"Wait. What?" I asked.

Iris stepped forward and handed the agent her phone. "I recorded his confession here." She grinned at me. "My dad is Bill Sitterly, and this definitely proves his innocence. And if that isn't enough, I have the paperwork to back up all of Mr. Isaacs's claims." She was practically singing.

My head was spinning. "What is happening? Who was that?"

"My dead first husband," Alice said.

I gasped, remembering something. "Jeremy Isaacs. Dan Isaacs's son?" I pointed to Iris. "He set Dad up?" I was just guessing.

"Ms. Bailey, Miss Sitterly," the agent said, "I think we need to talk."

"Not without an attorney present!" I chimed in.

"Why?" Iris asked. "It's not like we did anything wrong."

"Doesn't matter," I said. "Wait until Oliver gets here."

"Oh!" Alice said. "I accidentally grabbed your phone this morning. I put it back in the pouch."

I walked over to the leather pouch and retrieved my phone,

hugging it to me, then dialed Oliver. When he answered, I said, "I have no idea what is going on, but you need to get to the mommune stat."

"So does this mean my dad gets to come home?" Iris was asking.

I shushed her, suddenly noticing how incredibly pale Alice was. I sat down beside her and took her hand. "Alice?" She was trembling ever so slightly. "Iris, get Alice some water, please."

Alice's eyes were wide as she whispered, "I have mourned that man for almost twenty years. Is he honestly not even dead?" Tears rolled down her cheeks, and I held her to me.

Any notion I might have had that she was somehow involved in this calamity suddenly flew out the window. This was not a woman in on the scheme.

"Could you come back tomorrow?" I asked the agent. "I think I'd like to get her to bed."

"No," she said, shaking her head. "Bill deserves to be free, and no one is going to have to wait on me to see that that happens."

My turn to tear up. I wanted to ask Alice why she hadn't told me about Bill and her money, but this obviously wasn't the time.

"Mom," Iris interrupted huffily. "Can I at least play my recording for the agent while we wait for Oliver? You're going to want to hear this." She crossed her arms and gave me that *None of you would even be able to process oxygen into carbon dioxide were I not here* look.

I gestured like, *Be my guest.*

And, as I listened, that tiny 1 percent of me that was afraid my husband was guilty floated away into the ether. He was innocent. He was going to come home. And I had a feisty fourteen-year-old to thank for all of it.

@junipershoressocialite

Sharing bad behavior and delicious drama in North Carolina's most exclusive coastal zip code. DM with tips, pics, and juicy deets.

SEPTEMBER 17, 5:41 P.M.
35 Posts
11,946 Followers
32 Following

You didn't hear it from me, but . . .

PIC 1: Well, the feds can't get enough of the Sitterlys these days. But this time their visit just might spell freedom for our poor, falsely accused Bill. FBI, if our #freebill posts helped, drop an emoji in the comments. Juniper Shores Socialite: solving crimes—and crimes of fashion—since August.

PIC 2: If we hadn't seen him with our own eyes, we wouldn't have believed it . . . but . . . Jeremy Isaacs, Alice's poor departed first husband (formerly victim, so we thought) isn't dead. Nope, the man who spent his honeymoon years with Alice charming all of Juniper Shores is as alive as a, well, what's the opposite of a doornail? He's alive, he's here, and he was conducting a securities fraud scheme for the ages. Alice, we'd like to take this moment to formally apologize for all those Black Widow jokes. We're sorry and we're #teamalice all the way forever and always. Looks like the man was to blame after all. *Who would've thought?* (Cue eye roll.)

PIC 3: In lighter fare, Oliver-the-hunky-Brit and Julie-the-hot-single-mom were reportedly getting just a *little* cozy at the coffee shop this morning. The Sitterlys might have united them. But will love keep them together?

PIC 4: Say it isn't so. Rumor has it that our perfect ten of a Mommy Blogger is getting back together with her five (rounded up to a seven because he's so rich) of a husband. Grace, you are the glue that holds the mommune together. You are the reel that we save daily to our Insta. You are the haircut we take to our stylists. In short, Juniper Shores needs you more than Tokyo does.

TNT ('Til Next Tokyo Takeoff—first class, of course)
JUNIPER SHORES SOCIALITE

Brotherly Love

When the dust had settled and it was just us in the house again, Alice, who looked like a wrung-out dishrag, said, "Well, girls. You saved the day!"

I turned to Mom. "Oh my gosh, Mom! And we got our house back! We can go home!"

I was surprised at how torn I felt. I mean, yes, sure, of course I couldn't wait to go home. But also, we had had so much fun here. It was kind of like, now that I knew it was over, I wished I'd taken more advantage of the moments we had together.

Mom bit her lip.

"What? You have been acting so weird about the house."

Mom grimaced. "It's just that, we maybe, might have been able to go home, like, a while ago."

"What?" I was shocked. "And you didn't tell me?"

"Dad was worried about our safety, and I knew if you knew, you'd try to talk me into going home and . . ."

She trailed off. And I started to be mad but then I realized that, really, I wasn't. "Actually, I said. "I wouldn't have wanted to go home even if you'd told me."

"Really?"

I nodded. "Yeah. I love being here. It has been so awesome." I turned to Alice. "Thank you for giving us such a great place to stay."

"Alice, you have been so gracious to us," Mom said. "We can never ever repay you."

Her eyes filled with tears. So did Alice's. Then mine did too because I couldn't let them cry alone. "Wow. We've had so much fun."

Before I could get too weepy, Merit came tearing up the stairs in full-on football pads, spotted me, and yelled, "Are you insane? Are you serious? You just sat here and recorded a total lunatic? You could have been *killed*."

I tried to look nonchalant. "I'm fine, Merit."

"Well, that is the last time I ever leave you alone. You have no sense, Iris."

Mom and Alice shared a look. I knew that look. They thought Merit was in love with me. Alas, if only they knew the truth. Merit was in brotherly love with me. For the first time in hours, my mind flipped to Ben. Had I totally blown it with him? Would he ever try to make a move again after I'd stopped him?

Then I had a really great thought: just because Ben might never make a move didn't mean *I* couldn't.

Social Life

I don't know why, but ordeals like these always call for a shower. I wasn't dirty in the traditional sense, but I felt it all the same. I let Iris go first since, come on, she was the real hero of the day, a fact that made me nothing short of nauseated. I wanted to wrap her in bubble wrap with a small nose and mouth hole for breathing and keep her in the closet so nothing bad could ever happen to her. That should really be an option parents can choose at birth. I was proud of her moxie. But it also terrified me. Why was it that our best qualities could also put us in harm's way?

The phone rang beside me. I picked it up, recognizing the number right away—wishing that I had never had to recognize the number, feeling in the depths of my bones that I wouldn't have to see it much more.

"Hi, babe," I answered.

We had discerned that he could hear me even as the voice was playing asking if I would accept the charges for the collect call from the correctional center.

"I'm coming home tomorrow!" the ecstatic voice on the other end of the line said.

I had pictured this moment so many times, held a vision for it.

And yet, it wasn't at all what I expected. As tears streamed out of my eyes, I flopped back onto the mattress. "Tomorrow is the best day of my entire life!" I said through my tears.

"You're telling me," Bill said.

I was so overwhelmed with joy and relief that I couldn't even respond.

"So, how is it being home?" Bill asked.

Iris walked into my room, wet hair in a towel, wrapped in a fluffy bathrobe. "It's Dad!" I said, putting Bill on speaker, biting my lip, wondering why, now that we knew we were safe. Shouldn't Iris and I have rushed home immediately? Showered in our own showers? I reasoned that it was because all our stuff was here, but that didn't seem quite right. All of our *real* stuff was at home. I knew Iris and I hadn't discussed going home yet for bigger reasons than that.

"Iris!" Bill said. "How is it to be home?"

She was obviously quicker than I was because Iris said, "Mom and I decided that we want to spend our first night back at home with you, as a family."

I could hear that Bill was choked up when he said, "Oh, girls. That is just the best thing I've ever heard. I'm counting down the minutes until I see you tomorrow."

"Tomorrow!" Iris squealed back at him.

"We can't wait to get you back," I said. "Love you, Bill."

"Love you both," he said.

Iris flopped down on the bed beside me. "You did that," I said. That wasn't 100 percent true. The feds and Oliver had both independently solved most of what was going on by the time Iris did—hence the FBI's truly perfect timing—but she was at least on their heels, which was pretty impressive for a fourteen-year-old who had never even really been that into Nancy Drew.

"Yeah. I'm like that," she said. She paused and turned her head to look at me. "Should we unpack why we haven't gone home yet, or just let it ride?"

I sighed. "Pretty smooth how you lied there. I didn't just *love* how easily that slid out."

She raised her eyebrows at me. "You should be thanking me for saving you instead of scolding me for lying. What would Dad think if we told him we didn't want to go home?"

"It's not that I don't want to go home," I said. "It's just that we've had a nice time here, and it's going to be different going home alone."

"Quiet," Iris chimed in.

"But I am excited to go home," I said, "especially now that it means going home with Dad."

"Same," Iris said. "And it's only, like, two blocks away. We don't need to be dramatic. We'll still see everyone all the time."

"Right," I agreed. "Want to go see what they're doing?"

Iris nodded. "Last night at the mommune."

"Last night at the mommune." It was weird how now, knowing it was over, that made me so sad.

When we walked downstairs, Julie, Grace, Alice, Emma, and Merit were all waiting to hug Iris. Grace put her arm around her and said, "I've made you fresh warm cookies and milk. You've had quite the ordeal today. And you were quite the hero."

"Grace, I really was."

We all laughed.

Iris looked around. "Julie, where are the girls? It's our last night!"

She smiled. "They're at ballet, but they'll be home in time for dinner."

"So what I want to know," I said, "is how exactly you came to obtain the phone you used to record Jeremy."

Alice shook her head. "Jeremy," she whispered. "It's going to take a while to come to terms with that one."

Merit and Iris shared a look that I found very interesting. It was a secret look, a brother-and-sister one.

"Oh, no, no," Grace said. "Whatever it is, you two need to spit it out."

Iris scrunched her nose.

"Honey," I said, "I'm so happy you're safe and Dad is coming home that I don't care about much else right now."

"Well . . ." Merit started.

"They have burner phones!" Emma exploded. She reached into her pocket and handed Merit twenty dollars.

"What?" Grace and I said at the same time.

"Like drug dealers?" Alice asked.

"That's what I said!" Iris added.

Grace looked at Merit. "So, on the one hand, you should technically be punished for the burner phone. On the other, you might have saved Alice. Bill too."

"I vote no punishment for Merit!" Julie said with the voice of a warrior.

I jumped in. "I mean, it is a little unrealistic for teenagers to have to be without their phones from six p.m. on anyway. Eight or nine? Sure. But I vote that this wasn't Merit's fault."

Grace sighed. "Fine. No grounding, but also no burner phones. I mean, the things you don't even think you would have to say."

"While everyone is being so forgiving . . ." Iris said. "Chloe, Daphne, and I sort of broke into our house a few weeks ago. And Jeremy was in there stealing statements, and we maybe didn't tell you—"

"What?" I protested, feeling like couldn't breathe.

"But you didn't even tell me that we could get back into our house," Iris said. "So I think we're even."

"No punishments!" Merit said. "Now walk away slowly," he whispered to Iris.

It occurred to me then that, for just a few weeks, my only child had experienced what it was like to have five siblings. I hoped this experience would bond them, that they would stay in touch. I was holding the glee of having Bill back in my life in one hand and the sadness of leaving these people who felt like family in the other. It was hard to reconcile the two. But I would, I knew. Because tomorrow was a fresh start. Tomorrow was the new beginning we had hoped and prayed we would get. And now, it was only a day away.

Alice

Cinematic Display

We were all on the floor in our pajamas, a fire that our Boy Scout Merit had built roaring in the fireplace, even though it wasn't particularly cold outside.

"Your real strength," Charlotte said to Grace, as she dipped a cookie into milk, "is in knowing exactly what people will need, at exactly the right time."

"Even if it's before dinner," Iris agreed. "I have never needed a warm cookie or a glass of milk more than right now."

"How are you feeling?" Grace asked me.

"Vindicated," I said.

"Vindicated?"

I nodded. "I don't know if any of you have ever experienced this, but there is this thing that happens to you when someone has told you something about yourself for a really long time. You kind of start to believe it." I took a sip of milk. "So, for almost two decades I have believed that I somehow killed the men I loved. And now I know that isn't true."

Charlotte reached over and squeezed my arm. "No more Black Widow for you," she said.

She was giving me a lot of grace tonight when she should have been blaming me, at least a little, for this situation.

"So, you two are good?" Julie asked.

My face got hot, and not from the fire.

"Maybe it's Charlotte's place to say it and not mine," Grace chimed in, "but, Alice, this is a bizarre series of coincidences."

I wanted to jump in to defend myself, but, well, they weren't totally wrong. All eyes were on me.

Charlotte shook her head. "Look, Alice, I'll be honest, I was panicked and frantic, and Iris didn't have her phone, and I couldn't find mine, and you had that crazy 'vengeance is mine' Bible verse on your mirror, and I'd had no idea that you were one of the people Bill had supposedly stolen money from and—"

"Wait. What?" Julie asked, sitting down on the couch. "You were one of the people who lost their money?"

I just sighed.

"Why didn't you tell me that?"

"I didn't want you to worry." I paused. Today had been harrowing and eye-opening. And it seemed like a good day to tell the truth. So I was going to. "First of all," I said, "the Bible verse, if you read all of it, is about how we don't need to take our own revenge because the Lord does it for us. I saved it to remind myself that it's not my responsibility to settle the score."

"Ohhhh," Charlotte said, looking sheepish. "But you can see how once I found out you were on Bill's list . . ." She trailed off. Then she picked back up. "Why didn't you say something?"

"Because I didn't want you to be suspicious of my kindness toward you."

Charlotte didn't respond.

"Look, Grace isn't totally wrong that I had something to do with all of this. I kind of did. Because I did seek you out," I said, focused on Charlotte. "I didn't follow you into the bank that day, but I planned to find you, to invite you here. It wasn't random, and I should have told you that."

"But why?" Grace asked quietly.

I shook my head. "Because, for all these years, I've felt like I had some curse on me that made all my husbands die. If I could only right this huge karmic debt, I could make things good again. I have spent most of my life trying to earn some sort of invisible forgiveness for crimes that I didn't willingly commit. If I could take in and love the wife and the child of the man who had stolen the only bit of security I had ever had in this life, then I was really doing something. Surely that would be enough to make things right." What I didn't add, because it made me sound so pathetic, was that everyone would know I wasn't guilty. Everyone would quit talking about me.

All eyes were on me now, staring in disbelief.

"It seems to have worked," Merit said.

"What? Don't give in to my mad ravings. Tell me how crazy that is!"

"It's not crazy," he said.

Iris shook her head. "Nope. You took us in, Jeremy came back, your name is cleared, your karma is righted."

"And we're definitely going to get your money back," Charlotte said. "So, I agree with the kids. The plan worked."

Julie laughed. "Y'all are all nuts."

"We're all nuts, and we found each other!" Grace said.

"Alice," Iris said tentatively. "Maybe it isn't any of my business. But do you think that will make you feel better about moving in with Elliott? Now that you know you aren't the Black Widow?"

"I'm not sure about anything yet." But wasn't I? Hadn't today given me an awful lot of clarity? I had spent years clinging to this sainted image of a man who wasn't even real. Or, at least, he certainly wasn't who I'd thought he was. I had bought this house because it felt like some sort of invisible tie to him. Knowing what I knew now, it wasn't hard to let it go. Knowing what I knew now, I was ready to move on.

Iris stood up and stretched. "Well, no looking back, Alice." She paused. "Mom, can I go see Chloe and Dabney? They're probably worried since I left school early."

Charlotte looked aghast. "Are you kidding me? No. I am Velcroing you to my side. I will be going to school with you and sitting in the desk beside you for all eternity now."

"I'll go with her," Merit said.

Charlotte sucked in her breath. "Fine," she said. "But I want your phone on, and when I text or call, you better answer within two seconds or I'm calling the police. And be home by dinner."

Iris hugged her mom and then me. "Our last supper."

My eyes filled.

As the kids went upstairs to change, I said, "I don't know if this helps, but I don't think we were ever in any real danger. Jeremy is obviously mentally unwell, but I don't think he's dangerous."

Julie shook her head. "How about you don't defend the husband who has caused you almost twenty years of misery? That'd be great."

"How did that feel, Alice?" Grace asked. "I mean, to think this man that you loved was dead for all these years and then . . ."

I let out a small laugh. "He said he wanted to get back together! Like this was some great act of love that was going to bond us. We were going to flee the country together and make a new life with his stolen money. What a joke."

"I strongly suggest that you do not get back together with him," Julie said.

Charlotte nodded. "Having had my fair share of experience with trying to make a jailhouse relationship work, I concur wholeheartedly."

"What is so weird is that I have spent eighteen years pining for him, remembering him as this great love that no one else could ever measure up to. And now I realize that I dodged a bullet." I shook my head. "I'm not spending another minute looking back. Not on any of it. Only forward now."

Julie, frank as always, said, "Well, Grace, what will you do? I mean, if I go live with Mom and Charlotte goes home and Alice moves in with Elliott . . ."

Grace laughed and said sarcastically, "Thanks for clarifying, since I have given this no thought at all." She looked down at her hands. "Well, things are going well for all of us, it seems. I talked to Troy today," she said quietly.

I almost dropped the glass in my hand. "Like, Tokyo Troy? Like, your ex-husband?"

"Well, he isn't technically my ex-husband. We've never gotten divorced. But, yes." She smiled. "He wants me to come with the kids when they visit." She bit her lip and grinned. "He wants to talk about us and how we can fix things."

Charlotte gasped. "Grace, that's amazing!"

She shut her eyes and one perfect tear slid down her gorgeous face. "It is my only prayer and greatest wish," she said. "And it's coming true." She took a deep breath. "I am going to be a wife and mother so perfect for him that he can't help but want me back."

Julie put her hand on Grace's forearm. "Grace, you are one of the most extraordinary humans I have ever met. You don't need to prove your worth to anyone, husband or no."

She shook her head. "You just don't understand."

"Then help us understand," I said.

"All of you are brilliant and confident and not afraid of the world. I married Troy because I needed him. I needed him to take care of me. And now that he's gone, it's just really hard."

"Is it?" Charlotte asked. "Because you seem to be killing it. You keep an entire house full of people alive, you're an incredible mother, you have one of the most successful corners of the internet, and *Growing with Grace* was a huge bestseller."

A smile played on her lips. "I just sold a cookbook to my publisher too."

I put my hands up in the air. "What? And you didn't tell us! We need to celebrate!"

She shrugged. "I don't know. None of it feels like that big of a deal."

"Well, it is," Julie said. "It's a huge damn deal."

Grace smiled at me, this time her eyes lighting up.

"And you are so beautiful on top of all of that," Charlotte said. "If I didn't love you, I'd hate you."

"I hate you, like, twenty percent despite my love for you," Julie said seriously.

Grace laughed. I wanted to say more, but, in a great cinematic display, the door flung open. "Alice!" Elliott yelled. He turned and saw me and ran, scooping me into his arms and kissing me. Not letting me go, he said, "Thank God you're okay. I'm never going to let anything bad happen to you ever again."

He kissed me again. He was looking at me so intently that I wasn't sure he noticed anyone else was in the room. "I know you have said over and over that you don't want to get married. And I get it. Kind of. But, Alice, I love you and I'm not letting you go again. It's you and me. Okay?"

I smiled and nodded. "Okay," I whispered.

Then, in a day of shocking things, he did something that was perhaps the most shocking. He got down on one knee, reached in his pocket, and pulled out a beautiful gold and mother-of-pearl ring that was engraved *AP*. "I know what you've said, Al, but I want to be all in. I don't want to just move in together. I want to be together forever. I want it to be you and me, and I don't care if I'm sharing a bed with your ghosts or your fears. Because I'm not afraid. And when I found this ring yesterday, I knew it was a sign. So, Alice, I might be crazy. But I'm leaving it all on the table tonight. I want you to marry me. I want to be your husband. And I don't give a damn what Juniper Shores Socialite has to say about it. Will you marry me?"

That elicited laughter from the women around me, reminding me that Elliott and I weren't alone here. Had he asked me this this morning, I probably would have said no. But everything seemed different. Jeremy hadn't died. I hadn't been the bad luck charm. In fact, looking down at that beautiful ring with my future initials—perfectly selected by this wonderful man—I couldn't help but feel like good luck was all around.

I nodded at him and started laughing. "Elliott, I didn't kill Jeremy. He's alive!"

He gave me a puzzled look. "Right. So I've heard." He gestured around him. "Um. Kind of on one knee down here, babe."

I leaned down and kissed him. "Sorry. So what I'm saying is that, if I didn't kill Jeremy, then I won't kill you. So, yes! I'll marry you," I said. Then, in a very serious voice, I added, "Why did it take you so long to ask?"

Elliott let out this relieved and shocked little laugh and picked me up, kissing me. "Seriously?"

"Seriously," I said. "He stole eighteen years of my life. I'm doing whatever I want from now on. And I want to get married. To you."

Elliott slid the ring onto my finger. "I'm really glad to hear you say that because I made an offer on a house today."

I gasped. "The one on the sound?"

He shook his head. "Nah. The one on the beach."

I gasped again, covering my mouth. "Really?"

He nodded. "It's so beautiful, the view is perfect, and it's super close to Charlotte and Iris."

"But what about your boat?"

"That's why God made marinas." He smiled.

Then I had a brand-new thought. I looked at Charlotte for some reason. "Wait. If Jeremy is alive, am I still married to him?"

A stunned expression crossed her face.

"Were your other marriages illegal?" Julie asked. "Are you a polygamist, Alice?"

"Oh, the heyday Juniper Shores Socialite is going to have with this one!" Grace said.

We all started laughing, though it wasn't that funny.

"How about we sort all that out tomorrow," Elliott said. "Tonight, let's celebrate."

Moving forward, I thought. Moving forward. Sometimes that meant moving altogether. The mommune had been the most magical time of my life. But it was time to move on. For all of us. It shocked me to realize that I couldn't wait.

@junipershoressocialite

Sharing bad behavior and delicious drama in North Carolina's most exclusive coastal zip code. DM with tips, pics, and juicy deets.

SEPTEMBER 17, 8:49 P.M.
36 Posts
12,107 Followers
34 Following

You didn't hear it from me, but . . .

PIC 1: Third time's the charm, or so they say . . . and we are counting Elliott P. as Alice Sitterly's third husband because that Jeremy positively does not count. This is her mulligan marriage. (We make the rules here. Don't argue.) Did you *see* that estate ring he gave her already monogrammed *AP*? We know a fairy tale when we see one!

PIC 2: Iris Sitterly rules the day! Juniper Shores Prep's own darling daughter solved the crime, recorded the confession, and found the evidence to free her hunky daddy! Okay, okay. So maybe, just maybe, the FBI was on the trail too, but we give Iris all the credit. Iris for president! Or at least homecoming court.

PIC 3: We've heard that our dearest Julie is working late tonight, crafting the perfect front-page story. What, oh, what could she be writing about? And—send us some tips— we still want to know if she's writing a *love* story too!

TNT ('Til Next Tabloid)
JUNIPER SHORES SOCIALITE

Shooting Star

"So, are you going to tell Ben?" Merit asked when we got in the car.

"Are you going to tell your mom?" I asked.

He shot me a look. *"Iris."*

"I'm sorry, I'm sorry. Okay. Your truth is bigger than mine. I just want you to be happy and no one is going to care."

As he pulled out of the driveway, he said, "Iris, I want you to be happy and no one is going to care."

"Well, I hope Ben cares," I said under my breath. Then I sighed. "But, like, it's just going to change the dynamics of everything. You know? Chloe, Dabs, Ben, and I can hang out now and it's normal and—"

"No offense, Iris, but Ben has zero interest in hanging out with your girl squad. He hangs out with them because he likes you."

I got those fluttery butterflies. I knew Merit was right; I knew Ben liked me. And I could say for certain that I liked him too. "So maybe I should have learned the lesson today in my near-death experience that life is short, and you have to take risks?"

"Your near-death experience? Would we really classify recording someone from the stairs as a near-death experience?"

I nodded seriously. "We should make posters to keep something similar from happening to other people."

Merit glanced over at me. "I think I'm going to tell my mom."

I gasped. "Really?"

"Maybe around Christmas when she's in her peak Grace mood." He paused. "Do you think it's better if I tell her alone or with everyone?"

I pondered that. "Well, it might be a nice moment for the two of you. But then again, if you tell her in a group, you don't have to come out, like, a whole bunch of times."

He raised his eyebrows. "That's a good point. And it might feel like less pressure on her to say the perfect thing?"

"She's Grace. She'll say the perfect thing."

He smiled.

"Hey," I said. "I heard about this kid who told his parents he had a brain tumor. And then he was like, 'No, just kidding. I'm gay.' And then they were so relieved he wasn't dying it put it all in perspective."

I expected Merit to laugh. Instead, he said, "Huh. That's not a bad idea. Tell everyone something else so shocking that my being gay seems less shocking."

I scrunched my nose and studied him in the dark. "Merit, I was kidding! That's a terrible idea. Please don't do that."

We pulled into Chloe's driveway, and I said, "Merit?"

"Go see your friends!"

I guessed this conversation was over. Well, whatever. It was his life, his decision. So I jumped out, hoping I hadn't given him really bad advice.

When we got to the back door, Chloe threw it open and Chloe, Dabney, and Ben engulfed me in a hug. "You're our hero!" Chloe said.

I put my hands on my hips like Wonder Woman. "Yup. I found the masked man in the closet!"

"You're amazing!" Dabney said. "We're so happy your dad is coming home!"

They pulled away, but then Ben hugged me again.

"I'm so sorry, Iris," he said. "I was rude to you every time I saw you today, and you were out fighting crime."

I nodded. "I was. I am a modern-day knight, and you ignored me."

Merit looked from Ben to me. "Hey, Chloe and Dabney," he said. "I'm starving. You got anything to eat?"

You could almost see them swooning. I smiled to myself. If only they knew the truth. "Of course!" Chloe said, talking really fast. "We have everything! Do you want, like, a snack or pizza or—"

"Can you make me cookies?" Merit said. "Or brownies or something?"

I knew for sure that he didn't want those. We had just had Grace's cookies, a.k.a. the best cookies in the world. Anything else would pale in comparison. But he was buying me twenty minutes, and I was grateful. As they walked toward the kitchen, he glanced back over his shoulder and winked at me.

Ben visibly rolled his eyes, and I glared at him. "Ben! Honestly! Five minutes and it's back to that already?"

"I'm sorry," he said. I took his hand and led him out the door to Chloe's porch. It was dark, but I didn't bother to turn on the light.

We stood, leaning over the railing. I was looking at the stars, but I could feel Ben looking at me. And it made everything inside of me feel like hot liquid. I had thought about what I would say to him on the ride over here, how I would explain that the other night I was torn, but now I had had time to think and on and on. But now that we were here, I didn't want to break the silence.

"Ben!" I gasped, pointing as a shooting star streaked across the sky. It was so dark here on the beach, the sky was so full of stars, that it wasn't uncommon to see them. But it was still magical, and at this particular moment it felt like a sign, like God or the Universe or some unknowable, unnamed force in the cosmos had set all this up so that I could see how I truly felt.

I turned toward Ben, and he turned toward me. "You have to close your eyes and make a wish!" I said, with the same enthusiasm Brenna or Jamie or Audrey would have. I felt giddy.

He closed his eyes, smiling, and as soon as he did, I wrapped my arms around his neck and kissed him, gently at first, then longer. He wrapped his hands around my back, and I realized that I was glad I hadn't done all that talking. There was nothing to talk about. Ben was my best friend, and it felt right that now he would become something more.

I knew right away as I kissed him that this was going to work; maybe this was what we should have been doing all along. I let him go, but he kept his arms around my waist. "My wish came true," he whispered.

I laughed. "Mine too."

And the two people who usually couldn't stop talking seemed suddenly out of things to say. It felt perfect. We walked back into the house, into the kitchen with the others, holding hands.

Dabney noticed immediately. "So, is this a thing now?" she asked, pointing to our hands.

We looked at each other and shrugged.

Chloe rolled her eyes. "It's always been a thing. They just wouldn't admit it."

I wasn't sure that was totally true. But it didn't matter. I had been through the dark, scary part of my fairy tale today. So it seemed fair that now I would get my Prince Charming.

~~~~~~~~~~~~

The Most Roundabout Way

I knew that now was my time. Julie was moving in with her mother; Grace was, in all likelihood, getting back together with Troy, Charlotte was going back home—or, who knew, maybe even back to New York. And I loved Elliott; I did. I was ready to let go of this house, but it was hard too. It held so many memories for me.

I was sitting at the kitchen island after a night of sleep so good I couldn't believe it. I could have slept later, but, well, it was a school day, and the show must go on. Grace was making pancakes, and I was sipping orange juice. She scrunched her nose. "It's going to be weird, isn't it? All of us living apart?"

I nodded. "It will definitely take some getting used to. How will I manage to feed myself?"

Grace laughed, and I heard footsteps down the stairs that I recognized as Julie's. "Good morning, beautiful niece of mine!" I sang. But when she appeared, I could tell she had been crying.

"What's wrong?" Grace asked, pausing her mixing and pouring and flipping.

"My own mother," she said with a little heaving sob.

When it came to her mother, there was no telling what had happened. But I had guesses. "Your own mother what?"

"She just called to ask if she could borrow five thousand dollars to get things ready for us to move in!" she said, her sadness turning to anger. "Do you know how long it took me to save five thousand dollars? And we all know she's never going to pay me back!"

"Oh, honey," I said. "Sit down." She was correct. Of all the times Delia had "borrowed" money from me, my sister had paid me back precisely never. But I knew the rule: never lend money that you expect to see again.

Her face was stony. "Now I know she only wants me to move in with her because she needs my rent money." She shook her head. "I'm not doing it. I'm financially stable now. I can afford a small place of my own. And I don't need help with the girls." At that, she started crying again.

I got up and hugged her. "What, honey?"

"I do need help with the girls!" she said.

I laughed and wiped her tears, swamped with guilt. Mina would never have left me. I couldn't leave Julie, even if it meant sacrificing a piece of my happiness. "Well, you don't have to, sweetie. You will all just stay right here. With me."

She shook her head. "Nope. You're marrying Elliott. It's right; it's time."

I sighed as Charlotte came down the stairs. I felt so deflated, but I thought of Mina again, of what she had sacrificed to take care of me. "I don't have to, honey. Family first. You can stay here. I promise."

"Really?" Charlotte asked as she made her way to the coffeepot, jumping into the conversation like she'd been here the whole time.

"She's just saying that," Julie said, "because she doesn't want me to feel guilty about not moving in with my mom."

Charlotte nodded.

Grace poured more batter on the griddle, and it sizzled. "Alice, you're marrying Elliott. Because I was up all night crunching numbers and doing a little thinking, and, Julie, well . . . I have a proposition for you. For you and Alice, really. About how we can stay right here."

"Wait a minute," Charlotte said. "I thought you were beside yourself about getting back with Troy?"

She shrugged. "Some good friends of mine made me realize that my self-worth is not tied up in Troy. I'm back on my feet, I'm stronger than ever, I can take care of myself and my kids, and I don't want him. You all made me see that I didn't want him, really, but I thought I *needed* him." She paused. "And if it's time for us to go, we will. We can." She paused again. "But honestly, life is just more fun when we live it together."

"So what are you proposing?" I asked.

Grace turned off the burner and wiped her hands. "Alice, I would like to buy the mommune." She looked at Julie. "Jules, I want you and the girls to stay here and help me turn it back into a bed-and-breakfast. I'll do the cooking, obviously. And you would be in charge of all the managerial things. Booking, social media, etcetera."

Julie's jaw dropped. "No. Really?"

Grace looked at me. "Alice?"

I could feel myself tearing up, and I jumped up off my stool to hug her. "Yes! Absolutely, one hundred times yes!"

"It just goes so smoothly when we're here together, Jules," Grace said.

"And there's always a best friend to talk to or a kid to make you laugh," I added, maybe a little sadly.

"And some weeks, you aren't even doing laundry," Charlotte added, winking at me.

"This way, we keep some of that, but we also move forward. You know?" Grace said.

"Totally," I said. "I love it."

"Wait," Charlotte said. "But how will you guys do math homework without me?" She took a sip of coffee.

"You're just down the street!" Julie enthused.

Charlotte laughed. "This should have been one of the hardest times of my life, but, because of all of you, it's been one of the happiest. Thank you for that. I love you all so much."

"Well, it isn't over," Grace said. "Because one of my conditions is that we all congregate once a week, right here, for a great meal and a little forced family fun."

"Yay!" I said, clapping my hands. "I love this idea!"

Three little sleepy-headed nieces appeared from their bedroom around the corner. Audrey climbed into Julie's lap, Jamie crawled into mine, and Brenna said, "Yay! Pancakes!"

"Should we wake Merit, Emma, and Iris to celebrate?" Grace asked.

"We're coming!" Merit called.

The three of them padded down the stairs, still in pajamas.

"I'm so excited Dad is coming home!" Iris said.

There was a tentative knock on the back door, followed by Oliver's "Hello?"

I shot a knowing look at Julie.

"Oliver!" Charlotte said. "Is everything okay?"

He nodded. "All is well. Julie invited me to breakfast. I hope that's okay."

Grace laughed. "Julie, you dog. Juniper Shores Socialite calls it right again."

Oliver laughed and put his arm around Julie. Well, well, well, maybe someone had fallen into her lap after all.

Grace stacked plates full of pancakes, Charlotte poured glasses of milk, and everyone piled into their seats at the table.

"I can't believe this is our last family breakfast," Iris said.

"Well . . ." Julie said, "maybe not our last. Grace and I want to host everyone as often as you'll come."

Iris gasped. "What?"

Grace nodded. "We're buying the mommune!"

"So, you aren't getting back together with Dad?" Emma asked.

Grace put her hand on Emma's. "I'm sorry, sweetheart. I know this is hard—"

"Dad's a total jerk," Emma said. "And I don't want to leave my school. I'm *glad* you're not getting back together with him."

"Same," Merit said, his mouth full of pancake.

I laughed. "In case I don't get the chance to say it again, I want everyone to know how happy you have made me. I love you all deeply, and you have given me my life back when I truly didn't think that was possible."

"We love you too, Anally!" Jamie squealed.

"Alice, I honestly do not know what Iris and I would have done without your kindness and compassion. You saved us. You gave us not only a place to live but also people to sustain us." Charlotte paused. "And no matter what anyone else says, I believe with all my heart that all of us coming together played a huge part in Bill getting out of jail."

"Hey!" Oliver protested. "Ye of little faith!"

Charlotte laughed and raised her milk glass. "To the mommune!" she said.

"To the mommune," we all repeated, clinking glasses of milk.

In a few minutes, the kids would scatter to get ready for school, the sticky, syrupy dishes would need to be cleared (my week for dishes!), Elliott and I would go sign paperwork for our official offer on our new house, and we'd each have more than a few personal dramas and traumas to handle. But for now, for the moment, life was perfect.

I looked around this table at all these people I loved, and I realized that the rituals and routines of family life hadn't saved me; the people had. With their love and support, listening ears, and guidance. They had given me that family I had always wanted most. And I would always put them first.

It might be unconventional; it might not always be easy. But nothing truly great ever is. I thought of my mother, the woman who had loved and nurtured me so fully until her life had been cut short, of Mina who had cared for me and taught me in the very best way she knew how. I hoped that the little girls around this table would look back one day and think the same of me.

I had never gotten children of my own, but it seemed that I had become a mother anyway. And if these past few years had taught me anything, it was that, when we put our heads together, when we join forces, there's nothing that moms can't do.

"I think we need to do our dinnertime ritual right now, at breakfast!" Emma shouted gleefully.

"Oh, yes!" Iris agreed. "Alice, you start because you're the one who brought us all together."

"Okay," I said, clearing my throat. "Well, the best part of my day, obviously, is getting to have breakfast with all my favorite people in the world."

"And what do you need?" Merit asked.

I smiled at him, at all of them. So much in life had happened to us. But this, our time together, it seemed, had happened *for* us. In the most roundabout way, we'd all ended up exactly where we needed to be. I didn't have to answer Merit. He already knew; they all did. For the first time maybe ever, I was certain I had everything I could ever need.

Yes, we might be moving on physically, but we would always be connected in our hearts. Some people spent years searching for the perfect person who understood them, who made them whole. I had found nine.

Charlotte

Home

Iris and I wanted to pick Bill up from jail, but he insisted that we didn't. He said he wanted us to meet him on our own front porch, that that was the image that had gotten him through the past few weeks. Sitting on the small porch that faced the road, rocking in rocking chairs, Iris and I were silent for a few minutes. I finally broke the quiet. "Do the last few weeks feel like a dream to you?"

She nodded. "Yeah. I was kind of thinking that. Like we were plucked out of our normal life and had this totally crazy experience, and then we were just dropped back at home." She looked over at me. "Mom, I know Juniper Shores is small, and people will be talking about us forever, but I don't want to go back to New York."

I gasped. "Bradley! I need to call him and tell him I'm not taking the job."

"You're not?" she practically squealed.

I shook my head. "No. I love working at Montoya and Sons, and I love how happy you are with your friends here, and I love that Alice and Elliott will be three houses down and Grace and Julie are two blocks away. I think I found something here that I never even knew I was looking for." *Best friends*, I thought. I had found best friends. And I wasn't going to give them up.

We both jumped up when Oliver's car pulled up in front of our house. I ran down the steps, Iris hot on my heels, and practically knocked Bill over as I jumped into his arms. He squeezed me tight and kissed me hard before turning to hug Iris and kiss her on her cheek. "My little detective," he said. "I think you've earned yourself a paid internship."

She nodded seriously. "Dad, I think I'm going to follow in your footsteps." She paused. "Or maybe I can track down Jeremy Isaacs and learn a little more about securities fraud and embezzlement, you know?"

Bill groaned. "It's too soon for jokes."

"It was a little funny," Iris whispered. She said, "Dad! I'm going to go turn on a really hot shower for you!" and ran ahead of us.

I waved to Oliver, who waved back and drove away. I wasn't sure if he was giving us alone time or if he simply needed a break from our family. I wouldn't blame him. Bill put his arm around me and kissed my forehead. "I can't tell you how this feels. This is the best day of my life. Thank you for never giving up on me."

My heart swelled. Maybe it was true that absence made the heart grow fonder. Or you didn't know what you had until it was gone. Clichés were clichés for a reason. I had taken Bill and our happy marriage and life for granted. I certainly wouldn't do that now. Every day was a gift; no time was guaranteed.

I turned in the driveway to hug him again, to feel my full weight going onto him. These last few weeks, even if it wasn't physical, I felt that I had carried Bill. I think he knew that. Now, with this nightmare coming to an end, it was time for him to carry me. At least for a while.

I pulled away, wiping tears from my eyes that I didn't even know had fallen. "Go get in that hot shower," I said. "You deserve it. I'll make you something amazing to eat."

"Can we go out tonight?" he asked.

"Anywhere you want," I said.

"And then I need to meet all these women you've been living with," he said. "Thank them for their support."

I smiled, thinking of Grace and Julie and Alice, wondering how it was that that life, which had ended only a few hours ago, already seemed so far in the past.

I followed Bill inside and, as he walked upstairs, I continued on through and out the ocean-side doors and walked down to the beach, to this spot of sand in front of our house that, as much as our bedroom or our living room, felt like home to me. I wiggled my toes in the sand, squeezed my eyes closed, lifted my face to the sun, and thanked God for bringing Bill back to me. It was a miracle.

When I opened my eyes, I saw Grace striding through the sand, holding a big bag in each hand. "Hi!" she called.

"Hi!" I said, waving and running toward her.

"I thought you might need some food." She scrunched her nose. "I even made meat for Bill."

I laughed. "That's true love. Well, come in. I want to introduce you."

She shook her head. "Another time. Today is your day."

I smiled. "It sure is. I've never felt this way before."

Seagulls dove overhead and the waves sounded particularly soothing. It was a perfect day by all accounts. Grace bit her lip, then said, "But, hey, really, I just wanted to thank you."

"Thank me?" I asked.

She nodded. "You showed me something really important, and I think you're right. It never occurred to me that I was enough, just me, just as I am. You gave me that. Thank you."

I put my hand to my heart. "I'm shocked by that. Thank you, Grace. But I should be thanking you. You kept me breathing."

"That's what best friends do."

Best friends, I pondered as I took the bags from her, as I walked back to my house. Only a few weeks ago, I would have said that friends weren't necessary, that they were nice but didn't make that much difference in a life. Wow, had I ever been wrong. I watched Grace making her way back down the beach. Then I looked up at my house. With my husband. And my daughter. And all the things that were right with the world.

I thought of the past few weeks, the ups and downs, the things I had tried that I never even thought possible. Selling insurance. Being vegan. Having female friends. Moving in with my nemesis. We hadn't just survived, Iris and I. We had thrived. And, maybe, we had even helped save my husband. I gazed at our house, feeling such pride and joy.

You could go home again. You most certainly could. And I was going to go right now.

Iris

~~~~~~~~~~~~

Secret

I had learned in our time since leaving the mommune that Grace's perfect tables and amazing meals were even more perfect, even more amazing, now that the mommune was the White Ibis. We, as promised, all had at least one meal a week together as part of the continuance of our forced family fun, but usually two or three. Merit, Emma, and I were often back and forth between houses, I babysat the girls every chance I got, and I saw Alice every day. As I passed the platter of pesto tomatoes to Ben, I wondered if that got on Elliott's nerves. I looked across the table at him as he laughed at something Jamie had said while I wasn't paying attention. He took Alice's hand and kissed her cheek. Nah. He seemed pretty happy to me.

Ben squeezed my knee under the table. The past three months had been pretty darn great. He leaned over and kissed me. "Ewwww!" Audrey squealed. "No kissing!"

"I agree wholeheartedly," Dad chimed in.

I looked around the table. The whole gang was here. Julie, Oliver, Brenna, Jamie, Audrey, Alice, Elliott, Mom, Dad, Ben, Grace, Merit, and Emma. Somehow the warm family feeling of the mommune had carried over into this new existence where Dad was back, where Alice was getting married in three months, where eternally single Oliver had fallen head over heels for vivacious Julie and the three girls he never knew he wanted. I loved being back in my bed, in my room, in my house; even so, no place would ever feel quite as much like home as the mommune with these people around this table, laughing and joking and living lives that were richer because we shared them.

"Can you believe we are totally booked through the entire holiday season?" Julie asked.

"I can," Oliver said, his beautiful British accent dripping. "Because you are absolutely brilliant, and this place is heaven on earth."

She gave him a coquettish little grin that made me think of Sophie—who, by the way, Merit still had not broken up with. I hounded him about it constantly, but he couldn't bring himself to do it.

"Don't forget, Christmas at our house!" Mom said. She had come alive since Dad came home. She was working part-time at Montoya & Sons, and it seemed like the perfect fit. And Dad's business had come back 100 percent—with tons of credit to both Julie and Juniper Shores Socialite, who were instrumental in piecing his reputation back together.

"Forget Christmas," Alice said. "How about don't forget our wedding at your house?"

"The most important day ever of all time," Elliott said with an enthusiasm that brought tears to my eyes.

Dad put his hands importantly to his chest and said, "My first time officiating a wedding. I'm basically a man of the cloth."

Merit said, "Well, you did bring us all together." Then he cleared his throat. "Um, guys. I have something to say. And it's kind of a big secret, so you can't tell anyone outside this room."

I looked at him questioningly. Was this it? The big moment?

Please, God, don't let him tell them he has a fake brain tumor. I smiled and winked at him encouragingly.

Merit took a deep breath. "I'm Juniper Shores Socialite."

"What?" I said. Then I realized this must be the big shocking lie before the real truth. *Well played, Merit.*

Grace dropped her fork. She put her hands out. "I'm sorry. I'm having so many feelings right now."

Panic roiled in my stomach. If she was upset about this, how would the real announcement go?

"I don't believe that!" Julie said. "You write bad stuff about yourself all the time!"

"You made all of our lives much harder than they had to be," Alice said, scowling at him.

The supportive coming-out therapy friend on Team Merit, i.e., me, said, "He's kidding."

I looked at him, and he shook his head. "You're not? I'm sorry, what?" I asked, anger rising in me. "You absolutely roasted all of us!"

"Did I?" Merit asked. "Or did I clear all your names? Did I put public interest on you so that everyone believed Bill was innocent and Alice wasn't a murderer and Mom was more than just Dad's ex, and Julie wasn't an opportunistic tattletale?" He looked over and pointed at Ben and me. "These two would never be together."

I locked eyes with him, and I knew, in the way a best friend does, what he wasn't saying: *And everyone would continue to believe that he was a player who couldn't commit to one girl.*

He made it impossible to be mad at him.

Or, well, *almost* impossible. "I'm sure I'm so mad for a lot of things you wrote about me, but I can't remember what they are right now, so I will detail them in a list later on."

Ben leaned over and kissed my shoulder supportively, and Emma said, "Gag."

Alice clapped. "Guys! This is going to be so great! Julie can do an exposé on this!"

"Yes!" Merit said. "I can see the headline: 'Does the Mommune Turn Boys to a Life of Social Media Crime?'"

Everyone laughed.

"All right, all right," Julie said. "You are all so lucky to have me. I keep you cultured and informed."

"But you guys can't tell anyone," Merit said.

"You're trusting a group of this many people to keep your secret?" Ben asked.

"Not people," Merit said. "Family." He looked at all of us. "You can't tell! Beach house rules!"

"Beach house rules," we all said in unison.

He looked over at me, and I winked at him. *Beach house rules*, I mouthed again. I could keep his secret as long as he wanted me to. Because that's what best friends did. No, that's what *family* did.

I'd never been a part of a big family. It wasn't something I ever thought I'd have. But now, here, in this sleepy, gossipy little town with its beautiful houses, Botoxed socialites, and bronzed teenagers, I had found everything I never knew I wanted. People could complain about their moms and dads embarrassing them, their siblings getting on their nerves, but the past few months had given me a gift, a secret, a look into an inner world that I never would have had otherwise. And from all that, I had learned a lesson that it might take my friends years to understand: forced family fun was the very best kind.

@junipershoressocialite

Sharing bad behavior and delicious drama in North Carolina's most exclusive coastal zip code. DM with tips, pics, and juicy deets.

DECEMBER 23, 9:08 A.M.
97 Posts
16,402 Followers
57 Following

You didn't hear it from me, but . . .

PIC 1: Which Juniper Shores B&B is hosting one of TV's most famous personalities, far from the mean streets of New York City, for a refined New Year's Eve by the shore? Rumor has it that the whole gang will be in attendance for the oceanfront New Year's Splash and Bash to support Juniper Shores Prep. If you thought Belle Epoque at the Beach was scandalous, just wait. This event is *casual*. When the high heels and bow ties are off, so are all bets.

PIC 2: One Laura Lucas was spotted at the end of Juniper Park Road with the golf pro who, we might add, as Juniper Shores Country Club president, she hired. Was it for his great résumé? Or his great abs? We hope for Paul Lucas's sake, this one is a swing and a miss.

PIC 3: *Everyone* (read: no one) is surprised to learn that Merit McDonald and Sophie Parker have gone the way of Jen and Brad. With Iris Sitterly cozily coupled with her BFF Ben, will the star quarterback's heart go on? Stay tuned. The answer might just surprise you.

PIC 4: The mommune family has been spotted on the sprawling front porch of the Sitterlys' gracious, gorgeous beach home to celebrate—what else?—the impending nuptials of Juniper Shores' favorite redeemed murderess. The Black Widow landed the whale, and it's a match made in animal kingdom heaven. The whole crew has reunited to celebrate—and it feels so good! Sure, we adore a good scandal. But, come on: Who doesn't love a happy ending?

TNT ('Til Next Tide)
JUNIPER SHORES SOCIALITE

Acknowledgments

Here's a sentence that doesn't get written enough: thank goodness for in-laws! Because, without mine, this book wouldn't exist. When I set out to write about a mommune, I knew that I wanted Charlotte to feel like she had no choice but to go live with relative strangers because her husband had committed a financial crime and she didn't have access to her house. Enter: Taylor Coleman, CFP, CLU, CHFP, and brother-in-law, who I just so happened to work for before I was a writer. I should preface this by saying, Taylor is the most honest, forthright person I know. But he sure whipped up a great, sneaky crime for me. Now we needed to figure out how Bill would be punished for it. Thank goodness Amy Bower, my cousin-in-law, (We are much closer than that fake title implies!) is an Assistant United States Attorney. Let me tell you, figuring out how to punish someone when he is guilty of a crime isn't so bad. Making him innocent but keeping him locked up long enough to let this story unfold? Well, we had our work cut out for us!

All that to say, I did take some liberties to get my characters where I needed them. Isn't that the beauty of fiction? And, of course, all mistakes are my very own. But huge thanks to Taylor and Amy for all your help on this book and making me sound somewhat competent. I am eternally grateful!

This book is, in so many ways, an ode to female friendship and the ways in which it enhances our lives. I kept hearing about "mommunes" all last summer—on the news, on the radio, in my news alerts.

But it wasn't until the fifth or sixth time that one had been in my path that I thought: I wonder what people would say about a mommune in a small southern town? The idea gripped me right away and the first people I ran it by were my "summer friends," the five women who were there when this idea took flight: Jessica Wilder, Dorothy Coleman (my sister-in-law!), Heather Wiggins, Caroline Mooring, and Megan Fader. I'm not sure it *necessarily* takes a village to raise a child, but I'm positive it's a whole lot more fun. Thank you, ladies, for being mine for all the years I've been a mom! (And even before!)

Kate McDermott, Kate Denierio, Drew Leonard, Millie Warren, Lee Taylor, Leeanne Walker, Booth Parker, Shelley Smith, Marci Godwin, and Margaret Robinson, you are the most supportive friends, and I'm so grateful for all the memories we have made and will continue to make together!

Speaking of moms, I have the *best* mom. Thanks, Mom, for being an amazing mother and friend and business partner and modeling all the right ways to do things even if I don't always do them as well myself! And thanks to my dad for being so involved in everything I ever did, now and always. The older I get, the more I realize how few truly wonderful dads there are. I'm so lucky to have one of them! Love you both so much. Thanks for being the best support system and my biggest cheerleaders.

I have to thank my husband, Will, for being the most extraordinary father and husband. I wouldn't trade you for all the mommunes in the world! Little Will—who is a good five inches taller than I am and not-so-little anymore—thanks for being the greatest thing that has ever happened in my whole life. I never imagined that my favorite way to spend a day would be at your games and matches. I'm so proud of everything you do!

Growing up, every summer, my grandparents took our whole

family on a beach trip, and, in some ways, life at the mommune reminded me of that. Nancy and Tommy Sanders, Cathy Singer, Anne O'Berry, Catherine Adcox, Raymond Smith, Sidney Patton, Rutledge Smith, and Thomas Sanders, our family has grown by leaps and bounds, but we're the originals. Love you guys so much, and I will always, always be grateful for those special summers together. (Speaking of . . . I know there are like thirty of us now, but can we please do it again?)

Fellow authors Mary Kay Andrews, Kristin Harmel, and Patti Callahan Henry; our managing director, Meg Walker; and podcast partner, Ron Block: Y'all, we created a community with a quarter-million members. Can you even comprehend that? *Friends & Fiction* has been a life-altering corner of the internet, and, if you're a reader and you haven't joined us, don't wait another day! Lisa Harrison, Brenda Gardner, Annissa Armstrong, Shaun Hettinger, James Way, and Rachel Jensen: from the official book club to tech to web to everything in between, you guys are the most amazing. Thank you to our fabulous, tireless *Friends & Fiction* ambassadors, who show up online and in person. Amber Prater, Anne Floccari, Barbara Wojcik, Bubba Wilson (the lucky coin queen!), Clare Plaxton, Dallas Strawn, Dawne McCurry, Debby Stone (the countdown queen!), Francene Katzen, Irene Wenner, Jill Mallia, Jodena Pysher, Kathy Saccamano, Laurie Brown, Lesley Bodemann, Linda Burrell, Maria Lew, Marilyn Rumph, Marlene Waters, Mary Vasquez, Meredith D'Agostino, Michelle Marcus, Mindy Ehrlich, Molly Neville, Nicole Fincher, Rhonda Perrett, Robin Klein, Sharon Person, Lysette House (and Biscuit, dog F&Fer!), Susan Seligman, Susie Baldwin, and Taylor Lintz, you are the heart of *Friends & Fiction* and watching the relationships that you have made is such a gift!

Carrie Feron, how fun is it that this is our first official book together? I truly loved editing this one with you. Thanks for your great insight and your great faith in me, in the perfect amounts! Elisabeth Weed and Olivia Blaustein, I would be nowhere without your agenting expertise. What a year we have had! Jonathan Baruch, I'm so grateful for your support and guidance and all the energy you have brought to my books and career. Lauren Carr, putting aside the book and all your hard work on it and how incredible you are in every way, let's just remember that this is the year you let me share a stage with Kelly Bishop. Best. Night. Ever. (Champagne and burgers after were pretty great too!) Kell Wilson, thanks for all your marketing prowess and hard work on all my books! Jennifer Bergstrom, can you believe this is our tenth book together? Wow! Thanks for being such an amazing publisher for all these years! Aimee Bell, Jennifer Long, Sally Marvin, and Eliza Hanson, thank you for the million things you do behind the scenes to make these books come to life. I adore you all! Ali Chesnick, it has been such a joy to work with you on this one. Here's to many more! Gabrielle Audet and Sarah Lieberman, listening to the audio versions of my book is always like a new dream come true. I can't possibly thank you enough!

Kathie and Roy Bennett; Susan Zurenda; and the Magic Time team, Angela Melamud, Tamara Welch, Ashley Hayes, and Ashley Edmondson . . . What on earth would I do without you guys? You make so very much happen every day, and I'm the luckiest to have each of you in my life.

I am so grateful to the incredible, amazing, fabulous, spectacular book influencers who hold me up and float these books along. I could fill a book with all of them! So, to all of you, you know who you are, and I can't wait to share your fabulous content. I love you so much! Special shout-out to the amazing JoAnna Garcia Swisher and The Happy Place, Kristy Barrett of A Novel Bee, Ashley Bellman, Stephanie Gray,

Zibby Owens and the Moms Don't Have Time team, Maghon Taylor of All She Wrote Notes, Grace Atwood from The Stripe, Andrea Katz, Cristina Frost, Susan Roberts, Susan Peterson, Susan McBeth, Emmy Griffith, Judy Collins, Meagan Briggs, Courtney Marzilli, Jennifer Clayton, Chase Waskey, Kristin Thorvaldsen, Randi Burton, Melissa Steele-Matovu, and Jess Williams for being by my side and being so supportive!

A special thanks to Alissa Redmond and my hometown bookstore South Main Book Co. in Salisbury, NC, for always going above and beyond to celebrate. Laura Taylor and Oxford Exchange in Tampa, FL, thanks for not only always hosting me but for all your amazing work on this year's *Friends & Fiction* subscription. Tim Ehrenberg and everyone at Nantucket Books, I just love you guys! Sue and Dave Lucey and Page 158, Kimberly Daniels Taws and the Country Book Shop, M Judson, Book Love . . . Okay. I could go on and on. My tour wasn't set yet when I wrote this, but thank you to each and every store that has hosted me for this book and the ones that came before. I get to be here because of you! And you too, Patricia Suggs. Beaufort Historic Site has supported me perhaps more than any other organization. Thanks for all you do to keep our town vibrant—and historic!—and for the massive amount of love you give me!

Now, to you, my fabulous, amazing, incredible readers. I get to be here because of you! I get to do this thing I love because of you. I can never thank you enough for picking up my books, for reading them, reviewing them, recommending them to friends.

So, call one of those friends now. Maybe share a copy of *Beach House Rules.* If I've learned anything, nothing connects friends across miles and years quite like bonding over a book. I hope this one helps you do just that.